Praise for

"I can always trust Lexi Blake's Dominants to leave me breathless...and in love. If you want sensual, exciting BDSM wrapped in an awesome love story, then look for a Lexi Blake book."
~Cherise Sinclair USA Today Bestselling author

"Lexi Blake's MASTERS AND MERCENARIES series is beautifully written and deliciously hot. She's got a real way with both action and sex. I also love the way Blake writes her gorgeous Dom heroes--they make me want to do bad, bad things. Her heroines are intelligent and gutsy ladies whose taste for submission definitely does not make them dish rags. Can't wait for the next book!"
~Angela Knight, New York Times Bestselling author

"A Dom is Forever is action packed, both in the bedroom and out. Expect agents, spies, guns, killing and lots of kink as Liam goes after the mysterious Mr. Black and finds his past and his future… The action and espionage keep this story moving along quickly while the sex and kink provides a totally different type of interest. Everything is very well balanced and flows together wonderfully."
~A Night Owl "Top Pick", Terri, Night Owl Erotica

"A Dom Is Forever is everything that is good in erotic romance. The story was fast-paced and suspenseful, the characters were flawed but made me root for them every step of the way, and the hotness factor was off the charts mostly due to a bad boy Dom with a penchant for dirty talk."
~Rho, The Romance Reviews

"A good read that kept me on my toes, guessing until the big reveal, and thinking survival skills should be a must for all men."
~Chris, Night Owl Reviews

"I can't get enough of the Masters and Mercenaries Series! Love and Let Die is Lexi Blake at her best! She writes erotic romantic

suspense like no other, and I am always extremely excited when she has something new for us! Intense, heart pounding, and erotically fulfilling, I could not put this book down."
~ Shayna Renee, Shayna Renee's Spicy Reads

"Certain authors and series are on my auto-buy list. Lexi Blake and her Masters & Mercenaries series is at the top of that list... this book offered everything I love about a Masters & Mercenaries book – alpha men, hot sex and sweet loving... As long as Ms. Blake continues to offer such high quality books, I'll be right there, ready to read."
~ Robin, Sizzling Hot Books

"I have absolutely fallen in love with this series. Spies, espionage, and intrigue all packaged up in a hot dominant male package. All the men at McKay-Taggart are smoking hot and the women are amazingly strong sexy submissives."
~Kelley, Smut Book Junkie Book Reviews

Spy With Me

Other Books by Lexi Blake

ROMANTIC SUSPENSE

Masters and Mercenaries
The Dom Who Loved Me
The Men With The Golden Cuffs
A Dom is Forever
On Her Master's Secret Service
Sanctum: A Masters and Mercenaries Novella
Love and Let Die
Unconditional: A Masters and Mercenaries Novella
Dungeon Royale
Dungeon Games: A Masters and Mercenaries Novella
A View to a Thrill
Cherished: A Masters and Mercenaries Novella
You Only Love Twice
Luscious: Masters and Mercenaries~Topped
Adored: A Masters and Mercenaries Novella
Master No
Just One Taste: Masters and Mercenaries~Topped 2
From Sanctum with Love
Devoted: A Masters and Mercenaries Novella
Dominance Never Dies
Submission is Not Enough
Master Bits and Mercenary Bites~The Secret Recipes of Topped
Perfectly Paired: Masters and Mercenaries~Topped 3
For His Eyes Only
Arranged: A Masters and Mercenaries Novella
Love Another Day
At Your Service: Masters and Mercenaries~Topped 4
Master Bits and Mercenary Bites~Girls Night
Nobody Does It Better
Close Cover
Protected: A Masters and Mercenaries Novella
Enchanted: A Masters and Mercenaries Novella
Charmed: A Masters and Mercenaries Novella
Taggart Family Values
Treasured: A Masters and Mercenaries Novella
Delighted: A Masters and Mercenaries Novella
Tempted: A Masters and Mercenaries Novella

Masters and Mercenaries: The Forgotten
Lost Hearts (Memento Mori)
Lost and Found
Lost in You
Long Lost
No Love Lost

Masters and Mercenaries: Reloaded
Submission Impossible
The Dom Identity
The Man from Sanctum
No Time to Lie
The Dom Who Came in from the Cold

Masters and Mercenaries: New Recruits
Love the Way You Spy
Live, Love, Spy
Sweet Little Spies
The Bodyguard and the Bombshell: A Masters and Mercenaries New Recruits Novella
No More Spies
Spy With Me
Love and Let Spy, Coming March 24, 2026

Butterfly Bayou
Butterfly Bayou
Bayou Baby
Bayou Dreaming
Bayou Beauty
Bayou Sweetheart
Bayou Beloved

Park Avenue Promise
Start Us Up
My Royal Showmance
Built to Last

Lawless
Ruthless
Satisfaction
Revenge

Courting Justice
Order of Protection
Evidence of Desire

Masters Of Ménage (by Shayla Black and Lexi Blake)
Their Virgin Captive
Their Virgin's Secret
Their Virgin Concubine
Their Virgin Princess
Their Virgin Hostage
Their Virgin Secretary
Their Virgin Mistress

The Perfect Gentlemen (by Shayla Black and Lexi Blake)
Scandal Never Sleeps
Seduction in Session
Big Easy Temptation
Smoke and Sin
At the Pleasure of the President

URBAN FANTASY

Thieves
Steal the Light
Steal the Day
Steal the Moon
Steal the Sun
Steal the Night
Ripper
Addict
Sleeper
Outcast
Stealing Summer
The Rebel Queen
The Rebel Guardian
The Rebel Witch
The Rebel Seer

LEXI BLAKE WRITING AS SOPHIE OAK

Texas Sirens
Small Town Siren
Siren in the City

Siren Enslaved
Siren Beloved
Siren in Waiting
Siren in Bloom
Siren Unleashed
Siren Reborn
The Accidental Siren
The Reluctant Siren

Nights in Bliss, Colorado
Three to Ride
Two to Love
One to Keep
Lost in Bliss
Found in Bliss
Pure Bliss
Chasing Bliss
Once Upon a Time in Bliss
Back in Bliss
Sirens in Bliss
Happily Ever After in Bliss
Far from Bliss
Unexpected Bliss
Wild Bliss
Brooke's Bliss, Coming November 11, 2025

A Faery Story
Bound
Beast
Beauty

Standalone
Away From Me
Snowed In

Spy With Me

Masters and Mercenaries
New Recruits, Book 5

Lexi Blake

Spy With Me
Masters and Mercenaries: New Recruits, Book 5
Lexi Blake

Published by DLZ Entertainment LLC
Copyright 2025 DLZ Entertainment LLC
Edited by Chloe Vale
ISBN: 978-1-963890-11-2

Masters and Mercenaries ® is registered in the U.S. Patent and Trademark Office.
Lexi Blake® is registered in the U.S. Patent and Trademark Office.

All rights reserved. No part of this book may be reproduced, scanned, or distributed in any printed or electronic form without permission. Please do not participate in or encourage piracy of copyrighted materials in violation of the author's rights.

This is a work of fiction. Names, places, characters and incidents are the product of the author's imagination and are fictitious. Any resemblance to actual persons, living or dead, events or establishments is solely coincidental.

Sign up for Lexi Blake's newsletter
and be entered to win a $25 gift certificate
to the bookseller of your choice.

Join us for news, fun, and exclusive content
including free Thieves short stories.

There's a new contest every month!

Go to www.LexiBlake.net to subscribe.

Family Trees

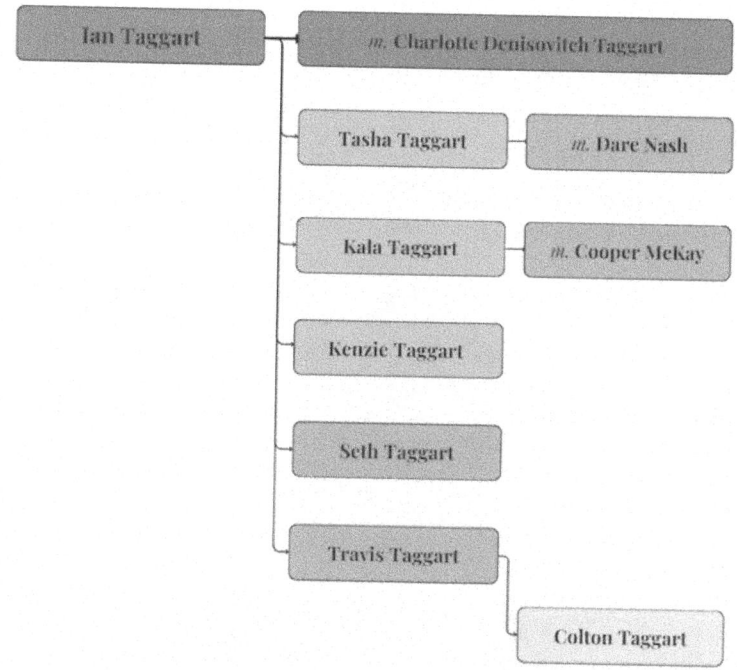
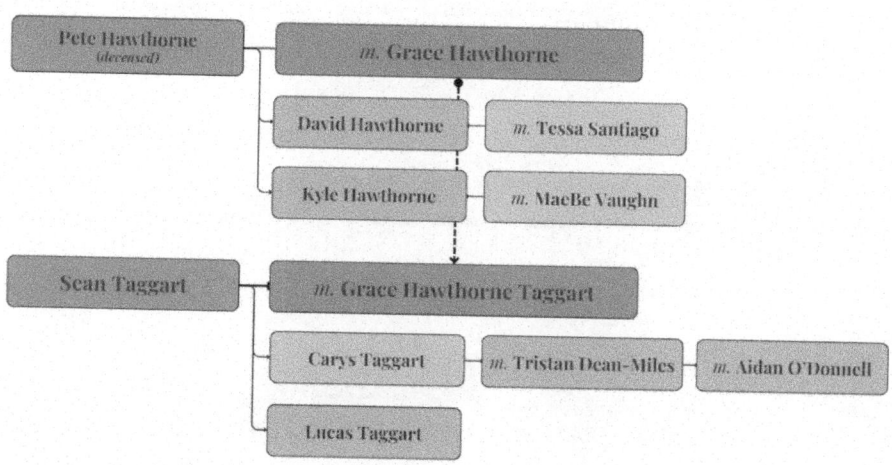

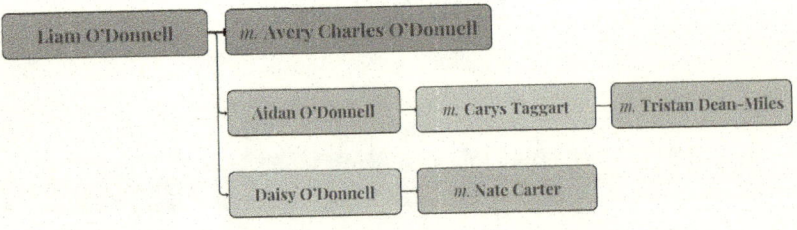

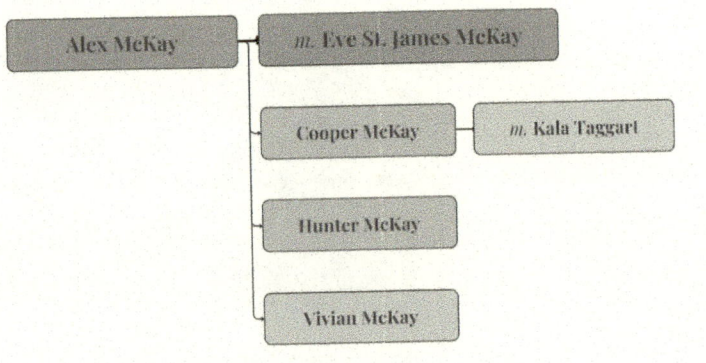

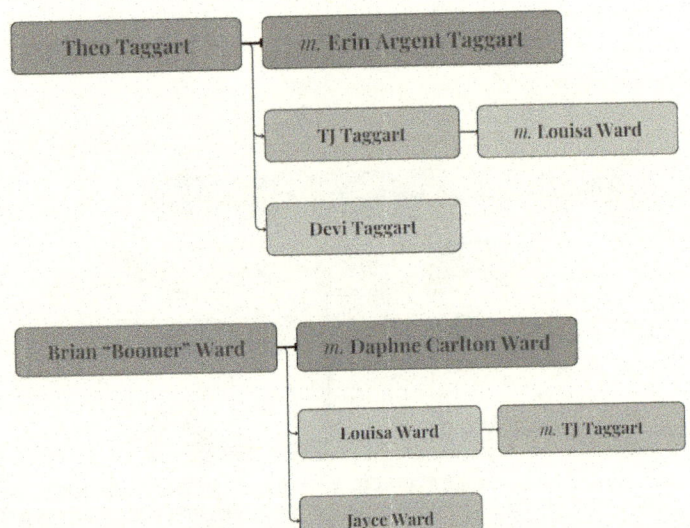

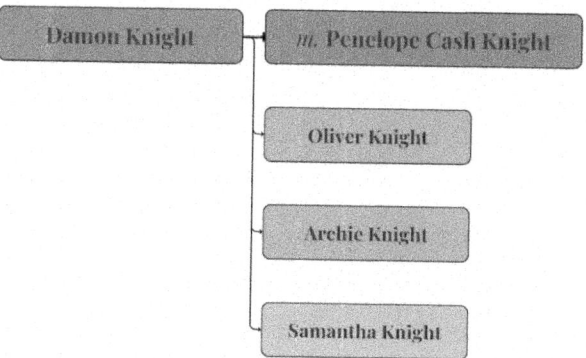

Acknowledgments

This book was a bit of a surprise. In my first notes on the team that forms the core of New Recruits, Zach didn't exist. A close friend told me I needed a man of mystery to balance out the second-generation characters. As usual, she was right. Zach gave the story what it needed, an authoritative figure who wasn't one of the team's parents. A hot soldier who might not be as great a guy as he seemed.

I'm going to be honest, I really thought I was going to have Zach's allegiance be a huge twist in this storyline. I toyed with him working for Huisman and against the team. Then I wrote him. And he...longed. Longed for a family, for a real place with his team, for a woman to connect with, for the brother he didn't grow up with. Yeah, that was a surprise to me, too. So that is how five books became six, and Devi fell for the "bad" boy. All thanks to one little suggestion from one of my favorite people. Just another way our worlds and work are better when we have friends on our team.

There's another little twist that comes about in this book. I don't want to talk too much about it because I don't want to give it away, but it's another character who didn't exist before a friend suggested I really, really needed her. Turns out I did and this character is now my new obsession, so look for her to show up often and in the funniest of ways.

So this book is for friends who help, for our circles who keep us close and share their imaginations and wisdom with us.

For Liz and Lucy

Part One
Dallas, TX

Chapter One

Zach Reed loved The Hideout. At first he'd come to the BDSM club because it was part of his job.

Scratch that. He was trying to be honest with himself since he couldn't be honest with anyone else. He'd come because he wanted to know what made Cooper McKay tick.

His brother.

He was with his brother. The brother he hadn't known existed for the longest time. The brother he never intended to do more than look up, make sure he was doing okay. He definitely hadn't meant to become his brother's military liaison on a CIA team. Hadn't meant to hang with him at a sex club. Nope. Not on his life plan.

He liked it. It helped that his brother was fairly private about his play.

"Well, I'm surprised Kala's standing after that kick to the..." Dare Nash settled the vest over his chest and gave his aforementioned brother a pat on the shoulder. "Does she have a piercing there? That's the rumor. Has anyone checked to make sure she's okay? You know. Down there."

Cooper snorted. "She's fine. Trust me. It's not the first time she's taken a hit downstairs. My baby likes to get into fights. Also, maybe don't tell her I call her my baby. She would take offense."

His brother was madly in love with Kala Taggart, the single deadliest operative he'd ever worked with. He wouldn't cross her if he didn't have to.

He'd started to wonder if they ever needed to know the truth. He'd managed to hide working with Tristan Miles to bring down the infamous Jester.

Who he'd actually killed first, and for his own reasons. He'd sent in an asshole for Tristan to murder and let him think he was in control. Yeah, they didn't need to know that either.

"At some point you have to make a move, right?" Dare asked. "I can't imagine being close to Tash and never making a move."

Oh, Zach could. He'd been rather enchanted by the lovely Tasha Taggart since the minute he met her, but she was on his team and honestly, he never felt like it was the right time to see if she was interested. First she'd had a fiancé, and then she'd needed space. Then she met Dare, and he no longer had any kind of a shot.

He'd come to believe it wasn't love. It was more like wanting to belong. He might have started all this because his bosses at the CIA wanted shit on Ian Taggart and his unique team, but the truth was Taggart was a better man and better operative and ran a better team than any of those assholes ever could.

Would they cut him loose if he didn't come through with something? Anything? Would they decide he was on the wrong side now and ship him straight back to the military where he wouldn't be part of this family he found himself in?

He had to give them something or he was going to get cut, and right as he was finally getting close to his younger brother.

His brother was saying something about Kala needing time, but Zach's head was on all the balls he was juggling.

Lying about why he was on the team. Lying about who his mother was—well, he hadn't truly. He simply hadn't mentioned that she was the elusive bombmaker everyone was hunting. Lying about who Cooper was to him. Lying about what he knew about Huisman.

That was the one he was least proud of. He could give them good intel, but it would mean blowing his cover.

"I think Zach is distracted," Cooper said with a chuckle.

He needed his head in the game. He hated that. Hated that he couldn't simply relax because the game never took a break. It was waiting to expose him. He shook his head and stood, stretching. "Zach is tired because he was on a red eye from DC this morning after someone's dad pulled strings and forced me to leave my hermit house."

Cooper shut his locker and leaned back against it. "I'm sure that was fun for you. Did Adam call, or Jake? Is it true that they bound Tristan in plastic wrap in order to force him to attend a family brunch?"

That plastic had been surprisingly effective. Also, Tristan's mom, Serena, made a hell of a Bloody Mary. "Yeah, I got to witness part of that come to Jesus. They did not hold back. There were tears and everything. Those were from Serena and Bri. Adam used logic. Jake growled a lot. Does that dude talk?"

"I don't think he has to. Adam talks enough for both of them," Cooper explained. "And I'm happy someone finally knocked some sense into Tris. He's been in love with Carys forever. If Aidan and Carys got married without him, he would regret it."

Dare put up his hands as though ceding the fight. "I live in this world now. This world where it's perfectly normal for two dudes to decide to marry one girl. I do not get it, but they seem happy. Adam and Serena and Jake, that is. Tris, Carys, and Aidan are a mess."

"I don't see why it's weird," Coop admitted.

Dare gave Zach a shake of his dark head. "Because you grew up around it. Zach and I didn't."

Zach shrugged. "Dude, I grew up in a trailer park. Let me tell you there's a lot of drama in a trailer park. Honestly, I think there would have been way less if Suzy Nelson hadn't cheated behind her husband, Gorge's, back. Not a nickname. The dude was legally named Gorge. If she'd walked to old Gorge and told him she wanted to screw Bubba Ham, maybe they would have tag teamed her instead of trying to shoot each other with BB guns. Also, Bubba *was* a nickname, but where I come from if you have several siblings, your momma looks around and decides one of the males is Bubba. He's usually the one who says 'hold my beer' a lot. There's always a Bubba, and if you don't know which one it is, it's probably you."

Cooper grinned. "I love trailer park stories."

"It wasn't all bad," Zach admitted. Cooper never had to know that when he told those stories, he was doing it so Cooper knew a little about the childhood that was almost his, too. His mom was awesome when she was around. She was smart and funny. She also happened to be a wanted criminal. "It was good to have a roof over my head and food in my belly, so I can't complain."

Except it would have been better with a brother.

He shook that off. Cooper loved his parents. He loved his life here in Dallas, and the Agency team that took him around the world. If their mom hadn't given him up, Cooper likely wouldn't have learned to fly, wouldn't have had the big found family he'd grown up in. Wouldn't have fallen in love with the most complicated woman in the world.

And that would be a shame because Kala Taggart was a hell of a woman. Zach genuinely loved her like a sister.

"Well, that sounds more fun than…" Dare began.

Zach snorted and stopped him since he knew what was coming next. "Rich boy, I know your dad was a massive ass, but really, let's not compare childhoods. I would totally win."

Even if he didn't tell them about his mom who was in and out of jail, and his aunt who loved him but also had some mental health issues. He had plenty of stories about growing up poor and being called white trash. Dare Nash had a nasty dad who was now doing time in jail—though it was Canadian jail, so there was that—but otherwise the world had been his oyster. And he'd gotten Tasha. And Ian Taggart kind of loved him.

Dare pretty much had everything Zach wanted. He was now the head of sales for McKay-Taggart. He would be part of the family, and no one would ever threaten to take it from him. His place was set.

Cooper glanced down at his watch. "I should get out there. We've got a couple of scenes to run tonight. Julian sent over one of his problem children. Not a real problem. He just hasn't gotten what he needs, and I don't think he's going to find it at The Club. I already set up the space, but I want to walk Kala through it and make sure it's everything she needs."

His brother might not be sleeping with the woman he loved, but he knew how to take care of her.

"I wasn't trying to…" Dare began as Cooper walked toward the door that would lead them out.

It was awkward to be around the guy who ended up with the girl, but Zach had no regrets. Tash was happy. That was all that mattered. "It's okay, man. We all have shitty childhoods. We probably shouldn't turn it into a competition. How's the wedding prep going?"

Dare seemed relieved to have something to talk about. It was probably weird to hang out with a dude who used to have a crush on your fiancée. Dare was a good guy. They followed Cooper as Dare talked about venues and how he mostly sat back and nodded and let Tash and her mom pick everything.

He was also a smart man.

"You can totally get Aidan killed," Kala was saying as he walked into the hall. "Like go for it, buddy. But if you think I'll let you hurt my cousin, you haven't met me. Would you like to meet me, Tristan?"

So this was going well. He was here for the drama. He used to be the dude who would say he wanted peace and calm, but he was pretty addicted to the scenes they ran at The Hideout, and he wasn't talking about all the public spankings.

Aidan frowned. The doctor was dressed for play and curled an arm around his fiancée's waist. "So says the woman who punched her in the gut not three hours ago."

The hall was crowded. The ladies had emerged from their locker room as well, and they seemed to be facing off with the guys. Well, except for Carys, who was huddling close to Aidan. Tristan Dean-Miles, however, was staring Kala Taggart's way. She stood there with her sisters, Tasha and twin Kenzie.

And her cousin.

Damn, her cousin looked good. Devi. He was pretty sure it was short for Devon. Devon Taggart. He stared at her for a moment. She had natural red hair and the cutest smattering of freckles across the bridge of her nose. So much hair, and it was curly and wound down to brush the tops of perky breasts. She wore a pair of boy shorts that barely covered her and an emerald green corset that made her skin practically glow. She always wore such pretty fet wear. There were roses embroidered on the corset, like they bound her up in beauty.

How had he never really looked at her before?

Oh, yeah, because she was his teammate TJ's sister, and TJ might smack him.

It might be worth it. Besides, TJ was totally wrapped up in his girlfriend, Louisa Ward, right now. He probably wouldn't even notice.

He shouldn't do this. It was a bad idea. He was a bad bet, and little Devi shouldn't be in his line of fire.

And yet he wasn't walking away.

"She'll back off," Tristan was saying. "Or she'll meet me."

Kala had been in the middle of the Tristan/Carys/Aidan drama. It was precisely how she'd gotten kicked in the cootch earlier today. Naturally Kala had taken it like a champ. It looked like Coop's well-planned-out evening might be in jeopardy.

Cooper groaned. "She's wound up enough as it is. Could we notch down the testosterone, please?"

"He's talking to you, sis," Kenzie said to her twin.

He rarely got them mixed up, despite the fact that they were perfectly identical. They worked hard to stay that way. When Kala got a scar, Kenzie made sure she had one, too.

It was a bit disturbing, but he understood. The twins were dedicated to the mission.

A low snarl came from Kala's mouth. Despite that predatory sound, Zach knew they were dedicated to each other, too.

His brother got into Kala's space, putting a hand on her back. "Come on. I've got a scene set up for you along with an imported pain slut. Julian sent this guy over because he claims no one can give him what he needs."

"Sounds like a challenge." Kala no longer looked like she wanted to murder someone. She leaned back into Cooper for a brief moment and then straightened up, obviously sinking into top space. "Are you watching or helping tonight, Master C?"

Cooper only had eyes for her. "Oh, I think you'll need help with him, Mistress. Let's go make sure the space is up to your standards."

Kala turned to him, her gaze going as soft as it ever did. "I have no doubt."

And then his brother was following her out onto the dungeon floor.

Damn, but he wanted that. Not the years' worth of slow burn. He would way rather get it going. Mostly because he would probably die soon. It was the nature of his business. If his bosses didn't kill him, then Huisman would, or any number of his mom's associates.

His gaze went back to Devi. So freaking pretty.

She did something artistic for a living. He tended to pretty much stick to his team, but he had the most insane urge to get to know Devi Taggart. It was a mistake. He was a mess and didn't have any right to drag her into what might turn out to be a nightmare.

But he could also try to be positive. He'd been with the team for years now. They never had to know he was anything but exactly who he said he was. The truth of the matter was his team was in the middle of something big, and if they delivered Huisman, Taggart would be locked in. There would be nothing those assholes could do to him.

"I wouldn't hate a session," Kenzie announced. "I think I'll go see if any of The Club guys are here. Gabe won't try to get into my thong."

Tasha sidled up to her fiancé. They made a lovely couple. "I thought you wanted someone *in* your thong."

Was Devi looking for a partner? He seemed to remember the Doms joking about her being a nun. She didn't play often, but she looked like she was ready for it.

Maybe she wanted a Dom for the night.

His groin tightened in a deeply pleasurable way. It had been forever since he truly wanted someone. Tasha… That was definitely more about how kind she was and how if she cared about him, he would be in.

Devi though… He just wanted her.

Kenzie put a hand on her hip, her magenta-colored ponytail swinging. "I think I'm choosing sanity for a while. And by sanity I mean celibacy. How about it, Zach? You know you've wanted to slap my ass for a long time. I mean that in an I'm-annoying way, not a you-think-I'm-hot way."

Oh, that was a terrible idea. Wow. Yeah, his dick withered at the thought, and it wasn't like she wasn't his type. Kenzie Taggart was a gorgeous woman with a near-perfect body and the sweetest smile. And yet… "Too much like my sister. Nope."

Turned out he wasn't one of those Doms who could simply service any submissive.

Kenzie gave him a flouncy pout. "Your loss."

She strode away and then the only one left was Devi. Well, the only one he wanted to spend time with tonight. Carys and Aidan and Tris were still there. But he pretty much only had eyes for Devi.

Zach gave her his best "I'm harmless" smile. Now that... That was a real lie. "How about you? You're Devi, right? You need a scene partner?"

She kind of squeaked and then she was gone, disappearing back into the locker room.

Well, that hurt. First woman he'd wanted in forever and she was obviously terrified of him.

It was a good thing because the truth of the matter was he'd never been into mousy women. He liked a sexually submissive woman, but he pretty much wanted a badass bitch outside the bedroom. He liked a brat.

He'd thought Erin Taggart's daughter would be both. But then she was also Theo Taggart's daughter, so there was that.

"I guess that's a no. Do I smell bad or something?" He looked to the trio, but they had no advice for him. Tristan was actually laughing. He could handle it. They were friends and friends ribbed each other. It was nice when he thought about it. "All right. Looks like I'm watching tonight. You three have fun and know you're going to have to deal with Kala in the field. She's serious."

Kala was always serious in the field.

He walked back into the locker room as he felt his cell buzz.

Cell phones were allowed on the floor, though only for emergency purposes. There were a bunch of members who had to be available at all times. CIA operatives. A fed. Aidan and Carys were doctors. Lucas Taggart was at least half of Dallas's booty call. So phones were a necessary evil. He pulled it out as he walked past Travis Taggart playing Xbox with Hunter McKay.

His brother's brother. Hunter was a good kid, but Zach felt awkward around him. Cooper loved his brother, was good to him. Hunter had taken his place, and he couldn't blame the kid, but he still felt weird about it.

He glanced down at his cell and frowned. Lacey.

Lacey was a contact in his mother's world. She was the daughter of a woman his mom had met a couple of times over the years, though miraculously, she trusted her therefore would actually talk to Lacey. She was a vegan, tree-hugging near anarchist, but she was excellent at digging up information and had contacts in the underground world his mom occupied that he couldn't match.

He liked Lacey. She actually kind of reminded him of Kala. But he didn't want to answer that phone. He wanted to pretend he wasn't who he was for the night. It would have been perfect to do that with Devi Taggart, but it wasn't happening.

So he moved past Lucas and Hunter and back toward the showers where he was absolutely certain no one would hear him. He slid his thumb across the cell to answer the call. "This is Reed."

Captain Zachary Reed. Soldier. Operative. Liar.

"Hey, Zach." Lacey's British accent came over the line. She'd been born in Liverpool and kept a house there. From what he could tell, Lacey Rook came from wealth, but she'd rebelled against her traditionalist parents and joined all kinds of activist groups. "I wanted to let you know I got in touch with a contact who swears he's seen our friend."

His gut tightened. "Where was she?"

"He wouldn't say. I'm working on him. He doesn't trust me," Lacey replied. "Not yet, but you know I can calm the most paranoid conspiracy theorist. Personally, I think she's here in Europe somewhere. The man I talked to is what I would call a procurement specialist."

So he basically worked logistics for underground groups and criminals, which often were a perfect Venn diagram. "He trying to buy something from her?"

Always her and she. He never said her name or called her *mother*. Lacey wouldn't either. He'd been working with her for over a year, and she was the closest he'd come to actually getting in the same room with his mom.

"You know everyone loves her pottery." Lacey followed their code words even though he trusted she would be on a somewhat secure line. "I'm sure he's trying to make a sale to a high-value client."

He didn't want to deal with this tonight. Whenever he tried to handle his mom, he felt fucking helpless. Likely because he was helpless. His mother was excellent at hiding. She was even better at building bombs that could shake the world—precisely the reason Emmanuel Huisman was looking for her. "Is it for the Canadian gallery? I know she wasn't interested in showing there."

His mother was terrified of Huisman, hence her going to ground for the last couple of years.

"I can't be sure. It was a hurried conversation," she replied. "When do you think you can get back across the pond? There are a few spots I'm looking at that might be a better fit for her."

So she had some places to check out. The problem was if he left now, it would be noted. "I'm afraid I'm pretty deep in the weeds at work. I've got a new project. I'll be in Canada next week."

Aidan O'Donnell had been invited to a medical conference by one Dr. Emmanuel Huisman. Aidan was a resident in trauma surgery, and the Huisman Foundation sponsored a whole lot of research in the medical world. Unfortunately, they also sponsored terrorism.

"Then I'll check it out myself," she replied.

"Hey, you need…" he began.

"I'll be careful. And you do the same. I'm worried about some movements I've seen recently, but we can talk about that later. I'm sure it's late where you are," Lacey said.

"It's almost dawn where you are." If she was in Liverpool, it would be five in the morning. "Are you up early or late?"

A husky laugh came over the line. Lacey was a gorgeous woman with long hair she changed as often as the twins did. The last time he'd seen her the long tresses had ended in a beautiful jade green color. And yet he didn't feel a pull her way. They'd worked together for months, and he'd never made a move on her. He wasn't even sure she liked guys, but it was weird he'd never felt anything for her when she was very much his type.

A vision of Devi brushed across his brain.

Maybe she needed to get to know him better. Or she didn't want to get involved with a guy who worked with her brother. He couldn't fix that. He might be able to convince her though. He just had to get some time with her.

Why was he thinking about this when he should be getting dressed and heading back to Cooper's, where he was staying for the week? He could get on his laptop—the encrypted one—and get some work done. Maybe track down some of the leads Lacey was offering.

But he wasn't going to do that. He was here. He was going to spend a couple of damn hours being the man he wanted to be. And if Devi wouldn't play with him, maybe she would let him buy her a drink at the end of the night. There was so much to catch up on. He'd missed the wedding where helicopters sent by Huisman nearly took out the wedding party. All he'd gotten was a stupid report that left out all the fun stuff. He would bet Devi had some stories.

Yeah, that might be his in.

"I'll sleep when I'm dead, mate," Lacey said over the line. "Well, I'll let you know if I come up with a workable plan for our friend. Until then, keep me up to date on whatever I need to know. If you find yourself in Liverpool, I'll buy you a drink."

"I'll keep you to that," he replied. "Bye, Lace."

He hung up.

"I didn't know you had a girlfriend." Hunter McKay stood at the end of the lockers. He was a couple of years younger than Cooper, and while they didn't look a lot alike, they both held themselves in similar fashions. His shoulders were straight, his arms crossed over his chest and a judgmental look in his eyes.

"I don't." How had he missed someone walking up on him? Devi. He'd been thinking about Devi. Another reason to take her rejection as the good thing it had been. She made a smart decision. He needed to make his own by not pursuing her further.

She would be one more person he had to lie to.

Maybe he got to the other end of this and he could have some kind of a life, but for now he had to be happy just getting to know his brother.

And praying Cooper never found out he *was* his brother.

Cooper's adopted brother stared at him warily. "I suppose it's none of my business."

"It's not." It was clear the kid had some serious instincts. He would bet Hunter wasn't quite sure why he didn't like Zach, couldn't put his finger on it, but the distrust was there. "However, if you need to know, I was talking to Lacey. She's a friend of mine in England. She's looking to help one of my relatives with an art showing."

Cover was a good thing. Keeping it was even better.

Hunter caved. Zach would bet it would be hard for the kid to stay mad or suspicious of anyone for too long. Hunter McKay was too happy to hold on to the more bitter emotions. "Sorry. I'm just... Well, I was worried, but my brother says you're a good guy so I'll let you know that someone is waiting for you in the hallway. I guess she changed her mind."

Devi.

Every single reason he had to take that rejection like a champ flew straight out of his brain, and he couldn't get to that door fast enough.

It was a bad idea. A horrible mistake.

And he was making it.

* * * *

"How about you? You're Devi, right? You need a scene partner?"

Devi Taggart felt like a deer in the headlights. Zach. Zach Reed. Captain Zach Reed. The single most gorgeous man she'd ever seen had asked the question, and she was standing in the middle of the hallway wearing fet wear and generally hanging out like a creeper gathering information for her besties. She had meant to find out what was going on with her cousin, Carys, and those two men of hers, not get an invitation to play with that glorious hunk of Dom.

He was one of the spy guys. Oh, she was well aware there was a part of the membership of The Hideout that called the group the spy kids, but this was not a kid. Zach Reed was all man, and her whole body clenched at the thought of being a badass bitch and claiming him for herself. She was Erin Taggart's daughter. Badass bitch was in her DNA.

Except she flaked. She meant to say something, but she kind of squeaked and then felt herself turn a brutal shade of red—another DNA gift from her mother was pale skin that hid nothing. And then she ran.

She slammed the locker room door behind her, barely breathing.

Not her finest moment.

Her two best friends were standing in the lounge portion of the women's locker room. Daisy O'Donnell was studying for some kind of test, but she was scheduled to address the new training class at some point this evening. Devi was pretty sure the studying was for a college entrance exam. Bri was hanging out working on the plot for her latest story. Daisy usually played on Saturday nights, but her Dom was on assignment as a bodyguard for McKay-Taggart.

"You okay?" Bri was wearing jeans and a T-shirt, her golden brown hair piled high atop her head. She'd been scribbling in a notebook, a sure sign she was plotting and not writing since she did that on her laptop. Sometimes Bri's room was covered in sticky notes covering all aspects of her stories, from characters to plot lines to dialogue she wanted to put in a future story. She loved being around Brianna Dean-Miles and her glorious brain. And Daisy's kind heart.

They were her closest friends since before they could remember anything.

So it was okay to tell them how idiotic she'd been. "No. I am not okay. I am… I don't know what I am. I might need a drink. Don't the twins keep cold vodka magically around at all times?"

Daisy stood. "Was someone mean to you? Was it a Dom? Because I can call Nate. He's had to work with my dad all week. He would love to beat someone up for you."

"Or we can be women and beat him up ourselves," Bri said with a nod like she was giving herself badass affirmations in her head. It came from being around her cousins too much. "We might have to find a way to drug him and then tie him up and then do something to counter the drug because we want him to be awake for his torture."

Daisy stared at her for a moment. "You need to get out of the house more, sweetie."

"We're not beating anyone up." She loved her friends, but they could go off on tangents. "No one was mean to me."

"Then why aren't you out on the dungeon floor? You said you were determined to play tonight, and you didn't care if your brother had to bleach his eyeballs," Bri pointed out.

She had a plan for that. She and her brother had done what other siblings did. They carved up the club, and that map was sacred. Besides, she was pretty sure TJ would take his girlfriend Lou to a privacy room, so he wouldn't have to bear witness to her glorious, slutty night. Because while she'd told her friends she only wanted to play to blow off some steam, she intended for all that steam to blow her straight into some hot dude. She planned to ask one of the baby Doms if they were interested in a lesson.

Then Zach Reed showed up and her nipples had gone all perky and her libido went super charged.

He worked with her brother. He couldn't possibly be interested in her.

"Do you think she's okay? Do we need to find a way to reboot her?" Bri asked.

"I think that's what the vodka's for," Daisy whispered back. "I know it seems like vodka follows the twins, but I think it's just up in the bar. Should I go get some?"

Why had she done that? Devi crossed to the comfy couch and sank down. She should get dressed and run. All the way to New York. Where she didn't have a job or a place to live or a future since she didn't get any of the jobs she applied for there. She hadn't even told her parents. Or TJ. Only Bri and Daisy knew she was coming out of what should have been an extraordinary internship, and she had no offers.

LA. The LA design houses hadn't replied yet.

They would likely be the same. She was going to end up answering phones at McKay-Taggart, and there wasn't anything wrong with that, but it wasn't her passion. It wasn't how she wanted to spend her life. She'd wanted to design clothes since she was a kid and she used scraps of fabric to make gowns for her dolls. It wasn't the end of the world. She could still find a job. She simply had to work harder.

"I think she's thinking about the jobs," Bri whispered.

"She's definitely thinking about the jobs." Daisy sat down beside her, putting a hand on her arm. "Honey, it's okay. You still have all the LA houses and Paris."

She wasn't getting a job in Paris. Or London. They thought she was pedestrian. It was what one of those fuckers had called her work. They had mostly been polite and said she didn't fit their aesthetic, but a couple had pointed out that her work lacked sophistication.

Well, she showed them. Yeah, she'd shown enormous sophistication when she'd squeaked like a mouse and run like a rabbit when Zach Reed showed the slightest bit of interest in her.

"Damn it. I am not this girl," she said with conviction.

"Which girl? Because if it's the girl who downs vodka from time to time, you are definitely that girl," Daisy countered.

Bri chuckled and sat on Devi's other side. "She's freaking out because she got turned down by the New York houses. She's taking everything they said and making it really big and insulting and wondering if she even has a shot at this. And yes, I know because I do it all the time. Every rejection I get makes me wonder if I'm good enough or I'm wasting my time and I'm going to end up sitting at the reception desk at MT, waiting for the next time something explodes or they get raided—which happens more often than you would think."

"I almost got there," Daisy said with a sigh. "I was going to work, and that was when the assassins came and then Da wouldn't let me work and he locked me up in a BDSM club with the man of my dreams. Good times. But I still think I would have been good at answering the phones. I even worked on my phone voice. *McKay-Taggart, this is Daisy. How can I save your life and-or introduce you to the bodyguard of your dreams?*"

"I don't think Uncle Ian would let you say that," Bri pointed out. "He has a strict script."

Devi waved that off. "When I used to answer the phones on summer break I said some crazy shit and Uncle Ian fist bumped me as he walked by. Said he had enough business as it was, and I was giving him nap time. And yes, I'm thinking about the jobs, but I'm also thinking about the fact that I made a complete idiot of myself in front of Zach."

Her besties gasped in perfect harmony.

"What happened?" Daisy asked. "Did you fall? I fall a lot. Nate thinks it's cute. If Zach doesn't think it's cute, he's being a jerk. You know clumsy is totally in these days."

"I didn't fall." It might have been better if she had, but no, she was good in five-inch heels. To her mother's never-ending dismay, she'd started wearing them at thirteen, and she could jog in those fuckers. But still, if she'd broken a leg, it would have been less embarrassing.

Bri stood, tears in her eyes. "You asked him and he turned you down. You got all of your courage together to ask the man of your dreams to simply play with you in the sex club you both belong to. And he brutally turned you down. He wasn't even polite about it. He probably laughed."

Okay, sometimes Bri's imagination took over and Devi could see she was playing the entire scenario out in her head, and that was bad for Zach. Bri was usually quiet and private, but when she felt like a woman had been dealt an injustice, she could build an army. Prom night had been a real revelation.

She couldn't have Bri rallying the subs against poor Zach. The man might be in the military and on a CIA team, but somehow she didn't see him fighting back against that. "He didn't laugh. He asked me."

Daisy sat back up. "He asked you what?"

"He asked if I wanted to play," Devi admitted.

Bri sat back down. "Well, that changes things. Why are you here and not getting your ass happily spanked by the military hottie?"

"You do not look thrilled to get what you've wanted for months," Daisy pointed out. "Was he rude about it?"

"Not at all." She was starting to calm down, but the lack of flight or fight adrenaline was also making her feel more like a moron. "He was… I don't know. He was casual about it. I think he wanted to play and I was breathing."

"And?" Daisy asked.

Bri huffed. "Come on. You know how you would feel if Nate had looked at you and been like *sure, you'll do*. She's crazy about Zach."

"I don't know that I would say crazy." Except she kind of was. It had been lust at first sight, but she didn't want to be the kid sister who pined for her brother's friend. Although it wasn't like they were close. TJ hadn't been working on the team for long, and he spent most of his free time with a hot dog in one hand and Lou's boobs in the other. They really should be more circumspect. Uncle Ian might deserve to walk in on them doing it in a conference room, but she'd been a good sister, damn it.

Daisy stood, brushing back her dark hair and pacing as though thinking through the problem. "You have talked about that man since the day he walked into this club. You practically drool when he's around. I don't get why you would say anything except Sir, yes, Sir. And Nate kind of did. He didn't even know it was me. If he'd known it was me, he would have run the other way, so I don't get why Devi doesn't want to shoot her shot. I mean at least you would know. And if it doesn't work, you got some hot sex out of it. I've heard rumors. He's kind of hard core. Is that what you're afraid of?"

Zach wasn't a big player, but he had spent some time with several of the subs here at the club. Usually outside of his friend group. He'd played with a couple of the subs Gabriel Lodge had brought in, and some of the hostesses/servers from the restaurant group. They had seemed deeply satisfied with his services.

She didn't want to be serviced.

Except that was exactly what she'd been planning for the evening. She'd planned to do what he did—go outside her friend group, pick a Dom, ride him to some sweet stress relief.

"I'm not worried that he's hard core. I like it rough," she admitted. She was known as one of The Hideouts hard bottoms. It took a lot to make her cry.

Some Doms liked a challenge.

"Then why?" Daisy's head shook. "Okay. I know why. You're being cautious. It was okay for the sex to be casual if you didn't care about the guy."

"Yes." Bri nodded vigorously as though happy Daisy had gotten it right. "She's half in love with him."

She wouldn't say that. "I don't know I would use the word *love* yet."

Daisy pointed Devi's way. "That's my point, friend. You've spent so little time with him that the guy you like is mostly in your head. You're not in love with him. You're infatuated with the idea of him. He's got a pretty package and seems nice and smart, and you like how he tops a sub. That doesn't mean you know him. It doesn't mean you would even like him if you spent time with him, but how will you ever know if you don't spend time with him?"

Bri frowned. "I don't like it when she's all logical. I prefer my Daisy talking about soul mates and true love."

Daisy took Bri's hand. "But how can you find either if you don't try? I know what I felt for Nate as a kid was a crush. Believe it or not I only intended to spend one night with him. One night to get him out of my system."

"And now you're engaged." It was how things went with Daisy. She could walk into a perfectly normal situation and it would upend almost immediately. In this case it led to assassins and being stuck at Sanctum for days, but also with her being engaged to Nathan Carter, who did turn out to be the love of her life.

Had she walked away from her chance to do the same?

"Yup, because when the opportunity presented itself, I was open to it." Daisy sat back down, looking at Devi with a serious expression on her usually sunny face. "The whole love thing is not for the faint of heart. It doesn't simply happen. We make it happen. Or at least we open ourselves up to the possibility. We don't run away from it. Even when you know it can break your heart. You know what our Aunt Grace says."

"It's better to have a broken heart than an empty one," Bri said quietly. "It's easier on paper. I watch my brother. I love him so much, but he's screwing up with the two people he's loved since he was a child. I keep thinking if those three can't make it, no one can."

"But they will," Daisy vowed. "This is a bump in the road. You have that attitude because we're in one of the hard parts. Note I said one. I'm not so unrealistic that I think it's easy going from here out, but the beginning is hard. It's normal to want to protect yourself when you see heartache all around you. When you see how the people you love long for something they think they can't have. When you watch them screw up again and again and there's nothing you can do about it. My brother is at fault, too. So is Carys. They've all made mistakes, but they're finally confronting them now. It's a good thing. It's why I think Devi should confront what's really bugging her."

"I thought it was Zach," Devi said. "I mean I've got a lot going on right…" Damn it. She figured it out. Daisy had been studying way too much. She was going back to college to get certified to work with kids on mental health. "It's not because I didn't get the jobs I wanted."

Bri sent Daisy a look. Like they'd talked about this and came up with a plan to handle it. To handle her.

"Fine." She sat back with a sigh. It looked like her hot evening was going to turn into a girl-talk session. "My deep desire to get railed by a hot and forgettable Dom tonight does have something to do with the job hunt. Dais, I know you've run through a lot of jobs and it's got to hurt when you get fired…"

Daisy held a hand up. "It does, but I'm not putting my soul into what is essentially art and having it judged by everyone. I know, sweetie. It's why Bri won't let anyone but us read her incredible novels."

"They're just not ready," Bri argued.

What wasn't ready was Bri, and that was okay. She needed to take her time and learn her craft. She could do that because she was a writer. Devi wanted to do the same, but designing clothes wasn't a solitary job. Not the way she wanted to do it. "You'll know when they're ready. But I'm definitely letting the rejections get in my head. I thought I was feeling confident. I walked out that door feeling hot and sexy, and then Zach was looking at me and all I could think about was the fact that I designed this corset and the shorts, and they called my work pedestrian and unflattering and worst of all, safe."

Daisy and Bri both winced.

Safety wasn't a bad thing, but none of her friends wanted to be safe when it came to the things they were passionate about. They came from families of spies and military operatives and bestselling authors, and extremely fierce people. Being called *safe* hurt worst of all.

"You are not safe," Daisy said. "You make some of the coolest fet wear I've ever seen. I would bet you didn't send them those designs in your portfolios."

Devi sighed. "Fet wear isn't exactly what these companies make. But I do get your point. I might have played it safer than I should have."

"You still have so many applications out there," Bri said encouragingly. "You'll find the right place. I just wish it was here in Dallas."

"We're not a hotbed of design." The thought of leaving these two made her heart ache. They'd been apart during college and the year she'd spent in Paris doing an internship. These last couple of years spent at home working on her portfolio and doing custom pieces for weddings and clients in the lifestyle had been fun, and being with her friends inspired her. "But I need to be in LA or New York or Paris if I want to make a real name for myself. London, maybe. You're right. I let myself freak out over something I've wanted for over a year. I should have smiled and had a wild night and walked away at the end, satisfied that I tried."

Because there was no way they worked. He would end up being cocky and full of himself and into video games and sports ball like most of her brother's friends. At best they might work as a D/s couple, and not a monogamous one since he was gone most of the time. He didn't even live here. Unlike the rest of the team, he lived in DC. He was only here every couple of months.

Why hadn't she leapt in? She was smart and capable and not clingy. She didn't need a man. Well, to spank her. She couldn't spank herself, and honestly, she preferred an actual man to a vibrator when it came to sex.

"I blew it." She'd had one shot, and she wouldn't get another.

"Or you change your mind," Daisy offered. "It's been a couple of minutes. I scarcely think he's already found another sub for the night. Go back out and find him. Tell him you changed your mind and need a good hard session. Have fun with him. He's not going to judge you."

"How do you know?" Devi asked.

"Because he's a dude, and all he's going to be thinking about is getting into those super-hot boy shorts of yours," Bri replied, looking lighter than before. "Tell me. Are they tearaway?"

Devi grinned. She did have fun designing fet wear. "Of course. You know I love it when I get my clothes torn off, but I don't like losing the clothes. So I found a simple solution. I spent a couple of months designing a whole fet wardrobe for Aunt Charlotte. My uncle is tight fisted when it comes to cash, but he opened the wallet for this one. All tearaway. I managed to make the Velcro completely unnoticeable if you line it up properly."

She'd made a pretty penny off that commission. She'd also made some cosplays and Ren fair costumes, and she was super popular around Halloween.

She designed Carys's wedding gown and the bridesmaid dresses. That had been fun, too. But was it too safe? She was designing for her family and friends. They wouldn't tell her if something sucked. They would be gentle and maybe wear it even if they didn't like it.

She didn't want to be safe.

Devi stood up. "I'm going to find him and stop being someone I don't want to be. I'm going to tell him what I want."

"To marry him and have him love you forever?" Bri asked.

Bri was sometimes way too romantic.

Daisy leaned against Bri. "It does sound nice, doesn't it? We could have a double wedding."

So was Daisy. Devi had always known she was the realistic one. "I'm going to tell him I need some stress relief and nothing more. But that doesn't mean I won't talk to him and figure out if I actually like him."

"And then you'll fall in love and marry him," Bri added.

Daisy nodded. "This is going to be a beautiful love story." She sniffled. "Like me and Nate."

She hoped not. See assassins. Devi just wanted a wild night with the hottest man she'd ever met.

She strode to the door and walked out into the hallway. She was confident and knew what she wanted.

Captain Zachary Reed.

For a night.

Hunter was walking out of the men's locker room. He gave her a masculine once-over and a big old sunshiny smile. Hunter McKay was slightly older than she was and he'd gone to a different school, but they'd known each other since they were kids. "Hey, Dev. You're looking good tonight."

Hunter always seemed too happy to be a Dom. She liked a little frown in her men, and he rarely did. At least not around her. They didn't spend a ton of time alone together and ran in different groups, but he was like family.

"Thanks." She looked over his leathers. Which she'd worked on. Everyone at The Hideout came to her when they had wardrobe malfunctions. Hunter had dropped some weight, and she'd taken in his leathers. "They look good on you."

He grinned and put his fists on his hips. "Yeah, I've been working out with the new guy. He's a great trainer. Luckily, thanks to you, I don't have to buy new."

Hunter often worked as the dungeon monitor, and he took his role seriously. Which meant he knew a lot of things and kept his eyes open. "Hey, have you seen Zach?"

Hunter nodded. "Yeah, he's inside."

So he hadn't headed to the dungeon. He hadn't gotten her rejection and moved on to the next sub. "Could you ask him to come out here?"

A brow rose over Hunter's green eyes. "He do something I should know about?"

And he could be protective. "Not yet, but if I get my way, that could change."

"You sure you know what you're doing? I know he works with Coop and the twins and your brother, but there's something off about him," Hunter said. "I can't put my finger on it, but he's... I worry he's not who he presents himself to be."

"He's a spy, Hunt. I assure you Kala doesn't walk into a new situation and punch people the way she does here." She wasn't worried about Zach being a spy. Her brother was one, and TJ was perfectly harmless to anything but a hot dog. Or a burger. Or honestly, any kind of food. Her brother had the wildest metabolism. "I know what I'm getting into. It's nothing more than a fun night."

Hunter seemed to consider it for a moment and she got ready to go in and get Zach herself because Hunter McKay wasn't about to make decisions for her. But right before she was about to make her way into that sacred male space, Hunter opened the door. "I'll get him. You be careful, kid."

"Kid?" But the door had already closed. He was like a year and a half older than she was and he called her kid. He was a kid. He worked for his dad and everything, and just because he could fly a plane didn't make him more mature than she was. Kid. He was a kid.

The door opened and a man walked through.

Whoa. Zach Reed was at least six foot four and had broad shoulders and a six-pack to die for. Dark hair and the warmest brown eyes and a jawline cut from granite. And lips. Damn he had gorgeous lips that were curling up. "You change your mind, sweetness?"

The nickname didn't apply, and yet somehow it threatened to make her toes curl. She moved into his space. He was finally looking at her, and she wasn't going to waste his focus. She got in close and tilted her head up, looking at that cut jawline and wanting to run her lips over it. "I'm looking for some stress relief tonight, Sir. Do you think you might be able to help me? I'm sorry for my first reaction. It's been a rough couple of days, but I assure you I'm not normally one to run away from something I want."

Was that a gun or was he suddenly happy to see her?

He eased back slightly since guns weren't allowed on the dungeon floor. "That is good to know, and I would be happy to play with you. Let's sit down and set some ground rules."

She followed him, ready for her night to begin.

Chapter Two

Zach closed the door to the privacy room and had to take a steadying breath. What the hell was this woman doing to him? They had stood in front of the main stage where Aidan and Tristan tortured their sub, but all the while his whole focus had been on the woman in front of him. They stayed toward the back since he needed to talk to her while they watched, and he hadn't wanted to gain the attention of Gabriel Lodge, who was training a bunch of kid Doms who looked like they should be back in high school.

And when the scene was finished in perfectly filthy style, she'd suggested they go to a privacy room.

He'd asked her questions about how the scene made her feel.

Horny, she'd replied in that bratty fucking way that got his motor running.

He had not planned on coming to a room with her. He'd thought they might find a play space and he would spank her and probably get her off and deal with a righteously unsatisfied dick.

He turned and hoped he had his Dom face on and not the puppy-dog eyes he was kind of worried he had.

Everything about this woman did it for him.

"Are you worried about something, Sir?" Devi sat on the bed, one long leg crossed over the other.

She liked to challenge him. It made him realize the subs he'd been topping were a little too…well, submissive for him. He didn't even think that was some weird contradiction. If there was one thing he'd learned here at The Hideout, it was that figuring out what worked for a person and accepting it was important to contentment. He could absolutely run a scene with the subbiest of women, but when it came to engaging his emotions, he preferred someone like Devi.

Or he might just prefer Devi period.

"What makes you think that, sub?" Yeah, that sounded like he was in control. Which he was. Body-wise he was totally in control. There was something going on that made him worry emotionally he was sliding off the deep end.

Which would be a terrible idea. This was a one-night thing.

"Well, you've been very circumspect, Sir. I don't know if you noticed but a lot of the tops were touching their subs quite intimately out there. It was a hot scene. I was surprised you didn't touch me. Are you worried about my brother?" she asked, her head tilting sideways as though assessing him.

Did she think he hadn't thought about cupping her breasts as she stood in front of him, practically leaning back against him? "I'm not worried about your brother. TJ is actually a pretty reasonable guy. If I stepped out of line he would deal with me and probably be pretty mean about it, but I could say the same thing about your cousins. I don't want Team Taggart deciding I'm fucking over their cousin and burying me six feet under. I've heard a lot about pools."

Her lips turned up in a slightly evil smile. "We were all taught that from a young age. Getting a body in right before the frame and gunite go in is chef's kiss when it comes to handling your enemies. I will start to worry when the twins finally buy a place and talk about pools. So if you're not anxious about my brother, then maybe you're not attracted to me and we should call this what it is."

She wanted to push him? She knew damn well he was attracted to her since his erection had pressed against her ass most of the night. He knew she felt it because she rubbed those sweet, round cheeks against him, making it hard to focus. "What is it, Devon?"

A brow rose over her eyes as though she felt challenged by the deep tone of his voice. "A miscalculation on both our parts."

He thought about it for a moment. She obviously needed more from him, and not in a beg-for-your-attention way. Even though he kind of felt like it. "If what you need is a Dom who reads your mind and is only involved in a scene for your good, then yes, you have miscalculated, brat. While we've known each other for a while, we don't know each other well. Do you want a quick lay? I'm probably willing to do that. I was attempting to gauge what you like and what you don't. You were busy teasing me and making sarcastic comments."

She flushed slightly. "I wasn't."

He crossed his arms over his chest, feeling more in control now because she wasn't exactly running from him. He was deeply attracted to her, but if the brattiness was all there was to her, then that attraction would fade quickly. He needed some balance. "Your response when I asked you what you liked about the scene was all the dicks."

That flush grew deeper. "Well, it was weird. I'll be honest, Sir. I've never watched a scene with a top before. No one's ever asked me to watch with them. I'm not a newbie or anything. I've run scenes with Doms, but mostly in a training capacity. I was distracted by the scene and Gabe trying to keep the dumbass new Doms in line. And apparently I'm self-conscious in a way I'm usually not."

Sweet honesty. There she was. "And the teasing?"

"Well, that felt good, Sir," she admitted.

"We went over the rules before we watched that scene." He knew exactly where this was leading. He was going to take this night with her. Hell, he was here for at least a couple of days. If she wanted to play, he would be up for it. Literally, and in a painful way. But Zach welcomed it because it meant he wanted something. Someone. He utterly dismissed his previous puppy love for Tasha. It had been exactly that. An infatuation with a kind, lovely woman who belonged to a family he wished was his. He wanted to belong and Tasha would have given that to him, but there was a reason he hadn't truly pursued her. "Honesty is important. I told you how much I need communication, and you ignored that rule. I asked you questions so I could get to know what you like and don't like. Now you're going to find out what I do to pretty subs who try to manipulate me."

"Manipulate you?"

This wasn't the same situation as Tash. Devi was different. He didn't care that her last name was Taggart. It was kind of a drawback since TJ might have a problem with it if he noticed. It didn't matter. He was going to run Devi to ground and give her everything he had. Starting with the flat of his palm on her pretty ass. "Yes. You haven't been honest with me all night. Let's see. First you act like a fainting virgin when I ask if you want to play."

Her jaw tightened and she stood, head tilting up. She wore ridiculous heels, but he still had two inches on her. He liked that she was tall. A lot of women barely came to his shoulders, but Devi would be able to go on her toes and brush her lips against his with ease. She looked like she was going to spit bile his way, but then she backed off. "That's fair."

Good. Another round of honesty. "Why?"

"I didn't expect an invitation from you, Sir."

"Why?" He wanted to be fair. "Not that I think you've been sitting around thinking about me. But you were standing there looking hot as hell in the middle of a BDSM club. You didn't expect a Dom to ask you to play? Or you didn't expect me to ask you? Is it because I work with TJ now?"

Her nose wrinkled, and she was the perfect mix of hot and adorable. He wanted to brush his lips over the freckles there. "You give me the perfect excuse, and I can't take it. I want to say yeah, it's all about my brother, but I grew up in a stupid household that preached stupid honesty. Fine. Zach, I have thought a lot about you. I was attracted to you from the moment I met you. Don't think I'm sitting around pining or anything. Just attracted. I had a rough week. A lot of rejection to process. So I walked into the club tonight planning on finding one of the new Doms to play with. Mostly for stress relief."

"Stress relief or to get some of your confidence back?" he asked.

"Both, I suppose, but the stress relief was in there."

He couldn't help it. He put his hand under her chin, getting her into the right position. "I like it when you're honest with me, sweetness."

"Good, then you should know I'm not that sweet."

He doubted that. "I'll be the judge of that. Tell me something.

Have you ever eaten out your own pussy?"

She flushed but she didn't back down. "I'm flexible, but I think that's beyond me, Sir."

He leaned over and kissed the bridge of her nose and all those adorable freckles. "Then you have no idea how sweet you are."

"You don't know either, Sir," she replied in a breathy tone.

"Not yet, sweetness, but I will before the night is over. Now I thank you for all that honesty, but it's not going to save you," he said, his mouth hovering above hers. "Pull your pants down and lay over my lap."

She groaned. "You're going to spank me when I did what you asked?"

"I'm going to spank you for disobeying the rules." He was well aware he was a bastard, but it didn't matter. This was what she wanted. It was all play. "I'm going to eat your pussy and make you forget about everything else because you were honest."

"You the carrot and the stick, Captain?"

She was a quick learner. "Only in here. Only when we're playing. I think you'll find I can be perfectly amenable to being a large lap dog at times, too. It's been a while since I took care of someone."

Hadn't he said this was for one night? He was already pushing the boundaries.

She stepped back and for a moment he worried she would walk or at least try to reset those boundaries. Instead she stood there, watching him as she reached for the waistband of her boy shorts. He expected she would push them down those long legs of hers but instead she pulled, a steady, strong motion, and the shorts split at the sides with a Velcro sound.

He felt a smile cross his lips. "They're tearaway? Like I could pretend to rip your clothes off but I wouldn't destroy them?"

She held them up. "Yep. Cute, huh?"

He could see her pussy. Fuck. He was so hard he could barely breathe. This was what happened when he let it go for way too long. He hadn't had sex in months, and it was making him a little crazy.

Or it's about her, dumbass.

When had he started hearing Ian Taggart's voice in his head? He had daddy issues.

"Is the corset?"

Her eyes heated up and the brat was back. The gorgeous fucking sexy brat. "Why don't you find out?"

He was not letting that invite go unanswered. He moved in and put his hands on either side of her corset. It was a gorgeous emerald green that made her skin glow and set off the natural red of her hair. It was beautifully made with laces up the back and hooks and eyes in the front. Or were they? He ripped the corset off her, and it split in two easily.

She was grinning even as those perfect tits of hers were perking up before him. "I found this real trick with the Velcro. No one can tell. I use thin material but it's strong. It looks like the hooks and eyes hold it together, right?"

That's what she did. That's right. TJ mentioned she was a designer. He hadn't been sure if it was graphics or interior. Clothes. Fashion. It fit her. "It's amazing, sweetness. You need to produce a whole line of these. Doms love to rip clothes off."

She was smiling so brightly and so comfortable with her nudity. "I know. And corsets are expensive. I once overheard my mom talking about how many times she had to buy new laces for hers because my dad would get impatient and take a knife to them. I know. It was a weird childhood. But it got me thinking. Most of the time tearaways look like crap."

He sat on the bed and held a hand out. "You tell me all about it, sweetness, while we get the discipline portion of the evening out of the way. I want to play with you, Devi, but I think I want to fuck you more. I think I might need to get the fucking part out of the way before I tie you up and see how much edging you can take."

He could actually see her nipples tighten. She was a little hard core. Good. He could be rough.

She nodded, her eyes a bit unfocused. "Yes. I could use that myself, Sir, and I'll take you up on the play, though I don't know how much time we'll have tonight. It's getting late."

"Then we'll have to try this again tomorrow."

"I thought this would be a one-night thing."

He gave her a shrug. "It might be. I could be terrible at this, and you might walk away."

Her eyes rolled. "Sure, you are. Tell me something, Captain, are you terrible at sex?"

"No, sweetness. You might think you were going to steal a night from me, but you'll be in my bed tomorrow, too. Now lay over my lap. Your safe word is red." They'd gone over this before watching the scene. She had few hard limits. He wasn't worried he would scare her. She was used to the lifestyle. He believed she would use that safe word if she needed to. He wasn't going to give her a reason.

She took his hand and let him help her down. "It's been a while since I had sex, Sir."

He stared at the globes of her ass. So fucking pretty. He cupped one, and a shudder went through her. "Me, too, and the last time I had sex it was for intel. You should know that. I've fucked for intel before. I want to be honest with you."

"I don't know that I like the sound of that," she admitted.

"I don't either. I did it because I didn't have anyone who mattered to me. Not in that way. I suppose I really did it because I had a bunch of people who did matter to me in other ways. But I don't think I want to do that again. I didn't like how it made me feel."

She sighed and relaxed. "Well, I haven't had sex in six months. I've been focused on getting the job I want. Which I didn't get. Hence the need for stress relief."

He stroked the cheeks of her ass, from the dip in her lower back to her thighs, learning her gentle curves. "It sucks to work hard and not get what you want. I'm sorry to hear it, sweetness, but it still won't save you."

He brought his hand up and then down in a sharp arc, the crack sounding through the small room. Her skin immediately pinkened, and she gasped.

"I don't want to be saved," she admitted. "We both know this punishment is going to get me hot as hell and ready for you to do everything you said you would. Now ask your questions again and I'll be honest."

He slapped her ass again. And again. This was going to be fun, and he liked how fair she was. He had tried to get a read on her during the scene, but she'd been snarky and elusive. "What do you like about D/s?"

Two more smacks.

A laugh huffed out of her, and though he couldn't see her expression he was sure there was a self-deprecating smile on her face.

"The honesty. Which I know how that sounds. I like that I can ask for what I want and at least here, no one will make fun of me for it. I can be who I am."

The irony was not lost on him, but he pushed the guilt aside. He wasn't lying to hurt the team. Just to hopefully save his mother, and his secrets wouldn't touch Devi. If he had his way, they wouldn't touch anyone. He gave her another two smacks, and she hissed at the pain but almost immediately relaxed. "Then why the walls?"

"You know why, Zach. I told you. I was way more attracted to you than I should be, and those hard slaps of yours are not helping. Damn Doms are always too soft. They think I'm fragile or something."

She liked it rough. If he'd had worries she didn't understand the word, they were overwritten now because he wasn't holding back and she was taking it all beautifully. "You're not fragile, but you need to understand that there's a place for sarcasm, Taggart. I know it's your family's love language, but I don't want it here. Not when I'm trying to get to know you."

"Yes, Sir," she offered sweetly.

The sarcasm was part of her DNA, but there was a well of sweetness in this woman that it seemed like no one had tapped yet, had been smart enough to wrap around himself and get warmed by. "What did you like about the scene we watched?"

Another smattering of slaps across her backside. Her skin was getting a hot sheen to it and yet there was nothing but a restlessness to her slight movements. As though she wanted more, wanted to tempt him to give her everything.

"It was raw. It was real. They didn't hold back. Well, Carys did at first, but then she went for it. I don't know. It gave me some hope for them," she admitted. Her hand wound around his ankle, steadying herself for the blows she knew were coming.

He gave them to her. Hard smacks that had her stiffening and releasing, breathing unsteady gusts of air. He liked the honesty. All she'd been willing to tell him before was she found it hot. So he now felt better about asking the questions he was interested in. "Did you like the ménage?"

Her hand moved on his leg. "Yes."

Another smack and then he caressed her, tracing the red spots with his fingertips. So pretty. "Is it something you're interested in?"

"I don't think that's for me, Sir. I like watching it, but I've never wanted to participate. I think I'm a one-man woman. Unless you have someone in mind."

Three smacks. He did not. Actually, the thought kind of made him violent. He'd spent a whole two hours with this woman, and he was already possessive as hell. "I'm definitely a one-woman man. I can't handle two subs, and I would struggle to share with another dominant partner. I'm not that patient or tolerant. I'm going to touch your pussy, sweetness. Spread your legs a little."

Her hand tightened around his ankle but she did as he asked, her thighs spreading slightly so he could get his hand between her legs.

And then there was zero doubt she liked what he was doing to her. Her feminine flesh was soft and wet and practically begging him to take a taste.

Not how he'd meant his night to go. He'd thought he would maybe spank a sub and send her on her way and meet up with his brother in the bar after. Sometimes he went with Coop and Kala to get burgers or waffles after the night's play. He hadn't meant to spend the evening with a woman as intriguing as Devi.

But he was going for it. And fuck the whole one-night thing. He wanted more.

He stroked her pussy, lightly at first, and watched as her breath hitched and she moaned lightly, hips shifting to accommodate him. "I'm here in Dallas for a couple of weeks. At least until we ship out again, but I'm going to be honest with you, I'm thinking of changing things up and living here in Dallas for a while. Coop has an empty room, so there's space for me."

"Really?" she asked quietly.

He couldn't read her yet, wasn't certain that *really* was a good question or a *damn, I thought I wouldn't have to see you so often* query. He found her clit and ran a finger over it, gently and then with more pressure. "Really. So if you're serious about the whole one-night stress relief thing, we should think about this. I'm worried if I get a taste of you, it won't be enough. I don't want to pursue a woman who isn't interested in anything but one night."

Who the fuck was he? This was insane. He should be running, but his whole body was focused on one thing and one thing only—

her. "Yeah, I work for more than one team, but Ian's told me if I want to pull back, he can make it happen. If I'm only working for this team, then there's no real reason for me to be located in DC. I like it here. And when I say here, I mean this club. I mean I like these people."

He worked at her clit, gently pressing and rotating while she squirmed on his lap.

"I think that sounds nice, Captain," she replied.

He liked the way she called him captain. Even if he could lose it all easily, he liked the way she said it. "So maybe we're not bound by this whole one night of stress relief?"

He wasn't sure he could walk away from her no matter what her answer was. He might take his chance and hope he was good enough in bed to bring her back at some point.

"I have a lot of stress," she said, her palm running up his calf. "It could take you days and days to relieve all of my stress. Maybe weeks."

He felt a smile cross his face and he withdrew his hand, smacking that pretty ass one last time. He had not started his day thinking to find a sub—a girlfriend—but he liked the thought. It was way too early, but he got the feeling this relationship was going to be intense. They would either burn out or maybe if they were lucky, find something lovely. Either way he was going with it.

"Then we should get started."

* * * *

Devi's ass felt like it was on fire, and she liked it. Her captain didn't play around. He went for it. So often she had to coax a Dom into going hard, but Zach seemed to know exactly what she needed. She'd longed for someone who would push her boundaries, but what she'd found was she was constantly pushing theirs, and it didn't work. Not so for Zach Reed. He didn't hold back, and that did something for her.

Except when he stopped stroking her clit right as she thought she would come. Shitty timing. Or perfect timing given he was a Dom and they liked to fuck with a sub. He lifted her up and kind of tossed her lightly in the air, turning her over and catching her in strong arms. Her sore ass landed against his forearm. His muscular forearm that she kind of wanted to lick, but then she wanted to lick every inch of this man.

She was naked in his arms, and it felt fucking perfect. There was no awkwardness. She should feel awkward, right? It wasn't like she hadn't had sex or even some fairly kinky sex before. She'd had boyfriends over the years, but she'd never once felt this spark, this instant connection. They'd been in each other's circles for two years, but it was like someone flicked a switch on and the world was brighter, better, more exciting. This was what she heard about, read about in romances. It might not be true love, but it was chemistry, and she was here for it.

And he wanted more than a night. She could do that.

He laid her out on the big bed that dominated this privacy room. It was one of the more masculine rooms, done in dark colors and on the Spartan side, but all that mattered was the man in the room with her.

The whole night had been weird and wild, and she kind of loved it. She knew it wasn't like any night she'd ever had before. Probably wouldn't again.

He stood over her, all six foot four inches of hot Dom staring down. If she was dressing him, she would put him in clingy shirts and tailored trousers that would show off how toned and masculine his body was. She would use dark colors but with pops of greens and yellows and baby blues to bring out his eyes and hair and skin tone.

"You're gorgeous, sweetness," he said, his voice husky.

He made her feel gorgeous. She'd told her besties that this was about stress relief, but there was a confidence boost in there, too. It was hard to get rejected. Especially when it was her work. Her life's work.

She wasn't thinking about that tonight. Nope. She wasn't going to think about the fact that she might soon be a whole adult living with her parents, and that the money her parents and uncles had spent putting her through a private Manhattan college and paying for her life during several low paid but highly sought after internships seemed to mostly have gone to waste. She only had another six weeks on the apartment she rented. She hadn't signed a long-term lease because she was going to be in LA or New York.

She was going to have to move back in with her parents.

A brow rose over Zach's dark eyes, and a commanding look came into them. "Stop thinking whatever you're thinking or we can start again. I wouldn't mind tying you up and torturing you for a while. My dick would, but I'm not being led by him."

He put his big hands around her ankles and pulled her to the end of the bed before dropping to his knees.

Oh, fuck. He was going to do it. He was going to put that dirty, sexy mouth on her and she wouldn't be able to breathe.

"You can tell me to stop, Devi," he said as he ran his palms up her legs. He bent them, placing her ankles not on the edge of the bed, but on his shoulders, spread wide. Her pussy was on full display, and all the reasons that was a bad idea flew out of her head.

Nothing mattered except the way that hot Dom was looking at her pussy. Like it was a magical thing and he wanted to be a wizard really bad. She was sure Bri would make this super romantic and emotional if she was writing this scene, but all Devi could think about was sex and how good she would feel when this man put his mouth on her.

"Just because I do this for you doesn't mean you owe me sex," he said in a serious tone.

He was going to be that Dom. "I know my safe word, Zach. I want the sex. I want more than your tongue on me, though I want that. Unless I say that safe word, you need to understand that I am enthusiastically consenting to sex. Take me. Make me forget all the shitty stuff that's happened lately. Be the good thing that happened to me."

"Your fucking wish, sweetness." He lowered his head and covered her with his mouth.

She damn near came off the bed. Might have if he wasn't holding her down. He was so strong. She couldn't fight him if she wanted to, and a thousand kinky fantasies went through her head. Things she shouldn't think about. Dark, dirty scenarios played through her brain. How she could play with this man.

He licked at her delicately, playing around her labia and teasing her mercilessly.

When she looked down, his eyes were up, and a feral look came into them before he speared his tongue inside her.

Her eyes nearly rolled to the back of her head. She let herself fall to the bed, let her eyes close as he fucked her with his tongue and mouth and fingers.

The first orgasm rolled over her and she clutched the comforter, twisting it in her hands as she fought not to scream. It had been so long since she'd felt this way, sexy and vibrant and alive. Sometimes the only way she felt alive was when she was working. Now she felt that confidence pouring into her along with the pleasure.

Zach stood, her arousal still on his lips. He dragged his vest off and tossed it aside before going to work on the ties of his leathers. "You sure, sweetness? Because I don't think I'm going to want to let you go. We don't have a contract, but I'm already thinking about what I would put in one."

She could barely see straight. Her whole body was suffused with pleasure, but still his words were sweet. "You should know I don't sign any contracts without my attorney. Even D/s ones. You wanna be my Dom, you'll have to go through my cousin. It's okay. He sometimes falls asleep during negotiations. He was negotiating the rental agreement between the twins and Brianna, and he fell asleep on the couch. Apparently Colton had an ear infection and kept him up all night."

A brilliant smile came over his face. He was a little fallen angel-like most of the time. Gorgeous and a bit brooding, but when he really smiled it was like the sun came out. "I love your weird family. So much better than mine. There's never a dull moment. Well, then I'll have to make sure Travis is tired because I want to take serious advantage of you, gorgeous. Come here and kiss me. Touch me."

She could do that. Mostly. Her limbs were still noodley, but he was wrong. She did owe him. He'd done everything he promised, and she wanted to give him some payback. Of course that payback would almost certainly lead to another orgasm for her. She sat up and rolled to her knees. He stood at the end of the bed, his body on full display. Damn, she was with Zach Reed. She might wake up in a couple of minutes and she would be back in the locker room helping Daisy study for whatever test she was about to take and talking plot lines with Brianna.

She put a hand on his chest. It was sculpted beautifully, the skin warm and soft under her hand. He had the lightest dusting of hair over his chest, coming to a *V* at his six-pack abs and trailing down to… That was a gorgeous cock. Long and thick and already weeping with arousal.

"Yeah, you do that to me, sweetness." His tone was low and guttural, as though he was forcing himself to stay calm and not throw her down and fuck her hard.

They would get to that. Eventually. He would discover she liked to role-play. A lot. She let her hand move down his body as she tilted her head up and he devoured her lips. His tongue invaded, stroking against hers even as she found his cock and wrapped her hand around it. He was so fucking hard, and she gently caressed his cock with one hand and wrapped the other around his strong, broad shoulders.

She could kiss this man forever. If this was some desperate dream she was having, she didn't want to wake up.

He eased her back, spreading her legs and making a place for himself there. He stared down at her as he managed to rip the condom wrapper open and start sheathing his cock. "You are too gorgeous for me. Say it again, Devi. Tell me you want me. I'm nothing but a soldier in the end. I don't have much to offer you, but I promise if you let me, I'll worship the damn ground you walk on."

It sounded perfect to her, and she was surprised he was so romantic. It made her heart flutter, but she didn't want this to move so fast he got scared off. He was in the heat of the moment. He didn't mean it. "I think you have a lot to offer, Sir. I think it's going to be lovely to be your sub."

He moved over her, and then that big dick of his was pressed to her pussy. "You're going to be my sweet sub. I'm going to take care of you."

He thrust inside her, and she gasped at the fullness. She was so wet there was no pain at all, but he was big and filled her up in a way she'd never been before. She wrapped her legs around his waist as he pushed inside her again.

"You feel so fucking good," Zach groaned. He stared into her eyes. "So right."

She let her arms drift around his neck, looking back up at him. He was so lovely. If he wasn't in the military, she would talk him into letting that jet black hair grow out so it would be slightly shaggy and she could run her fingers through it. "Back at you, Sir."

He fucked her in earnest now, his big body working over hers. He let himself go, and it was feral and wild and everything she hadn't known she needed. She held on while he pushed her higher and higher. This time she'd didn't hold back. When his cock hit the right place deep inside her, she let out a shout. She let her nails bite into him, and he simply growled and fucked her harder.

She came twice before he gave over and let himself go. His hands tangled in her hair as he held himself deep inside her, giving up everything he had.

That big body came down on hers, his head finding the crook of her neck. "That did not suck."

Oh, but he had, and it was glorious. "It did not suck, Sir."

She smoothed her hands down his back.

He lay there for a moment and then another, and a feeling of peace settled on Devi. He was correct. This felt different. It felt right. How could she fit so effortlessly with this man when most of her other relationships had been awkward, at least in the beginning?

Were they starting a relationship? Or had that been play, too? They hadn't set parameters.

He sighed and shifted off her. "Be right back. Whatever is going through your head now, stop."

"What's that supposed to mean?"

He stood and pulled the condom off, tying it neatly. "Sweetness, it means you are easy to read and while you were perfectly happy for a couple of minutes there, you got stiff, and I could feel the distance. Stop it. I don't like it. I know it's fast, but I don't like you pulling away from me, especially when I don't know why."

He walked into the bathroom. She heard him turn on the sink.

Well, he didn't hold back.

And he didn't like distance between them.

She sat up but didn't bother covering herself. She wasn't going to fuck this up with her insecurities. When he walked back in, she let him pull her into his arms and lie back.

"Tell me what you're thinking, Devi."

She let herself listen to the strong beat of his heart for a second. "I was wondering if all the contract talk was just play."

He squeezed her tight, like he didn't want to think about letting her go. "No. And I know it was too soon. I knew it the moment I said it. I don't want to scare you off. We don't have to have a contract. We don't have to be anything but friendly, if that's what you want. I would really like to see you again. Not in the club. I mean I want to see you in the club, too, but I want to… I don't know, be out in the world with you. My life is a series of scenes. At least that's what it feels like at times. I'm always playing a role. I don't want to do that with you."

Or she was completely wrong and he was being honest and vulnerable with her. "I like a contract, Sir. I don't think I need wholesome dates to know I would like to sub for you."

"But I want the dates, too." He sounded a bit hollow now. "Unless you don't want anyone to know."

She sat up, breaking his hold on her. She needed to look at him, make him believe. His back was against the headboard of the bed, so she straddled him and felt his cock start to come back to life against her inner thigh. She put her hands on either side of his face and looked him in the eyes. "I love my family. They do not have any say in who I see or date or sub for. TJ and I are close, but we stay out of each other's dating lives. Otherwise, he would have gotten many a lecture from me over how he treated Lou. Of course now that they're finally together, he's so into her I doubt he'll even notice I'm dating someone. My father, on the other hand, will be twelve kinds of up your ass, and not the way you think."

"I think he'll probably want to know what I'm doing with his daughter. He'll likely want to know why a spy is hanging out in his baby girl's bed," Zach replied. "He's a Taggart. He'll be overly protective and probably sarcastic about it."

Oh, it was nice that he didn't know everything. "Haven't spent much time with my dad, have you? No. That's my mom. She's the one who'll ask how this whole thing works since you're playing the spy game. My dad will want to know when the wedding is and what's your favorite Taylor Swift song."

Zach winced. "Really?"

She nodded. "Oh, yeah. You'll love Mom. She'll growl a lot and threaten to bury you alive if you hurt me. She means that, but she's pretty reasonable about what constitutes hurt. The torture and death thing only applies in the most dire circumstances. But my dad is serious about wedding planning, and he's not getting a lot from TJ and Lou. They seem happy to wait for a while."

"All your brother needs to be happy is Lou and a never-ending supply of snacks." His lips had curled up. "But your mom would be right about the spy thing. I'm gone a lot, but I want to see you when I'm here. I'll be here more often if I have my way. And honestly, this is not a job I plan on doing forever. At some point I want to put down roots and enjoy a life that doesn't include people shooting at me."

"Well, then you should rethink seeing me, Sir, because that seems to be a theme lately." She frowned. "I don't like being kidnapped and threatened with death all to get my bestie's attention."

He flipped her over and loomed above her. "What?"

She thought everyone knew about her dance with death. "A couple of weeks back Daisy got into some trouble with a cartel, and they ended up doing the whole gun to my head thing because I wanted some fresh air. I was babysitting that night for Sanctum, and I don't know if you have been informed but sometimes babies make a lot of poop. I needed the fresh air because Michael and Vanessa's baby girl recently started solids. It was a lot. A lot, Zach. But not like so much I would be willing to be kidnapped to not have to change another diaper."

He was perfectly still. "What?"

He did not seem to be following her. "It was cool. Daisy distracted the bad guys with her boobs, or maybe it was her hootch since she was full-on unclothed, if you know what I mean. Then Nate killed a bunch of people and my uncle laughed his ass off and my mom yelled at me about something called situational awareness and my dad brought me a glass of wine and everything was okay."

Zach rolled off her, his arm going over his eyes as though he couldn't stand to see the world for a moment. "We're not going to do that again. I can't take it, sweetness. No one's after Bri, right?"

"I think Bri is safe. She's like a nun. That's what they call us. The nuns of The Hideout." She hated that nickname.

His arm came down, and the sexiest smirk hit his face. "You are not a nun. Let me prove it to you and then we'll go get dressed and I'll take you out for waffles. I heard it's what a bunch of the Doms do."

And he wanted to be normal. It was clear to her that he wanted a break from the dangers of his life. He wanted her to be a safe place for him. "I think that sounds lovely. Both ideas."

He was on top of her again. He moved with the grace and quickness of a predator in his prime. "But first, you're going to tell me the whole story. All of it. Except you can skip the poop part. And then when we go out you're going to tell me why I might be the one good thing. I want to know everything about you, Devi. Everything."

He leaned down and kissed her, and she was pretty sure he was too good to be true.

Chapter Three

"Do you know what you're doing?"

Zach stopped shaving and looked over to where his brother stood. Cooper was already dressed to go into the office. "Getting ready to go to brunch and then trying to figure out how to get my reports done asap so I can spend the afternoon with her, too. After the conference meeting, of course. Can't miss that, but then I think Big Tag won't care if I have everything done that I need to do."

He was feeling optimistic, but then a night of ridiculously hot sex with a woman he was crazy about put him in a good mood. It hadn't simply been the sex. It had been the real intimacy. She'd been open and honest with him. They'd really talked.

He'd really lied. But not about the important stuff. Just the stuff that could get her killed.

"I meant with Devi. Hunter told me you played with her last night, and Tris mentioned you two left the club together. I happen to know you didn't walk into this house until about an hour ago," Cooper pointed out.

Damn. He washed the shaving cream from his face and dried off before turning to Cooper. "I stayed at her place. We went out for waffles and ended up talking all night. I didn't realize there was a curfew. I'm sorry. I'll let you know next time. I appreciate you letting me stay here. I hate getting stuck in hotels."

"And if I ask you to back away from Devi?" Cooper asked.

Wow. He felt himself stand up straighter, felt his fists threaten to clench. He kind of thought he would pick his brother over anyone, would do whatever it took to make Cooper feel comfortable around him but this…no. He liked Devi. He felt good when he was around her, and even if this wasn't going to last forever, he wanted the time with her. She was important.

Before he could formulate a response, a slow smile crossed Coop's face. "You like her."

He breathed a sigh of relief. His brother was pressing a button to see how he would respond. He could understand. Cooper had known Devi his whole life. "I like her. I like her a lot. I…I don't think I've liked anyone in a long time the way I like her."

"I think that's great," Cooper said, leaning against the wall. He looked all happy and carefree now. "Devi's a great girl, and she's been looking for a play partner for a long time."

It felt too good to have his brother on his side, but he should make his position clear. "It doesn't bother you I want to date Devi?"

Cooper sobered. "Date? As in see her outside the club?"

Why did everyone think he only wanted a club relationship? He liked regular things. He liked movies and waffles and hanging out in places where there were no spanking benches. "Well, I definitely saw her outside the club last night. I'm planning on the same tonight."

Cooper nodded. "I like it. Devi needs someone with a firm hand when it comes to D/s and an indulgent one in life. But you know she's planning on moving, right? She wants to get back to Manhattan."

He thought Coop was wrong. They'd spent several hours in an all-night diner talking about this. She'd told him what was going on in her career. "It's not about the city. It's about the job. She's been applying at a bunch of design houses. That's what she called them. The New York ones didn't pan out. She's trying to get into sportswear or something. I think she should do fet wear. The stuff she does is stunning and easy to use, if you know what I mean."

Cooper nodded. "She did a couple of Kala's corsets, and she designed Carys's wedding dress. Not that she got to wear it for long."

Zach winced. He'd heard about what happened at the failed wedding of Aidan and Carys. He was kind of glad since he knew how much Tristan loved them both. Tris was trying to distance because of the secret op they were involved in. The one none of their team knew about.

But then Tristan didn't know the whole story either. Tristan had no idea how Zach manipulated the situation, and he was going to keep it that way. "She showed me some of her work when we went back to her place. She's so talented. If she ends up in LA or Paris or wherever, the good news is I can travel."

"I'm glad you're serious. Devi's great. You should know though that Kala loves her cousin and if you fuck her over…"

"She will kill me. I'm cool with that. I have zero intentions of fucking Devi over. I'm going to get to know her."

Cooper stepped back, shaking his head. "I do not know who you are right now. It's the smile."

He rolled his eyes. "I smile, asshole."

Cooper shrugged. "I mean is it a smile?"

He smiled. Sometimes. He intended to smile way more.

"I'm heading over to pick up Kala before we go into work. She's a beast without a pitcher of coffee and a chocolate croissant," Cooper said. "You need a ride?"

This was something they should discuss. "Nah, Devi's picking me up in half an hour. We're going to some brunch place she likes and then she'll drop me off. We were talking about maybe seeing a movie or something tonight. I should get a car."

Cooper shrugged. "Why?" Then his brows rose. "Are you talking about renting something or buying a car, because you pretty much don't need one in DC."

Dangerous ground, but he was feeling like pushing his luck since it seemed to have changed the night before. "Well, that is something I wanted to talk to you about."

"I am shitty at buying cars," Cooper admitted. "I'm a complete walk in the door and pay whatever they want because haggling seems rude. But if you take Kala with you, they'll give you a deal just to shut her down. She can be brutal, and she knows way more about engines than you think she does."

He knew a lot about them, too, but he wasn't supposed to be that smart. Like they didn't realize he spoke a couple of languages. He was the military grunt. They didn't need to know he was actually a hell of a hacker and had fooled Tristan Dean-Miles a couple of times. Kala's best friend and the team's resident tech expert, Louisa Ward, thought he was a moron who could barely turn a computer on, and that was the way he needed it for now. "Well, then I'll have to ask her to go in with me. I might not need a car to get around DC, but Dallas is another story. If I want to go anywhere outside the city, I need a car."

"Seriously? But Zach that would mean…" Cooper left the statement open ended, as though trying to figure out if Zach actually knew what he was saying.

His himbo cover worked way too well. "I'm going to talk to Big Tag soon. I know they want active military to work with these teams, but like Tristan, I don't want to spread my focus too much. It gets messy. I can still liaise with military even if I give up my active status and work strictly for the Agency and for our team. Which means I would move to Dallas and probably have a cover job with McKay-Taggart. I hear they're always looking for bodyguards."

Cooper sighed and seemed to consider the problem for a moment. "I think your timing is impeccable. I was wondering how I was going to justify staying here without a roommate. It's kind of a big house. You looking for a place to stay?"

This was actually happening. Everything he'd wanted was right in reach. "I was hoping you would say that. It is a good time because after that scene last night, I think those three are going to figure it out. Eventually, but don't Tris's parents own this place? Are they willing to be our landlords?"

"Serena actually bought this place a couple of years back," Cooper explained. "She was clear that I could stay as long as I want, and she's open to me buying her out over time. I like it here. It's comfortable."

More importantly Kala liked it here. She'd mentioned a couple of times how much she liked what she called the boys' place. Of course she'd also mentioned one of the reasons she liked it was the backyard had plenty of space for a pool.

Yeah, he knew what that meant. "Then I would love to take one of the empty rooms. Let me know what my share of rent is and I'll start handling half the bills until you bring in someone else."

There were four bedrooms in this big rambling house, though Cooper had only ever had two roommates. Tristan and Aidan once had rooms here. Nate Carter was supposed to move in, but he'd only been around for a week or so before he ended up engaged to Daisy O'Donnell and living at her place.

"The only person I might invite is my brother if he needs a place to stay, but he seems happy in my parents' pool house for now. I think that might change when he finishes up his masters and goes to work. But he could surprise me and move states for all I know. He promised my dad he would get his education and then he could roam around the world for a while. So it might not happen. He might be like our sister and never come home again."

Vivian McKay lived in London, and he knew Coop felt the distance. He loved his siblings.

It made him wonder what it had been like to grow up with Alex and Eve McKay as parents. In that big comfy house with a brother and sister and a found family that never let him down.

"Hunter's a good kid. I wouldn't mind at all. I promise I'll be a quiet roommate with very little drama." He would be Cooper's steadfast brother even if he never knew.

Coop nodded and pulled his cell out. "See that you do. And the room is one hundred percent yours. Maybe when we get back from the Montreal op we can find you a car. I need to go. You're sure you don't need a ride?"

He'd already gotten three adorable texts from his sub. Oh, they didn't have a contract, but she was his sweet sub and he was going to enjoy it. "She'll be here soon. And just so you know we're going to a showing of old-school *Star Wars* tonight. Devi's only seen the prequels."

Coop's eyes lit up. "You know Kala loves *Star Wars*. She mentioned something about it. If you two don't mind, we might tag along. Like a not double date since we won't mention that I'm dating her without her acknowledging it."

"A not double date sounds great." Everything was falling into place. He wasn't even tricking Devi into a double. Last night she'd been the one to mention Kala loved old-school Star Wars, and wouldn't it be fun to show her how nice it was to date. She loved her cousin, knew her cousin loved Cooper, and was trying to make it as easy as possible for Kala to fall into a relationship.

Kala could be complex.

"Then I'll see you at the office where I'm sure we'll get a shit ton of lectures on how to protect Carys and Aidan," Cooper said with a grin.

He strode off, and Zach could hear him pick up his keys from the tray near the front door. It opened and closed, and he heard the lock slide into place.

Zach moved through the house that would soon be his home, contemplating the fact that when he asked Big Tag to move him fully onto the team, he was going to tell him why he'd been assigned to the team in the first place.

He poured himself the last cup of coffee and switched it off. He needed to get dressed. She would be here soon.

Would Ian be upset? Or would he roll his eyes and say he already knew and had some plan to make him a weird in-house double agent against his military enemies?

He moved to the hallway and saw Devi's graceful form silhouetted in the opaque window of the door.

Damn. He'd do it. He would pretty much do anything Big Tag asked him to because he wanted to be part of whatever family that woman was in.

He set his mug down and wished he wasn't about to open the door wearing his sweatpants and nothing else. He was supposed to be ready. He was supposed to be on time and prepared. It was kind of his brand. Zach Reed. Not too smart, but damn the man is on time.

He opened the door and she stood there wearing jeans and a cute top that showed off her midriff. She was beautifully put together. Casually elegant with a hint of "look, I go to the gym."

She'd dressed for him, and he wasn't even ready on time. "Hey, sweetness. I'm so sorry I'm running late. I'll be two minutes."

She stepped inside, and her eyes roamed his chest, a fine flush coming over her skin. "Oh, I think you can do way better than two minutes, Sir."

She leaned in, her hand going to his chest and her mouth tilting up in invitation.

All thought fled and utter lust took its place. He locked his mouth over hers, kissing her like she was all he needed in the whole fucking world.

Brunch would have to wait.

* * * *

One week later Devi pulled up to the private airfield and wished she knew more about this secret mission her Dom was going on. He'd told her the bare minimum. They had a good shot at getting a bunch of information on some doctor guy they'd been checking out. He was a bad guy according to Zach, and Aidan had an invite to his house because of some kind of medical conference, and they were all flying into Canada.

She parked the car and Zach turned to her, reaching for her hand and pulling it in both of his.

"I don't want to go."

Only a few days and she was in so damn deep. They'd spent pretty much every minute of the week together when he wasn't working. While he was at the office, she worked on commissions. She had three right now, two corsets and a catsuit. Being with Zach, though, had inspired her, and she'd designed several fet wear costumes that would bring her Dom to his knees. She liked him on his knees. When he was there he usually had his face buried in her pussy. "I don't want you to go. I want to walk in there and tell my uncle he sucks because we haven't even had a second night at The Hideout."

He squeezed her hand. "I promise when I get back we're playing every night it's open. You need to think about what kind of scenes you want." His voice went low and that tone went straight to her pussy. "I want you to write down your darkest fantasies. Write them down and send them to me and I'll make them happen, sweetness. All those dirty things you dream about, I'll give them to you in a safe fashion. But I promise, it won't feel safe."

Yeah, she was pretty crazy about him. The *L* word was creeping into her brain. "I should warn you that some of my fantasies are complex."

He brought her hand to his lips. "I can handle it, Devi. I can handle you."

She was a lot. Could be a lot. She could be overly emotional and passionate when she thought she was right. She pretty much mostly thought she was right and could be super stubborn about it. How many times had someone told her she was too much? The only reason she wasn't considered the Queen Bitch of her friends' group was the fact that her cousin was in the group. Kala often made her look good.

Zach liked Kala. Liked her. Liked complex women. "I can handle you, too, you know. I can handle this. I'll be okay without you, and I won't ask questions when you come home. This is your work. Both my parents were military."

"Not when they had you. You didn't have to watch them leave. What if I get pulled from this assignment and deployed?"

"Then we have some decisions to make," she replied honestly.

"I would leave. I would see if Ian would hire me on at MT, and I would be here with you. I would let all the rest of it go and see the whole thing as fate."

"Or I could go with you," she said quietly.

He shook his head. "No. I want you to have the life you want. I don't think you can find that on a base, and if I'm out in the field we wouldn't even see each other. We're lucky it's all short-term assignments right now. If it gets worse, I'll look into pulling that lever. If I hate leaving you right now, how am I going to feel in a couple of months?"

"You might be sick of me in a couple of months," she pointed out.

He leaned over and kissed her. "I won't."

She believed him. Zach Reed seemed to know what he wanted, and he wanted her. "Well, I can give you something more to look forward to. I think when you get back you should come to dinner at my parents' house."

His lips spread in a slow smile. "And we'll introduce me as…"

"My boyfriend," she admitted. "They can extrapolate the Dom part. It's weird talking about the lifestyle with my parents."

"Boyfriend is good." He kissed her again. "For now." He sighed and glanced down at the clock. "I should go."

She didn't want him to go. She was like a love-struck teen, desperate to keep the object of her affection close. But she was a whole grown ass woman, so she sucked it up. "We're getting you a car when you get back. I talked to Kala about it and everything."

He snorted. "I'll do as she says." He sobered slightly. "You like double dating with them, right? I ask because I really like it, but we can slow play that if you want to."

"I love it. I love watching them date when neither of them will admit they're dating. It's so weird. Are they like that in the field?"

He sighed. "So much worse. Coop is useless because he can't even pretend to flirt with anyone else. Huh, I guess that's going to be hard for me now, too. I didn't think about that."

He was adorable. She kind of loved that about him. It was honestly hard to think of him as some scary spy who did in the bad guys. He was Zach. Sure, he could be a hardass Dom, but that was all about play. When her cousins talked about Zach it was like he was some larger than life killing machine, and that just wasn't Zach. He was like her brother and her dad. Yes, they were military, but in a huggy, Golden Retriever way. She kissed him again. "No flirting in the field. I like that rule. But seriously, you have to come to dinner. My mom wants to get to know you better. She likes you. She was the one who suggested—and I mean that in the Erin Taggart definition of the term—I haul your ass to family dinner. Her words, not mine."

His grin amped up. "I like her, too. Your mom is a legend. And I'm glad she married your dad because I've heard he makes a mean brisket."

Oh, she was going to miss him. "I'll make sure he knows you're looking forward to it."

He opened the car door and got out, grabbing his bag from the backseat. "Well, come on, sweetness. Let's get this part over with."

She was unaware there was another part. She looked at him through the open door. "I thought I was just dropping you off. Aren't we supposed to play this cool?"

He snorted and closed the door, jogging around to open hers. "Kala knows. And we haven't exactly been playing it cool with her and Coop. They know we're serious, so everyone knows we're serious. Although I don't think your brother knows, so he might punch me. I can take it."

She took the hand he offered her and grabbed her purse with the other. "He will not punch you. But my uncle might be surprised I know you're leaving on a classified op."

Zach held her hand as she locked the car and then started to lead her toward the terminal. "Then he shouldn't have made this a whole family thing. Everyone knows. We're the worst kept secret ever. Look, it might be different if your last name wasn't Taggart, but I'm not going to pretend to keep things from you. Mostly. I mean, baby, you know…"

She waved him off. "I do not need to know. If I needed to know my brother or my cousin would tell me, so I'm going to add you to that list. I'll trust you to tell me the things that would affect me or us."

He stopped in front of the doors to the lounge. "I'm crazy about you, Devi. Don't forget that while I'm gone."

"Promise, and same to you," she said, her damn stupid heart so full. She was falling hard for this man. So hard.

She already pretty much loved him.

He guided her into the lounge. The overflowing with her family lounge. It wasn't only the team. Uncle Sean was here, and so was Liam O'Donnell. She glanced over and her brother was half asleep on one of the benches, wrapped around Lou. Such a cute couple. She should have taken more pics of her and Zach. She had a couple of selfies, but looking at Lou and TJ she wanted a phone full of pics so she could remember him when he was working. She didn't get to tag along like Lou.

Uncle Ian stared at them, his eyes narrowing. So neither her mom nor her cousin had told on them. It was a little surprising since they both were on the gossipy side. "Dude, did you not get the not-a-family-reunion memo? You brought my niece to an Agency meeting? You know she's not supposed to know who you work for."

Zach's arm tightened around her shoulders, and she leaned against him. "Everyone knows, and every day with this team is a freaking family reunion. Devi gave me a ride."

"I just wanted to say hi, and y'all go and get whatever bad guys need to be gotten." She could be the cheerleader. Go team spy.

Her uncle sighed, his head shaking. "We're leaving now. Zach, we're going to have a talk."

"I expected we would, sir." Zach turned to her and didn't even hesitate. He leaned over and kissed her, lightly at first, and then like he was going to make her remember him while he was away.

When Devi came up for air, she remembered she was supposed to remind him. He'd done some work while he'd been at her place and mentioned he was worried about something. "Hey, don't forget you were going to warn them about the Tara person."

Zach winced. "Yeah, uhm, we're going to have to be careful with the twins because Tara's already in Montreal. I'm sorry, Tris. I just found out about it. Did she call you?"

Her cousin Carys looked to Tristan. "Tara?"

"She works as my technical assistant when I'm dealing with The Jester missions." Tris moved into her space, cupping Carys's face. "There's no reason for any jealousy. She's nothing but a woman I work with."

"Oh, I wasn't warning anyone because I was worried she would upset Carys." Zach's hand moved over her waist as though he didn't want to stop touching her. "I've worked with them both for years. Nothing there but work. However, she doesn't have clearance to know about the twins, so we need to be careful and make sure she's not waiting at the airport to give us a briefing. She said she's already met with CSIS, and they're going to have an operative liaising while we're in Canada."

She did not understand the alphabet soup of intelligence agencies. When Zach, Coop, and Kala started in on shop talk, she usually let her mind drift or ended up sketching. At first it seemed to worry Zach and he tried to pull her back into the conversation, but the truth was she liked it. It had been a long time since she'd felt so inspired. She was working on a corset with wings. Like a fairy. Who was going to get hard railed by a hot Dom.

"It better not be Ben." Kenzie stood and sighed. "Someone tell me when I have to hide. I hope she's not there because I'll have to hide in the stupid plane and get an Uber. A Canadian Uber."

Kala started for the door to the terminal. "Hey, if you get an Uber, you can stop at Tim Horton's. Dad won't let us. There's an upside."

Her cousins were a hoot.

"It's only because they didn't have lemon donuts the last time, and now Dad won't forgive an entire country," Kenzie pointed out. "But you're right. I'll totally grab some donuts. And maybe stop and get some crêpes. You know, now I see the advantages."

Tasha huffed. "Now she's going to try to sight-see, and I'll be the one who has to point out all the CCTV cameras and that other intelligence agencies also know how to use logic and technology. Mom, maybe I should stay and make sure Uncle Alex and Uncle Li don't burn down the company."

"I won't burn anything down. You know I've been running this company for a long time while your parents gallivant around the world," Uncle Liam replied in his lyrical Irish accent.

"She's trying to stay with Dare." Aunt Charlotte followed her daughters toward the door. "He can't go with us this time because he's actually working and not using his job as a cover. It's refreshing. Come along. TJ, wake up. Your sister's being manhandled."

"Am not." Though she totally felt Zach's hand dangerously close to her ass. He might want to get one more squeeze in. "I mean not in a way I'm not happy about."

Her brother yawned as he straightened up. "Is it time to go?" His gaze shifted her way. "Hey, sis. What are you doing here?"

She was going to throw her brother right into the fire. Everyone was moving into the terminal, but her brother stayed back. "Dropping my boyfriend off."

Lou elbowed TJ as she stretched and grabbed her bag. "I told you I thought something was going on between them."

"Dude, you know she's my sister, right?" TJ put the question to Zach. "What is happening? I'm very confused. Dude takes one little nap…"

Devi broke away from Zach and moved in to hug her brother. "I'm sure he'll fill you in. And we're going to have family dinner when you get back. All of us. The parents are excited about both of their kids being in stable relationships."

Her brother hugged her back, but when he released her, his eyes were on Zach and there was all kinds of suspicions there. "It can't be too stable since I happen to know he wasn't with you a couple of weeks ago when he…"

Nope. They were not going there. The terminal was empty with the exception of the four of them, and she shushed her brother. "I don't care about what he did before we got together. Go and take out the bad guys. I'll see you when you get back."

TJ leaned in, his voice going serious and low. "Dev, we should talk about this. He's… Do you know what he actually does? I'm not sure he's telling us everything. I think he might be working for someone else."

Who else would he be working for? Her cousins liked him. Her mom liked him. TJ was being overprotective. "I'm good. I know everything I need to know. If you don't like the fact that I'm dating one of your teammates, then you'll have to get over it because I'm not going to leave him to make you more comfortable."

TJ frowned and looked over to Lou, who was shaking her head like he was on his own here. "I'm only trying to look out for you."

Zach was quiet during the conversation, but she could practically feel his discomfort. Like he was on the outside and worried the door to that warm, nice place with all the food and love and fun was about to be slammed in his face and locked. She moved back to him, putting her hand in his and showing her support.

She loved her brother, but she wasn't about to let him dictate who she saw and who she didn't. He never had before, so this was a bit of a surprise.

Lou took her brother's hand. "How about we let them say goodbye and I'll see if I can find you a snack. You know Aunt Charlotte always has the best snacks."

TJ frowned Zach's way. "Yeah, I think I'll need it since it looks like I'll be having a conversation on this flight."

They turned and walked away but only after Lou had thrown her a sympathetic look.

Zach winced. "Well, it seemed to be going way too smoothly."

She shook her head and went on her toes to kiss her gorgeous captain. "My brother will get over it. Share a beer with him and tell him how much you like me and everything will be fine."

She kissed him again and then watched him walk off.

It would be okay. A week or two and he would be back and they would move him into Coop's and get him a car and start their lives.

She stood there until the plane took off, a weird feeling of anxiety in her gut.

She shook it off because it would all be okay.

Chapter Four

It was blown to hell, and Zach had no idea how it had gone so fucking wrong.

Twenty-four hours before he was sneaking Facetimes with his girlfriend from the tiny room in the safe house in Montreal he shared with his brother and her brother. TJ had calmed down after a beer and various snacks and Zach having a long discussion with him about everything he adored about Devi.

And now he was covered in blood and in Toronto and his whole team was going to know about how he betrayed them.

He glanced back at the big mansion Huisman had brought him and Tristan to. Kala and Carys and Tris were still in that house, and his gut twisted at the thought of leaving them there, but it was clear to him that Huisman knew exactly who he was, who his mother was, and had some dated knowledge of how to get to him.

He hadn't meant to kidnap Kala. Huisman had been going for Tasha. Carys to get Tristan to talk. Tasha for Zach. He meant to torture the women so the men would talk. He hadn't been happy his henchmen had mistaken Kala for her sister.

They'd picked up him and Tristan in the suite Tris, Aidan, and Carys were staying in. They'd been cleaning it out when Huisman's men showed up, drugged them, and dragged them to Toronto.

If only Huisman had kidnapped him before he'd fucked everything up with a few casual words.

You couldn't know you were going to walk in and find The Jester face down on the floor, man. You did what you had to do.

The trouble was by the time Zach had joined Tristan, The Jester had been on his back. The only one who could have known how he started face down was the man who'd actually killed him. Zach.

When they'd gotten to the Toronto house, Huisman had explained that he hadn't truly wanted Tristan at all. He'd really wanted to talk to Zach.

Because he knew. He knew who Zach's mother was, and if he was allowed to bring Shannon Reed in, the world would burn in ways he didn't want to imagine.

Huisman had tried to bring in Tasha Taggart because he had intelligence that stated Zach Reed was in love with her. It was outdated intelligence but at one time he'd thought he was.

If Huisman knew about Devi...

He forced himself to walk around the backside of the house toward what he hoped would be an alley that led away from the garage. The men assigned to take him to what Huisman called a remote site had hauled him into that garage. He'd offered to go quietly if Huisman let everyone else go.

The bastard hadn't, and Zach had done what he had to.

Now he needed to find a fucking cell phone. He needed to call Lacey and get out of the country.

There would be no going back to the States for him. No going back to Devi.

She was going to hate him.

He looked down at the blood on his hands. She would be right to do it.

We'll come for you, brother. Tristan had said the words to him as he'd been hauled back toward the garage.

He'd replied the only way he could. *Tell Devi...fuck...tell her I'm so fucking sorry. And Coop...just tell them all I'm sorry.*

If his team came for him, it would be to put him in some isolation room and question him. Even if he told them everything at this point, he was still looking at jail, and all that would do was leave his mother at Huisman's mercy. And the world to the weapons she could build.

He wished he believed his mother would fight Huisman, but he was realistic. She'd often chosen the path that made her more comfortable.

There was no way out. Not if he wanted to protect the people he loved.

He carefully eased around the cameras. There were some clear blind spots, and he used them. He had a few problems to solve—the handcuffs that dangled from his left wrist, the fact that he had no ID and no phone—none of them compared to the terror he had if Huisman figured out his connection to Devi Taggart.

His girl. His only girl. Oh, he'd had girlfriends before but not the way Devi was. She fit with him.

And she would never speak to him again.

It probably didn't matter since he was going to die or get shoved into prison somewhere. He might end up underneath whatever fucking pool an MT employee was building this week.

He missed her. He didn't want to be here, sneaking around and trying to survive. He wanted to be laying on the couch at her place, his head in her lap while she read some romance novel about fairies fucking and stroked his hair while he watched baseball.

He was not going to fucking cry.

He was not going to think about the fact that he would miss that woman for the rest of his life. She was in danger every second he was close to Huisman. If he got away and stayed away from her, she would be safe. No one in that house would give up their connection. Never.

He was losing so much more than a job. He was losing a whole family.

He stopped before making the turn to the alley. Someone was moving to the west. He could hear the sound of shoes against the pavement. He glanced around the fence and saw a sprinter van parked on the side of the alley, tucked away as though it was trying to be as inconspicuous as possible. A guard was walking up to it. One of Huisman's. He didn't know why that van was there.

Zach breathed a sigh of relief. His team was here. Ian and Charlotte Taggart weren't about to let their daughter and niece die. Adam wouldn't let his son go. So now all he had to worry about was who had been left in the van.

Almost certainly Lou. She would be manning whatever communications they had going and ready to drive them out when the time came. Someone else might be in that van, but he knew Lou was there.

The guard had a gun and a weapon that was far more dangerous—a walkie-talkie.

Luckily Zach had taken a knife off one of the guards he'd murdered. He was pretty sure they were dead. He was covered in a lot of blood, and none of it was his. He had a choice to make, and it wasn't a difficult one. He could do his team one last solid before they became the ones hunting him. Before they started a game he didn't want to play.

He moved on quiet feet, holding the handcuffs out so they didn't hit anything and make noise. The guard lifted his walkie and Zach pounced.

It was his fifth kill of the day. But it was the only one where he had a witness he cared about.

He couldn't see her because the van had some privacy features Lou had obviously engaged, but he knew she was there. The blood splattered all over the van.

He let the body drop to the ground, sure he hadn't connected to anyone in the big house.

The van door slid open and Zach went still, adrenaline pumping through his body. Aidan O'Donnell was there.

"Hey, Zach." Aidan's tone was quiet, soothing. Probably the tone he would use if he found himself in front of a hungry lion.

The doctor was looking at him like he was a monster. And he was. "Aidan."

The window rolled down and there was Lou. "And me. You need to get in the van and let Aidan look you over. The team is inside the house. We need to be ready to go."

He couldn't do that. If he got in that van, he put everyone at risk. Even if they would potentially listen to him, all it would do is put his team on the radar. There was more than Huisman out there looking for him. "Good. Huisman sent half his guards with me. They're dead now, so it'll be a fair fight. Doc, Kala's going to need you. Carys, too, if Huisman decides to fuck around with Tris. I have to go."

"Go?" Lou sounded shocked as she scrambled out of the van. "Go where? You're hurt."

He loved his team. He was going to miss them so fucking much.

He wanted to hug her, but he wasn't going to mess her up with all the blood. Lou was clean and she should stay that way. "Back to hell, sweetheart. Should've known I wouldn't belong here. Take care, Lou. Aidan, you can get in through the garage. No one's guarding it anymore."

Zach jogged away, forcing himself to keep going when every cell in his body screamed at him to go back in that house and finish the mission.

But this mission was over. He had a new one.

Staying alive. Finding his mother so Huisman couldn't.

He slipped away into the city, found a bathroom, stole some clothes and a cell.

And started his new life.

* * * *

Devi looked up from the sewing machine at the sound of her doorbell chiming. It was late for visitors, but she stood up.

Zach.

She felt a smile cross her face. If that was her gorgeous man, he was early. She'd talked to him a couple of days before, but he'd warned her the op was starting up in earnest and he would have to go radio silent for a while. They were going to talk about what that meant since he could have absolutely given her a heads-up that he was on his way back.

She stood and moved out of the little office that served as her sewing and design room. She was currently working on some commissioned fet wear. A Dom at The Club was spending lavishly on his new sub, and Devi was here for it. This commission alone meant she could stay in her apartment for at least four more months. By then she would have heard about her applications.

She was thinking positive, which was why she stopped in front of the mirror and made sure she didn't look terrible. She unbuttoned the top button of the shirt she was wearing, showing off some cleavage. Zach liked her boobs, but then he seemed to like almost everything about her.

She took a deep breath and threw open the door.

To her brother.

Her incredibly weary-looking, grim brother.

Devi's heart sank. Zach was... His job was dangerous. He was in the line of fire most of the time. Tears sprang to her eyes. If something happened to Zach, TJ would want to be the one to tell her. The world blurred. "Zach?"

TJ reached out a hand, putting it on her shoulder. "He's alive, but we have other problems. Devi, I need to talk to you."

He was alive. She breathed a sigh of relief. He might be in foreign custody. She had to be ready for it. But as long as he was breathing, she could deal with it. It would be okay. "Come in."

TJ moved inside the door, and when they sat down she found it wasn't okay. Not even close.

Part Two
One month later

Chapter Five

Outside of Winchester, Virginia

"You need stitches," a voice was saying.

Devi tried to follow it, but she was so tired. The voice sounded far away. She was warm and cuddled up against something. Where was she? What happened?

"I don't need stitches. It's a nothing wound. I barely notice it. We're going to look after her first. She hit her head or something. I'm not quite sure. She was out by the time I got to the basement." That deep voice. Zach Reed. The man she hated for what he did to her and her family. The man she couldn't forget.

Her life was shitty because of that man.

Her life had become bodyguards and sympathetic looks and nights spent sitting up pissed at him. Wondering why he'd had to pick her.

She knew why. Someone had told her why he'd selected her as his next scheme, but she couldn't remember. It was something about her family.

"I told you she's fine," the feminine voice said in a British accent. Not a posh one. "I checked her out before I gave her the sedative, and don't yell at me. I have to get us all the way across the bloody Atlantic, and I can't do that if she's screaming. She can scream all she likes once we're on the plane, but until then I need her quiet. We're only supposed to be a party of two, you know. The plane was gassed up and checked out for two. Lucky for you I bet she weighs one fifteen soaking wet."

"I'm sorry. I couldn't avoid it, but you should have known I didn't want her drugged," Zach said.

Drugged. Yeah, that was what she was. Nice and drugged. It would be so easy to go back to sleep. Or was she already asleep?

She thought about opening her eyes, but she didn't.

"Why would I have known that? Up until tonight I thought she was nothing but a girl you played at a club with," the woman shot back.

"I thought it was best no one knew how I felt. Lace, you have no idea what those drugs could do to her," Zach accused.

"I know they'll keep her calm until we can figure out where to stash her. Don't you get mad at me. I did not expect you to show up with a girl," the angry Brit said. "Besides, it's a light sedative. She'll likely be in and out of consciousness, but she won't scream and try to get away. I promise she doesn't have a concussion. She'll be fine when she wakes up, but you'll be dead because of that knife wound."

Knife wound? Who stabbed him? Had she stabbed him? She'd dreamed about stabbing him and tossing him in a shallow grave.

She missed him so much.

"I'm not going to die. It's superficial," he replied. "A couple of butterflies will close it."

"Well, the butterflies won't stop the infection you likely got from moving through those tunnels." The other woman's voice held a bit of distaste. "You have no idea what's down there."

She felt arms squeeze around her and realized they were moving. In a car or something, and she was on Zach's lap. Oh, she could smell him, feel the warmth of his body.

"I know Huisman was keeping a stash of stuff. I'm pretty sure some of those boxes were weapons. I gave Coop a heads-up, but I'm worried the fire will take everything out," Zach admitted.

The woman he called Lace was quiet for a moment. "Did you open the boxes? Get any footage of what was in them? Perhaps collect a couple of samples?"

It was Zach's turn for a pause. "I had to get her out. That fire was going, and no one was putting it out. I doubt Cooper had a chance to get down there."

"So what you're saying is even if by some miracle the fire doesn't destroy what could have been incredibly valuable intelligence, the Agency now has it. Not your old boss but his boss," she pointed out in a terse tone.

"Yes. I know what a fuck-up it was, but I wouldn't take it back. I couldn't leave her there," Zach insisted.

Leave her? He was talking about her. The "her" in question was Devi Taggart. What had happened? Everything was fuzzy. Her brain was on the fritz. She might be dreaming this. She dreamed about Zach all the time. Dreamed about him not turning out to be the biggest mistake of her life. Dreamed that he'd come home when he was supposed to, and the betrayal was actually the dream and she needed to be way less insecure because they were perfect for each other.

"Zach?" Devi managed to say his name. It felt weird. She had to concentrate to talk.

"Sweetness?" He gently smoothed back her hair. "Thank god, you're awake. You're safe. You're in a car, and we'll be on a plane in an hour. What's important is that you are safe and you're going to stay that way."

She understood nothing except he was here and he shouldn't be. He ran. He hadn't come home from Canada. He had taken off and was now AWOL, and every intelligence group in the world might be hunting for him because he betrayed his team. "How are you here?"

"That is a long story and one I'll tell you when we get to the safe house and I'm sure we're secure," he replied, his voice a low rumble.

A huff came from the Brit. "It's secure. I told you. It's safe as houses, and no one will think to look for us there. I've been working on our cover with the locals. Though I would like to point out there were only supposed to be two of us, and I'm going to need a cover for her."

"She's my girlfriend. That's all they need to know," Zach shot back and then his hand was on her hair again and she fought the urge to sigh at his touch.

There was something so wrong with that statement. "Not your girlfriend."

He sighed, and she felt his weariness. "You sleep. You're okay, and I'm going to make sure you stay that way. When you wake up, know I'm going to take care of you. I promise."

Take care of her. It was all she wanted from him. Zach was the one, but he'd been gone for so long. Something played at the back of her sedated brain, but it didn't seem important now.

"You should have told me you were extracting a Taggart," Angry Brit said.

"Why does it matter that she's a Taggart?" Zach asked, a bit of suspicion in his tone.

"They're trouble for us, and you know it," she said after the slightest hesitation. "You should have told me this was your plan. I've trusted you with my life for a while now, Zach. This feels like you don't trust me."

"I do, but I didn't know I was going to do it until I was there," Zach shot back. "I planned to let her uncle take her, but it's obvious to me he can't handle her. We'll have a talk about that."

Bodyguard. She'd had a bodyguard. She hated having a bodyguard. Not Landon in particular. He was an okay guy. He was even attractive, and she'd thought seriously about trying to wipe Zach from her memory with him.

She couldn't do it, so she acted out. She acted rebellious and gave Landon the slip, and something terrible had happened and that was why she was in this car with the man of her nightmares.

"You still should have told me, and you shouldn't have carried her like that when you've got a hole in your side," came the reply, and Devi felt the vehicle turn. "Lucky for you I've got a kit in the plane. I'll stitch you up before we go."

"Lucky for me you found a damn plane," Zach muttered. "I'm sorry I didn't tell you. It was a gametime decision. I appreciate you coming all this way for me. I know how hard that must have been and what strings you're having to pull to get me out of the country."

"It wasn't that hard." The Brit's voice was softer now.

He was leaving again? Thoughts seemed to flow in and out. Time, too. For a moment she remembered standing in the private terminal with him, their arms around each other. Saying good-bye had been hard, but she'd loved showing him off to her family, letting them know she'd snagged that gorgeous, funny, amazing guy. "You just got here."

She didn't feel good. Well, maybe she felt too good. She couldn't tell. One second she wanted to wrap herself around Zach, and then she thought she would puke and then her head was pleasantly floaty.

What the hell had happened?

"I know," he replied, his voice going low. "And I'm not letting you go this time. I should have done this weeks ago."

"Done what?" She managed to get her eyes open, and he was every bit as gorgeous as she remembered. Except worse for the wear. He had a cut on his cheek. Not deep, but a bit bloody. His face was still lovely. Like a model but rougher, his life experience showing in the lines of his face, the hard, chiseled jaw. She liked to kiss him there.

They'd been together for a week. How could it feel like a lifetime?

He looked down at her with such tenderness. Such softness, like he'd missed her terribly and only now felt right again. "Kidnap you."

Not what she expected to hear. And the words reminded her that something was wrong with this scenario. Something beyond the blood and drugs and obviously annoyed British lady.

Zach had betrayed his team. Her family. He'd lied and nearly gotten Kala killed.

She hated Zach.

She loved Zach.

How was she here with Zach? She wasn't supposed to be anywhere near Zach for multiple reasons, the chief one being she wasn't about to be that pathetic girl who let a man walk all over her and then ask for more the minute he seemed sweet again.

She tried to shake her head. "Let me go."

He sighed. "I can't. I did it once. I don't have it in me to do it again. Devi, it's going to be okay. I'm going to keep you safe."

"She's probably confused." Angry Brit sounded less ragey. "She'll sleep soon. You can tell her now, but you might have to tell her again. I gave her enough to keep her out for a couple of hours once she stops fighting it. Taggart, go to sleep. Trust me. There's nothing luxurious or fun about the flight we're about to take. I wish I could be sedated."

What was Angry Brit doing with Zach? Realization flooded her. It was a tale as old as time. She should have known the liar would also be a cheater. Of course she would have to figure out who he cheated on since it sounded like he knew the Brit pretty well. Devi could be the other woman. "Tell your girlfriend I'll stop fighting when hell freezes over."

"There she is," Zach said with what sounded like affection. "There's my fierce baby. She's not my girlfriend, Devi. Her name is Lacey Rook, and she's been helping me for over a year now. She has connections I need to find what I'm looking for, and we're getting close. I'll explain it all to you when we get where we're going. I promise I won't hold anything back this time."

Liar. He was a liar, and she shouldn't be cuddled against him. She tried to get her arms to move but they wouldn't. "Where am I? What happened?" Kala. It came flooding back. Kala was in trouble. She had been with Kala, and her cousin was in serious trouble with that French man. What was his name? House something. Had they fought?

Her head felt so heavy.

"Don't worry about it, sweetness. I'll tell you everything when you wake up. I promise."

"Liar." She managed to push the word out of her mouth.

Another stroke of his hand over her hair, and damn but that felt nice. "Yes. I'm a liar, but I'm never going to lie to you again. You'll understand when I tell you everything."

"Kala." Her cousin. She'd been drugged, too. And that man…that awful man had promised to torture her. But she saw another picture of Kala in her head. One of her brilliant, brave cousin trying her hardest to make her limbs work, trying to save them both.

"She's fine. Cooper got her. I'll tell you the whole story when we get where we're going," he replied.

Kala was okay. She could breathe a little better. Cooper had her. He would take care of her. "Home. Go home."

Though she couldn't sort through it all right now with the drugs in her system, she knew she'd been through something traumatic, and she wanted her mom. She wanted her dad.

There was sympathy in his eyes as he stared down at her. "I'm afraid for now your home is with me. There's no way Huisman doesn't know about you now. None. That bitch who took you would have told him everything."

A vision of a dark-haired woman in her forties came over Devi.

She had definitely fought with that woman. What was her name?

Why couldn't she remember anything?

Why did it feel so good to be in his arms? His hands on her body. Tired. She was so tired.

"Just rest," he said. "It's going to be okay."

It wouldn't, but there was nothing else to do. The drugs were winning, and she gave in to the velvety darkness.

* * * *

Zach held her in his arms and didn't give a fuck about the wound he'd taken while he and Cooper had fought their way through Huisman's mansion to get their women. When he'd learned Devi had been kidnapped along with Kala, he'd almost lost his mind, but he'd known he had to do something. He'd put everything he and Lacey had been working for in jeopardy, but he wouldn't take it back.

Devi had been acting out and putting herself in danger again and again. She wanted his attention? She had it.

"Is she finally asleep?" Lacey asked.

"I think so." He was pissed about the drugs even though he knew he would probably have been forced to do it himself. Devi was mad, and a mad Devi was a chaotic Devi, and he couldn't have chaos right now. When they got to the farm, Devi could get as angry as she wanted. For the most part the cows and the chickens wouldn't give a damn.

"You could have gotten arrested." Lacey was driving, and she wasn't happy about it. "Taggart should have taken you in the minute he saw you."

All the intelligence agencies out for his blood were a point of contention for Lacey. She had her own work to do, and Zach was fucking it all up. It was precisely why he'd spent the last couple of weeks in the Colorado wilderness with his aunt. He understood her frustration. "I knew he wouldn't."

That was a bit of a lie. He'd *thought* Big Tag wouldn't arrest him. He hadn't been certain. Coop was more of a risk. His brother had discovered the truth about their relationship in Colorado, and he had not taken the news well. Naturally Kala had, and she'd listened to him and chosen to leave him be.

For now.

But when he'd walked up to Cooper and his former team this evening, there had been nothing but affection for him. Well, Big Tag called him a dumbass, but that was practically a declaration of love from him.

It filled him with hope, and wasn't that the most dangerous of all emotions because he knew deep down this didn't end in a white picket fence and two point five kids with the woman of his dreams.

There was a reckoning coming, but not until the people he loved were safe. Once he'd found his mother and gotten her to a secure location and ensured all of her research and notes were destroyed, he would deal with the fallout. He didn't intend to spend the rest of his life on the run. He would stand in front of the people he cared about—the family he could have had—and reveal all of his secrets. Every single one.

"You were lucky, Zach. I'm surprised you're being this reckless."

"That's what happens when you're in love."

She groaned. He should have expected it. Lacey Rook wasn't much of a romantic. She was far more practical. In the two years he'd known her, he'd never actually seen her hit on anyone. He still wasn't sure what her type was. Man. Woman. No idea. He did know she had specific tastes when it came to food. She was a vegan. They were likely in for some meatless living in the place she was taking them to.

"Now I think you're even more reckless," she replied as she turned down the road that would lead to the private airfield. Super private. Like the Agency hopefully didn't know about it private.

His life now revolved around hiding from the Agency, and that meant going to some unsavory places. Was he doing the right thing? He immediately answered his own question. Zach Reed followed his instincts, and he knew this woman.

"I couldn't leave her. She's on Huisman's radar now, and she's been ditching her guards. She's here apparently because she wriggled out of a bathroom window to prove she didn't need one." He sighed and stroked her hair. Damn but he'd missed all that curly red stuff. And her freckles. He gently traced the line of them that went across her nose and cheekbones. So fucking pretty. "I think if I let her uncle take her back, she would try again."

"Well, now you know why I sedated her," Lacey said with

another huff. "Zach, you have to know we can't keep her."

"I don't see why not." The farm was private and quiet, and he rather thought Devi would prove reasonable when she remembered what had happened tonight. She loved her family. She wouldn't want them in the line of fire.

Of course maybe she would wake up and be so happy he saved her from Huisman that she fell into his arms and proclaimed her love and willingness to be a wanted criminal with him.

Sure, that was happening.

Lacey snorted. "Because it's called kidnapping, and it tends to get nasty. Her parents are going to lose their shit when they don't know what happened to her. Unless she doesn't have the kind of Taggart parents you so often describe."

"Kala was conscious when I took Devi out of there, but I get your point. It's not the same as knowing she's being taken care of." He would have to deal with that. "You gotta burner in here?"

She popped open the glove compartment and tossed him a small cell. It wasn't smart. It wasn't luxurious. It would get the job done, and no one would be able to trace it. Even if they could, the signal would put them in Virginia, and they would be gone in an hour. "Are you going to call her uncle and tell him where we are so we can both go to jail?"

He wasn't the only one with the authorities after him. Lacey had a long rap sheet and her own reasons for staying underground.

"No, I'm calling someone who will be reasonable about this whole thing." He dialed the number, and it immediately picked up.

"This is Erin. Who the hell is this?" The woman he wanted as his mother-in-law sounded irritated.

"Erin, it's Zach."

A pause came over the line, and she sighed as though relieved. "Well, hello, Zach. You have some explaining to do, son. A lot of it, actually. But first, do you know anything about what's happened to my daughter? Ian hasn't called yet."

Zach wasn't surprised she was calm. Erin Taggart had been Army intelligence, and she was cool under pressure. "I have her and she's safe."

"You? What were you doing with Huisman?" She stopped. "Damn it, Zach. Did you hear about it and go in?"

Another relief. She hadn't immediately thought he was working with Huisman. "I monitor several sites Huisman works with when he needs muscle. I also might have someone on the inside with the Disrupt organization, and she tipped me off that something was going down. You should also know that I had someone watching Devi. She managed to give him the slip along with her bodyguard. I wasn't going to leave her there. Erin, I know I have a lot of things to explain, but the one thing I have never once lied about is how I feel about your daughter. I walked into the op knowing I might be arrested because I was not going to leave her in his hands. I won't allow that fucker to touch her again."

"Well, good luck because she's proven to be stubborn when it comes to her own safety. Can I talk to her?"

"I can't believe you rang up her mum," Lacey said under her breath.

He ignored her. He could see the small runway up ahead. They would take off from there, land at a private airfield in upstate New York, and make their way to the UK from there. "I'm afraid she's asleep."

"You mean you drugged her." The sound became muffled as though she put a hand over the receiver. She still talked loud enough he could hear her. "Theo, calm down. I don't think he wants to hurt her."

Devi's dad would be way harder to deal with. "I don't. I'm trying everything I can to make sure she doesn't get hurt."

"Well, you could turn yourself in," Erin pointed out. "Then Huisman wouldn't need to grab Devi."

She didn't know the whole situation. "Oh, but he would. I assure you he would grab her, and I would find myself needing to break out of prison. He doesn't want me in prison, and he'll do what it takes to have me out here in the field where he wants me."

"Why does he want you, Zach?" Erin put the question out there. The question he hoped to never have to answer.

"Because my mother is the bombmaker."

A whistle came over the line that proved Erin knew more than she should. "Damn. All right. This is probably already way more classified than I should be involved in."

"I can send you everything I have. My career is already over, and we both know there are two ways I get out of this."

"Prison or a coffin," Erin answered with a weary sigh. "I'm sure that's what you think, but you have to know Ian has some pull."

"Which he isn't going to want to use on me. I lied to my team. I had my reasons, but I lied to them." Here was the big one. "I lied to my brother for years."

"No one cares about that." He heard Theo talking in the background, so it was a pretty good bet they were on speaker. "Who doesn't have a sibling or two who shows up out of the blue? It's the kidnapping my daughter part that I'm upset about."

So everyone knew.

"Zach, what my husband is trying to say is you handled the situation the best way you could, but now it might be time to come in and let the family figure out what to do," Erin said in that reasonable tone.

"I'm close to finding my mother," he told her. "I'm working with some people I trust, and once I make sure she's safe from Huisman, I'll do exactly that. I'll turn myself in to Langley."

"You will fucking not turn yourself in," Erin practically snarled. "Zachary Reed, you listen to me. I am trusting you with one of the most precious people in my life. If you are lying to me or playing her then you should turn yourself into Langley because they might, and I mean might, be able to protect you from what I'll do. If you're not, then all you will be doing is putting your team in the position of having to break you out. You fix this and you come to Dallas and we will find a way out."

"Or he could drop our daughter off with her cousins and go about his business," Theo said in the background.

He was not going to cry. Nope. He'd been alone and hungry and cold for freaking weeks. He'd felt his singularity in ways he never imagined before, and the fact that Erin Taggart wanted him to come home… Home. That fucking word. Had he ever truly had one? "I can't, Theo. It's too dangerous. I'll find a way to get what intel I have to Ian, and I'll set something up so you can talk to Devi. If I think she'll take her safety seriously, we can talk."

"I expect a call tomorrow," Theo said.

"When you settle in," Erin corrected. "Tell my daughter I love her and we're going to have a long discussion about what it means to have a bodyguard. Or apparently two. She got away from the one she knew about and the one she didn't. So there's that. Don't take your eyes off her, Zach. I will hold you personally responsible for her safety from now on."

It was how he wanted it. "I'll take care of her."

"Also, tell her Eve survived. Barely. She's going to be okay."

His heart squeezed at the news. Cooper had only told him part of the story since they'd been preoccupied with saving their women at the time. Devi had been through a lot of traumatic shit today. "Good. I'll let her know. Talk to you soon."

He hung up, rolled down the window, and let the burner fly out to the highway.

"Well, she seems like an interesting woman," Lacey commented.

"Like you don't know her. I'm sure you have a file on all the Taggarts." Lacey kept copious files on everyone she came into contact with, and that didn't have to be physical contact. In her world, Lacey was considered an expert on intel gathering. She knew where all the bodies were buried, who buried them, and how much dirt they got under their nails while doing it.

"Not for the reasons you think," she admitted. "They're not on my organization's radar. Look, the Taggarts don't have anything to do with the people I work with. They're strictly about saving lives, and I appreciate that. I have nothing against them, but they are Agency and have ties to law enforcement across the globe who could try to stop my friends from doing what they need to do."

Save the planet. It was what Lacey Rook wanted to do. Even if she used some fairly illegal tactics to do it. It was precisely how she had contacts who knew his mother. "The Taggarts have never been involved in the green underground, so you have intel on them because they're connected to me."

She turned slightly and gave him that uptick of her lips that always made him think she knew more than she was saying. "They're connected in ways you haven't thought of yet. But I do trust them to do the right thing for the most part. What I worry about is the people who want to take them down. Wasn't that part of your job?"

He looked at the woman on his lap. How much did Devi know? What had his team told her? She knew he'd lied, but did she realize how far it went? "It was how I got the position. I was supposed to spy on them, gather evidence to help bring the team down. I did a terrible job, and that's why no one at the Agency will save me."

No one except his team. Maybe.

Lacey took a deep breath and seemed to settle down. She took the exit ramp that led to the small airfield. "Then we have to save ourselves. Let's start with getting you stitched up and then I'll give you your new ID. I'll have someone meet me in New York with ID for our guest."

This was what Lacey did best. She could be in the middle of a Bulgarian wheat field and pull a hacker out of her ass. Or something like that. Lacey always knew how to get out of bad situations.

Maybe she had some advice on how to handle Devi. "Thanks. I am sorry for the trouble, but I couldn't leave her."

She sighed. "Well, I suppose it's nice for you to find a woman to love. Not brilliant timing, though, since no matter what Erin Taggart thinks, you're in a hell of a muddle, mate, and we haven't even gotten to the bad part yet."

He was. And his side hurt. He didn't think he was bleeding out, but he might not notice.

The only thing that mattered was the woman in his arms.

He went silent as they approached the airfield, simply reveling in being able to hold her.

It was the quiet before the inevitable storm, and he wanted to enjoy it. But he still asked the question. "What's the bad part?"

Lacey looked at him through the rearview mirror. "I didn't find your mum. Not yet. But I did find someone else. Someone who could be way more dangerous to you."

He didn't want to know but he did. There was only one person in the world who could unsettle him more than his brilliant, troubled mother, and that was the man who troubled her. "What's dear old Dad up to?"

"Well, I'm almost certain he's working for Huisman now."

And just like that all his peace was shattered.

His father was back, and his world was infinitely more dangerous.

Chapter Six

Devi woke to the feel of light on her face, warm and inviting. Not annoying, like she didn't want to wake up and smell the coffee and get to work light. No, this light was soft, and she shifted in the bed, reaching out for...

Nope. She shot straight up, the events of the night before exploding in her brain.

"Hey, easy now," a voice with a distinctly British accent said. "You slept way longer than I thought you would so you're probably a little woozy. Don't try standing up too soon."

"Where the fuck am I?" She turned her head, catching sight of the woman sitting in a comfy lounger across the room. She looked roughly Devi's age. Late twenties, with golden brown hair and dark eyes that looked slightly ethereal. She could be a fairy queen sitting there drinking her tea. Lovely and graceful, and now she remembered she'd been the one to drug her. "And take one step toward me and we'll have a problem. Don't think I've forgotten what you did."

Those warm brown eyes rolled, and she set down her tea and the book she'd been reading. "Well, I'm terrified. You might pull my hair. You know for a Taggart you're fairly easy to take down. In my world, you're practically kings, but you must be one of the slow relations, if you know what I mean."

And she was evil. "You drugged me. What did he call you? Where is Zach? What is this place?"

"Such a curious lass. All right. Yes, I drugged you since I had to smuggle you out of the country on short notice and quite frankly, I didn't think you would cooperate. Second, he called me Lacey. My name is Lacey Rook, though I go by several aliases. It's such a good way to avoid being arrested. As for Zach, he's getting checked over by a friend of mine. Arthur came out to check on my hillycoos, but he can make sure Zach's all right, too. I think antibiotics work on both animals and people. To answer your last question, you're in Wales. Some people I know run this farm as a sanctuary, and members of my group take turns keeping it up and taking care of the animals. Lucky for all of us, it's my turn, and I explained I wouldn't need helpers. I was bringing my American cousins along. We've got six weeks here and then we'll have to find someplace else."

Wales? Her brain started making connections. Wales was bordered by England, and London was in England, and that was where Vivian McKay lived, and Sophy Weston, too. She knew people here. People who could help her escape.

"If you're thinking about running, feel free." Lacey stood and picked up her cup and book. She wore faded jeans and a soft-looking knit sweater. "The Irish Sea is to your east, and England to the west. I think the nearest bus stop is twenty-four kilometers away. Good luck."

"Kilometers? Is that far?"

A brilliant laugh huffed from Lacey. "Oh, I love Americans. Look it up, darling."

Her head was starting to hurt. "Do you have to be such a bitch?"

She seemed to think about that for a moment. "I suppose not, but it's more fun this way." She sobered. "Is your head hurting? You don't have a concussion but that doesn't mean you're going to be comfortable. According to Zach, you were unconscious when he found you. Someone hit you."

Lena. Her cousin's stupid evil therapist. That was just wrong. "My cousin's therapist kidnapped me to make her do what she wanted. She knew she couldn't take Kala out herself, so she used me."

"Her therapist. Well, that's not fair, is it? Though I'm sure with a name like Kala she probably needs it," Lacey said briskly. "Now are you going to be stubborn and run or would you like me to tell you what's happened? And perhaps give you something to get rid of your headache. I've got some herbal teas my mum sent with me. Don't make fun of them. According to her, they come straight from the fairies, and the wee folk know how to take care of a person."

She was still dreaming, right? This was… Was that a chicken? There was a chicken staring at her from the side of the bed. It stood there looking up at her.

"Don't mind Miss Rachel," Lacey said, scooping the chicken up. "She's every bit as curious as you are. So which way are we going? If you hurry, you could sneak past Zach and perhaps get to the back field before he realizes you're gone. Be careful. There's a testy bull in that field. Abused terribly, and he's easily startled, but then you would be, too, if they used you to train bull fighters. Poor Ferdinand."

The last words were said to the chicken, who clucked as though she was entirely sympathetic to her bull brethren's situation.

"Why am I here?" Devi pushed back the covers and then realized she was down to her undies and an oversized T-shirt. Although she suspected it wouldn't be oversized on Zach Reed. It would fit just right. "Who undressed me?"

"Well, it wasn't me. It was the bloke who put his entire life and work on the line to save you. It's the reason he's being looked over by a veterinarian instead of a real doctor, though I will say I would put my life in Arthur's hands." She looked down at the chicken in her arms. "He saved you, Rachel. Poor baby had terrible stomach issues when she came here."

Devi was starting to get the idea Lacey wasn't about to give up anything. She was going to have to ask. "Can I have my clothes back?"

Lacey gave her a smile as she headed for the bedroom door. "Of course. When they dry. I hung them up this morning. Should be nice and dry in a couple of hours. If it doesn't rain."

"Or you could throw them in the dryer," Devi suggested.

Lacey turned in the hallway, an intimidating look on her face. "Do you have any idea what kind of energy conventional clothes dryers use? Not to mention how hard they are on actual clothing. Do you care about the planet in any way?"

Devi was not going into this. "Look, lady, you're the one who kidnapped me. Are you planning on lecturing me on climate change for torture? Because that would be a good way to get me to walk into the sea."

It wasn't that she didn't love the Earth. She did, but this woman was irritating her on a base level. And also, where the fuck was Zach? She glanced around the bedroom and noted that his bag was on the floor by the bed and someone's head had definitely lain on that pillow beside her. Asshole thought she was sharing a room with him? That was not happening.

Although she was his prisoner. Was she not being scared enough? Prisoner. She'd been a prisoner, and Kala had been, too.

"Are you okay? You went pale," Lacey said, sounding like she gave a damn.

But Devi was stuck because it all flooded back. The night... She'd wriggled out the bathroom window because she didn't need a damn bodyguard. This Huisman person was coming after Zach, and no one seemed to understand that Zach didn't give a shit about her.

I thought he was in love with Tasha. It's good to see he's moving on.

Careless words. Words she wasn't supposed to hear. He wanted a Taggart. It wouldn't be the first time an intelligence officer tried to use her family name to get a leg up. Tasha's first fiancée had done the same thing.

Zach didn't give a shit beyond her last name. He'd lost his shot at her cousin, the twins had their eyes on other men, and her cousin Carys had recently married. So she was the only female Taggart left for the picking. And she'd been such easy prey. Yes, that had been boiling through her system as she made her way to The Hideout. And then Lena had been waiting with big guys and guns, and they walked into the club and told her cousin they would kill her if she didn't do what they wanted.

Again. She was the pawn. She was being used to gain a particular outcome.

She felt a hand go to her chest as she heard the shot in her memory. Aunt Eve. Aunt Eve had been with Kala. She'd tried to protect her and Lena shot her. Shot her in the chest. Devi watched her go down and knew...

Screaming. She could hear her cousin screaming in pain, and there was nothing she could do about it. When they brought her back, Kala had been paralyzed and then Lena had been there again and it was Devi's turn to protect her cousin.

She failed.

"Devi? Sweetness, what's going on? You're safe." Zach's words penetrated the horror movie playing through her brain. She could feel the way they tossed her around. How they'd treated Kala like she was a fucking doll. They tossed them into the plane like cargo, and she'd held onto her cousin's unconscious body so she didn't roll around. She'd lain there holding on and praying that Zach would find them. That she wouldn't lose Kala this way, wouldn't die without seeing him again.

His arms were around her, and she was sitting on his lap in the same cozy chair Lacey had been in when she woke up. Just for a second, she breathed him in, let his familiar scent comfort her.

"Kala?"

She felt him kiss the top of her head. "She's fine. Cooper got her out and I got you out. From what I can tell she's on her way back to Dallas with the rest of the team."

"My Aunt Eve…she…she…"

He stroked her hair. "Is alive and well. She's going to pull through. Everyone is alive, Devi. Well, Lena isn't. Kala took care of her. Tell me what he did to you. Lacey and I both looked you over and we didn't see any bruising except around your wrists. But we both know he doesn't have to leave scars to hurt you."

Oh, she felt pretty scarred. It was time to be an adult and not a clinging child. She had to remember that all this affection was for show. It was to trick her and make her fall further for him. Now he had even more reasons to draw her in. He was AWOL. Her uncle might be able to handle the situation if she cried prettily and begged him to take care of the man she loved.

And she did. But that love didn't go both ways, and she wasn't going to let herself be used. She sat up.

"Hey, go slow. You almost passed out." His arm tightened around her waist as though he was afraid to let her go. "Just rest for a minute. The sedative she gave you is probably making you woozy."

"Reliving the torture I went through is making me woozy, Zach.

Please let me up. I don't want to be here."

He took a long breath and moved his arms so she was free. "I know, sweetness, and that is one hundred percent my fault. I should have come after you the minute Huisman made his play. I shouldn't have left you behind."

Her head hurt and she wanted to cry. Was crying, but in an inactive way. She needed a big sob fest to get rid of the anxiety anvil that sat on her chest. She swiped at the tears and tried to shove the turmoil down deep as she slid off his lap and forced herself to stand on her own two feet. "Are you saying you wish you kidnapped me earlier?"

He had the grace to wince. "That sounds worse than I meant it. I'm just saying I didn't handle this well, Devi. I should have come to you. I thought it was better to leave you with your family. I thought they could protect you. Now I'm going to do the job, but I should have come to you and told you the truth."

"About how you want to marry a Taggart and you weren't going to let a little thing like being a criminal and betraying your team stop you?" Anger was far easier to deal with than the horrible vulnerable feeling she'd gone through.

She was weak. She was lesser. No one wanted to hire her even after all the money her family put into her college. She had been kidnapped. Twice. Neither time was the actual kidnapping about her. One had been to force Daisy O'Donnell out into the open, and the other she was leverage against her brilliant, deadly cousin.

He went still, his eyes pinning her. "That is not true."

"So you didn't have a thing for Tasha?" It was stupid that she was stuck on this. He betrayed everyone. Put his whole team in danger, and she didn't really know why but this was what she pushed at him.

Because once again she was small and insignificant, with the exception of her family name.

"I had a kid-like crush on her in the beginning." He seemed to think through every word. "I never touched her. Never once made a move on her."

"Not like you did with me. She was the beautiful, perfect woman, and I was available." It was how she felt. "I was convenient and had the proper last name."

"This is where we're going?" His lips curled up in a slightly self-satisfied smirk. "I kidnap you, haul you across the ocean and away from your family, and you're jealous. Not angry. Jealous. Baby, we're already halfway there."

"What is that supposed to mean?" She took a step back as he stood and loomed over her.

It was too bad she'd been wearing sneakers when they caught her. Not that she had them now, but she longed for some four-inch heels. They wouldn't put her on eye level with him, but they would help.

He simply stood there, that stupid, sexy smirk on his face. "It means I thought it would take weeks to get back into your bed, but if I was betting now, I would say a couple of days and you'll need more than you can give yourself. We're stuck on this nice but weird farm and oops, there's only one bed."

"Zach, I am not fucking around with you. You sought me out because I was the last Taggart you could hit on."

He frowned, a look of pure consternation coming on his face. "Why would you say that? Look, the thing with Tasha was probably more about her dad and wanting to belong than I want to admit. But you... I looked at you and I wanted you. I know we met before and I always thought you were beautiful, but that night we connected in a way I have never connected before."

"Because my cousins wouldn't give you the time of day," she shot back.

"I didn't want your cousins," he said in an altogether too calm voice. "Kala and Kenz are like sisters to me. As for Tasha, I'm now pretty sure it wouldn't have worked. She's too calm and polite for me. I seem to have a thing for brats."

She shook her head. "No. I don't believe a word you say."

"And I can understand that. Devi, I wish I could let you move on with your life. I wish I was a good enough man to not touch you again because there's no happy ending for us. I'm going to die or go to prison, and if I was a better man, I would hand you back to your uncle. But I'm not. I'm a desperate man, and I need these weeks with you because one way or another this is it, and you're the best thing that ever happened to me. Ever will happen to me. I'll do pretty much anything to get back into your bed and have these last days with you."

He sounded so serious, like he'd spent weeks thinking about what he would say to her. She wanted to sit and talk to him and work this out. What if he was telling her the truth? What if he honestly wanted her and this was a tragic misunderstanding? What if she was his real love?

She needed to kill this part of herself. The part that wanted to believe the best in everyone. The part that thought she should try one more time and everything would work out. "You can go to hell. I consider myself your prisoner, Zach. Every bit as much as I was his prisoner last night, and honestly, for the same reasons. You need something from my uncle. I don't buy for a second that you're willing to die or go to prison. You're a user, and you'll use me to save yourself from whatever is going on here." She was feeling mean. Her head hurt, and she wasn't even sure they were telling her the truth about where she was. Or if Lacey was only a friend. She was probably Zach's mistress and she was helping her man save himself. "What's wrong, Zach? Were your mommy and daddy not good enough for you and you need a new family? Poor little boy wants mine? Is that it?"

His eyes closed, and if he was acting, he was damn good at it. "I suppose I deserve that. I'll leave you alone then. I'll find another place to sleep. Be careful when you're walking around. Lacey doesn't believe in penning in the cows. I'll see you at dinner."

He moved around her, leaving the room. The space was suddenly quiet but her mind wasn't.

"Wow, now I believe you're a Taggart," an unwelcome voice said. Lacey stood in the door with a mug of tea in her hand. She walked in like she owned the place, setting the tea down on a coaster on the table by the chair. "It's something my mum has used since she was a kid. It always helps with headaches. I don't think it will make you less of a bitch, though."

"Yeah, because the kidnapped girl should be polite to the people holding her. Sure thing." She looked back to the door where Zach disappeared. Was he trying to play on her sympathy? Did he think looking like a hurt boy would bring her around?

"Well, you weren't exactly polite to the men guarding you, were you? So it feels like you're a bit nasty to everyone." Lacey frowned and moved to the corner of the room. She opened the door to the closet. "Come on, kitty. I don't think she wants you in here. Will you let me pick you up?"

The cat hissed and retreated.

Lacey sighed. "Someone found her out in the woods starved and obviously abused. She likes dark, small places. She's also pregnant, so I have to worry if she'll let me close enough to help with the kittens when they come. And now I have to deal with you. I'll get her out of here. I wouldn't want her abused further."

"Why would I abuse a cat?" Devi asked.

Lacey shrugged. "Well, I watched you tear apart a person you supposedly loved, so I thought perhaps a cat would be a way to take out your frustrations. You seem to do that a lot."

"You don't know me, lady."

"Don't I? I know the reports. I know you were a thoughtless child more interested in throwing a tantrum than honoring the people you say you love."

Oh, this was what she needed. A stranger to tell her what a shit person she was. "I am not a child, and I'm not the one who kidnapped a person. I'm a fucking victim like I always am."

"Boohoo, love," Lacey said almost absently. "It's your fault you're here, though I doubt you'll take any accountability."

This woman was deranged. "Accountability for my own kidnapping?"

"Oh, I think you should take accountability for most of what happened. Not the Huisman rubbish. He's pure evil, but you gave him the way in," Lacey pointed out.

"Excuse me?"

Lacey stopped and seemed to decide whether or not she wanted to continue. "Did you or did you not ditch your bodyguard?"

"You know I did."

"And how did that work out for you?" Lacey asked, an elegant brow arched over her eyes as she turned Devi's way. "Because let me play out a couple of scenarios for you. If you had been with Landon when you walked into the club, he could have taken out Lena and her crew. At the very least he would have realized something was happening and called in the troops."

Guilt twisted inside her because Lacey wasn't wrong. "I didn't think anyone was coming for me."

"Zach didn't warn you?"

"He didn't call me. He talked to my cousins. They went to my parents, and I got the bodyguard." He hadn't talked to her at all.

"So your parents love you and your cousins love you and Zach…"

She would only let this woman go so far. "Don't you say it."

"I don't have to. We both know the truth. You're the beloved daughter of a tight-knit family who wants you to be safe, and you repay them by getting someone shot."

"I didn't shoot my aunt."

"Didn't you?" Lacey seemed determined to poke every wound. "I mean I know you didn't pull the trigger but—again—what if you hadn't ditched your guard and they hadn't been able to use you to gain entrance to the club? I read the reports. Your team thinks they're safe from hackers, but I'm quite good. What would have happened?"

"They would have waited for Eve and Kala to come out and they would have shot her there."

Lacey's head shook. "That is not the most likely scenario. It's the one that takes the blame off you."

"Fine. What's the likely scenario?" Devi asked, not wanting to hear it.

"Well, the most likely one is that Eve McKay and the young Miss Taggart would have still been in the club when it opened and Lena wouldn't have been able to get in once people started showing up. Another scenario, they do get inside but they only have Eve. They need her then. They needed someone or something to force that badger you call a cousin to comply. Eve would have worked. So then she is unharmed and tossed on the plane and sent to Virginia instead of fighting for her life and potentially losing a great deal of lung capacity, but it's all right since you were feeling… How were you feeling?"

Angry. Alone. Stubborn. She'd stood in that dumb bathroom and she'd needed to find some freedom, needed to show everyone that she wasn't this target because Zach Reed didn't love her. She wanted her parents to hate him. Her mom worried about him, didn't believe he would ever truly hurt his team and wanted to wait for more of what she called intel.

Devi heard her brother's girlfriend talk about Zach and how good he was.

Her mom was an excellent judge of character.

"I didn't mean for anyone to get hurt."

Lacey gently closed the closet door. "I'm sure you didn't mean to hurt your aunt or cousin, but you absolutely meant to hurt Zach, and good on you. You scored a perfect hit since both his parents are wanted criminals and they're the reason he's in this position, though you know everything, so I'm sure you knew that. Way to kick a man when he's down."

Oh, she knew nothing. "He didn't talk about his father. He just told me his mom was in and out of jail and his aunt raised him."

"I'm surprised he mentioned them at all. He was vulnerable with you, and you stabbed him right where he told you to. Like I said, now I believe you're a Taggart. Should I move the cat or can you leave her be?"

Devi blinked back tears. He had told her about his mom. They laid in bed between bouts of ridiculously hot sex and he talked about his childhood and how hard it had been.

And she'd slid the knife in.

But damn it, he lied to her. He wrecked her damn life.

"I'm not going to hurt the cat."

"Then I'll let you be. Like I said the sea is that way," she said, pointing to the east. "You can walk right in and swim your way back to your fabulous life where you don't have to worry about the world exploding or burning, or well, any of the tragedies we're on the verge of. You can swim off and go back to your happy life. If you don't, we have tea at four and supper at 7:30. I'm off to town to pick up the list of shite Zach thinks you need. I should also apparently pick up something stronger than Mum's tea since Zach is going to end up on the couch, and it won't fit him. He was right about the one bed. I'm certainly not giving up mine."

Lacey walked out and shut the door.

Guilt swamped Devi but she took a deep breath and sat back on the bed. To the side, the cat hissed again.

Yeah, she knew how that feline felt.

*****

Zach was still reeling three hours later as he looked out over the peaceful pasture. It was all green and covered in grass and wildflowers. Beautiful. There were goats and chickens and a number of alpacas, and the weird shaggy cows Lacey gushed about. There were mangy dogs hanging out with kind of mean geese. It was not a place he ever thought to be. Most people thought he was a country boy when he mentioned he grew up in a trailer. Nope. He was urban white trash. Land cost money, and his family never had that, despite all the crimes his parents participated in. Shouldn't there have been some kind of upside?

A horse wandered by, huffing as he moved. The horse was old and probably slated to be glue when Lacey's group swooped in and brought him to the farm so he could eat grass and fart and die peacefully.

Zach wished there was a farm for spies.

After the debacle with Devi, he'd gone over the reports concerning the night before. None of them mentioned that Zach had been at the Virginia estate that burned to the ground. Devi's name hadn't made the reports, either. According to the reports filed by his former team members, it had been Cooper McKay who saved the day and the team.

Kala Taggart had done pretty much everything she promised him when they met in the Colorado woods, and Cooper finally figured out who he truly was. Instead of arresting him, Kala had listened and told him she would help. Made him promise to come home when he had what he needed.

It was almost surely Kala who sent him the writeups of the fallout from burning down Huisman's place in Virginia. He sent her a single name.

Raymond White.

His dad. Biological dad. That man hadn't given a real damn about him except in how he could use his son to manipulate Shannon Reed.

And it looked like nothing had changed with dear old Dad.

Kala would put it together quickly, and he had no doubt she would have Lou on it before they got back to Dallas.

Had he made a terrible mistake? Devi hated him. Hated him. Somehow he hadn't thought she would hate him. He'd known she was mad. He'd kind of viewed her acting out as a call for him to pay attention to her, but what if this wasn't about him beyond the fact that he was the bad guy?

He stood outside the pretty cottage he was going to have to share with her for now. He should call her mom, send her home, and pray she followed directions this time.

"Well, Miss Stella is looking perfectly fit, and you are as well, so I think I'll be heading out. Unless you want me to look at your new…guest." Arthur Beddoe was the vet Lacey worked with when it was her turn to watch over what her group called "the farm."

"She's not a guest and you know it, doc."

Arthur was an older man. Probably sixty or so, but he looked younger. He was fit, with neatly cut dark hair and warm brown eyes. He wore cargo pants and a short sleeve button-down, all of which might be normal looking until you got to the socks and Birkenstocks. They were a dead giveaway that this was a man who cared about the environment and probably smoked a little weed in his time. A brow cocked over those kind eyes. "Are we not playing games, then? Sometimes when Lacey brings…friends…around they like to pretend. I think the last one asked me to call him Mr. Noir and pretended to be an attaché with the French embassy."

That made Zach chuckle. "Yeah, I suppose that's a dig at the Agency, but I understand it. How much do you know and are you former or current?"

Because there was zero way this man wasn't intelligence or had been.

Arthur studied him for a moment. "I was SAS in my youth and worked a bit of intelligence, but I've been out of the game for a while. Raised my kids. Got back in for them, I suppose, though I changed teams. I'm not involved in any state-sponsored intelligence agency, and I'm strictly logistics and aid now. I'm the one who brought Lacey in. Consider me her mentor, and I pretty much know everything except who the young lass in the big bedroom is. I need to know if she's going to take us down."

He would have said no an hour ago. He would have said Devi Taggart would never want revenge. "I don't know, but if I get even a hint that she's going to bring in the authorities, I'll take her and we won't bother you or Lacey or the group again."

"I don't think that was your plan, Zachary." Arthur set his kit down and leaned against the fence posts. "I thought we were trying to find your mum before Huisman gets to her."

"I know, but I also know finding my mom is only part of what you and Lacey are trying to do. Lacey has a much larger mission, and she's been working on it for a long time. If bringing Devi here is going to upend her ultimate goals, then I'll figure something out. I don't know what yours is. I know you're here to help Lacey, but I still haven't figured you out yet."

Arthur shifted the Tilley hat on his head, setting it back slightly. He wore a pair of glasses and had a wedding ring on his left hand. "Believe it or not my mission is to make this world a bit better. I do that by helping people like Lacey and others, and by helping these animals find a home where they aren't abused. Where they can live a natural life. I believe Lacey would say that your mission is important to our work since Shannon Reed is the only one in the world with the detailed plans on how to build her bombs. We have some intelligence about Huisman buying property in Asia. Nepal, to be exact. There are a lot of rumors as to what he's built there. I'm worried about what he's planning, which is why I don't think this is a good time for you to be working out your personal relationships. Especially when they could bring the world down on us."

"I'm not calling in the cops," a soft voice said, and he turned.

Naturally Devi was standing there, and she seemed to have found a robe and some socks. She looked young and pretty and vulnerable.

He wasn't good enough for her, and she knew it.

She sniffled slightly and her shoulders went back, chin coming up in a stubborn expression. "I'm not a snitch, Zach. I might not work in the same world my cousins do, but I understand it." Her eyes caught on the animals standing together by the water trough, and she gasped a little. "Highland cows. That's what she meant by hillycoos. They're so cute. Are they like the cat in the closet?"

He was unaware there was a cat, though it didn't surprise him. The chickens walked around like they owned the place. He found himself standing up straight, fumbling for words. "The whole place is an animal sanctuary. Lacey works with a group that saves animals from bad situations and takes care of them."

"The cows were sick and scheduled to be put down because they're old and the farmer didn't want to waste money on their healthcare. Our organization paid him to let us take them. They're doing well now," Arthur said. "Are you talking about the pregnant calico who won't let anyone touch her?" When Devi nodded he went on. "She's got a week or so before those kittens arrive. I worry she'll abandon them or not let anyone near."

"She seems to like the closet in my room. Well, the room I'm in," Devi said.

"Do you want me to move her? I can find another place for her," Zach offered.

Devi sent him a frown. "You think I would evict a traumatized pregnant cat from the only place she feels safe?"

And he couldn't win. "I was only trying to make you comfortable."

She stared at him for a moment and seemed to make a decision. She turned to Arthur. "You in charge of the animals?"

He shook his head. "Just their healthcare. Lacey does the heavy work when it comes to the farm. Members of the group take turns. She spends six weeks here, and then she's back to Liverpool or off to wherever Disrupt sends her."

Not a single look of recognition hit her eyes. So her cousins had really kept her out of it. Disrupt was the main organization that Huisman used as a front for his many schemes to burn down civilization.

"Well, I'm going to require a litter box and some warm blankets and probably some thick gloves because kitty likes to scratch, but she'll need more room if we're turning that tiny closet into a feline homestead. And some cat treats. I'm befriending her. Slowly, of course." She looked to Zach, a bit of challenge in her eyes. "I volunteered in shelters most of my life, and I've fostered both cats and dogs. She needs patience. She was hurt, and she has to process that pain and figure out if it's worth it to risk herself again."

Were they still talking about the cat? He wasn't sure.

"I don't believe I'm needed here anymore. As we say here in Wales, *tan y tro nesaf*." Arthur tipped his hat and picked up his bag. "Tell Lacey I'll be back to check on Mel and Cass in the morning. Until then, I'll be in town. Remember what I said. There are more people at risk than you can imagine."

Arthur walked away, disappearing behind the cottage which led to the dirt road that would lead him from the farm.

Devi stared after him for a moment as though trying to figure out where she'd seen the man before. Or putting off the moment she had to deal with Zach. Yeah, it was probably the latter.

It was afternoon, the soft light playing over her red hair and bringing out the gold in it. "I'm sorry about your clothes. They're not dry yet. Lacey has some specific ideas on what appliances do and don't harm the Earth. She's picking you up some clothes in town. If you like I can get you a laptop and you can order some things. I've got a couple of IDs we could use."

She turned his way, her lips curving down. "Because you're a criminal."

There it was. That twist of the knife he hadn't expected from his sweet sub. They hadn't fought even once while they'd been together. They had harmony between them and a peace he'd never known. Like most things in his life, it had been an illusion. "I assure you I had them from when I was an operative."

"But you were lying while you were an operative." She wouldn't allow him to get away with anything.

"I was, but not until later. I went into the Army because I wanted to. As I approached the end of college I realized... I don't know why I'm telling you this. You don't want my personal history."

"I thought I knew your personal history." Devi shook her head. "I thought you went into the Army because you wanted to serve your country. Now I know... Look, none of this matters."

She was right. It didn't. He'd fucked up with her, and he wouldn't be given a second chance. "I'll call your mom and she can coordinate how to come get you. I can take you to London and leave you with your uncle's team there."

McKay-Taggart had an office in London, though unlike the US office it had an extra name attached. McKay-Taggart and Knight. Of course, he might get his ass arrested if he walked in there with her since there was an Interpol Red Notice out on him.

"My mom will hunt you down," Devi vowed. "I don't think you should call her. It would be a mistake."

She thought he was such an asshole. "I already did. I called her before we left the States."

Her eyes widened, and she looked an awful lot like her mom. "Why would you do that?"

"I was never going to let them worry about you. I wasn't going to not let you talk to them, Dev. I know you think this is some brutal kidnapping where I tie you up and starve you for days." Now that was a point. "Although you might want to because I'm fairly certain the only groceries in this place are vegan. But that's not being done to torture you. It's what happens when you work with underground animal rights activists. The point is I promised your mom you would talk to her today. To make sure she knows you're okay."

"She's all right with you taking me?" There was a slight tremor to her voice that let him know she was emotional. "She didn't threaten you?"

Another thing he hadn't considered. He was fucking this up entirely, but that was what he seemed to do. "I explained the situation to her, and she believes I'll do what it takes to protect you. I will, you know."

She sniffled again and turned away from him, looking back out over the pasture. "Or I caused enough trouble that she thinks I deserve whatever I get."

"You didn't cause anything."

"Not what your friend said."

"Lacey? Look, I'm sorry. Lacey can be harsh, especially when she's worried her mission and her people could be at risk." How had it all gone so fucking wrong? He shouldn't have called Lacey. He definitely shouldn't have hauled Devi off like some prize of war. He should have remembered that he was alone and there was nothing he could do about it. "We can go to London in the morning. I need to make some arrangements."

He would roll the dice and call Kala to see what she could put together. And then he would hope Huisman didn't realize their connection.

"Arrangements?"

He shrugged. "It's not easy to travel when all of the intelligence world is out to get you. And a big portion of the criminal underground. I might have a Red Notice out."

"Zachary." She said his name like an admonition. Like he'd done something terrible to embarrass her.

"It's what happens when you try to chase down your criminally minded mother," he admitted with a long sigh. "Now I have to deal with the fact that my father is involved somehow and pray they don't know who my brother is."

"Your brother?"

He took a long breath. He shouldn't do this. It was bringing her further in. "None of this matters. You should stay as far away from my problems as you can. Honestly, the less you know the better for you."

"Is that your excuse for lying to me? You were trying to protect me?" She crossed her arms under those pert breasts of hers. They weren't big. They were gently curved and had pink nipples that tightened into buds he liked to suck on. "You know it's considered the worst trope."

Now he was lost. "Trope?"

"Bri writes romance novels. We've read them since we were teens, and guy protecting the fragile girl flower from the horrible truth by lying to her and pushing her away is the worst trope. It's like a recurrent element. Something that happens in the genre over and over again. Like surprise pregnancies."

He barely managed to not let his jaw hit the floor. "What? But we were careful." His heart started to race. This changed everything. If Devi was pregnant, there was no mission beyond protecting Devi and his kid. At all costs. Except she'd taken a hit to the head and been fucking drugged, and he was pretty sure that was not a recommended activity for pregnant ladies. "I need to call Arthur back. He should look at you. I told her not to drug you."

She stepped in front of him, her hands going to his arms where she held him back. "I was talking about tropes in romance novels, Zach. I'm not pregnant. We *were* careful. Are you okay?"

He was shaking slightly, and he wished he could hug her. Instead he steadied himself and stepped back. "Sorry. I guess I just…"

"Freaked out at the thought of getting me pregnant?"

He shook his head. "No. That part didn't bother me. That part would be wonderful even though I know the timing would be hard, but the thought of you and our baby in Huisman's hands got to me for a moment."

"Well, I suppose if I was pregnant, you would get your Taggart connection."

They were back to that. Every time he got a second's worth of hope it came crashing down, and it irritated him. He knew he was in the wrong, but could she give him a second's grace? He was tired and hadn't eaten and his damn side hurt. "Which am I, Devi? First, I was the horrible asshole who got you pregnant and would leave you high and dry, and now I purposefully got you pregnant so I can join your clan because once your uncle discovers the pregnancy, he'll drag me to the altar and force me to marry you."

"Other way around, buddy," she shot back.

"No way around, buddy." He gave her back her words and couldn't help the bitterness. "No one is going to force Devi Taggart to do anything she doesn't want to do. No one would blink an eye if you told them you were having a baby, and oh hey, it's that asshole's, so could you bury him, uncle, so I don't have to put up with him anymore and I can go find the pure-hearted man of my dreams without that piece of trailer trash in my life?"

"I never said that, Zach."

"I'm sure you'll get around to it. Don't think I haven't heard it all." He needed to breathe. He'd gone from terror to a weird high of having his brother actually work with him, to the revelation that none of this was going to work. There was no tender place for him at the end of this. There was horror and death, and that was likely the happiest of outcomes. "When Lacey gets back, we'll call your parents and get you out of here."

He started to turn.

"I don't think that's a good idea," Devi said quietly.

He was going to miss her, but right now he couldn't handle more bile. He felt weirdly fragile, and one more nasty word from the one woman he'd ever really loved might break him. He was sure his father would give him a smack and tell him to be a man, but he couldn't right now, and he sure as fuck wasn't going to take it out on her. "Your mom isn't mad at you. I'm sorry she wasn't as angry with me as you want her to be, but she's a pragmatic woman. It would have been difficult for Cooper to get you and Kala out. I made a call. It was the wrong one."

"I am so fucking angry with you," she said, her gaze intense as though she was holding something back.

"I know. I'll leave you alone."

"I don't want you to. I don't… Zach, I don't know what I want right now beyond going back and not leaving Landon in that restaurant." Tears filled her eyes. "I could have killed Aunt Eve. I got my cousin kidnapped. I think they did terrible things to her. They wouldn't have if I hadn't been stupid and gotten myself caught, and I did it because I was mad at you."

His heart softened immediately, and he knew this woman was his Achilles' heel. "I'm sorry."

"I don't want your apologies."

"Baby, what do you want? I'll give it to you."

"I can't go home," she said with surety. "If I go home, I put everyone in my orbit in danger. I was foolish and not thinking. I was going to show you. I was going to show everyone that I didn't matter."

Every word made him ache. "You matter. You matter so much."

"I understand that you have done a good job of taking the focus off Tasha and putting it on me."

He stilled. It was like she took a knife to him. He couldn't quite process the words. He knew they were deadly but…she couldn't think he did that intentionally.

"Zach, you're bleeding."

He was. He was bleeding, and he didn't care. If he bled out, then it would all be over and he wouldn't have to worry about it anymore. He'd lived so long in survival mode that the brief time he spent with her had been the best of his life. He had his girl and his brother and a place in a world he loved.

He had none of those things now. Did it matter if he bled out? It would make things easier for everyone he cared about.

"You're bleeding. Whatever the doctor did you opened it up again."

He couldn't. He just couldn't. He put a hand to his side. Sure enough, there was some wetness. The butterflies had likely come apart when he moved the boxes from the front porch inside. Arthur told him not to pick up heavy things, but he didn't listen because he wanted everything to be in place when Devi woke up.

"Zach," she began in that irritated tone that seemed to be the only one she used around him. She reached out and grabbed his arm.

And stopped when she got a good look at him.

Tears slipped from her eyes, and she shook her head. "That's not fair."

He was crying. It was dumb and unmasculine, and he likely never would have if he hadn't done all the therapy Big Tag required. Therapy had done nothing except teach him how much he longed for another life. Unfortunately, therapy couldn't change his circumstances.

He thought she would walk away, but she moved in, fingers coming up to caress his cheeks, wiping the tears away.

"Not fair," she whispered and then laid her head in the crook of his neck, and he felt a shudder go through her. Then her arms wrapped around him, careful to avoid his injured side. "I don't know what to do, Zach. I can't go back. Not home and not to what we were before, but I also can't… I can't stay this mad at you. It's become everything I am, and I'm hurting people I love because I'm hurt. I'm going to stay hurt if I don't make things right with you. Be evil. Make it easy on me."

And just like that he hoped again. Such a dangerous thing to do, but she was in his arms telling him she wanted things to be okay between them. He reached up and stroked her hair, holding her close and ignoring the pain. "I can't. I know I should let you go, but I won't do it by being mean to you. I won't lie again. I promise. I love you, Devi. I love you so fucking much, my sweetness."

It made her cry harder.

He held her and for a moment felt like he had a place in the world.

Chapter Seven

Devi stared at the screen on the laptop. "This is safe?"

Her mother sat in front of her own screen. She looked tired but then she probably hadn't gotten a ton of sleep. "Zach assures me he's pinged it across the globe and no one can find it. Do you want me to call in Adam? I would call Lou to check but she's asleep and your brother is...also asleep."

So they were doing it somewhere. Good for TJ. "No, I think it's safe to say that when it comes to evading the cops, Zach knows what he's doing."

It was two hours since she cried on his shoulder and held him and then forced him to let her fix his bandages and nag him about not picking up stuff when he was healing a freaking knife wound. How was this her life?

Then she'd worked with Lacey to fix up the cat palace, and now she was talking to her parents.

It was all so unreal.

"I think Zachary has skills none of us imagined." Her father was there, too. He leaned in. "How are you, sweetie? Has someone looked you over? Kala told us you took a pretty hard hit from that Lena person. Who should be glad she's dead now. I wish I could say the same of Huisman."

"I'm fine, and the woman Zach is working with is pretty good with herbs, so I didn't even need an aspirin." The tea had worked wonders, though she still got the feeling Lacey didn't want her here. She could understand that. Lacey Rook had a mission, and apparently Devi was cursed to be kidnapped every couple of days. It was Groundhog Day except with torture and regret. "How is Kala?"

Lacey had returned with clothes and food and a couple of bottles of what she called responsibly sourced wine and a six-pack of beer. Devi had taken a shower and changed into comfy clothes, sat with the cat for a while before trying to introduce some warm blankets and nearly getting her fingers taken off. But the cat had eaten the treats she left, and they were in a holding pattern.

Like she and Zach were.

He cried. The sight of his gorgeous face with tears streaking down his cheeks as he tried to hide them from her… She wasn't sure he could have done anything that would have gutted her more.

Were those the tears of an excellent actor?

"She's got an appointment with a cardiologist. Whatever that fucker did to her might have damaged her heart," her father explained.

Her mom sent her dad a "we talked about this" look before turning back to the camera. "Kala is fine and very feisty, and you need to tell Zach to fix this shit because Cooper and Kala are getting married in three weeks, and you know there's going to be some drama."

She heard a gasping sound and frowned toward the door. "You might as well come in, Zach. It must be hard for you to spy out in the hallway."

He eased in the bedroom, an apologetic look on his face. "Sorry. There's only one bathroom, and I heard that news. I'm surprised. Well, I'm not surprised they're getting married. I'm surprised Charlotte is letting it happen in a couple of weeks. She's been working on Tasha and Dare's wedding for months and we still have months to go."

"Hey, Zach," her mom said with a bright smile.

"Zach," her father growled.

He knelt down beside her. "Hi."

If looks could kill, her father would be doing murder right now.

Her mom seemed...okay with it.

"Want to tell me where you are, Zach?" her father asked.

He looked to her. "What's the call, swee...Devi? It's up to you. If you want to leave, I'll give them coordinates on where to pick you up."

The Garden. While she'd replaced his bandages they had also talked about the possibility of her going home. The only place he was willing to take her was to McKay-Taggart and Knight in London. She couldn't go, and for more reasons than she was willing to admit. "I think I should stay where I am for now."

"I can protect you," her father insisted. "Devi, your uncle has promised bodyguards and a safe house for all of us until this thing is over. We could use a vacation, your mother and I."

"Speak for yourself," her mom said with a huff. "She didn't like the bodyguards. They didn't work for her."

She couldn't let this get too heated. "Mom, I was awful to Landon. Please don't let Uncle Ian fire him. I purposefully tricked him so I could prove a point, and it got a lot of people hurt. It's why I think I should stay here for a while."

"I'm not worried about myself," her father insisted. "Your mother and I can handle whatever comes our way."

Her parents were badasses. Her dad was a former Navy SEAL and her mom had once been Army intelligence. They could still handle themselves, but they shouldn't have to. "Dad, I think it's for the best."

"I will protect her," Zach said gravely.

"Well, you're the reason she's being hunted by a fucking megalomaniac determined to bring the world down." Her father had clearly had a lot of stimulation the last couple of days.

"Theo," her mom said. "We talked about this. Why don't both of the guys go and find something to do? I'd like to talk to Devi alone. Please, Theo. I know how you feel, but you need to remember what your brother said."

Her dad took a long breath and then nodded. "All right. Devi, I love you. I want you to come home but... Well, I want you home and safe. I'll talk to you the next time Zach allows it."

"Not allowing anything. She's not a prisoner." Zach was shaking his head. "I will set this up whenever she needs to talk."

She needed to channel her mom. She looked his way. "You should go check on dinner."

He stood. "Okay, but I want to know about Kala and Coop. And honestly, all of them."

He strode away and her dad was suddenly absent, though she was sure he would be somewhere listening in. Or not. Her dad was the best guy she knew, and he would honor her wishes and definitely her mom's.

"How are you really, baby girl?"

She needed to get past all these tears. "I'm physically okay. The place Zach took me to is actually pretty cool. I have a pregnant cat neighbor, so I'll have kittens soon."

Her mom got that mom smile on her face, the one she had for the soft and young and weak of the world. "Aww, that's sweet. Are you and Zach getting along?"

"I'm mad at him."

"Of course you are, but that doesn't mean it's not a complex situation with complicated feelings. Anger can cloud things, but I know it's there. I'm hoping you can take a deep breath and use this time to figure things out. Not only with Zach, but with your life."

"I thought that's what I was doing at home." But even as she said the words she knew her mom was right.

"You're drifting. You came home from college and wanted some time off and I was happy to give that to you, but it's been a couple of years and I know you're working on commissions and trying to find internships but…"

She knew where her mom was going. "It's not what I wanted. I wanted my own line, but it's hard. I guess I got caught up in life."

"Working part time at McKay-Taggart or Top is not what you're meant to do, baby." Her mom sighed and put her elbows on the table where they'd eaten meals growing up. Her and Mom and Dad and TJ. Sometimes Bri or Daisy would join them.

Precious, precious time. She hadn't realized it then, but every moment had been precious.

Her friends were moving on with their lives and she was stuck. Sometimes the best way to get unstuck was to completely change the circumstances. For a little while at least. "I know and that's one of the reasons I want to stay here, but there are others."

"Zach?"

She nodded, not able to actually say the words. "And other reasons. Mom, I did ditch Landon, and I knew it would get him in trouble. I didn't realize how much it would cost Aunt Eve."

"She's doing well." Her mom got a bit teary. "Your Aunt Eve is tough, and you have to know that she would do it all again to save you. The first words out of her mouth when she woke up was to ask about you and Kala."

Not a surprise. "Please tell her how sorry I am."

"She doesn't need an apology, baby girl. She needs to know that you are okay, too."

Devi nodded. "I'm as okay as I can be right now."

"That's all we can ask for. How is Zach?"

Devi wiped away her tears and felt herself go mulish. "I'm mad at him."

"You did mention that and rightfully so, but how is he?"

"Aren't you supposed to be on my side?" She'd expected her mom to be a Valkyrie warrior, bringing death and destruction on all who thought to harm her.

She hadn't thought that maybe her mom didn't think Zach wanted to harm her at all.

"Always. I can be on your side and still care about how Zach is," her mom said in an altogether too reasonable voice. "Do you want me to turn this over to your dad? I assure you he'll let you talk shit on Zach for hours. He's been planning where to hide his body."

Did she want that? Maybe if it was Bri and Daisy and they had margaritas. They would let her trash Zach, and still at some point Bri would push her to be honest about how she felt.

Angry. Angry. Enraged. Sad.

Longing. She felt longing when she looked at him. Ached when he cried because she'd been brutal with him and he couldn't take it. Not from her.

Why? He'd told her some of his past, a sanitized version constructed to get him where he wanted to be. There were likely some truths mixed in, but a lot would have been hidden. What happened to him that he couldn't be the hardened operative around her?

Or was it all one more act?

When she thought about it, she knew little that was real about him.

"What do you know about Zach?" There was zero way her mom didn't know everything her uncle did at this point. Classified intel be damned, Ian Taggart wouldn't leave her parents in the dark. Not about the basics.

"I know you should talk to him. I know some of his past, and it's painful and cruel and he didn't deserve it. I can tell you, but it might be better if you ask him."

Because if he told her, he would be opening up to her. "What does Uncle Ian think?"

There had to be a reason her family wasn't banging on doors and threatening the world. Her parents had gone to Germany with the team when her brother had been taken. They'd made sure he got home.

So there had to be a reason her mother was calmly sitting there while she was in… Everyone told her it was Wales. They could be lying.

"I'm pretty sure your uncle knows more than he's saying, and I know he did not arrest Zach when his dumb ass walked right up to the team in Virginia. I need you to think about that. He didn't hide. He didn't run. He walked up to them knowing they have orders to bring him in. I believe he did that for you. Now you're probably sitting there thinking it was all about Cooper, but I don't, and I have several reasons why," her mother began.

She was confused. "Why would it be about Cooper? Because of how close they are and he didn't want him to have to save Kala alone? I don't understand. Uncle Ian could have gone in with him."

Her mother went still, like she hadn't anticipated the question. "He didn't tell you. Damn it. I thought for sure he would have told you that."

Really confused. How much worse was this going to get? Or did her mom not understand? "He and Cooper are friends. At least they seem to be. When we were together we spent a lot of time with Cooper and Kala."

Who were getting married. She always dreamed of designing dresses for her cousins' weddings. She'd made all the dresses for Carys's wedding. Well, for the one that got busted up with gunfire. She was supposed to start Tasha's wedding dress soon. Well, after her cousin figured out to the very last detail exactly what she wanted. But that was probably done now that she was stuck on a Welsh farm. Someone else would get to lovingly sew the dress. Not her.

Was she going to end up being the cursed wedding dress designer? Not like "hey, you'll probably get divorced if you wear that Taggart original." Nope. More like "your wedding will get raided and there will be bombs."

"Sweetie, Zach and Cooper are biological brothers."

She'd had such plans for Tasha's wedding and the bridesmaids' dresses. Wait. What? "Brothers?"

"Yes. It's one of the things he told Cooper and Kala while they were in the woods."

"Why were they in the woods?" She had been left out of so damn much.

Now that she thought about it, they did resemble each other. Same coloring. Same nose. Same build.

Brothers.

"They were tracking down Zach's aunt. The one who raised him after his mom went to prison." Her mother seemed to be carefully measuring her words. A thing she almost never did. "Zach was there, and they all had a showdown. You'll notice that Kala didn't bring him in either. As a matter of fact, I believe Kala is still feeding him information."

"How?"

"Well, there's this thing called the Dark Web and…"

Her mother was starting to irritate her. "How are they brothers? I swear I will hang up if you start explaining sex to me."

Her mother sometimes spoke only sarcasm.

"I wouldn't do that. Not now. Baby, I know you are hurting. I know it feels like you're on the outside looking in, but that's what happens when you're involved with a person who works intelligence. I should know. I've been on both sides."

Her mom's words kind of flowed over her because her brain was moving in quick speed. "Cooper was adopted. Zach's older. His mom kept him but not Cooper? Or were they both adopted out?"

"You were right the first time. Our mom wanted to hide Cooper from our father," a deep voice said. Zach was back in the doorway. "Sorry. It's not a big cabin and you kind of screeched. I'll tell you everything if you give me the chance. Or I can give you the reports I sent to your uncle. Either way, I'll be in the kitchen. Dinner's ready. I'll warn you. It's beets. Do you want me to make a plate and send it to your room?"

Where she would get no information?

She felt her mom watching her. Waiting for what she would do. She loved her mom, but she could be judgey when she thought her kids were doing something dumb. Devi wasn't sure which would be the dumber path, but she knew which one she was taking. "I want a debrief. That's what you call it, right? Look, Zach, if I'm staying here for safety, I want to know what I need safety from. I will not be kept in the dark. If you think I'll sit in my room and be a good girl, then you don't know me. I'm smart and I'm strong and I can make decisions myself. So set the truth out in front of me and I'll decide if I'm part of this team or if I'm going to hide somewhere on my own."

"Nicely done, sweetie," her dad yelled from the kitchen.

Good to know his hearing was still excellent.

"Can you handle that, Zach?" her mom asked, clear challenge in her tone.

Zach nodded. "Yeah, I can handle it. I've been telling this story a lot lately. But I'm going to pop open some beers if we're doing this."

He walked back out into the hallway.

"Listen to him, baby girl," her mom said. "I think he cares about you, and he's definitely in trouble. Your uncle is in the background trying to help him, but a lot of this work is going to be done on the ground."

Meaning Zach had to handle it with his "team." And she'd opened the door to becoming a part of it. The good news was she liked beets. Aunt Charlotte made an excellent borscht. Hopefully Lacey knew how to cook. If she didn't, then that would be something Devi could take over. Like she'd never cooked for vegan models. But there were still problems. "How can I trust him?"

Her mom seemed to think about it for a moment. "I've looked at his actions, and I would trust him. I think he's a young man in a bad situation for the right reasons."

Her mom wasn't considering all the scenarios. "I think he likes me because I'm a Taggart."

"So you heard the rumors about Tasha."

She couldn't seem to get away from them. She nodded.

"Consider the fact that from what I've heard he never once made a move on her. He made several moves on you."

Oh, like she hadn't thought this problem through. "I was convenient. He didn't have a play partner and he was bored."

Her mother sighed. "You don't know that. Don't let your insecurities overwhelm you. It's time to ask some questions and to take a real measure of the man. He called me from the car that night. Before he even had you on a plane. He called your parents because he couldn't stand the thought that we would worry. He's taking the risk of getting caught by letting you talk to me now."

All of which could mean that becoming a Taggart was worth the risk of jail time.

How would she know until she truly understood Zach Reed's story? Until she pulled the veil back, it was all supposition and gossip.

He was Cooper's brother? She was still floored by the revelation. Brothers. And Cooper knew. And Kala knew.

Did she trust them? "I wish they would have told me. Kala and Coop, that is."

"That's part of it, and you need to decide if it's worth it to stay close to the people in your life who owe their secrets to the Agency. You know a lot of the time I thought your father was dead, your uncle had some inkling that he wasn't."

"And he didn't tell you?"

Her mom's head shook. "Nope, and I thank the universe for that. Uncle Ian sent Uncle Liam out on several ops to figure out where your dad was being held, and neither mentioned it to me. Not because they didn't care about me or want me to know, but because they weren't sure. I was pregnant with your brother and starting to figure out I could live a life."

Devi didn't see how her mom's past related to her own. "That's not the situation here."

"No, but it is a situation where they have to decide what you need to know versus the risk of you knowing. Also, a lot of this happened recently. Kala's only known since Colorado. She just got back and oops, kidnapped. Would you like me to play the part and explain why she hasn't taken the time to tell you?"

Oh, she could hear her cousin in her head right now. *Sorry, cos. Was way too busy getting my ass kicked and then valiantly trying to save us both to give you a debrief on what happened with your ex-honey in Colorado.*

"Okay, I'll give you that, but obviously Zach knew." And she wouldn't understand why he didn't tell her until she talked to him. "Sorry. I'm mad, but I get it. I don't know the whole story. Even when I do, I don't know that I can trust him."

"All you can do is try and listen and trust your instincts. Look, there's a big part of me that wants to tell you to come home. We can hide out somewhere until the heat is off, and you don't have to risk having your heart broken. Because there's still a big risk of that. He's in serious trouble."

Trouble she didn't understand. "Mom, I love you. I'm going to go talk to Zach."

Her mom nodded. "Good. I think you should do that, and tell him you're going to need a tablet or something you can work on because I've already got a text from Tasha. She wants you to send her some more design ideas for her dress."

"More? I've sent her five already." Her cousin was turning into a bit of a bridezilla.

Her mom shrugged. "She might have mentioned that it's not like you have a lot else to do. Unless you're coming home."

That didn't seem like a great idea. On a lot of fronts. Including the one where she hated Zach and still couldn't stand the thought of not being around him. To torture him and get revenge.

Yeah, sure. That's what she was doing.

"I'm staying. It's safer for everyone." Still a lie, but closer to the truth. She couldn't leave until she had some closure.

"I love you," her mom said and cut the connection.

And Devi stood ready to figure out what the hell was happening with the man she definitely shouldn't love.

* * * *

Zach walked back into the kitchen, his heart heavy. How had he forgotten? In all the drama of the last day and a half, he hadn't told her the biggest secret of all. "I didn't tell her about Cooper. I…should have. Her mom told her and she's angry all over again."

Lacey looked up from the stove where she was stirring something that absolutely would not include a side of beef. "When were you supposed to tell her? She pretty much woke up and started yelling at everyone. Honestly, not what I would have expected from a Taggart."

"You keep saying that. Almost like you know a few." Zach was confused. Lacey was normally completely cool under pressure. Her calm demeanor was one of the reasons he trusted her and had for more than a year. Lacey knew a bit about the team he'd been on. She knew about Big Tag and his daughter Tasha. But as far as he knew she thought what the rest of the world did. That Ms. Magenta was Kara.

Lacey shrugged. "Only by reputation, but I would expect her to have a bit more fire."

"She's fiery enough." He should know since she singed the fuck out of him. He could still feel himself bleeding. He had to be stronger than this. He wasn't supposed to…feel this deeply. This was why he should never have touched her. He shouldn't have brought her into his world.

"No, she's bratty and privileged. She's not thinking about any situation but her perceived one."

He thought she was being a little harsh. "She's been through something traumatic. I lied to her about a lot of things."

"You had to. Look, Zach, if you want me to assign blame, I can do it. You shouldn't have started a relationship with her. Your life is far too dangerous with your mother unwilling to come in and your father in play now. This is not the time to look for love." She glanced over to the door that led out to the hallway and then focused on the task of plating again. "In fact, I'm going to say you were much more reasonable when your affections were directed at the other Ms. Taggart."

He did not need to talk about that. "It was a crush. I never meant to make a move. Devi is different."

"Different how? Because I don't understand. From my perspective she's nothing but trouble. She was annoyed by the cat."

Despite the fact that he'd recently had the revelation that he shouldn't have brought her in, Lacey saying it bugged him. Seriously bugged him. And he didn't like the way Lacey was talking about Devi. He had a deep protective instinct when it came to his sub. "She was not. She was surprised, and then she made a whole plan of how she's going to befriend the damn cat. You don't know her. You met her on what must be one of the worst days of her life. She had to watch her cousin get taken away by Huisman. She fought. She was brave. Don't talk about her like that. I won't listen. If you dislike her so much, we can both leave. Don't forget. I help you out, too. Well, I'm calling in those favors for her."

"See, just when I'm ready to hate you," a soft voice said. Devi walked in. She shot Lacey a look. "You shouldn't do that to him."

"Do what?" Zach was confused. She looked awfully pretty in her new jeans and button-down. Her sneakers were the only thing left from her previous outfit. She'd taken something plain and made it interesting by rolling up the bottom of the legs, showing the difference in color and tying off the bottom of the shirt so it clung to her curves and exposed a bit of her midriff.

Devi walked a few steps into the kitchen. A bit wary, looking around like she needed to know where the exits were. "She knew I was standing here, and she baited you into saying a bunch of nice things about me. She knows damn well I'm fine with the cat. She helped me set up the bedding for her in the closet. Her name is Sunny, by the way."

"Not how I would have gone," Lacey said, taking two plates to the small table and setting them down. "Did you want to know what he honestly thought or not? I was trying to do a sister a solid."

Yep, still confused. "I thought you didn't like her."

Lacey shrugged. "You're right. Our first meeting was awkward. Also, sorry about the drugs. They can affect you long after, but when I got back from town with her clothes and all of the supplies, we had a fine time. Well, we had a painful time because Sunny has sharp claws."

"So he never tried to bring my cousin to meet his underground warrior woman?" Devi asked.

Lacey grinned. "See, that's why I'm fond of her. I really am an underground warrior woman. I should get a tattoo. Mum would be so proud."

"How did you two meet?" Devi sat down like they were having an everyday regular meal.

"Devi, we should talk."

She nodded. "And we will, but I have questions. I have been utterly out of control for weeks now. Give me this. How did you meet? I'd like an answer, and I'd like it to be detailed and thorough."

A snort came from Lacey. "She wants to know if we've shagged."

Zach grimaced at the thought. He had never viewed Lacey that way. There was zero between them except work and a friendship he'd come to rely on. "No."

Lacey grabbed a third plate and sat across from Devi, leaning over conspiratorially. "Not that he's been a saint. Quite the opposite. He's a horny bastard."

"I am not. I am a regular sex drive bastard." She didn't have to put it like that. "I've been single and quite frankly, despite her uncle's rules for his daughters, he's willing to throw me out as man meat a lot."

"What is that supposed to mean?" Devi's brow had arched, and she looked a lot like her mom in that moment. Her mom when she was trying to figure out if it was time to kick a little ass. "Because I happen to know that my uncle has a honey pot rule, and yes, I know what honey pot means in the spy world. It's flirting for information and potentially having an entire sexual relationship to work a target. I happen to know my cousins are forbidden from doing that, and I'm fairly certain my uncle would never ask Cooper or Tris. You're telling me he'll toss you in?"

And she sounded as fierce as her mother.

Lacey grinned. "Oh, from what I can tell Big Tag often throws Zach to the wolves, and by wolves I mean any target who finds him attractive. Once he flirted with a man in an airport for over two hours so a member of his team could steal his laptop, download the information, and get it back in his bag. The bugger had shown zero interest in Miss Magenta, but he perked right up when Big Tag sent in Zach."

Devi frowned and looked at Zach. "She knows about the twins?"

Fuck. Big Tag was going to kill him. "No."

Lacey's eyes narrowed. "Twins. Bugger all. That's what I've been missing. You keep talking about your cousins. I thought you were using the plural because you grew up with them. I knew Tasha Taggart was on the team. Is Kara a Taggart, too? Did the Agency scrub her? Or them? Twins explains a lot."

Devi had gone pale. "Oh, I did that."

He reached out and took her hand in his, guilt threatening to swamp him. "Sweetness, you are not an operative. I don't blame you. Your uncle won't blame you. The twins won't blame you." He squeezed her hand and looked her right in the eyes. "You have done nothing wrong. You're in a world you're not used to. Look at me. Your cousins are fine. Lacey is an ally, and one I assure you Big Tag will vet thoroughly if I bring her in. Which I'll probably have to at this point."

Lacey's head shook as though that was a terrible idea. "I don't think we need to do that at all, but Zach is right about one thing. I'm not about to go out and shout it to the world. The truth is I don't care. I have my job and that is to infiltrate an organization called Disrupt. Particularly Disrupt Europe."

"I don't know what that is," Devi admitted.

She wasn't alone. Outside of politicians and some think tanks, it wasn't a wildly advertised group. "It's a bunch of wealthy people who got together with intellectuals and politicians to create new ways to solve problems. Like water in Africa. They basically brought together a group of innovators and are working on real solutions to bring water to dry areas of the continent."

"That doesn't sound bad." Devi sat back, seeming to find some calm.

"Yes, it certainly seems fine from the outside," Lacey agreed. She scooped up some of the beet, carrot, and kale salad she made.

Zach sighed and wished he had a burger. "There's a second level to Disrupt. A darker one."

"And that man who took my cousin is involved." Devi winced. "I need to stop saying cousin."

"You don't. I was serious. I have a vague interest in some of the stories Zach has told me about Ms. Magenta. I won't talk about it to anyone," Lacey promised. "I owe Zach a lot. So to answer your original question, I have to talk a bit about my mum. She's a legend in activist circles. She works mostly on the environment, but she will champion animal causes as well. One of her friends was working with Disrupt Europe on animal testing. She called my mum one night and said she found evidence that there was a group within the group, and they were buying bombs."

"Why would they need bombs?" Devi asked.

"A good question, and very specific bombs." Lacey passed Devi the wine she bought. "Do you recall the terrorist attacks in Jakarta a few years back?"

She nodded. "Yes, because I was working on a project with a company at the time. It was some post-grad work I did for a professor designing a sportswear line. Our manufacturer was in Indonesia, and we ended up having to shift to Vietnam because the shipping lines were screwed up for months."

"Yes, the word *disrupt* works for both parts of the organization," Zach agreed.

Devi looked thoughtful for a moment. "Why would they want to blow up some transportation sites in Asia?"

"Because of what comes out of Asia. An enormous amount of merchandise, and more importantly, parts we use to build things here come out of Asia. Disrupt those shipping lanes and you disrupt the world," Lacey explained. "I know it's hard to understand, but what I've uncovered is a group of extremely wealthy people behind the front-facing organization who use the legitimate parts of Disrupt to do what they actually want to do. Which is burn the world down so they can make a profit and rule over what's left."

"What happened to your mom's friend?" Devi asked.

Lacey stopped and put her fork down. She took a long sip of wine. "She disappeared. She was supposed to meet my mum in Munich to give her the files and the evidence she found. She didn't make it. Three weeks later her body was dragged out of a river in Croatia. Any reports you read will claim she was drunk and fell in. She didn't drink."

"So she was murdered," Devi surmised.

"She was, and my mum was heartbroken. She's strong but she's not capable of violence. It's not in her soul. It is in mine. My father had another life before he married her, and it seems I take after him. My original plan was to find her killer and bring some justice. I brought blood and pain. I don't think it qualifies as justice, but it did feel good," Lacey said, her voice steady. "However, I found nothing that would stand up in a court of law, so I decided to keep my cover and go further. And that is when I met Shannon Reed."

"Zach's mom."

He nodded. "I've told you about her. True things, like she was in and out of jail."

Devi studied him as though she could see to his soul. "For drug possession. You told me she cooked meth."

Not exactly what he'd said, but he could understand her confusion. "She created designer drugs. My mother was...is a gifted chemist. My father met her while she was on a full ride to Stanford. He was a low-level drug dealer who started to move up the ladder once he convinced his girlfriend to make his product. My mom managed to refine his drugs. She did some time in California. When she came out, she went right back to my bio dad, and I was conceived. She managed to stay out of jail while she was pregnant with me."

"When did she have Cooper?" Devi asked.

Lacey whistled. "You are excellent at putting ice on your words. Zach, do you need a jumper?"

He frowned Lacey's way. "We don't need your sarcasm." He turned back to Devi. "After she got tagged the second time, my aunt left the military so I wouldn't go into the system. I was very young. I don't remember much about my father beyond the fact that he would show up every now and then and scare the hell out of my aunt. The longest time my mom did was for my dad. She took the fall. Not like she had a choice. She was in jail when she found out she was pregnant. By then she had figured out Ray sold her out to the cartel they were working with, and she was terrified. That was when she and my aunt decided to find a family for the baby."

"They sent him away to protect him but kept you in the line of fire?" Devi managed to sound irate on his behalf.

The inequity was something he let go of a long time ago. "Ray already knew about me. My aunt managed to pay off enough people in the prison that they kept my mother's pregnancy secret. From what I've been told she didn't show until late in pregnancy, and she spent the last six weeks in solitary. The baby's adoption was arranged by a private broker."

"Did Uncle Alex buy a baby on the black market?" Devi asked.

"All right, how big is this family?" Lacey asked. "And does that make you cousins in some way?"

"No," he and Devi said at the same time.

"Alex McKay is my uncle's best friend. He was very much a part of my childhood. We had a lot of adults around who we weren't biologically related to, but they were family," Devi explained and then frowned. "And now I realize how I could have handled talking about my cousins. Anyway, I don't expect you to understand. I know the world values blood."

"I think I understand more than you can imagine," Lacey replied quietly. "From what I've been told the adoption was perfectly legal, and Mr. McKay had no idea he was adopting the child of someone who knew who he was."

"My aunt worked with Big Tag in the Army. She liked and trusted him. She heard from some of their Army buddies that his best friend was trying to adopt," Zach explained. "So she made it happen."

And now she would put it all together in her angry brain and come to the conclusion that everyone in his family was trying to use everyone in hers. She would be right back to the whole he was going down the line of Taggart women looking for a way in.

He only wanted inside one of them, and she would probably shoot him if he tried. Or sic her recently acquired attack cat on him.

"So your mom was worried Coop would be one more thing your dad could hold over her head?" Devi asked carefully, as though weighing her words.

It was better than the bile she'd been spewing all day. "Yes. I was a toddler at the time, but everyone in the cartel knew I was her son. She thought if she could get Cooper out, he would be safer."

"And your aunt went to the man she trusted," Devi continued.

"Ian doesn't know. I mean he does now, but he didn't know at the time," Zach explained. He didn't want her lumping her uncle into the lying pile of shit men she had now. "Ian had no idea I'm Cooper's biological brother. I didn't know he existed until years and years later."

"Did your dad use you against your mom?"

He didn't like to think about how shitty his childhood had been. "Mom was out for a couple of years while he was in South America working. He came back to the States and picked me up from school one day. Charmed his way in, explaining he was my dad and only had a few days before he had to be back to work. I'm fairly certain the woman thought he was being deployed or something, though I assure you my father would never join the military. Too much sacrifice. He took me to a motel, and I don't remember a lot except that I ate pizza and watched cartoons and my mom cried and shook when she finally got me back. And she agreed to start working on a project for my dad's new bosses. She drifted in and out of my life after that until I was fourteen. I didn't see her again, though she would send money back and talk to me every now and then on the phone. I didn't lay eyes on her until I was twenty-two and starting to work intelligence."

"That's when he found out about the career change," Lacey pointed out.

"So your dad's new bosses were terrorists," Devi surmised.

Not exactly. "They were arms dealers. They didn't have a political agenda. They were into making money," Zach replied. "By this point my mother was no longer with my dad. She was paranoid and involved in several underground groups that I'm sure a couple of governments would label as terrorists."

"Including the one my mum's friend was heavily involved in. It was an animal rights group that operated out of Liverpool." Lacey took over her part of the story. "It was Shannon who told us about the strange requests she was getting from an arms dealer called The Jester. She did some work for him, and he had a client who was deeply impressed with how she reworked certain aspects of her bombs."

"She made them smaller. Easier to carry and conceal. Her bombs are also capable of handling small nuclear devices. Think of them like a bullet that goes off without needing a gun to deliver it." Zach was well aware that his mother was one of the most dangerous people walking the earth right now. "They used her bombs in the Jakarta attacks and in some more focused assassinations that were played off as accidents."

Devi took a sip of wine as though she needed the fortification. "Did she know what was happening?"

See, there was his hope. Her deep belief in people. Unfortunately, he couldn't play up her optimism here. "There's no good way to use one of her bombs. She didn't know exactly what they would be used for, but she accepted the money for them."

"She did it for more than money," Lacey countered. "Devi, I've met Shannon. I consider her something of a friend. Shannon has faced an enormous amount of trauma. It's affected her mentally. She sold those bombs because she was trying to protect herself and her sons. I believe the people around her used her family to put her in terrible positions."

"My mother is paranoid. Not on some funny level. She's taken shots at delivery people because she forgot she ordered a pizza and decided the man was coming to kill her." He wanted Devi to know the whole story. "So to say tracking her down has been difficult would be an understatement. Now after all of that, I met Lacey when we were both looking for the man known as The Jester. He worked with Disrupt and was responsible for her mother's friend's death. This is where you'll likely hate me again. Lacey and I worked outside of the Agency to find The Jester. We found him, fought him, killed him."

"I think that was more me than you," Lacey argued. "Men. They come in and take all the credit."

He ignored her because this was the bad part. "At the time I was working with Tristan Dean-Miles on the same case for the agency. I couldn't let him know about Lacey, nor that I killed The Jester, so I sent an assassin up. I wasn't about to let Tris die. I had it planned perfectly, and Tris killed the man he believed to be The Jester and then took over his identity."

"You used Tris to find your mother." Sure enough, her icy demeanor was back.

"I did." He wasn't going to lie or prevaricate. "By this point in time Lacey and I had drawn some conclusions about the Disrupt subgroup."

"We believe they were behind the attempted assassinations of certain heads of state in Europe a few years back. It didn't work because they were attempting to replicate Shannon's bombs." Lacey was all business. "They failed. The man we believe to be the head of the group decided the best way to fix the problem was to bring Shannon Reed in."

"That Huisman guy," Devi said.

"Yes. He's been looking for the bombmaker for a long time. It was precisely why we had to take out The Jester. Apart from my biological father, he was the only person connected to that world who knew her name." Zach had not started the day thinking he would end it with a debrief of his girlfriend.

She frowned his way. "Why didn't you go to my uncle?"

"Because while I trust Ian implicitly, I know there are those in the Agency who would do anything to see him fail, including screw with ops he's running and fuck with intelligence he brings to the table." He would love more than anything to dump this whole mess on Ian's lap, but he couldn't, and he had another confession to make. Somehow it was easier to make it to the man himself than it was to Devi. "I was sent in to gather intel on the group and make it easier for the bosses I worked for to dismantle the team."

"You did what?" Devi pushed back her chair.

"He did nothing." Lacey's eyes went steely. "He took the place on the team because he knew Cooper was his brother at that point and he was curious. He wanted to meet his brother, but he was cautious and didn't want to disrupt his life if he didn't have to. Zach Reed helped his team."

"Tris might disagree," Devi challenged.

"It took two of us to take that man out." Lacey didn't back down. "Tristan Dean-Miles was reckless and stubborn, and if he walked in and faced the real Jester himself, he would be dead now. Zach gave him the opportunity to look like the big man and take all the credit. Devi, I wasn't lying before. I do see your point of view, but you don't understand this world. You said you were kidnapped because of your cousin. I'm assuming you're talking about Ms. Magenta."

"Lacey," he began.

Devi nodded. "Huisman tortured her."

"And did she blame Zach?" Lacey asked.

"No. She didn't. Neither does my mom," Devi replied.

Lacey pushed back her chair and stood, grabbing the wine bottle. "Look, forgive him, don't forgive him, but understand he did all this because he thought it was for the greater good. He's trying to balance saving his mother with being true to the team he came to love, and then you have to throw in the fact that he's madly in love with you. He's juggling a lot of dangerous balls."

Devi's mouth opened, that stubborn look coming into her eyes.

Lacey was having none of it. "Believe him. Don't believe him. I honestly don't see why you think he would be playing you at this point. Your family trusts him. His life and career are on the line, and he risked the entire mission to save you and bring you here and put my mission and Arthur's on the line. You want to play out some drama in your head that you're the poor little wallflower he had to choose because your more glamorous cousin was taken, go for it. If your life is so boring you have to make up drama in your head, good on you, but I'm not wasting my time dealing with this. If you stay, you'll have a list of chores. If you don't, like I said, you know where the sea is."

"Hey, I don't..." Devi began.

Zach put a hand out. "Don't. She's done. She's apparently overstimulated and should probably go read in her room."

She shot Zach the finger. "I think I'll do exactly that, and you and the princess here can argue, but we have the problem of your father to deal with, and I'm hoping your mum responds to one of my messages in the next few days. The good news, Devi Taggart, is this might all be over soon and you can go back to your dating apps and girls nights and all the fun things an overly privileged girl like yourself loves. He'll more than likely be dead or in jail, so he won't bother you anymore. Marrying a Taggart wasn't going to keep him from that fate. It would simply make his last days of freedom sweeter. Think about that while you're in a comfy bed and he's on that ratty couch. He's trying to save his mother and the bloody world. You're trying to spare your pride. Weigh them and see which one is more important."

With that Lacey marched out like the bitter queen she often was. Followed by a mangy part pit bull and a three-legged terrier.

"She took the wine." Devi sat back. "I think I needed the wine. That woman is very judgmental."

He couldn't argue with that. He passed her his second beer.

She popped the top and drank half of it in one swallow, an impressive display. She sat back with a huff. "So the answer to my question is no, you aren't hiding some relationship with her."

"I was absolutely hiding a relationship with her. A working relationship that is sometimes friendly and absolutely never romantic. She's like that cousin who is helpful because she's got mob ties and doesn't mind busting some ass."

"So she's Kala." Devi took another drink. "I'm sorry about telling her Kara is twins."

"She knows a lot of things she doesn't tell me. Don't worry about it. Once we take down Huisman, Lacey wants out," he told her.

He stared down at his food.

"Zach?"

"Yeah?"

"There's no reason for you to sleep on the couch. I'm pretty sure one of the cats already claimed it for the night. It's not like we haven't slept together before. Though we're sleeping. Just sleeping."

She was letting him in bed with her? "I appreciate that."

"And I'll do the chores and stuff, but I need to talk to Tasha soon and see if I'm fired." She picked up her fork again. "I'm supposed to design her wedding dress."

"I'll make the arrangements, and I'll get you a tablet like the one you work on," he promised.

"Thank you." She picked up her fork.

Zach got to work on dinner. He was suddenly hungry again.

Chapter Eight

*W*eek One

There was a trick to making sure the irritable donkey Lacey called The Fabulous Miss K didn't land a kick. Oh, Devi had taken a couple to the shins at first, but she had it down now.

Keep the feed bag in her left hand. Use her right hand to distract the aforementioned angry donkey. For some reason jazz hands worked on her. While she was Bob Fosse-ing the fuck out of her right hand while singing "Defying Gravity" from *Wicked*—had to be from *Wicked*, she'd tried some *Six* on the girl and that ended with bruised shins—she managed to top off the feed and somehow fill the water trough.

The chickens were so much easier.

Three days on the farm and it felt oddly comfortable to walk into this barn and clean out the stalls and make sure that donkey that had obviously escaped from the bowels of hell got her feed.

"So you're sleeping with him?"

She had the cell on speaker phone and thanked the universe that Zach Reed was apparently way smarter than anyone gave him credit for. He assured her the line was safe and she could call anyone she liked. Lou, he explained, was doing the same thing on the other side of the world with some of the tech she had developed.

None of the tech they gave her put phone numbers in Devi's brain. She explained that she knew how to call people by pressing their names on her contact list or saying *hey, Siri, call Brianna*, and that didn't work here. So he had programmed her numbers and made this weird sat phone/cell hers. She could even text and had all the emojis.

He was getting annoyingly likable again. It had only been a couple of days, and she was fascinated all over.

Not that she was showing him.

"I am not. I mean I am sleeping with him, but I'm not doing anything else with him." Except eating every meal, watching British quiz shows while they drank afternoon tea, and playing games and spending most of her days with him. Only that. Nothing else.

After the first day, she sat in on the daily briefing that Lacey and Zach had—sometimes Arthur would join—and Lacey had gotten used to having a non-spy at meetings. She'd had a long talk with Devi about how she would play in her entrails if she betrayed them, but honestly, she was used to that. She'd heard many a lecture from her cousins, and her uncle was really invested in entrails and medieval torture.

But that was all.

It wasn't like she turned to him in her sleep and woke up with his muscular arm wrapped around her waist and felt safe and warm and whole for a moment.

"Well, let me tell you the spy kids are looking for you," Bri said in a hushed tone.

"They are totally looking for you." Daisy was there, too. "They've got a setup in the conference room at The Hideout because they don't want to use the stuff at the McKay-Taggart building. Mostly because Uncle Ian is all like 'give them some time; let Zach work this out.' But Kala is having none of that. She thinks Zach knows where his mom is, and she wants a word."

"Wait, is that a talk or is Kala going to kill someone?" Bri asked.

She wasn't wrong. Her murderiest cousin could mean either. "I'm hoping for talk. According to Zach, he and Kala have an understanding. Hey, what are you doing? That is not your feed, Miss

Rachel. Shoo. Damn chicken."

The chicken named Miss Rachel was the obvious alpha chicken, and she liked to wander everywhere and get into all the other animals' food. And they let her. Because she was kind of mean. She was absolutely the queen of the chickens.

Devi rather thought she could take some cues from Miss Rachel.

"You're dealing with chickens?" Daisy asked. "Did you get one of those egg aprons?"

"Oh, if only I could eat the eggs. I'm in veganville North Wales. Wait. Maybe you shouldn't tell Kala I said that." She was a terrible spy. Like awful. Oh, it wouldn't be pain or torture that made her talk. It would be gossip. All anyone had to do was set her two besties down, give them a bottle of tequila, and let the state secrets flow.

Lacey might have a point, but then if they wanted to keep their secrets, Zach shouldn't have brought her to this… She wanted to say hellhole, but it was a bucolic paradise where she sometimes sat and talked to the pigs. They were surprisingly good listeners. And they did not judge.

"Are you okay?" Daisy asked. "I could tell my da they're horribly mistreating you and he will find you."

Daisy's dad, Liam O'Donnell, was considered the deep thinker of McKay-Taggart. Uncle Li had been her mom's partner for years, and they now handled the trickiest of cases, the ones that involved some kind of mystery because between the two of them, there wasn't one they couldn't solve. Likely over a burger and some beer. "I need time here, Dais. Please tell everyone I'm fine. I can handle some vegan meals. Lacey is actually good at them." It was the first time talking to her friends, and she had to hope they would be honest with her. "Can you tell me how Landon is doing? Does he hate me?"

"Oh, he was in the doghouse for a while, but then he helped Harlow Dawson kill a bunch of what he called criminal douchebags, and now Big Tag likes him again," Daisy promised. "Nate said Landon is fine, though he is currently taking what he called the don't-lose-the-girl course. We're all helping out. Every couple of days he's supposed to watch one of us, and we're supposed to get away from him. I tried climbing out of my dad's second story office and managed to break one of the limbs on the big oak, but Landon totally caught me."

"Uncle Li is paying for his chiropractor because he didn't really catch her, more like she landed on him, but Big Tag gave him a pass," Bri explained. "I'm supposed to try to escape from The Hideout on Saturday. I'm going to have Marley Brighton distract him with her boobs."

She missed them. Missed the club they all belonged to.

Missed sitting in the lounge with Zach and pretending everything was perfect. It had felt perfect.

But she was starting to wonder what had been perfect about it. Had it been having her friends around her? Being in a place she loved? Not knowing exactly who Zach was?

Or had it felt perfect because Zach was the person she was supposed to be with, and damn all his problems.

"That sounds like fun," she said, shooing the chicken away again and easing out of the stall. She moved on to the sweet old race horse with the gimpy leg who loved treats and wandering around the fields. She pulled the carrot out of her pocket and offered it up. "Please tell him how sorry I am."

"You can tell him yourself when you come home," Bri promised. "Now let's talk because since you're gone, Kala is letting her sisters and her mom handle the whole wedding, and she said she didn't care what her wedding dress was like."

Oh, no. This was a drama that could kill the planet. "Kenzie and Tash will put her in something froufrou, and Kala will run. I have to fix this."

She hung up and immediately called her cousin.

"Tell me where you are. I told Zach I would keep him in the loop. I did not tell him he could kidnap my cousin."

Kala was smart, but the last time Devi checked her cousin wasn't psychic. "How did you know it was me?"

"Like I don't already have that programmed in. Zach did a good job, but I have smarty pants on my team. The number changes, but Lou's figured out how to ID it," Kala said in her grumpy fashion. "She hasn't figured out how to locate it, but she will. I'll be on your doorstep in a couple of days, and Zach and I are going to talk."

"He didn't kidnap me. I mean he sort of did, but it's come to my attention that I am not entirely innocent in all of this, and I suck sometimes. So I'm taking a time out. Trust me. I'm not under lock and key. I'm currently in a barn."

There was a gasp over the line. "He's keeping you in a barn? I thought at least he would be banging you in some luxury hotel."

She was confused. "I thought you didn't want him to kidnap me. Now you're mad he isn't banging me?"

Kala sighed. "I just thought at least you two could work a couple of things out because you, my cousin, have been brutally bitchy since he left. A couple of good orgasms and maybe you're happier."

She wished her cousin was wrong. "I did not call to talk about my lack of a love life, nor do I want to discuss why I won't sleep with a man who lied to me. I called to warn you."

"Shit." Kala's voice went low. "He's in trouble, isn't he? Is it that woman he's working with? He won't give me any info on her, so I think she's shady as fuck. Like I have a feeling about her."

Kala kind of had that feeling about almost everyone. "Lacey is fine. You don't have to worry about her."

"Her name is Lacey?" Kala asked, and then she sounded further away like she was holding the phone out. "Lou, we need to find a chick named Lacey. Probably not her real name."

Again. Terrible spy. The good news was she could distract her cousin. "If you let Kenzie pick your wedding dress you're going to look like Little Bo Peep. She will drown you in lace and put you in a hoop skirt."

"Wait. What? Why would she... Oh, shit. She won't be dressing me. She'll be dressing herself. She's in a whole 'woe is me, the world is against my love' phase because she hasn't talked to Ben in a couple of weeks. Devi, you have to help me."

She settled on a bale of hay. "That I can do."

* * * *

"As-tu reçu le message que j'ai envoyé?" Lacey asked over a breakfast that consisted of pretty good potato hash.

While Zach missed meat, he had to admit Lacey was good with plants, and Devi had started taking over some of the cooking as well. Her cornbread muffins were tasty this morning.

Did you get the message I sent? Lacey had asked. In French. Which Devi did not speak.

Devi looked up at Lacey. "Are you okay? You know he only speaks American. I would have called it English until I landed here in Wales, and it is not the same. Not in any way."

Lacey snorted. "It's simply a difference in saying and phrases. Everyone speaks English. Arthur is the only one clinging to his Welsh, and *il y a des choses qu'il vaudrait mieux garder entre nous.*"

There are things it would be better to keep between us. Yeah, probably, but he promised he wouldn't leave Devi out. He turned to her. "She asked if I got her message. She's got a good line on where my mom is staying."

Which was with a group of underground green activists somewhere in South America.

"Really?" Devi asked. "So you could find her soon."

Lacey sighed. "No, but we're closer. I think I might be able to make some kind of contact in the next couple of days." She looked to Zach. "You don't think we should have a way to communicate that doesn't involve her?"

"Rude," Devi said with a frown.

He pointed Devi's way. "What she said."

Devi sat up and gasped. "Wait. Zach speaks French?"

He could give her something else. It might not help his case much, but he felt like showing off. And not keeping things from her. Besides, this would give her something not even her cousins knew. *"Ya govoryu po-frantsuzski i po-russki. A Leysi ne govorit. Ya ponimayu, chto ty govorish, milaya."*

Devi stared at him. *"Znachit, my mozhem govorit', i ona ne poymyot, o chyom my govorim."*

He nodded her way. *"Nash sekretnyy yazyk."*

"Our secret language," she said with a smile, giving him back his words.

"Well, it's not secret." Lacey had her I'm-going-to-murder-someone face on. She really was a vegan version of Kala Taggart, which was likely why he got along with her so well. "It's Russian, and no, I don't speak it. You know the only reason he learned it was to be able to listen in on your uncle's talks. I've heard he speaks Russian, and so do many of his team members."

If Devi was phased by the accusation, she didn't show it. She simply shrugged. "Why do you think I learned it? Hey, if my cousins don't know you speak Russian, have you heard some shit you want to share?"

Oh, so much. "Yeah. Let's talk about that guy Ben your cousin likes."

Devi leaned in, and he knew he had her. If only for an hour or so.

Week Two

Zach turned over and stared up at the ceiling.

He might need to contemplate the sofa because it was rapidly becoming clear that it would be less uncomfortable than lying in this bed with Devi night after night.

He had made contact with his mom today. Well, he hoped it was his mom. Someone claiming to be his mother had sent an email to an address only she should know. It was something they set up years before. He'd sent so damn many letters there. Letters that told his mom he loved her. Detailed his Army life. Talked about meeting Cooper.

Somehow, he thought she would never actually read them.

Be careful. He's looking for me, too. Tell Lacey I'll be in touch.

The first words he'd heard from her in years.

"You're thinking too loud." Her voice was husky and sweet.

And just like that his cock was hard. Although it seemed like his damn perpetual state these days. She walked in a room, he got hard. He smelled the soap she used? Hard. Heard her laughing or yelling at the geese for scaring the massive mastiff with PTSD? Hard and harder. "Sorry. I'll try to stop."

The room was dark with a new moon and no city lights to provide ambient illumination. If they went outside there would be a blanket of stars overhead, but here it was all silky darkness made warm with her presence in bed beside him.

She sighed, and he felt her roll over. The bed was what passed for a double in the States, so she was always close. "Or you could talk to me."

"I thought we weren't doing that." It wasn't like they didn't talk. They had fallen into a completely congenial friendship. Or maybe they were two people existing in what passed for harmony now.

"I think you should go with my flow, Zach. It's late, and it's easy for me to pretend the rest of our shit doesn't matter. What if in here we're friends? Nothing more. Nothing less. Just friends. I don't think we've been that."

"I felt like you were my friend. I felt like… I don't think I've felt closer to a person than I felt to you." The minute the words were out of his mouth he regretted them. He should have talked about what she was working on or the game they played earlier tonight where she'd beaten the hell out of Lacey, who had tried to cover how much it irritated her. Yeah. They could have talked about Lacey and her weird vegan "I love animals but will assassinate a human" vibe.

She didn't like to talk about them. Oh, she would talk about things related to him. Like finding his mom and how his dad was embedded with Huisman and how worried he was about his aunt who was currently somewhere in the Pacific Northwest living out all her *Nomadland* fantasies. But when he tried to broach the subject of them, she shut him down.

"Sorry," he said, not waiting for her to ice him out or tell him he was pushing. "How did the dress design session go? Have you found someone who can actually make it?"

"I know a ton of seamstresses in DFW. Kala is finally happy that I put in some pockets so she can hide weapons, and I made it floor length but with a fuller skirt and a little place where she can tear it away in case she needs to fight hand to hand."

"Uhm, it's her wedding not a battle."

She was quiet, but he could feel her stare. "Tell that to my cousin Carys."

He winced. Okay. Her cousin's wedding had been interrupted by a helicopter attack, so he would give it to Kala for being prepared. "Heard. So she's happy with the design now? Can you get it done in time? I'm still trying to understand why they have to do it now. Shouldn't they wait until things calm down? The weird thing is I think my…Cooper is the one pushing."

"Well, when you chase after a woman for as long as your brother did, I'm sure you're ready to get things nailed down once she says yes. Sometimes less. I think you mentioned marriage on our fourth date."

He went super still. He remembered the moment. They were sitting in a diner after a movie they'd seen with Coop and Kala, and he'd made a passing remark that he and Devi would probably be married before Tasha and Dare. "I was joking about how long their engagement feels."

"Were you?"

"I mean I was, but I wasn't joking about marrying you," he admitted. "I pretty much wanted to do that when I woke up at your place after that first night and you fed me and immediately put me to work fixing your sink."

"You did not. You were terrible at it. How can you know so much about computers and stuff and nothing about sinks?"

"I guess because my aunt was sweet on the old dude who lived in the single wide next to ours, and he was always over fixing things. I didn't want to stand around and listen to the olds flirting. I was more into sports."

"Sportsball. I can see you playing various sportsballs. Cooper did, you know. Played a lot of sports," she said quietly. "I played soccer when I was a kid, and I did some karate. My brother played football for a while, but then he got a concussion and my mom freaked out and his playing days were over. I think that was a good thing because my brother hits his head a lot."

He chuckled because TJ Taggart was on the klutzy side. Oh, he was athletic and deadly when he wanted to be, but there was a lovable goof side to the man. "He needs to stop walking into dosers. Did I ever tell you how Lou accidentally knocked him out with a sedative she was supposed to use on the bad guy?"

Her laughter went straight to his dick. "No, but Lou did. I also heard something about you giving them a lecture about making out in the middle of an op. Tell me, have you ever made out in the middle of an op?"

"If I did it was because making out was cover for the op." He felt tired again. Now that he looked back at the last couple of years, he realized how often he'd put his body out there for the mission. At first it seemed very James Bond and hot, and now that he'd been with her... "It wasn't glamourous. It wasn't sexy. It was a job, and at the end of it it's hard not to feel used."

"Yeah, I'm going to talk to my uncle about that."

"Don't." The last thing he wanted was to get Ian in trouble. "Your uncle never forced me to do anything. I was young and dumb, and it all sounded like fun. Sex was a game until... Well, until I realized it's important. Being at The Hideout taught me a lot."

"There's a lot of casual sex at The Hideout."

"But it's agreed on. Everyone knows what their partner is willing to give and what they won't. Sex is talked about. I'm not proud of those nights I spent fucking someone so I could later on download their laptop." He took a long breath. "And that's why I didn't talk about the job with you. I guess there's a lot of things I'm ashamed of."

"My mom always tells me shame is useless. Change is better. Acknowledge you did a wrong. Make up for it, and move on. Shame only brings you down." She sighed, and he felt her hand move to his chest. "Zach, I don't know that I can believe you when you say you love me, but it has also been pointed out to me that I might feel better if I did some of those casual sex things."

There was nothing he wanted more, but there was only one problem. It wouldn't be casual for him. "Let me guess who gave you that advice. Have you been talking to your aunt?"

"Do you understand how weird this is? We're hiding from pretty much all the authorities plus a bunch of criminal elements, but I'm still talking to my family like I did when I was in college. Like TJ called and asked if I had mustard because he was out and my apartment is close to Lou's work."

That did not surprise him. "Did you?"

"Of course, and I had a bunch of sandwich meat that was going to go bad, so I'm sure he ate that, too, but he also watered my plants. It's weird, and it's starting to feel normal. I'm starting to not be as angry as I should be. I'm starting to be curious."

A curious Devi was a dangerous Devi. Dangerous to his state of mind, to his peace, to his heart. "I'll answer any question and I won't hold back."

"Did you love Tasha?"

He should have known that would be her first question. "I thought I did. But it was a crush. It was more about wanting to belong than anything else. With you..."

"Not what I asked."

So they were playing this game. Well, he supposed it was a start. "All right. Anything else?"

She seemed to think for a moment. "Do you ever wonder?"

All the time. "About what?"

"What it would have been like if it had been you and not Cooper who was adopted? Or if Cooper hadn't been and he grew up with you?"

"No. Never. I wouldn't have wanted my brother in some of the positions I was in because of who our parents are." There was a scenario he thought about quite a lot. "But sometimes I wonder what it would have been like if Alex and Eve had the option of taking us both. If I'd grown up a McKay. I played sports because it was a way to get out of my house. I liked being part of a team. Even if it was temporary, it made me feel like I was part of a family, so I wonder if I would have given in to my nerd half utterly if I was a McKay."

"Because you would have been able to follow your interests since you would have had a stable family."

"I love my aunt. Hell, I love my mom, but they were both troubled in their own ways. And I was a lonely kid. So I see how my brother grew up and I can't help but feel some way when I think about what it would have felt like. I can't help but be jealous of Hunter and Vivian for getting to have him as a brother."

She shifted, and her head replaced her hand on his chest. "It was good. I only had one brother, but I had so many cousins and friends. I never had to be alone unless I wanted to be. I had a great childhood. I wish you had one, too."

They went quiet but when he realized she was asleep on his chest, he moved his arm around her, cuddling her close.

He was content.

* * * *

Devi was frustrated. She'd basically told him she was down to do the dirty and he ignored her.

"He's ignoring you?" Daisy sounded shocked. "Did you show him your boobs?"

Devi's boobs weren't as impressive as Daisy's, so no. She had not. "I can't lift my shirt and expect him to fall in line."

And she probably shouldn't, though Kala's words had been plaguing her. She should use this time to get him out of her system, but he was not complying.

"I don't know why," Bri added. "It's what Daisy does. Oh, hey, did you tell her about Harlow Dawson and the new guys?"

"No," Daisy replied. "I'm too busy trying to solve her Zach problems."

Zach, who spoke way more languages than she imagined and could do complex computer hacking and had a mom who might destroy the world.

Her Zach problems couldn't be solved with her boobs. Daisy's, maybe, but she had small, athletic boobs. Damn her boobs. "Wait. Guys? As in plural? Tell me about Harlow."

Hopefully someone was getting some.

Week Three

There was nothing sweeter in life than a purring kitten. Devi sat in the comfy chair, a mug of tea at her side and three kittens sleeping on her lap while their momma rested at her feet.

Well, maybe that was sweeter. When a small creature with no reason at all to trust a single human chose to trust her. It hadn't been easy, but days of sitting with her, feeding her, caring for her, and Sunny had come to Devi when she went into labor in the middle of the night.

Zach had gotten up, made some tea, and sat up with her while Sunny gave birth to four perfect kittens. Well, three perfect kittens and one she named TJ because he was kind of klutzy and always, always hungry. TJ the cat was currently trying to climb up the curtains, testing those deadly kitty claws.

"Hey, Lacey made some muffins. She thought you might like one." Zach put down a plate of what smelled like apple cinnamon muffins. He frowned. "Not today, TJ. Not on my watch."

He gently gripped the kitten, who mewled furiously at the taking of his right to unalive himself in the silliest way. Zach held him to his chest and TJ calmed.

Devi looked up. "Are you okay?"

She knew what today was.

"I'm glad for them." Zach sat on the edge of the bed. "I wish we could be there."

At the wedding of Cooper McKay to Kala Taggart. McKay-Taggart. As it always should have been. "Mom will send pictures."

She would. But it wasn't the same. Zach lacked all the family experiences that were normal to Devi. There had been no Sunday dinners, no lake house parties where the kids ran wild, no family vacations. This would have been his first family wedding, but that wasn't in the cards for Zach Reed.

She was like Sunny. Zach had been patient and kind and fed her while she hissed and clawed his way.

And she was softening, damn it.

She was wondering if he was ever going to make a move on her. She'd opened the door with the whole orgasm will make me feel better thing, but he'd been a perfect gentleman even when she woke up wrapped around him and she could feel his erection against her.

Damn man and his control.

"Tell me about her dress," he said.

Devi sat back and wished she could hate this man. She took a sip of tea and felt Sunny purr against her feet and couldn't find the will to hate anything at all.

* * * *

Zach stared at the picture on his phone.

Kala and Cooper were married, and they both looked so fucking happy. His brother was married and all he got was a couple of pictures.

He flipped through them. Erin Taggart had been the one to send them, but she explained it was Cooper and Kala approved.

"Zach, we should talk." Lacey stood in the doorway, and there was no possible way to miss the fact that she waited until Devi put on her boots and went out to deal with what she called that donkey. The Fabulous Miss K was kind of her nemesis.

"Have you heard something?" Zach asked since he knew damn well if this was a talk about Devi, she would have it out in the open.

Lacey had no filter and would simply say her peace.

But she did have discretion when it came to the mission.

She nodded and joined him on the porch. She stared out over the field, and in the distance Devi could be seen walking toward the barn. "Yes. Huisman liquidated one of his offshore accounts to the tune of fifty-five million dollars. I'm working on tracing the money, but I'm worried a portion of it is going to bounty hunters."

He sighed and slipped his phone into his pocket. "Well, that was inevitable. I'm surprised he waited this long."

"I believe he thought he could use you to bring her in, and then he thought he could use one of your old team to bring in you, and then you would bring in your mother," she pointed out. "I've heard a couple of rumors that your old team thwarted at least one kidnapping attempt."

His heart threatened to seize. "What?"

Lacey waved him off. "Idiot tried to send in a mercenary to take Charlotte Taggart."

He huffed at the thought. "So there's one more body on the farm, I suspect."

"Yeah. We won't hear from that mercenary again, but I think we're reaching a critical point," Lacey said. "Huisman is wanted for questioning by several intelligence agencies, but on paper he still looks good. I don't know how he's kept the press from reporting anything."

"That's the Agency as much as Huisman." Right now they were in a standoff, but Huisman wouldn't leave it alone for long. He would want to make his move and soon. The trouble was what kind of move would he make? That was what kept him up at night. That along with his aching cock.

"Well, I've sent a friend to talk to your mum. She's well known in those circles."

He nodded and realized he had a question because it had been days since he'd seen their friend. "Where did Arthur go? Wasn't he supposed to check in on the cows?"

She shrugged. "The cows are fine. He's on assignment, and I don't ask questions. As long as the group is giving me good intel, I keep my eyes open and mouth closed."

Well, that was pretty much what he was doing, too. His eyes were always on Devi and his mouth was closed so he wouldn't try to eat her like the fucking treat she was.

"You need to do something about that, mate. It's getting disturbing," Lacey said with an edge of snark. "I'll let you know when we make contact. We should think about heading to Liverpool in a week or two. I think that shark you call a teammate is sniffing around, and Devi is the world's worst spy."

Zach shifted because he realized she had been talking about his erection. Yup. This was his life now. Spy shit and anxiety and his unruly cock. He wished she would show him her boobs. He missed her boobs. Sometimes she didn't wear a bra and his whole body damn near revolted at the fact that his hands weren't on them. "She's not a spy at all."

"Well, you treat her like she's your assistant."

"I treat her like she has a stake in what happens, and she does." He wasn't leaving her out, though he also wasn't planning on putting her in danger, and it would be way harder to watch her in Liverpool. "How big is your place there?"

Lacey leaned against the railing. "Well, there will be more than one bed, so you should factor that in." She sighed when he didn't take the bait. "It's not my place. It belongs to my parents, and they are far wealthier than I am. It's big by city standards, and it's got everything we need to monitor the streets around us. We need to think about bringing in extra security if we convince your mum to come in."

"I have to tell Ian."

"Do you?" Lacey stood up straighter. "Somehow I think the man will know. He seems to have psychic powers. But seriously, you need to be sure of Devi before we go to Liverpool. I know she seems to have settled in here, but there will be a lot more opportunity for her to cause trouble in the city, and I would feel better if I knew she was loyal to you."

If she knew he was sleeping with her. "I'm not going to cause her a shit ton of emotional damage so you feel better."

She moved back to the door. "I also think you would be in a better mood, mate. But what do I know. I'm a lowly underground activist. Think about it. Time is running out. Just a couple more weeks and this should be done."

He wouldn't think about anything else.

Chapter Nine

He was going to die of frustration.

Not only had his mom disappeared again, but every day Devi gave him a reason to put his hands on her. Every single day.

He couldn't because it wasn't his place.

Or was it his place?

"I need you to hand me the syringe now," Arthur said.

Yeah, he was helping Arthur vaccinate a group of goats. Normally Lacey liked to be the one helping the vet, but she and Devi had gone into the tiny town for supplies. Those two were getting close. He'd heard them laughing and joking as they'd done chores around the farm.

He would never had thought Devi could handle farm chores. His baby was a deep well, and he would never learn everything he wanted to know about her.

Probably because he would be dead or in prison, and that was why he wasn't going to touch her.

Arthur huffed, and when Zach looked up the older man was staring his way. "You're not sleeping with her."

He wasn't sure why Arthur needed to know that. "There is a lot of sleeping going on between us."

He actually did think he slept better when she was beside him. She was cuddly and warm, and several times she'd lifted her face in the early morning light and all it would have taken was a little movement of his head to press their lips together.

She wasn't serious about him, and she shouldn't be.

Arthur took the syringe. "Are you going to let this opportunity go, son? She's softened up nicely. I thought she might be a problem in the beginning, but I think we all got to her and now she would fight for us, not against us. I also think she wouldn't run from the fight, so you need to get her ready for it."

The goat snorted as the syringe went in and then wandered off after Arthur gave it a pat on the back. They moved on to the next.

"I don't want her to fight at all," Zach admitted, carrying the big bag Arthur had brought.

"And if your father shows up?" Arthur asked, making his way over the soft ground. It had been raining a lot, and Zach had become accustomed to rain boots. "I know you don't want her to fight, but shouldn't she be able to?"

"She's had some self-defense training," Zach replied. Not that it seemed to have helped her since she'd been kidnapped by cartel assholes and then by Huisman's assholes. According to Kala she had tried to fight Lena but had lost. And Lena was a damn therapist. He should think about that. But the idea of rolling around with her made his cock ache. "Maybe Lacey could handle it."

"Oh, I assure you Lacey could train her, but I think she'll say this is your responsibility," Arthur replied. "We might have already talked about this."

"Really?" Why would they be talking about his relationship? Scratch that. He knew why, but he was trying so hard to keep things solid so they didn't jeopardize the mission. Missions. Could it be called a mission when it was pretty much his life at this point?

"Well, it's that or we talk about how The Fabulous Miss K is getting along with the pigs. I swear that donkey needs a therapist," Arthur said, gently holding the next goat. He ran a hand along its back and gave her a treat before asking for the next syringe.

Zach sighed. "Is there any way you could do it? You know training a person can get…personal."

Arthur smiled. "Yes, that would be the point, son. Train her and you'll wind up using that bed for something other than sleeping, and then all the awful sexual tension will be gone."

Zach heard himself growl. "I'm trying to avoid that."

"Why?"

A light rain began. That felt right. He was stuck in a muddy field with traumatized goats and a somewhat caustic veterinarian. His brother had gotten married, and he'd spent that time eating butterbeans, watching Brits win shockingly low amounts of money by answering trivia questions and rolling bocce balls, and trying to keep a kitten from killing itself. "Because I'm not going to hurt her again."

"So it's not because she isn't the other woman?"

Now Zach's growl was fully focused. "I am not in love with Tasha Taggart."

"But you are in love with Devi Taggart," Arthur pointed out, checking the goat's hooves.

"She doesn't believe me." And he was pretty sure she never would. He was almost certain she would accept a sexual relationship with him, but that was all it would be. Sex.

"Do you think not having sex with her is helping your case?"

"I don't want this to be a case. I want it to be a relationship." He wanted to be fucking normal. He wanted to be back in Dallas getting ready to go out with her, to go to the club with his sub and sit with his friends and not think about anything except how he was going to torture her sweet ass and who would go out with them for late-night waffles this week.

He wanted a future with her.

"You know I'm married, right? I lied to my wife about some of the more dangerous portions of my job." Arthur seemed to be focused on his patient, but every word was carefully chosen.

"Being that your job at one point was intelligence, that's understandable."

"And yet you've told Devi almost everything," Arthur pointed out.

"I didn't in the beginning, and you know why. I walked into that team thinking they were undisciplined and would fuck up everything and ended up being just like them. They talk more than they should, but they trust the people around them. Even the non-military friends and family are willing to help with anything they ask for. I've never known that kind of loyalty. But it's expected that we keep our loved ones out of the loop. It's what they signed up for."

"Well, she didn't, and she would argue with you about that. We almost broke up. And then my saint of a wife decided that what she needed was time. She couldn't forgive me, but she also couldn't stay away. Time is on your side. Even if you don't have a lot of it. For my wife and I it took the better part of a year, but I won back her trust. I did not do it by acting like her friend. Devi seems to be willing to have relations with you, to pretend things are normal. A funny thing happens when you pretend things are normal. They tend to become normal."

He stood there in the mist, Arthur's words penetrating his brain. "You think if I take her to bed and be a good boyfriend, she'll start treating me like a boyfriend?"

Arthur shook his head. "I think you should take her to bed and start treating her like a good husband, a great partner. Show her you trust her. Talk to her about what you can. You aren't beholden to the Agency when it comes to this."

"Oh, I assure you they will hold me responsible."

"Perhaps, but you can be open with Devi because you're not an operative for them anymore," Arthur pointed out. "You're on your own and get to choose your team. I think she would be a good team member if you let her."

"Isn't that putting her in danger? Shouldn't I protect her?"

Arthur looked up and winced. "Don't ask Lacey those questions. Seriously, it will get rough. You should protect her, but you shouldn't coddle her. She's not some child to lock away from the big bad world. Besides, she seems to find trouble."

He huffed. "Yeah, I get your point. But what if the Agency holds her responsible, too? I'm obviously more afraid of her in Huisman's hands, but I don't like the thought of certain elements of the Agency getting hold of her either."

"That's a chance she should be allowed to take. A choice she makes for herself."

"I'm not going to get to marry her. Or even to have a couple of years with her." He heard the sorrow in his words.

"Pessimist. You don't know that. I'm sure in your head this all ends poorly, but you know some powerful people, and they can move mountains when they want to. Besides, have you considered the fact that if you're the one to bring Huisman in, the Agency can use that to protect their own image?"

He had not. It was a long shot. But it was a shot. "They won't want to admit I tricked them. They could say they sent me out and then they look smart."

Arthur stood and pointed his way. "Exactly. If you don't think Ian Taggart hasn't already considered that exact scenario, then you don't know him well. Look, there's real chatter about something going down soon."

He nodded. "I think that's why my mom contacted me."

"She likely knows far more than we do. The question is will you tell Taggart what you know when you know it?" Arthur asked. "I understand that Lacey and I can't provide the backup you need. So are you going in alone or calling your former boss? Who happens to be Devi's uncle and will absolutely protect her from any Agency blowback."

He wasn't wrong. The Taggarts wouldn't allow Devi to be hauled off to some Agency black site to be questioned. "From what I can tell, the Agency is taking the reports about Huisman seriously after what happened in Toronto."

Arthur nodded. "Ah, so actual evidence worked. I might have mentioned that."

To a goat? He wasn't going to let Arthur second guess Ian Taggart. "Well, they're all in now."

"Are they? Or are they carefully working your boss?" Arthur asked, putting the stethoscope in his ears and listening briefly before settling it back around his neck. "One of the things my group is worried about is possible spies inside the Agency. I believe Huisman has his own people in high places across the world."

Yeah. Lena Gallagher proved that. "I'm confused. You talk like Big Tag is invincible and now you're worried he's being naïve."

Arthur started moving toward the barn, clearly in the belief that Zach would follow him. "I don't think a man with his background could be naïve about his work. I do think you could be. Look, all I'm saying is if you want any chance with the young woman, you're going about it wrong."

"You think I should sleep with her."

"I think you should fuck her. I think you should stop protecting yourself and be a man and give her what she needs. I have rarely met a young lady who is begging to be topped more than that one."

Zach stopped. What the hell had Arthur said? "Topped?"

Arthur turned and gave him a grin that made him look younger and way more potentially perverted. "Topped, Zach. As in sexually dominated, though I think you might want to take it a bit outside the bedroom with that one. I do so with my own sweet wife. Oh, she doesn't recognize it because I'm a sneaky Dom, but let me tell you it works. Give it a shot."

Arthur turned and started back toward the barn again.

The old Welsh dude was in the lifestyle? Huh. He and his wife. In the lifestyle and seemingly happy for years. Because there was more to marriage than youthful passion. There was peace and comfort and someone to grow old with. To spend his life with. To worship and be a partner to in and out of bed.

Was it worth the risk? Oh, he would risk his freaking soul for a chance to be with her.

Was it worth the risk for her?

He was making that decision, and it wasn't fair.

Zach let the rain fall as he thought about a possible future.

Hope was a dangerous thing.

* * * *

Devi looked around the small town and decided this was absolutely the best kidnapping ever. Five stars. Fully recommend.

"Get yourself a drink." Lacey chuckled as she closed the trunk of the SUV. Boot. Here it was called a boot, and it was full of feed and supplies they picked up at the store that also sold groceries. The horses had their feed, and she had scones and Welsh currant cakes and a lot of vegan stuff, but she was liking it. Lacey was teaching her some great recipes. "I've got some things I need to do, but it shouldn't be long. Hopefully this rain will stop soon."

Did it ever really stop? It rained a lot here, but she thought she might not mind if she could cuddle with someone.

With Zach.

"No problem." She was getting used to the spy stuff. Zach seemed to be more open and would let her sit in on debriefs and talked freely around her. But Lacey was involved in things other than Zach's mission. Probably saving cats and dogs and bunnies from testing of some kind. Or getting more hillycoos out of terrible situations.

Lacey looked her over and frowned. "Don't get in trouble."

Devi gave the other woman her best *what me, trouble?* expression. "Will do."

"I'm serious. You have your mobile, right?"

She had the burner Zach gave her before she left with Lacey. It was connected only to him and Lacey, he explained, and only to be used in emergencies. He then told her that an emergency did not include seeing a cute outfit and calling Brianna or Daisy to gush about it.

She was going to be honest. She liked Wales, but in this part of the country there was a lot of practical clothing.

"Got it," Devi replied, eager to walk around and see more of this teeny-tiny town. It looked a little magical. It looked like a place where she could get some inspiration. She had her tablet in her backpack, and sitting in a pub drawing out some designs sounded like a fabulous way to spend an afternoon. "Go do spy stuff."

Lacey frowned. "You know we don't call it that, right? Certainly not in public."

Devi shrugged. "Go do whatever you call it. I'm going to walk around a bit and then I'll settle in."

Lacey seemed to think about that for a moment. "Maybe I should…"

Nope. This was the first time she'd been alone in weeks, and she was taking it. Devi simply walked away. She heard Lacey curse, but she didn't follow.

She probably wouldn't wander for long since it was raining, but it was nice to be here, to pretend like she was a tourist.

Was she a tourist? Sometimes she felt like one. Like she was wandering through life looking for that place where she could belong. For a moment she'd thought she found it with Zach. She had definitely realized that where she belonged wasn't a place. It was a mindset. It was how she felt, not where she was.

Why did her "place" in the world have to come with jail time or losing him long before she was ready to?

She wandered for a while, looking into some of the shops and spending time in the tiny bookstore. She used some of the money Zach gave her to buy a book about Welsh legends and then made her way to the pub to wait for Lacey.

She was reading about the Welsh god of the dead when a man sat down beside her. She glanced up. He was older and American, from his accent. He ordered a beer. Not a pint. Definitely tourist.

"Catching up on local folklore?" the man asked.

She should have gotten a table, but no, she'd taken a place at the bar because it made her feel more like a local. If it had been some woman asking her questions, she likely would start up a conversation and have fun with it. Something about this man set off her internal siren. He was maybe six foot two with a lean build and graying hair, but it was his eyes that bothered her. They were a dark, flat brown with nothing animated about them.

They were the eyes of a predator, and suddenly she felt like prey.

"Yeah. I like to study the places I go and visit." She gave him a friendly smile. It wasn't like she'd never dealt with predatory men before. The key was to make them feel like you didn't recognize them and then dash as soon as possible. Lacey should be here soon, so he wouldn't have a ton of time to hit on her. She got the feeling Lacey would know how to shut a dude down.

Devi did, too, but she was supposed to wait here, and she didn't think this guy would take her normal fuck-off speech with aplomb. She was supposed to not make scenes.

Also, he was way not in her age group. She pegged him somewhere in his sixties, though he could be younger. He hadn't taken great care of himself. He looked haggard but in a hungry, burn-the-world-around-him way.

"Yeah, I studied a bit when I was younger. I knew a woman. So smart. She was into chemistry at the time, but she also loved folklore." He sounded smart, his voice somewhat melodic, but there was a menacing undertone. Like he knew something she didn't. "So I remember that the Welsh god of the dead was named Arawn. He had a bunch of hellhounds, and you had to be invited into his version of hell."

"His version of hell was most people's version of heaven," she replied and looked to the door. Damn. She wanted to leave. It was the strangest feeling.

"Well, I suppose everyone has their own take on things. It's all about perspective, isn't it?" He took the beer from the bartender, who then stepped back and moved to the customer at the end of the bar. "What some would call heaven others think of as hell."

She glanced at the clock. Only a few minutes more and she could go home.

She was not thinking of that rundown farm as home.

She guessed it was all about perspective. "I suppose so."

"I've always found it interesting how travel changes your perspective. Like what most Americans consider a complete hellhole is how a lot of the world lives," he said.

Oh, he was a philosopher asshole. "I assure you there are people in America who know what a hellhole is and who try to help. And plenty who don't. Like everywhere in the world. I know a lot of people who try to make the world a better place."

"Do you?"

Okay, so she was trying to be a better spy. "Sure. Like the people who feed the homeless, and I've got a friend who is studying to be a therapist who specializes in helping children recover from trauma." Daisy was starting school soon, and Devi thought this was going to be the job her friend stuck with for the rest of her life. Her calling.

"I've always thought therapy was a racket," he replied with what she was sure he thought of as an inviting smile. "You know there are things that happen to us that we should shove down and things we should use as fuel. That's what trauma truly is. It's fuel for change."

Okay, creepy and completely wrong, but she didn't care enough to argue. "An interesting take. I need to find the loo."

"You fit in well," he said with another smile. "Calling it a loo instead of a bathroom. When you get back you can tell me where you come from. I hear a little of a Texas twang in there."

Creepier still. She nodded and slid off the barstool. She wouldn't be coming back. She was going to find herself another way out. "You have a good ear."

She left her poor pint behind. She'd wanted that pint. She moved toward the back of the pub where the toilets were located according to the hand-painted signs. It was good to know that she could attract creepers even here in rural Wales.

Devi pulled out her phone and glanced down at it. Lacey was going to be a few minutes late, according to her text.

"Hey, lady," a masculine voice said. He had an English accent. He was dressed in a soccer—football—jersey that proclaimed him to be a fan of Glossop North End. Whatever that was. He looked to be close to her age, and his smile actually did seem friendly. He was probably a big old nerd. "Uhm, not sure how to tell you this but you shouldn't drink that beer."

Fuck. They were in the hall, out of view of the bar. "Why? I mean I can guess. Did he slip something in?"

The man nodded. He had curly, dark hair and wore jeans and sneakers. "Yeah. I mean I think he might have. I saw his hand move over the top of the mug. He's bothering you, right?"

"He is trying to pick me up, and now I know he's a criminal who was going to take advantage of me. Should I call the pol..." She couldn't. There would be far too many questions and paperwork, and Zach would likely freak out, and Lacey wouldn't like the cops looking at them when she was so close to her mission starting. "Uhm, maybe I should sneak out. I thank you... I didn't catch your name."

He held out a hand. "Tim. I'm down here visiting my cousin. He didn't see it. Told me I shouldn't get involved, but I couldn't let you walk into that trap."

She shook his hand. "Well, I wasn't going back. I was going to slip outside."

Tim let her hand go. "Good for you. Hey, you know what I'll do? I'll tell him I saw someone leaving out the back entrance. Then he'll likely find another target."

She didn't like the sound of that. "Maybe I should try to deal with him."

Tim waved that thought off. "Don't bother. There aren't any other targets. All the young women leave for bigger cities. It's probably why he pounced on you. I'll watch him and maybe have a talk with the local constable about what I saw. He can be pretty intimidating, and he doesn't particularly like strangers. Stay inside the loo until I give you the all clear. Or just in this hallway. I'll make sure he goes out the front."

At least there were some nice people left in the world. "Thanks, Tim."

He started to pass her but stumbled slightly and bumped into her. "Sorry. Bit of a klutz."

"No problem," she replied as she moved further toward the loos in the back. There were all kinds of pictures lining the narrow hallway. She glanced at them. They went all the way back to World War II. Pictures of men and women in uniform hoisting a pint. Some had careful notations on the bottom of the frames. Lieutenant Miles Bron and company. Catrin and Bethan Davies welcome their soldiers home. They gradually moved to later years, and Devi was fascinated with the clothes they wore, the way they held themselves. What history was here in this tiny pub? She could look at the pictures forever. She kind of wanted to sketch a few of them because there was a ton of inspiration here. She loved the lines of the WWII military uniforms and the elegant hairdos. But she was equally inspired by the bohemian vibes from the sixties. There was something cool and over the top about the eighties.

She could use those lines. Pair them with soft colors and fabrics from the sixties and the elegant makeup from the forties. A whole line sprang into her head. Day wear that flowed into evening looks. Casual wear that fit the vibes of formal wear.

She wanted to sketch and get the ideas down, but she couldn't exactly go back out to the bar until the coast was clear. If she had her own phone she could have taken some pictures, but she understood why Zach had brought this seemingly smart phone down to basic functions. It wasn't sending out a signal that let everyone know exactly where it was.

So she simply moved down the hall, studying the pictures that caught her eye. The last few years were filled with photographs of celebrating footballers and graduates with their proud parents. There was one of the same group from long ago. They'd been young soldiers at the beginning of the hall, and now they were old and gray and still hoisting a pint in their uniforms.

It brought tears to her eyes. So much life in those photos. Whole love stories seemed to play out. Children grew up as she made her way down the hall.

She was going to tell her Uncle Sean that they needed a wall like this at Top. It was where a good portion of Dallas celebrated, but more importantly it was where her whole family came together.

Almost every graduation and new job were celebrated. Where new babies were welcomed and reunions were had. Just a couple of months back they'd had a big celebration for her dad and Uncle Case's birthday. Uncle Case and Aunt Mia had come with her cousin Heath. She had sat with her besties and felt like she was at home.

A sniffle came from her. She was getting emotional, but it was okay. She'd felt numb for a long time, and emotion was part of who she was, what she did.

She caught sight of a wedding photo. It looked to be from the early 2000s if the fashions were on trend.

Dr. Arthur Beddoe and wife, Cecelia.

Arthur. She kind of loved Arthur. He was smart and funny and gave excellent advice. It was hard to believe he'd been a soldier at one point.

He wasn't wearing his uniform. He was in a morning suit, smiling gamely as he held his wife's hand in one and a pint in the other.

He was younger. Way younger. And honestly, he didn't look like himself. The coloring was right but the jaw was different, and his shoulders were less broad.

Something about the photo was wrong.

"Hey, he's gone. But I got a bad feeling about that one." Tim was back, a worried expression on his face. "I think he was going off to look for you."

The thought sent a chill down her spine, and all the questions about Arthur fled in favor of worrying if she'd attracted a serial killer. That wasn't supposed to happen to her. That happened to Daisy. She was the girl who didn't get into ride shares without checking the license plate and that the picture on the app matched the person doing the driving. She was the perpetual designated driver. The steady one.

"I should go." What she should do was call Zach, but if she did she might never be allowed to leave the farm again. As much as she loved it, she enjoyed the occasional bit of leave. He should understand that.

Tim seemed disconcerted at the thought. "Maybe you should come sit with me and my cousin. Do you have anyone who could take you home? I could follow you in my cousin's car. I don't like the thought of that man looking for you."

She didn't either, but lucky for her she had an out. "A friend is picking me up. I won't leave until she's with me. You're right. I should stay in a public place."

She walked past Tim and toward the bar. Asshole thought he could kidnap her? Well, she wasn't going through that again. She was through her kidnap-me era and into her girl-who-doesn't-get-kidnapped phase. Yeah. And she needed to train because this was a dangerous world, and she hadn't kept up her work-out routine lately. Though lifting feed bags was a great arm workout.

"There you are." Lacey stood at the bar, frowning, a bag over her shoulder. "Where were you?"

If she went into the whole might-have-been-stalked thing, she would definitely never leave the farm again. Also, she handled it. Well, she and Tim handled it. She glanced back and Tim wasn't there. Must have needed the loo. He was a nice kid, but it was time for her to go. "Just visiting the loo. I'm ready if you are."

Lacey stared her up and down. "You know you don't have to wiggle out of the loo window. If you're ready to escape…"

She knew this one. She rolled her eyes and started for the door. "The sea is that way. I'm not walking into the sea, Lace. If we hurry, I can be home in time to watch a bunch of celebrities I don't know answer quiz show questions. It's celebrity week on *Impossible*."

And that meant something to her now. Strange world.

She let go of all of her worries but one as they made it to the Jeep.

How to get Zach to put his hands on her.

Did she want his hands on her? It was casual. She could stay casual.

As they started to drive away she could have sworn she caught sight of the man from earlier. Watching her.

The danger, she feared, was far from over.

Chapter Ten

Devi walked out toward the barn, curious at the note left on the middle of the bed. It had been sitting there when she returned, folded with her name written in a neat, masculine hand. Lacey had informed her that she was going to be on the secure line for the next hour or so. Something to do with the package she picked up in town.

She was getting way too comfortable with criminal shit going on around her. It felt almost normal. She planned to put on a kettle, grab a couple of biscuits, and watch some telly.

She was becoming so British.

And then she found that note.

Come to the barn if you want to play.

The words had sent a thrill zinging through her body. Her damn nipples had gone rock hard, and she'd known that she wouldn't be shouting answers at the quiz shows this afternoon.

The rain was down to a light drizzle, and she could see the goats resting under the big poplar tree in the distance. The horses were out in the field along with the super-cute Highland cows, who almost never were more than a couple of feet from each other. Those cows had gone through something, and it seemed to have bonded them.

Like her parents went through something terrible. Her mom had found the courage to have a baby and build a life after she thought her dad was dead.

Zach was alive.

Maybe it was the fact that one of her best friends wrote romance novels, but she was starting to wonder if feeling the loss of Zach later would be better than this numbness she had been living in. Would she be less angry if she had a few weeks with him? Maybe she would realize it never would have worked long term, and he could be the passionate, wild affair of her youth. The one that taught her what she honestly wanted was stability.

The trouble was if one took out the Interpol Red Notice, the whole world wanting to drag him into an interrogation room thing, Zach was stability personified. In a brief time, he'd gotten to know her likes and dislikes and made sure she had the things she wanted. He was on time, always conscientious about her feelings.

Except for the whole lying thing.

She hesitated, standing outside the barn doors.

First because she had to think about what this meant. He used the word *play*, and she knew what he meant. D/s sex. He was the Dominant and she the submissive. He would treat her like his sub.

Wasn't that what he was doing already? He took care of her. He made sure she had "wellies" when it rained, and when she complained about her feet hurting because she spent hours standing while helping Arthur with one of the sheep giving birth, he'd shifted and gotten them in his lap and rubbed them until she sighed. He cuddled her and made sure she was comfy.

If she walked through that door, she was giving him the right to do all of those things. Up until this moment she could fool herself because the permission was implied, not spoken out loud. She wasn't his sub. She was his… She couldn't even say prisoner since at least once a day his cohort asked if she wanted to go to the sea. There were no locks meant to keep her in, no cuffs to shackle her.

But there would be if she walked through that door. There would be a contract between them. Oh, it wouldn't be signed and witnessed and filed in The Hideout's office, but it would be there.

What made him change his mind?

Why was he in the barn? Like there was a perfectly fine bedroom. That was full of cats.

So the barn it was.

And she wanted to know what he'd been doing in the barn. Her curiosity wouldn't let her walk away. She had to know.

It didn't have to mean anything. It didn't have to touch her soul.

She pushed through the doors and the barn was quiet, the sound of soft rain on the roof the only noise.

"I'm up here," he said, and she realized he was on the second floor. She rarely went up there. From what she could tell it was used to store things they didn't work with every day. It was mostly empty.

Except even from here she could see Zach had made some changes.

He had taken off his shirt. His big chest was on beautiful display, and his jeans hung low on his hips. His hair had grown out since he'd gone on the run. That dark silky hair had started to brush the tops of his ears, and she had the most insane desire to run her hands through it.

She took a deep breath and started up the ladder.

He was waiting to help her, big hand coming out to hold her own.

"What made you change your mind?" She was pleased with how solid she sounded. Like this was no big deal.

He made sure she was steady on her feet before he backed away. "A friend gave me some advice. He thinks I might regret never taking this chance with you."

She wasn't sure what the word *chance* had to do with it. "I told you what I was willing to do weeks ago."

He nodded. "Yeah, that's the chance I'm taking. You were open and honest that this is going to mean nothing. That you need a physical release and I'm handy."

"You're not fucking handy, Zach. There is nothing convenient about you or the situation we're in." It was a ridiculous assumption. "I only meant that I know this isn't going anywhere, so I'm not opening my heart to you."

"And I am. And that is what I am risking."

"You don't have to. I'm being honest with you."

His hand came out and he touched her, really touched her for the first time in days. Not a brush of his hand as they passed each other or a caring caress or those moments in the early morning when her brain was fuzzy and she wanted to stay asleep because his arm was over her waist. There was intent in the way he took her chin in hand, forcing her to look up at him. She was tall, but Zach made her feel petite.

He also sometimes made her feel like an idiot, so she should remember that.

"The question is are you being honest with yourself." He loomed over her, his big body so close all it took was to reach up to touch his chest. Feel the heat of his body, the softness of skin over hard-earned muscle.

"And if I am?" She wasn't going to lie and say she was sure. She wasn't. She wasn't sure of anything except the fact that her body was starting to heat up. From the minute she read that note, she'd felt again. Not fear or anxiety. She'd felt the slow hum of her body awakening, the anticipation of getting her needs met. Of letting go for a few hours. Letting Zach take over.

Her body trusted this man implicitly. She wasn't sure about her heart.

"Then I'll deal with the consequences, sweetness. I don't know how much time we have, but I want to spend it with you. Being with you the way we really are."

A Dom and sub. The man he was and the woman she was. "Then we start, Sir."

"Zach." His fingers tightened slightly around her chin, and he moved in. "No Sirs. I want to hear my name. I'm not some random Dom in a club who wants you for a night."

No, he wanted her for however long they had. "Then we should start, Zach. Is this our play space?"

He stepped back and gestured around. "I spent the afternoon renovating. I had to be creative, but the good news is I can be handy. Arthur helped. He's surprisingly good at building furniture, and we had some supplies I didn't know we had."

It wasn't like a plush sofa or a luxurious chaise lounge, but he and Arthur had created what looked like a spanking bench. She walked over and tested it out—comfortable, it was solid. "Did Arthur know what he was making?"

She felt like she could breathe again. Making the decision to take this time with Zach was a huge weight off her shoulders and her soul. The key was taking what she wanted and not giving up anything that would hurt.

Or maybe just understanding that this would hurt like hell, but it would be worse if she never had this time at all.

"Arthur, it seems, is in the lifestyle."

That got her attention. "Arthur?"

Zach shrugged those big, glorious shoulders. "Hey, they get kinky in Wales, too."

She still wasn't going to tell him about her near miss with a potential serial killer—she did not want to be the next Daisy—but she felt like she had to talk about what she'd seen. "There's something odd about him. I saw a picture of him today in the pub. It was his name, but it didn't look like him."

Zach seemed to think about that for a moment. "I promise he's been vetted, and sometimes we don't look like ourselves in pictures. It's all about angles and lighting. Lacey says he's solid, and he's been helpful. Also, it's a small community. I think they would notice if their vet got switched out."

He was probably right and she was looking for conspiracies that didn't exist. Which she shouldn't do because there were so very many real ones. She didn't need to make them up.

She also didn't need to procrastinate. It was obvious Zach had been working hard all afternoon while she was gone. He had set up a whole play space, including a cot that would be hard for the both of them to fit on. Unless they cuddled close. He had a table with carefully placed toys laid out. There was a crop and lube and... Yup, that was a plug. A too big but really probably wasn't too big plug. There were a couple of different styles of clamps. He had promised to dress her up the next time they played at The Hideout. He had gone to Canada before the weekend, so they hadn't had a second weekend at the club.

How could she have fallen so hard in so few days?

"Take off your clothes, Devi." Zach stood back.

She was right. It hadn't been long. This might be exactly what she needed. Time with him could prove it never would have worked, and then this whole thing could be a hot, fever fantasy, a time she spent with an on-the-run, wanted-by-several-countries Dom. It wouldn't hurt her whole heart if she figured out living with him wasn't something she wanted to do for the rest of her life.

Because living with him these last few weeks hadn't been awful, and he hadn't even been fucking her.

Yeah, she knew she was being a little delusional. She was comfortable with him. She was starting to wonder if she needed to live in Manhattan or LA or London to have the career she wanted. What if the career she wanted was to be happy doing her own thing? Building her own business, even if it meant working at her uncle's restaurant while she did it.

Being with Zach made her happy. Content. With herself. That was the part that killed her. Being with Zach made all those voices that normally screamed in her head quiet down, and she could hear herself for the first time in forever.

"Devi?"

She sniffled, trying not to get too emotional. "This isn't going to be casual."

His head shook. "Not for me. You will never be casual for me, Devi. It's why I stayed away these weeks. I don't want to hurt you, but I also… I don't want to go the rest of my life without touching you again, without making as many memories as I can."

He always knew what to say. The problem was she wasn't certain who was talking to her—the man or the operative.

Tonight, it didn't matter.

Devi frowned, realizing what she was wearing. "I should have… Zach, I'm sorry. It's a farm. As a proper submissive, I think there's an unwritten rule that you should never present yourself to your Dom while wearing Crocs, but it was these or Wellies."

He stopped for a moment, and then the most brilliant smile crossed his face and he laughed. He reached out a hand and grasped hers. "Come here, brat. I've missed you."

He kissed her, his hands steady on her waist while his lips moved over hers. He took his time, exploring her mouth, sliding his tongue along hers, drugging her with his nearness.

Oh, how she'd missed him. These weeks had been filled with quiet revelations, but none so big as the fact that she was in love with Zachary Reed.

But love didn't have to last forever. Love could come and go.

Or this could be the love of her whole damn life. She'd once asked her mom if she would have taken back the heartache of losing her dad.

Not even if he had never come home to me. Loving your dad made me a better person. No matter how it ended.

When she stepped away, she kicked off the aforementioned Crocs and pulled the jumper over her head. She was calling it a jumper now instead of a sweater. Like this time and place were so different from reality it had its own language.

This was their space. Their time. It wouldn't last long, but she was going to let herself revel in it until she had to give him up again. Until she had to watch him meet fate.

She wriggled out of her jeans and then did away with her cotton bra and panties. She normally had gorgeous fet wear and lingerie she made for herself, but it felt right to be in her own skin with this man. To feel primal and stripped down to her rawest self. A piece of her no one would ever witness. Only Zach.

She moved in and put her hands on his chest, memorizing the scars there. The long one that ran from under his right shoulder blade almost to his pec.

"Bulgaria. Knife fight over a piece of intel we were supposed to bring back," he said quietly.

"What was the intel?" she asked.

"I don't know, sweetness. That's part of the job. It was supposed to be a dead drop, but someone was watching," he admitted.

She found the round one on the other side of his chest. "That's a bullet wound."

He nodded. "Yep. Happened in Australia. And the one on my bicep was from getting caught under a shit ton of building when your cousin cut the wrong wire on a bomb. Took them hours to dig me out."

"And this one?" She touched the one on his cheek.

"Fell off my bike when I was twelve," he replied. "Probably needed stitches, but my aunt was a former soldier so she butterflied me up and we kept going."

So much of his life had been dangerous. Even his childhood, since every moment was about survival. About trying to outrun the past.

"Give me your hands, Devi," he commanded softly. "I want to play. I want to be in control for a little while. I want to know I'm taking care of someone rather than wrecking lives."

He needed this as much as she did. Needed her. It was enough for now. She held out her wrists. "I would like to play as well, Zach. Can we... You know the kidnapping thing is kind of hot when you think about it. In the right circumstances. It used to be a fantasy of mine, but then someone actually kidnapped me and it ruined it."

"You were kidnapped twice, sweetness. Twice."

Three times, but one of them was him so she was pretty sure he didn't think that counted. She wanted it to. In the sexiest way. "Please, Zach. Can't you make kidnapping hot like it was before?"

His lips curled up. "You want to role-play. Yeah, I can do that. How hot do you want it?"

"Singe me. Make me feel it. I want to be warm all the way until tomorrow," she admitted.

His whole demeanor changed, and he seemed to grow a freaking foot. "Devon Taggart. Do you know why I brought you here?"

Oh, her damn pussy responded to that. They could have been doing this for weeks. "You took me from my parents' home. No, I don't know why you took me. It was a mistake, but you can take me back. I'm sure my father would simply be happy to see me again."

He chuckled, a deeply satisfied sound. He grabbed the jute off the table and expertly wound it around her wrists, making her feel it, but not so much it would bite into her skin. "There was no mistake, sweetness, and we both know your father isn't the problem. However, I'll handle your mother. You're here to serve me. Would you like to know how?"

She knew and her nipples were so tight it was almost painful. Like she might be able to use them as weapons. Huh, she wondered if her cousins ever did.

"Devi," Zach said sharply.

"Yes." She could get distracted. She liked that she had a Master who would bring her back to him. Make her focus on the game they were playing. "I suspect you're going to want me to clean for you. You know there are maids. You could call one up."

He growled and moved into her space, gripping her chin and using more force than he had before. *"Ty ne uborshchitsa, dorogaya."*

Her heart rate ticked up. Damn. She would never forget that moment when he'd turned to her and told her they could have a secret language. One Lacey wouldn't understand. One only for them. Her aunt had deep ties to family in Russia. Mob ties. He'd told her she was obviously not a cleaner in low, sexy Russian. "Are you from a rival syndicate and you decided to make me pay for the war that's raged between our families with my sweet ass?"

He snorted. "You've spent too much time with Brianna. And yes, sweetness. Your family has disrespected mine for the last time. Now you're going to be a very good girl and spread your legs and take my cock. After I've bred you, your parents will know how this is going to go from..."

She winced.

He nodded. "Yeah, I'm going to leave your parents out of it. Let's go with your cousin. Kala's the leader of the rival syndicate. I'm going to show her who the real boss is by taking her precious cousin to my bed."

He knew her well. It was way better to not bring her parents in. She thrust her breasts out, shoulders squaring in a prideful pose. "My cousin will kill you for this."

His jaw tightened, and he gripped her hair. "Then I should enjoy you while I can. But first let me give you a taste of what happens when you defy me."

Before she could take another breath, he dropped her hair and had her in a fireman's hold. He moved her over to the spanking bench he cobbled together. It was surprisingly comfortable. Like it had been made by a man who knew how to take care of a sub. It was as comfy as one could get with one's ass prominently in the air.

And then it wasn't so comfy because his hand came down on her ass. Hard.

"You will obey me. You will not step out of line, and you will not run. There is nowhere for you to run that I can't find you." His hand came down again.

Sweet pain. She knew the difference. Knew this was all play, and she could stop him at any time. Knew if he thought he was hurting her he would want to die. Which is why it was okay. Deep down she even knew this was her way of processing some of what had happened. But mostly it was a way to connect to him. To show him she did trust him without having to say it out loud. No. Out loud she could be the brat she felt like. "I assure you, Zachary, that I will get away and I'll come back and show you what warfare is."

He moved in front of her. She still had to rotate slightly to see him. Her head was below his waist, so she was treated to the sight of his cock pressed against those jeans he wore. He had the crop in his hands. He slapped it against his open palm. "Then the lines are drawn, and we have to see where we come out when the explosion is over."

She couldn't even hold onto the padded bench she was draped over. He'd ensured her tied hands were secured around the bench, but that was her only stability. When he brought the crop down, she bit her bottom lip and rode out the flurry of strikes that went from the fleshy part of her ass down to her upper thighs. Fire lashed across her skin and seemed to run like lightning to her pussy, getting her wet and ready for that cock he was going to give her.

"I can promise you, Devi, you won't be able to keep me out. As long as you're here, you're mine." He ran a hand over her ass, skimming the places he'd struck. "Mine to discipline and fuck. You're my fuck toy, Devi Taggart, and I won't let you forget it. Open your legs."

This was all part of the game. He'd placed her face down on the bench, but there were two appendages where her legs could go, where he could tie them down, leaving her pussy and ass utterly vulnerable. Tears were pooling in her eyes, but it felt so good to…feel. She didn't want it to stop. This could be their refuge where they played and shut the world out.

So she played. She closed her legs, wanting to pretend for a while.

The crop came down again. And again. And again. He dropped to his knees in front of her, giving her a glimpse of steely eyes and a willful expression. "Devi, if you don't spread those legs for me, I'll ensure that I lube that plug up with something that you will feel for hours. Days, even. Have you ever had your asshole burn?"

Evil man. "Have you?"

"Have you met Gabriel Lodge? Take a Dom training class," he shot back. "I assure you we all know, and that's why I'm telling you it is in your own best interest to spread those legs and give me access to your asshole. If you think it will bother me to hear you cry for the rest of the night, it won't. I'll like it. You're fucking gorgeous when you cry. I'll give you a hint. Don't clench too hard."

Or she could go along with him. Yup. That was play, too. She shifted her legs open, letting them move down to the padded benches.

His smirk was more than slightly evil. "Excellent, but you should remember that in the future. I might not warn you again."

She wished that didn't send a thrill through her. They talked about anal play when they discussed hard and soft limits, but most of their time had been fairly vanilla sex.

This was more. This woke her up and made her long.

"I understand, Zach." She gave him her most breathless tone. It wasn't hard since she was kind of wildly anticipating what came next.

She gasped when it was his hands moving her down. The rope around her wrists caught on something under the bench. He'd built a peg into the bench to catch whatever fastening he put her in. It held her in place as he moved her torso down the bench until her ass was just off it.

His hand moved under her, fingers finding her pussy and sliding through the evidence of her arousal. "That's what I want. I heard you were a sexual goddess, Devon. This…this is fucking ambrosia."

She heard him groan and could picture him sucking his fingers into his mouth. It was something he loved to do. He would finger fuck her, get her hot and bothered and on the edge, and then he would carefully lick his fingers clean, like he couldn't stand the thought of missing a single drop.

"You be still and I'll let you have this while I play with your ass," he said from behind her. She could hear him moving, likely going to the table so he could grab whatever instrument of torture he intended to use next. "If you move and lose it, it's gone, and there will be punishment. Lift up for me."

She did as he asked and felt him slip something under her, something slightly squishy. It was odd and then it buzzed right on her clit, and her eyes nearly crossed.

Vibrator. One of the tiny ones. Small but damn mighty. The hum softened, and she realized he had a remote. Damn, him. He was going to kill her. She had to be still. So still.

The hum increased. Barely enough to make her desperate for more. That was when she felt him part the cheeks of her backside and dribble the absolutely not-exotic lube on.

"I'm going to have you," he declared. "In every way a man can have a woman, I will have you."

It took real willpower to stay still while she felt him rub the lube in, big finger rimming her before easing inside. It was so much. She could barely breathe, but then the vibe started really vibing, and she wasn't thinking about anything but the orgasm she was on the cusp of.

She was almost certain she heard the donkey huff, but that wasn't so surprising. She let it go, concentrating on him.

Over and over he fucked her with his finger, easing in and pulling out until he replaced warm flesh with the plug, sliding it in.

The vibe reached a crescendo, and she couldn't hold back a second longer. She gritted her teeth because The Fabulous Miss K was downstairs, and she could be sensitive to weird sounds. No idea what happened to that donkey.

The orgasm made her body buck, losing the vibe, but she clenched on the plug. She wasn't losing that sucker.

Her whole body felt alive and vibrant.

And she knew he wasn't done. Not even close.

* * * *

Zach moved back to the table and washed his hands in the basin he brought up when he set the whole scene with Arthur earlier today. It had felt oddly normal to plan a sex scene with the man. Like he was back at the club where he belonged, and no one would question why he would need to wash his hands in a barn.

Because he'd fucked her asshole with his finger before sliding the plug inside. It would be his cock before this whole thing was over. He would imprint himself on her.

He picked up one of the condoms he'd placed on the prep table because that was one thing he wouldn't do to her. He wouldn't leave her alone with a child. She would be a loving mom, but it wouldn't be with a father who was dead or in prison. Like his parents had been.

Fuck. He wasn't thinking about this now.

"Zach, I…"

She wouldn't do this to him. She wouldn't let him get to this point and then kill the play. "Do I need to gag you? I don't think I want to hear anything from you but *yes*. If you can't do that, then maybe we should rethink."

Her head tilted, and he saw the frown on her face. "Touchy. I was going to ask where you got all the toys. I was curious, babe. I wasn't stopping the play. I'm the daughter of a rival syndicate, and my cousin challenged you. The only way to make her see you're the biggest mafia king around is to fuck me hard, to make me your little sex slave. But I'm also curious about the toys."

She was going to kill him. He moved back between her legs. If she was his little sex slave, then he wasn't going to waste more time. "I kept a bug-out bag and some other important things in a storage locker in DC. Lacey helped get me back into the States after the Canadian debacle. I happened to have a kit there. I don't know why, but I brought it with me. Now hush unless you're going to say something super dirty. Do you have any idea how much I want to fuck you?"

Her pelvis tilted up slightly, the sexiest invitation he'd ever gotten. "I think you want to make me pay for everything my cousin has done to your family. It won't work. I'll find a way out."

She needed this. She needed this to be play. In some ways she wasn't lying. Not about the find-a-way-out part. But if it made her feel better to make him the bad guy... Well, he was the bad guy. If it made her feel better to make him a mafia bad guy instead of the spy who broke her fucking heart, then he would do it. His cock ached being so close to her. He moved between her legs, one hand stroking down her back as he admired the pink shadows on her ass, proof of his discipline. "There is no way out. I'm not giving you back. You won't see your family again, Devi. You belong to me now, and you'll find out I don't let what belongs to me go. Ever."

He lined his cock up to her pussy and pressed inside.

The groan that came from his chest felt like a pressure release valve turned on. So much tension, and it melted away now that he was inside her again. She was so fucking tight. He could feel the plug drag against him as he worked his way fully in.

She gasped and wriggled as she tried to get used to him. "Zach…"

He put a hand on the back of her neck, holding her in place. "Don't move. This is my time. You feel so fucking good." He pulled out slightly and then thrust slowly back in, letting the sensation soak into his veins. This was where he wanted to be all the time. Whatever he'd felt for any other woman it was nothing compared to her. Devi was both the trip and the destination, the person he wanted to be beside forever. Wanted to play with forever. *"Ty moya. Ne zabyvay, chto ty prinadlezhish mne."*

You are mine. Don't forget you belong to me.

"*Ya tvoya*," she replied.

I am yours.

Forever. He wanted forever. He pressed in and pulled out, controlling her with one hand on the back of her neck and the other on her hip. He closed his eyes and saw her the way she'd been that first night. Like him, she'd felt the chemistry between them. The magic. She had looked at him like he was important. Like he was everything she ever wanted in a man.

He fucked her, relishing in every gasp and groan that came from her mouth. He wanted to make this last, but he couldn't. She felt too good, too perfect. Like home.

He felt the moment she tightened around him, and he was a goner. He groaned and lost all control, fucking her with a mindless determination. The pleasure was a wave that took him to a place he never wanted to leave.

He fell over, his cheek against her back, his cock sliding out of her pussy.

Pure peace. It was what he felt when they were like this.

"Zach, I don't want to stop playing. I think you should clean up your little sex toy and we should have dinner and pretend like you didn't kidnap me. Lacey can't know. She might try to save me."

She was definitely going to be the death of him. "I wouldn't let her. I told you. You're mine." He reached down and cupped a breast, loving how soft her skin was, how hard her nipple got. "So I will pretend, *dorogaya*. But when we close that door tonight, you'll be mine again."

Unfortunately, she was right about the time. It was getting close to dinner, and Lacey would be looking for them. She'd sent him a text that something important had happened and they would need to talk.

Now that he thought about it, he was surprised she hadn't looked for him already.

He kissed the nape of her neck and stood. "Hey, anything interesting happen while you were in town?"

He moved to the trash can he set up for this occasion, pulling the condom off and tossing it aside. He would need to get them both in a shower before dinner, and he certainly wasn't turning on the hose they used on The Fabulous Miss K. One day Lacey would tell him what the K stood for.

Devi seemed perfectly content to lay on the bench, her cheek turned so he could see one side of her pretty face. Her eyes were closed, and a silly grin was on her lips. He wanted to see that expression on her face every minute of the day. "We bought a bunch of feed stuff and then I went to a bookstore and got some books on folklore. This creepy guy hit on me at the bar, but I went to the bathroom and that's where I saw all the pictures."

"Creepy guy?"

She sighed as though her fun time was truly over now that she'd heard his jealous tone. She managed to move her hands off the hook under the bench, but then she stopped and winced. "If I move too much this plug is coming out."

He chuckled and realized that he would have to get used to guys hitting on his girl. It wasn't like she said some hot guy hit on her. He gently helped her up so she didn't have to move too much. "I would rather take it out in the shower. I've got a robe for you, sweetness. Have I told you how gorgeous you are? It doesn't surprise me you got hit on."

Her lips curled up as her head tilted, and her arms moved to his shoulders. "You're going to get in that tiny shower with me?"

He thought he was going to fit just fine. He dropped a kiss on her lips. "Yes. But we need to make sure it's kitten free. I swear they get more adventurous every day. And shouldn't Lacey have worked her magic to keep the men away from you? I swear she's a terrible bodyguard."

"Oh, she had to pick something up, so I was alone." She frowned. "Maybe I wasn't supposed to tell you that."

He unwound the rope around her wrists, inspecting them to make sure he hadn't left marks. "It's a tiny town. I don't suppose there's too much trouble you could find, but I worry. I don't like you being unprotected. I think we're safe, but we can't know who's watching."

"I was careful," she replied and moved to where the linen robe he'd brought for her hung on a peg. She stopped and frowned as she tied the robe around her body. "Zach, how the hell do you expect me to keep this plug in on that ladder?"

He heard a snort. A feminine snort, if his ears weren't lying.

Damn it. Lacey had come looking for him, and she was a freaking voyeur. Did everyone in his life have to be so damn comfortable with sex? He wasn't going to point it out to Devi that they'd had an audience. How had she moved in so quietly? They needed motion detectors out here. Although Lacey pointed out there were a mega shit ton of animals who would set them off.

He pulled up his jeans and grabbed his T-shirt. Next time he would be naked with her. They would lay together skin to skin for hours, and nothing would stop him. He grabbed his cell. "We'll work it out. If I have to find a way to carry you down, I'll do it. I gave you that plug. You are not to lose it."

He glanced down at his cell.

No bars. Nothing. Which meant the security system was down, too. They were blind.

It was possible the system was accidently down. It had happened a couple of times, but not since Zach had worked on upping the signal.

A jammer would do the trick. Jam the signal, and then taking out the security system would be a breeze. A good hacker could do it all from a distance so the whole team could invade and the cameras placed around the farm would pick up nothing. He might have noticed but he had other things on his mind. Arthur was gone. Lacey… He didn't know where Lacey was.

A chill went up Zach's spine, and he looked at Devi, his voice going low. "I need you to hide."

A brow arched over green eyes. She mouthed the word. *Where?*

She wasn't wrong. They weren't exactly in a place with a ton of hidey holes. He moved in close to her, his mouth by her ear. "Someone is jamming the signal around the house. I need to go and find Lacey, and I need you to stay here. I think someone is downstairs. I don't want to tip them off. I'm going to see if I can figure out who's here. There's a window to your right. It goes to the roof. Shimmy down the rain pipe and get to the Jeep if you can. If they catch you, know I'll do everything in my power to get you back."

It was raining outside and she could slip and fall and break her neck, and that was a way better case scenario than Huisman getting his hands on her.

He should never have brought her here.

Her face had gone a stark white, but she nodded and whispered back. "I don't think I can do that with the plug."

He grunted and kissed her. He no longer cared about the damn plug, and it was sad. A few minutes ago her keeping that plug had been important. "Be careful. I'm going to see if whoever is down there will follow me. But for now, we need him to believe we don't know he's there."

"Zach, I'm not going anywhere with you." The brat was back, and it was clear she was clinging to their role-play. Her tone was sassy even as her eyes told him she was worried. She was handling it with grace. She wasn't falling apart. "I told you my cousin will come for me, and she will rain hell on your whole syndicate."

He moved to the ladder. Everything looked normal down below. He might be freaking out for nothing, but his instincts were kicking in now that the lust cleared a little. Someone was here.

Fuck, it might be more than one. Huisman might have sent a team. He had before.

What had happened? What the fuck had gone wrong? He slipped his SIG into the back of his jeans. If he was alone, he would try something different, try to draw them out so he could take them down one by one, but he was panicked at the thought of having Devi fall into their hands.

Huisman would torture her.

Was it best-case scenario if he was about to be arrested? If it was Interpol or some Agency black team come to drag him back? They would leave her alone. Her name alone would protect her.

His stomach turned as he started down the ladder. His back was vulnerable. It went against his every instinct, but he did it for Devi. He forced his voice to stay in that deep dark Dom place. "If your cousin shows her face here, I'll take her down. I promise that, *dorogaya*."

His feet found the ground, and adrenaline pumped through him. He had barely turned when he felt something cool at the back of his neck.

"I'd love to see you try, asshole," a familiar voice said.

Yep, maybe not worst-case scenario, but it was bad.

His team was here, and he had some explaining to do.

Chapter Eleven

Devi knew that voice.

She had been planning to do exactly what Zach told her to do. After she took out the plug. It turned out it kind of slipped out when she took that first step without thinking about it. She was picking it up with one of the handy towels Zach had stacked because no matter what situation she was in, a good sub never left a used butt plug sitting around. That was a D/s no-no she wasn't going to play around with no matter how close to death she was.

Although the bad guys might slip on it. No. Ewww.

Plug stored, she was moving toward the window she would likely fall out of when she heard her cousin's voice.

"I'd love to see you try, asshole."

She breathed the biggest sigh of relief. "Kala!"

"Hey, Dev. I'm thinking about killing your boyfriend." When Devi looked down Kala was dressed in all black and had a Glock to the back of Zach's head. Kala glanced up. "He was supposed to tell me where you were. I had to find out for myself."

Rude, but she could understand. It was hard for Kala to be on the outside. "Well, we're fine."

"You are not fine. You are doing gross, dumb stuff, and apparently I'm somehow involved," Kala pointed out.

Her cousin was taking things for granted. "You don't know that. Maybe Kenz takes over the syndicate."

Kala snorted. "Like Kenzie could run a syndicate. She would try talking to our enemies. Hell, she would probably fall in love with one, and while that is useful sometimes, not in the syndicate. Also, Tash would be terrible, too, but the point is what you're doing is weird."

"Hey, girl who wants me to wear bat wings to the next costume party. Or are we riding dragons now?" Cooper McKay stepped from behind the ladder. He smiled up at her. "Devi, don't let her shame you. She's a total pervert and into fairy porn. Role-play is a perfectly normal thing. Hey, brother. You've pissed off my wife and fucked up my honeymoon. We were supposed to be in the Bahamas."

"Well, I was supposed to be in Dallas concentrating on my nanite project, but it's cool. I'm pretty sure it works." Lou was standing by the horses' pen. Her brother's girlfriend had a wide smile on her face like this was all a magnificent adventure. She was also in all black. There was apparently a dress code. "I don't think the suckers will turn on the people who wear it and, like, eat them or anything. I didn't give them teeth, you know. I am a little worried, though, because they can rewrite code. What if they decide to give themselves teeth? The good news is I think I made the kill switch so they can't touch it."

"A smart play, bestie," Kala said with a nod. "Now someone get the doser because Zach's going to take a nap while I get my cousin out of here."

"No, you're not." Devi suddenly realized she was going to have to exert some willpower. She turned and started down the ladder.

Everyone in the barn groaned.

"Devi, dude, underwear," Kala barked.

And then whoofed because Zach used her distraction to turn and disarm her cousin. They did some twirly-whirly action-hero moves. Like they thought they were in a martial arts film.

At least someone was having fun.

They really liked punching each other. Weird.

"Hey, Dev," Lou said, walking up. "Way to distract. Did you know they have Highland cows? They're so cute. What is this place?"

"Don't kill each other," Cooper said, watching the fight, but he leaned against one of the stalls. If he was worried about his brand-new wife and, well, brand-new brother killing each other, he didn't show it.

"Kala, I'm not going anywhere so don't give Zach any of that sleepy stuff you use on people," Devi called out. "He's heavy, and I have plans for him later on tonight. Though you are kind of playing into our role-play, you know." She turned to Lou. "The cows are so sweet, but watch out for the donkey. Oh, Sunny just had kittens. You should come see. Hey, where's my brother? Did he let you run off with the team all alone? Where's Uncle Ian?"

"TJ decided to wait outside," Lou said, her eyes wide behind the big glasses she wore. "He kind of turned green when we figured out you were in the barn and you weren't alone."

She frowned Lou's way. In the back she heard Kala curse, and then the barn floors shook as something big obviously hit the ground. "Don't touch his face," she called out before turning back to Lou. "The rest of you couldn't do the same?"

Cooper yawned. "Nah. I figured it was like the club. Look, Kala wanted to snipe Zach from afar. I thought we should talk. She was unwilling to wait outside in case Zach had another way out. I was here to make sure she didn't lose her shit, and Lou wanted to see the animals."

"They're so cute. Is this like a sanctuary? I noticed the poor horse has scars," Lou said. "Also, when did Zach start speaking Russian?"

Her boyfriend was all kinds of surprises. "I think around the time he decided to be on a team full of people who spoke Russian. He didn't want to get left out."

"I'm married to one and I barely speak it." Cooper sounded aggrieved. "Way to show off, big bro."

"Kala, if you will chill for two seconds," Zach was saying.

"I chilled for weeks, Zach. Weeks," Kala replied.

"She's been talking to you and her parents," Zach argued.

"Not good enough." Kala threw another punch.

"This might go on for a while." Lou holstered her gun and started for the barn door. "Do you have anything I can feed your brother?"

Oh, she had questions that were going to come before her brother's never-full gut. "Where's Uncle Ian?"

Cooper winced. "Hopefully back in Dallas with no idea that we hopped a plane to here."

"He doesn't know you're here?" It was inconceivable that her uncle had no idea four members of his team had gone missing.

"Well, we really did fly to the Bahamas and stayed for two whole days to take pictures," Lou replied with a sad sigh. "I thought it would be more fun, but Kala was in full-on mission mode."

"Why were you going on Coop and Kala's honeymoon?" Devi asked.

"That was the funny part." Cooper shook his head. "No one batted an eyelash. Everyone accepted that we are weird, interconnected couples who sometimes end up all sleeping together without any swinging, thank the universe. Lou is Kala's emotional support tech goddess. Big Tag didn't say anything. So we took pics to send to the family to hopefully convince them we're sunning ourselves in the Caribbean and hopped a plane to Cardiff."

This was her fault. "Who told? Was it Daisy?"

"What the fuck is that?" Kala called out.

"I told you to stop bitch slapping me," Zach replied, frustration on full display.

"Then stop being a little bitch, Zach," Kala replied.

They might be at this for hours. Her cousin wasn't politically correct. Or polite in any way.

"It was Bri," Lou admitted. "And she doesn't know she told. She was explaining that she was working on this story where a beautiful fashion designer got kidnapped by her rogue CIA agent ex and taken to Wales. So it was a good bet you were in Wales. From there we might have sent someone to figure out where you were in Wales. It's a small country, but you still can't go knocking on all the doors."

"Zach is good at avoiding CCTV, but he's not perfect. We caught him on a camera in town buying, of all things, cat toys." Cooper tilted his head as though studying her. "Tell me those weren't for you."

Well, she could probably do some kitten play, but she wasn't going to admit that to Cooper. "No, they're for the cats. And please don't mention that to him because I'm the one who made him buy toys. They're babies. They need to play." She realized there was something wrong with this scenario.

"I swear I will beat you down if you use that on me," Kala swore.

"Well, if you didn't want to get roped, sister, you shouldn't have walked into my fucking barn," Zach practically roared.

"I should go check on that," Cooper said with a sigh as they heard the back door sliding open. He grinned. "Zach found a lasso, and it looks like he knows what he's doing. Hey, when you get her wrapped up, deliver her right back here, brother. I like the whole barn thing. It's rustic. Maybe we should do a barn add-on at The Hideout. We have a surprising amount of cowboys who come through."

"You've been monitoring every CCTV cam in Wales?" She wasn't going to blame her bestie. Brianna looked for inspiration in all realms of her life. And it would be cool to get a book before Daisy did.

Although Daisy's love story ended in happily ever after. She wondered how Bri would get her hero and heroine out of the whole death v prison inevitable outcome.

"Not exactly," Lou hedged. "We had some help from friends of ours. You'll meet them later, I'm sure, and we should talk about that because Kala is going to have to act a little weird."

Her cousin was acting weird right now. She was cussing up a storm. Not weird for her, but some people might find the mix of languages odd.

"Zach, don't do it," Kala warned.

Devi looked back, and the big barn doors to the south of the building were wide open and Zach had a lariat in his hand. Oh, it was a lasso in Texas, but she was doing the Wales thing now. Welsh.

"Are you going to be reasonable? Are you going to sit down and talk this out?" Zach asked, but not in his reasonable voice. He was using the voice that came out when he was a bit overstimulated.

She moved to stand beside Cooper. "I don't think either of them is going to sit and talk things out. Do you think they're going to fight to the death?"

"Nah, just until Kala stomps his balls or something. It's a thing she does," Cooper admitted.

And she had the intel she needed. "Take her down, babe. She's planning on going for your balls."

She needed his balls. She was pretty sure his cock wouldn't work if her cousin shoved his balls back up into his body cavity. She was not spending the whole night holding a bag of ice to her temporary Dom's crotch. Also, another thought hit her.

Zach let the lariat fly and proved he was damn good with rope.

Kala turned and tried to swerve away, but it did not work. The lariat landed around her and Zach immediately tightened it and pulled back, catching her around her waist. She ended up on her ass, back to Zach.

Kala sat there for a moment. She was still in that predatory way. She was also sitting in mud since it had rained all day. There was only a light mist now, but the damage had been done.

The world seemed to slow down as everyone waited for Kala to explode.

Devi knew her cousin better than that. Oh, it had looked like a terrifying battle was happening, and she would have totally crushed Zach's balls, but this was play for Kala. Not the sexy kind. More like the way dumbass boys teased and fought each other as a form of affection since their toxic masculinity wouldn't allow them to hug.

"Uh, is the weird sex stuff done?" Her brother came into view. Like the others he'd gotten the wear all black memo, though he wore a gun strapped to his chest. He frowned down at Kala. "You know he's supposed to be Devi's guy. He's not supposed to play with you."

Devi moved quickly, stepping out into the yard. Her brother could get the wrong idea. "He was trying to save his balls."

Disaster waddled into the scene as one of the big geese rounded the corner.

TJ smiled her way. "Hey, sis. Are you okay? I mean you seemed comfortable with him. Unless you seriously were upset and didn't want to be kidnapped. But there was rival mobster stuff going on, so I figured I should stay out of it. Honestly, I wanted to stay out of it entirely. Mom's going to be pissed. Could you talk to her for me? Let her know I didn't do any patriarchy things. Oh, hey. That's a big duck."

"It's a goose," Lou corrected. "You should be careful. They can be touchy."

Oh, that goose was seriously touchy. "That's Caleb. You should step back. He mostly keeps to himself, but when he gets scared, he can be obnoxious."

"Zach, you should get me out of this right now," Kala warned.

TJ leaned toward the goose. "This guy? Nah, we're going to be friends. How you doing, buddy?"

No one was listening.

"I'm not getting you out of this until you tell me what you did with Lacey," Zach announced. "She wouldn't have let you in. Tell me you didn't kill her. She was how I'm going to find my mom."

"Whoa, we didn't kill anyone," Cooper said, holding up his hands as though to say *see, I'm completely harmless.*

He wasn't. "TJ, I'm serious about that goose."

"I want to meet Lacey," Kala said in a syrupy-sweet tone. "I want to meet this so-called operative who thought she could hide my cousin from me."

"She didn't try to hide me. She didn't want me here," Devi pointed out.

"He's cool," TJ said, reaching a hand out.

"She didn't want you here?" Kala asked, one brow arched. "Who does she think she is? Is she too fucking good for my cousin? Have you put Devi in a place where some asshole insults her?"

"It's not like that." Lacey only told her to go to the sea a couple of times a day now, and it was mostly because she annoyed the other woman. Sometimes on purpose. But only sometimes. "She actually reminds me a little of you. I think you'll like her. TJ, he's about to attack."

She'd had a couple of run-ins with Caleb. And some of the goats. She'd learned.

"Devi and Lacey are friends." Zach had learned, too. He was staying back. He knew a dangerous animal when he was in proximity to one. "Lacey has been cool about it, and you guys need to tell me what you did to her. She's been helping me for over a year. She's an ally. She's close with underground animal rights and climate activists. They trust her. She's in the same groups as my mom. Lacey can get to her. It's what we're working on."

"Dude, okay, I get it," TJ was trying to say as he backed away from the now honking goose.

Miss Rachel the chicken walked her way into the scene, likely coming to enjoy the drama. She settled herself right on Kala's lap and watched as Caleb started in on the new guy.

That goose could move.

TJ let out what could be described as a horror-movie scream when that goose got one of his fingers.

"Don't you dare shoot that goose, TJ," Lou yelled.

That was when she noticed Kala had a hand on the chicken. She was petting Miss Rachel, and a big smile came over her face as TJ started running.

"You go, Caleb. Get him," Kala shouted.

"She's cool now." Cooper held a hand out to his brother. "You can let her go."

Zach sighed and took his brother's hand. "Sorry. I wasn't trying to hurt her. I was doing my best to not."

He looked awkward, and Zach almost never seemed awkward. Except when he was emotional. He was only awkward around people he cared about. Loved. There was no question he loved his brother.

Cooper's head shook, and he pulled Zach in for a manly hug. "I know that. She doesn't really want to hurt you either. She's worried about Devi and some of the shit we're hearing about Huisman. Come on. And Lacey was not in the house when we went in, so I would bet she saw us coming and ran. Probably thought we were cops or something."

Zach hugged him after a moment's hesitation. She could feel her Dom's relief as he passed the rope to Cooper.

Lou ran out to help TJ.

Devi did not because her brother could use the cardio. He ate a lot. The only way to counter the insane amount of food he ate was cardio.

"Lacey wouldn't have left." She was worried now.

Zach stepped back and let Cooper handle his wife. He got the rope from around her, and Kala managed to stand up with the chicken in her arms. Miss Rachel looked around as though approving of her suddenly heightened position. A couple of the other chickens were clucking like they were jealous.

"No, she wouldn't have," Zach agreed and reached for her hand. He threaded their fingers together.

"Who is Lacey? I don't want some cover. Who is she really?" Kala asked, brushing off her tactical pants with her free hand. "She's certainly not some sweet animal activist. Though you should know I do approve of the attack goose. It's kind of evil. Build a sanctuary for animals and train them all to be your army."

One of the big mastiffs lumbered up and walked to Devi, looking for a pet. She used her free hand. "Yeah, see, so brutal. Lacey didn't mean to get involved in international espionage. She just wanted to save a bunch of animals. And the planet. Her mom is active in...well, activism. And you should meet Arthur. He's the vet. Also involved in animal rights."

Kala sighed and turned. She was covered in mud but calmer now that she had something to pet. "Well, good for them. I would like to meet them. I can't find pictures of these people. She has no socials and no trace of her on the web. Lou can't find her. That tells me one of two things."

"It should tell you she's smart," Zach replied. "Do you think I haven't vetted her?"

"How can you vet her, Zach? How do you vet someone who doesn't exist?" Kala asked.

Devi didn't see the problem. "I mean you don't exist. Like your construct thingee does, but I was told they scrubbed you from existence. Your birth certificate doesn't exist."

And yet here she was.

"Of course my birth certificate exists." Kala frowned. "I mean I think my mom has it somewhere. What doesn't exist is any real information on me anywhere except in the records of the Agency. Which is precisely why I want to meet Lacey."

Zach looked worried for the first time. He was always so sure of Lacey. "She's been more than helpful. She's saved my life a couple of times. I don't think she's spying for some foreign agency. She's managed to work her way into Disrupt Europe. She's looking for Huisman, too. Now tell me what you did with her because if you didn't kill her, she would be here."

"She wasn't there," Kala said with a stare. And then she grinned, watching as TJ ran past the cows, goose still in full pursuit. "That's a Highland cow. Lou went on and on about them. Shaggy cows. Cute."

There were two things that could distract her cousin. Cooper and cute animals. Lucky for her they were both here. "Aren't they the best? Lacey names all the animals. That's Mel and Cass. And Lacey went into that room I'm not supposed to know about. She said she picked up some intel in town and might be a while. She wasn't sure she would have time to cook dinner, so I offered to make a salad or something."

Zach dropped her hand. "She's in the comms room. It's also a safe room. You need a code to get in and out. Fuck. You also need power. Did you turn it off, Kala?"

"I didn't. Lou did," Kala admitted. "It was the only way she could cut the phone and Internet, too. She said it's all wired weird. Or wired by paranoid spies."

"She's not a spy," Zach insisted as he started to move. "Not the way you think. I'm going to get the power back on and let her out and try to explain why my whole team is here."

Zach strode away.

Lou was a bit out of breath when she rejoined them. "TJ might be lost to us now. I'm going to be honest, when I read Jane Austen and dreamed about running around moors in the UK, there was never a goose involved."

"Should I follow him?" Cooper asked. "Zach, I mean. Obviously TJ made bad choices. I don't think I need to, but we did come here to look for him."

Kala waved him off. "Nah, he's not going anywhere without his *dorogaya*. Yeah, we're going to talk about that. He's not supposed to speak anything but some high-school level Spanish. Kenz, Tash, and I have had entire conversations we thought he didn't understand."

"Did you talk about how hot he is?" It's what Devi would have talked about.

"No. We might have talked about how we thought he was a plant," Kala replied. "And long detailed discussions of our periods. We switch to Russian for those to save tender male ears. Tell me about Lacey Rook. I'm serious, Dev. She doesn't exist."

"Again, like you don't exist," Devi reiterated.

"My point exactly. Zach isn't thinking straight." Kala glanced around. "Though I will admit, this place is cool. You know I've thought I would make a good bog witch. Like get a cottage in the woods and have a bunch of animals around me."

"That dream died when we got married." Cooper moved toward Devi, his arms out. "Did I thank you for all your help? She was both beautiful and comfortable. You did a fabulous job, and the lingerie was chef's kiss."

She hugged him. She hadn't realized how much she missed her family. She'd been so focused on Zach and her own pinging between misery and curiosity. She'd given her cousins permission to raid her apartment. She had lots of samples there, and she was happy they had gotten used. "I'm glad you liked it. I'm sorry you had to cut your honeymoon short to come find me. I really am okay."

"I'm not sure about that." Lou looked concerned, and not about her boyfriend. "I've discovered some unsettling rumors on the Dark Web. I know it sounds crazy that we went to all this trouble to find you, but Kala wants to make sure you know what you're getting into."

"A call might have worked." Devi was well aware that she needed some pants. Wales was chilly even at this time of the year.

"How could I know he wasn't influencing you?" Kala asked as Cooper managed to get the rope off her. He loosened it and let her gracefully step out. "Also, I didn't want to have this meeting over the Internet. I wanted to lay eyes on you. I mean not as much of you as I actually saw, but eyes. Babe, something's wrong here." Her cousin leaned over and gently eased Miss Rachel down. The other chickens clucked around her. "I have this feeling in my gut. Something's wrong."

"I do not understand this place." TJ jogged up. "First, it's the goose. Like I'm never going to think of geese as nice again. I'll eat that motherfucker if someone wants to roast him up. Then I finally get away and a goat tries to headbutt me."

Cooper was obviously taking his wife's instincts seriously. He had his hand on his gun and was taking careful measure of the area around them. "We should move inside. Kala has a bad feeling."

"Maybe we could go inside and get some dinner," TJ suggested.

"What did you say the chickens were named?" Kala asked, her hands in fists on her hips. She didn't seem deeply concerned they were about to be murdered. That wasn't her cousin's we're-in-physical-trouble face. It was her thinking face. She was putting things together.

Devi had zero idea what the chickens' names had to do with what was going on in Kala's head, but she offered them up. "You know Miss Rachel. That's Miss Callie and Miss Jen."

Kala's eyes closed, and her expression went blank. "And the goose who only gets violent when he isn't left alone is Caleb. The cows?"

"What's going on, babe?" Cooper asked.

"Mel and Cass," Devi replied, an uneasy feeling in her gut.

"Fuck me." Kala's eyes opened, and that was her I'm-going-to-murder-someone face. Yeah, she'd seen that expression a lot growing up.

"That is something you and Cooper should talk about." TJ had a hand on his gut. "I need a sandwich. Devi, do y'all have any ham?"

"I suspect there is no ham here, TJ," Kala said between gritted teeth. "Tell me something, cousin. Didn't you spend some time in Bliss? Do your eyes not work? Or has she gone the full-on *Mission Impossible* route and she's wearing someone else's face? I suppose she could have used her skills in the dark arts to change her appearance. It's what fucking demons do."

Lou gasped. "No. No. It can't be her. Didn't you see her dad a couple of weeks ago?"

Cooper moved near Lou as though they needed to stand together to face whatever was coming.

"I haven't been to Bliss in years. Gosh, I think the last time I spent any real time there I was like nine. I went to Carys's wedding, but I had an interview. I stayed one night and I was on a plane in the morning. TJ went with Seth and Travis more often than I did. I spent summers in Dallas with my friends." She was confused. Bliss was a small town in Colorado where her Uncle Ian owned a cabin. He spent many weeks during summers there and sometimes went to ski as well. So did the Dean-Miles family, and she'd gone with Brianna a couple of times, but when she was a teen she'd preferred to spend her summers at home.

Her sewing machine was at home. She would spend summers working with local theater groups making costumes. She kind of missed that. She'd really enjoyed those summers. Was she so determined to make it big that she was forgetting how much she loved small jobs, ones where she knew the people she was designing for?

"Isn't Rachel the name of Paige's mom? The one with the two husbands, and one of them is a little wild?" TJ asked.

"They all have two husbands." Kala shot out every word like it was a bullet. "Well, except Lucifer's mom, and yes, I recently talked to Henry and he did not bother to mention Lucifer was working a guy from my team."

"Oh, shit," Cooper said. "Baby, it's not her. That would be insane. Your dad would know."

"She is walking chaos, so insanity is kind of her thing. Also, I will be having a long talk with my father. I should have known there was a reason he and Mom took the whole 'Zach's in the wind thing' like champs," Kala said and started for the house. "We're going to need to blow the place up. Bullets won't work on her. TJ, do you have C-4?"

"Dude, no. I did not bring C-4 on the plane we recently traveled on," TJ said, catching up to her. "I don't, like, keep it on me at all times."

"And that is why you fail," Kala announced.

"I didn't fail," her brother replied.

Devi followed behind, noting that Lou and Cooper were whispering to each other. "Uhm, who are we talking about? Because Lacey is British. Definitely not from Colorado. She's from Liverpool."

"She's from the bowels of hell." Kala approached the main house, climbing the steps with purpose. "Also, changing her accent is one of her talents. If you heard her real voice you would turn to stone. Kind of like what happens when you look her in the eyes."

"I'm confused," Devi admitted. Her cousin could make some snap judgments about people, but this seemed extra even for Kala. "What is happening?"

"How about chicken or turkey?" TJ fell in step beside her. "Or cheese maybe. You make an awesome grilled cheese, sis."

"There is nothing good in this house," Kala announced. "Lucifer only eats the earth's excrement."

"She calls them vegetables." She had seen her cousin act weird, but this was a lot. She looked back to her brother. "Lacey is vegan and pretty hard core about it. But I think we have some tofu scramble left over from breakfast."

TJ went pale. "Tofu?"

Her brother was going to have to go with the flow. "I also have some protein bars. You'll be fine. It wouldn't hurt for you to eat a salad every now and then."

"I eat salad," TJ protested. "Lou makes me, but she puts meat on it. Maybe some fried chicken."

"We are not frying up Miss Rachel," Devi swore.

"I didn't say we should fry up that chicken." TJ followed Kala inside. "Just maybe *a* chicken. Like one from the grocery store."

"There's no animal products allowed. Zach still eats like a horse. You'll be fine," Devi promised. "Hey, Kala, I think we should let Zach handle Lacey."

Her cousin turned on her, an unholy gleam in her eyes. "Zach can't even smell the stench of brimstone. He is useless."

Devi didn't smell anything.

The lights came back on, and she heard the sound of a door opening upstairs.

"Zach, what's going on?" Lacey asked, her voice tight. "Is Devi okay?"

"She's fine, but we have company," Zach was saying as he moved down the stairs.

Lacey rounded the corner. Her hair had come out of its neat bun, like she'd been working furiously. Probably trying to get out of the safe room that became a cage. "Get rid of the... What the actual fuck?"

Oh, Lacey started off in the same British accent she'd always used around Devi, but the last part of that sentence had been said with a flat, American accent, and Lacey's normally placid face turned distinctly... What was the right word? Not exactly angry. Volcanic rage would be more descriptive.

Kala matched her dangerous vibe on every level, and suddenly Devi was almost certain this was how the world ended. Not with a bang but a girl fight.

"You." Lacey said the word like it was a warning. Or a threat.

"You," Kala said back.

Devi took a seat. This looked like it was going to be some excellent drama because she was pretty sure now she knew what she was dealing with. Was popcorn vegan? She glanced up and Zach looked every bit as shocked as she was.

Whatever was about to happen, he hadn't kept it from her. He hadn't known the secret. He wasn't going to take this well, and she was going to have to calm her Dom down. It was her job. He gave her wild pleasure and indulged her fantasies, and she calmed him down when he found everyone around him was lying about who they were. It seemed to happen a lot.

The one thing she did know was now that her family was here, their time was running out.

* * * *

Zach heard Lacey's accent slip.

What the hell was going on? How had his carefully planned evening turned into a pile of drama? He was supposed to take Devi back into the house and get her in the shower and start the whole process over again. He should be kissing her and washing her hair and fucking her again.

Instead, something was happening, and it wasn't good.

"What the fuck do you think you're doing with my cousin, Lucifer?" Kala asked. "Did you think you could hide her from me?"

"I was doing nothing with your cousin, you complete psycho. I was trying to keep things together since your team couldn't handle it." Lacey was still. Like preternaturally still.

He was confused. Oh, not really. It was super clear to him now that Lacey was Agency. A plant sent in to figure him out. The question was who sent her. And why did she and Kala hate each other?

Lou and Cooper rushed in, filling the small space. He noted Devi had taken a place on the loveseat, and she was watching with wide eyes. Almost like she lived for this shit.

His stomach was in knots. Had he fucked up again? Had Lacey been lying all this time about her contacts? He thought he was close to finding his mom but only because Lacey was working in the background.

"Kala, you need to stay calm." Cooper had his hands out like he was dealing with velociraptors he thought he could train. "Lucy, we should sit down and debrief. You have to know we were not informed you were working an op that touched ours."

"Of course you weren't because she would have fucked it all up," Lacey snarled.

Lacey. Lucy? God, he was a moron. What the hell had he done? He should use the chaos to leave. He could grab his go bag and be on his way out of Wales before anyone realized he was gone. He would go to ground. Maybe back to the States. Find his aunt. Hunker down until he could figure something else out. Yes, that was exactly the plan. The Agency was obviously using this Lucy person to keep tabs on him. She would be his arresting officer when she decided she had everything she could get out of him. Hell, she might do it tonight since her cover was blown. So the smart play was to sneak out right now.

He didn't want to leave Devi.

"I would fuck it up?" Kala asked, brows rising.

Devi looked across the room at him, a smile tugging her lips up, and she held out a hand. An invitation. He could practically hear her. *Join me, Sir. Come and sit with me, Zach. We'll survive the storm together.*

He should leave.

"You fuck everything up. Did you think I would forget how you assassinated that guy in Qatar before I could get the intel I needed out of him? Also, that bullet came close to hitting me," Lacey/Lucy declared.

"Yeah, I missed," Kala returned. "I did fuck that one up."

He didn't even pretend he was leaving. He walked across the space and took Devi's hand, gently pulling her up and moving so he was the one sitting on the couch. He then pulled her down, settling her on his lap.

Yeah. This was what he needed. The minute he was in contact with her he could feel his panic fading. He wrapped an arm around her waist and settled his hand on her thigh, holding her close. He leaned in. "I have no idea what's happening. I think I fucked up again, and we might be in trouble. I mean *I* might be in trouble."

She leaned her head against his shoulder. "You were right the first time. Okay, here's what I've figured out. I think Lacey Rook is actually Lucy Brooke Flanders. I obviously don't know her personally, but I've heard the rumors. She's from the same town where my cousins spent all their summers. She's younger than Kala, but something happened when they were kids and they despise each other. Like nuclear hate. Kala doesn't like to hear the sound of her name."

"How did she end up in the Agency?" Shouldn't it be more elite? Shouldn't there be people he met who had regular jobs? Why couldn't he ever meet a mechanic? Or a librarian?

His favorite person in the world designed fet wear, and he wanted to see her in it again.

"Oh, I'm sorry you think I'm mishandling the Zach situation. I'm under a little pressure here since I had to work overtime when he brought his girlfriend back to our damn secret base." Lucy had begun moving, edging around the room.

Kala mirrored her. "Poor baby has stress? I eat stress for breakfast."

"Yeah, and it makes you gassy and unpleasant to be around. You should try some vegetables," Lucy replied.

They really did hate each other. Maybe they were like magnets. Put together the north end and south end of a magnet and they attracted. Like Cooper and Kala. But try putting two north ends together and they repelled.

"It was her dad who got her in, though I don't think he wanted her at the Agency." Lou joined them, though her eyes never left the two predators circling each other. "Henry Flanders was Big Tag's mentor when he started his career. He's the only guy I know who Big Tag lets get away with pretty much everything. He's probably somewhere nearby. He only works with his daughter. They are a specialized team. The Agency gives him a lot of leeway."

Devi gasped. "He's Arthur. I figured something spy-like out, Zach. I think I'm getting good at this. Arthur is Henry, and that's why he doesn't look anything like the dude in the picture at the pub. What's the chance I would run into the vet? Or you would? I wonder if they had to scramble."

She seemed so pleased with herself. He couldn't take that from her by pointing out they'd both gotten tricked. "I met Arthur a few weeks after I met Lacey, so they've had this cover in place for a while. I didn't think anything about the fact that Arthur didn't have a bigger web presence than his website. No pictures of anything but cuddly animals. The time I called he wasn't in, but it seemed like a real vet's office. When would I run into the real Arthur? I'm kind of stuck out here."

"Hey, babe, she was serious. There's nothing but a bunch of beets and green stuff. I found a muffin though." TJ joined them and then frowned when he saw his sister on Zach's lap. "I can pull up another chair."

The instinct to back off…wasn't there. Normally he would feel weird being this affectionate around her siblings. He would never have kissed Tash in front of any of her family, even if she'd initiated it. He would have pulled away and respected her dad and sisters.

Damn, she really had been a way to be inside the family he

wanted. It had been more about who her parents were. He loved Devi's parents, but she was far more important.

All that fucking mattered was Devi. If her dad was here, he would tell Theo Taggart that he would die for his daughter, but he wouldn't pretend he didn't want his hands on her all the time. He wouldn't pretend like having her this close didn't calm and soothe him. Brought him a peace he was surprised to have. "She's fine right where she is."

Like TJ and Lou should care.

"I'm fine," Devi said with a smile to her brother. "Also, I figured out that the vet is actually Henry Flanders. Look at me. I can be a spy, too."

TJ's nose wrinkled. "I don't think you should change careers, although I would like to point out that for a fashion designer, you could wear more clothes. Like underwear. Underwear is a great thing to wear around your brother."

She crossed her legs demurely but didn't move to fix the situation. She was comfortable in her own skin, and he supported that. If her brother didn't want to catch her half naked and tied down in a barn with a plug up her backside, well then he should have called.

"So no one knows why they hate each other?" Zach asked.

They should be dealing with the whole Lacey isn't Lacey and what the hell is going on that he had an additional Agency team checking on him thing. But this was more fun, and all the gossip made Devi's eyes light up.

"No idea," TJ admitted as the two women in question continued to hurl insults at each other. "I stay out of that situation right there. I've worked with Henry and Luce a couple of times as support. They've brought in some scary assholes. They took down this cult leader who was about to Kool-Aid his whole congregation. Fun days. But I don't talk about that with Kala. I know better than to mention what she calls the unholiest name."

"I think they're both territorial assholes who rub each other the wrong way and don't like it when they get in each other's business." Cooper moved in beside TJ, arms crossed over his big chest. "From what I can tell, Lucy loves her big sister, Poppy, and Kala kind of got to be good friends with her and Lucy was young and acted out and Kala refuses to forgive her. There might have been a prank involved. I don't know. She kind of foams at the mouth when I ask her about Lucy." He sighed. "Is it weird that I find it hot?"

"It's like *Ghostbusters* but Kala and Lucy are the streams you're never supposed to cross," Lou added as she shook her head. "The funny thing is she loves Kenz. Like Kala loves Poppy and their parents. She genuinely adores Nell and Henry."

"Henry, who is Arthur." He was catching up.

"We don't know that," Cooper hedged.

His brother was careful. "Nah, I think Devi's right." TJ had finished the muffin, and Zach could practically hear his gut whining like the mastiff named Sawyer's did right before dinner. Such a big dog and such a pathetic cry for food. "There's beef jerky in my go bag. Second door to the right. Watch out for the cats. There's also some MREs."

The look of relief on TJ's face was nearly comical. "Thanks, man. Kala made us skip lunch when we got confirmation Devi was here."

He practically ran up the stairs.

"I'd like to know how you managed to confirm that." He had a suspicion. It was time everyone laid all their cards on the table and he got a full picture of what was going on. "I'm betting Lacey didn't tell you. Otherwise, she wouldn't have been so shocked. Unless this is all a play for my benefit. I've seen Kala act pretty brilliantly."

"Oh, you're going to see her act, and I'm not looking forward to it," Cooper said with a frown. "No. We did not know you were with Lucy and her dad. How long has this been going on?"

"I found out she had something of a relationship with my mother a year and a half ago." He thought he was the ultimate spy, but they'd all been playing him. He was still that dumbass kid in the trailer park. Still a bit of trash his mother forgot to sweep away because everyone knew she liked to make a mess. "She actually got me to reach out to her."

Devi's head nuzzled his neck. Like she could sense how upset he was. His sweetness.

"She's excellent undercover. Like she was born for it," Lou admitted and then stepped forward. "Hey, you will not go for each other's eyes. Come on, guys."

"They'll just grow back," Kala said, words laced with venom.

"I'll string yours up and decorate my cabin with them," Lucy promised.

"Or we could figure out what's going on," Cooper offered.

But they were off again. Kala got Lucy in a headlock, but Lucy flipped her, narrowly missing the end table and its fussy doily.

"You're surprisingly calm for a man who recently realized the Agency has been watching him all along," Cooper pointed out. "Shouldn't you be grabbing that go bag rather than letting TJ pilfer it? I was a little worried I would have to stop you once I realized Lucy was here. You didn't know."

"Nope." He should feel worse about looking like a fool in front of his brother, but Devi was practically purring in his arms. She rubbed her cheek against his. "And I would run but I would have to carry her out with me, and I've already had to replace her clothes once this month."

She snorted. "You did not replace my clothes. You bought me some new ones. Trust me. Your wallet would feel it if you replaced my clothes."

"It's time," Lou said. "They're going for soft spots now. I do not want to be the reason Kenz has to give her sister a kidney. Besides, they'll be here soon, and we have to deal with that. It would be better to put an end to it before the knives come out."

"Who is they?" Zach asked. "Am I about to be arrested?"

Devi sat up and scrambled off his lap. She faced her cousin and looked like a sexy goddess in her robe and nothing else. Her hair was wild and eyes slightly wicked. "Kala, you are not having Zach arrested."

Kala was currently back on her feet, trying to land a punch.

Lucy was good at evading. "She's not having Zach arrested. She'll be too busy in the emergency room. Though you'll have to find one. I'm planning on feeding your dead body to the pigs. Wait. I wouldn't want them to ingest all that bile."

"I'm going in." Lou reached into her backpack and came out with a water bottle. The spray kind.

"You're the one who's about to be in need of socialized medicine," Kala vowed.

"I'm serious." Devi wasn't backing down. "You are not taking him. He has work to do. I don't care what kind of oppy thing you're running."

Kala swiped out with her leg, catching Lucy's and sending her to the ground. "Oppy thing? I was trying to find you, damn it." She pounced, pinning Lucy. "I was worried about you, but here you are playing sex games in a barn."

"In my barn?" Lucy's gaze turned Devi's way. "Where the innocent animals are? What is wrong with you? Hey, Coop. Good to see you. Sad you have such awful taste in women."

"Well, I was taking your dad's advice," Zach shot back. "He helped me make the spanking bench. I should have asked why the vet knew so much about furniture building."

"Eww," Lucy said, bringing her knee up to catch Kala in the crotch.

"Way to confirm your dad's here," Kala shot back with a wince. "The good news is he can build your coffin."

"No. Bad Kala. No." Lou moved in, spraying her bestie with the water.

Kala growled but she moved off Lucy. "Lou, I told you that's rude."

"Yeah, Lou, don't be rude," Lucy said in a singsong, sure to frustrate Kala tone.

Lou turned the water bottle on her. "Bad Lucy."

"Hey." Lucy scrambled to her feet. "What the hell?"

Devi grinned as she turned to Lou. "Can I try it?"

"Not a good idea. Lou is trained." Cooper moved to the center of the room and looked the women over. "You two need to chill the fuck out because the Canadians are on their way. We need to get ready for a meeting, and that means keeping everyone's cover."

Zach stood because this was news to him. "The Canadians?"

Kala seemed to sober at the thought. "Yeah, how do you think we found you? Ben Parker has been looking for you. Zach, that is. Though I suspect he used Devi being missing as another starting point."

"The last time I saw Parker, he was still upset with Miss Magenta." Did everyone know where he was? Because it was hard to believe that if Henry Flanders knew, Big Tag didn't, and what was the game? It was obvious Big Tag was playing a long one.

"Miss Magenta, gag." Lucy said.

"It's better than Lacey Rook. You sound like some chick with an OnlyFans," Kala shot back.

But now that he understood all the relationships, Zach got Lucy's name. "Her dad went by John Bishop. She used Rook instead. Both chess references."

"Very good, Zach. I wasn't going to be a pawn." Lucy straightened her shirt. "And now I need to call my dad since apparently we're hosting the Canadians. It would have been nice if someone told me they were here."

"It would have been nice if you were never born," Kala shot back and then held up her hands because Lou was serious about the water bottle. "Sorry. I can be professional." She turned to Zach. "Miss Magenta and Ben Parker have made up and are working together well now. It's why he agreed to help us out. We couldn't look for you with Agency contacts because they would report back and be surprised when we don't arrest you. At least that's what we thought. Now I wonder how much my dad isn't telling me."

"The Agency doesn't know," Lucy admitted. "I mean they know I'm working on Disrupt Europe, but I'm hunting a terrorist with ties there. They don't know that I found the bombmaker, and they certainly don't know Dad and I are working with Zach. Hopefully your friend doesn't feel the need to update the Agency."

"Parker is going a little rogue on this op," Cooper admitted.

"Kind of like we are," Lou said. "There's a reason the whole team isn't here. We're doing this without Big Tag and Charlotte. I don't think Ben's going to rat us out."

"You found her? You made contact with her?" Zach felt his heart threaten to seize. They were missing the big point.

Devi's hand found his. "Your mom is here?"

"No, she's in South America, but she's coming here," Lucy explained. "That's what I was working on this afternoon. My mom made contact with her. She's been living with an underground group in Argentina. They call themselves climate warriors. They do things like make it hard and costly for companies to log in certain places, and I don't like to think about what they've done to convince certain governments to change their policies. Pretty sure they know how to blackmail a politician."

"Your mom is involved?" How far was the Agency taking this

whole familial thing?

"Yes, but not the way you would think. Some of these underground groups are focused on the environment. They're activists. Some, over time, turn to more criminal pursuits, and that's when my mom starts asking questions," Lucy explained. "She's got a lot of pull in that community. A few years ago, one of my parents' friends had a daughter who got involved in a bad group. My mom pushed my dad to help her find the kid and he talked to Big Tag, and we've been working with the CIA ever since."

Kala put a hand to her heart as though it was strained. "My own father betrayed me."

Lucy ignored her. "My dad said he thought someone was in town. He worried it was the Agency looking for Zach. He was going to do a review of all the CCTVs coming in and out of the village."

Devi moved in front of him. "My uncle won't let them take Zach."

They all looked at her like she was naïve. Damn, if he'd known how one session would change Devi's mind, he would have convinced her to play with him that first night. It felt good to have her on his side.

It was dangerous for her. If the Canadians were here, there was a chance they would want to get on the Agency's good side, and an excellent way of doing that was turning him in.

"Your uncle will do what's best for the op," Lucy replied, though not unkindly. "I mean I don't think he'll leave Zach there to rot, but if it comes to it and we have to choose saving the world and saving Zach Reed in the short term, his ass is sitting in a prison for a while."

"I'm going to turn myself in when this is all over," Zach said. "That was always the plan. I made a deal with Kala."

Devi turned, and she was staring at him like she'd never seen him before. "Turn yourself in?"

Oh, he fucked up again. He reached for her hands. "Yes. I've done some things I need to make right, and turning myself in is what I have to do."

Kala's eyes rolled. "Like I'm going to keep you to that, but we do have to deal with the Canadians, and that means I have a role to play." She looked to Lucy. "Are you going to fuck me over?"

"I'll fuck you up, but I won't fuck you over," Lucy admitted.

"Are you going to pretend to be your better half and make Parker think you're not all weakhearted girl for Coop? I take it he wasn't invited to the wedding."

"You can't turn yourself in," Devi said quietly.

He pulled her close and wrapped his arms around her, not quite sure what to say.

"No, he wasn't, and how the hell do you know all that?" Kala asked. "Not the wedding. The whole Kenz and Parker thing. We've kept that out of the reports."

"Oh, I know how she knows." Lou slipped the water bottle back into her pack. "Big Tag feels the need to gossip. Henry is the only one in his life besides Aunt Charlotte who has the clearance to actually hear his stories, so he talks to Henry."

Lucy nodded. "Dad gets sad and lonely when Mom's not around, so he gets chatty with me. I looked Parker up. He's hot. Way to go, Kenz."

"He's a douchebag," Kala complained.

"You think everyone is a douchebag," Lucy countered.

"Are they going to take me home?" Devi asked.

It would be for the best, and he was a selfish bastard to not turn her over right this second. Instead, he breathed in her scent. "Not unless you want to go."

"I think I'd like to stay a while if only to make sure you don't do something dumb."

And to explore this thing between them. Thing. What a stupid word. This miracle that seemed to be going on between them. He called it that because he never expected to feel this way.

TJ strode back in, a big piece of beef jerky in hand. And a couple of kittens clinging to his pants. He wasn't sure TJ even knew they were there. "Thanks, Zach. I was dying. So what's happening? Are we bunking down here?"

Lucy's eyes had gone almost comically wide. "Is that meat you're eating in my home, TJ Taggart?"

TJ shoved it down his throat so fast. He was still trying to chew when he shook his head. "Nope. All plant based. Yup."

The kittens were climbing TJ like a tree.

Lou moved in and carefully pulled one off him, her face going soft. "Oh, they're so cute."

There was a knock on the door, and Lucy moved to open it.

"Maybe we should go change." Zach wanted to get her alone. Even if they did nothing more than talk about what was going to happen next. Hell, he didn't know what was happening next.

He noticed Cooper had his gun at his side, and Kala did the same, both staring at the door. He should have been doing that, too, but he'd gotten soft. So fucking soft.

"Uh, guys, I think something's on my back," TJ said quietly, staying still. "Is this like Australia where everything wanted to kill me?"

Devi snorted her brother's way. "It's like a shelter where you're a perfect cat climbing toy. Come here, baby. You don't want to play with my stinky brother."

"I'm not stinky," her brother protested.

"Guys, it's my dad," Lucy announced. "And it looks like he's been hunting. Game faces on."

She opened the door and Arthur was there. Henry. Henry was there. It was plainly obvious that he'd been hiding a lot because the man was suddenly a predator. Gone was the mild-mannered vet who gave good advice and gently took care of all creatures great and small.

In his place stood an operative. And a pissed one at that.

He had also dragged two bodies to the porch. Some dude Zach hadn't met before and Ben Parker. Damn. He hoped the guy wasn't dead.

"We have a problem," Henry announced.

Yes, they definitely did, and it was getting bigger by the moment.

Chapter Twelve

Devi stepped out into the hallway freshly dressed and cleaned up because apparently despite the man's lifestyle, Henry Flanders was deeply disturbed by young women running around without undies. Even though he'd turned to Zach and congratulated him for following his advice.

She intended to figure out what that advice had been. She meant to ask Zach about it when they were alone, but he'd been busy helping Henry secure the Canadians, who were not dead like she worried in the beginning. She hadn't gotten a good look at them, but she'd recognized Ben Parker's golden hair. Kenz would be so pissed off if her honey was murdered.

She glanced down the hall and noted that TJ was standing guard on the bedroom Lacey used. Her brother was leaning against the wall and gnawing on what looked like a protein bar. Poor baby. This job had obviously been hard on her brother. "You okay?"

He looked up and gave her a grin. "Better now that you're dressed." He sobered. "You okay? Zach's treating you well? Mom told me not to worry, but I worry."

Like she had to every single time he walked into the field. She moved into her brother's space and gave him a long hug. "I'm fine.

Well, as fine as I can be. I'm glad you're here."

"I'm glad I'm here, except for the food parts," he admitted.

She chuckled and moved away. They should talk. "Is Dad okay?"

"He's freaked out, but Mom's working on him. She likes Zach. A lot," her brother replied. "You know Mom. She thinks this is one more adventure and we'll handle it. She's certain we can work something out. I'm not so sure. I'm worried you're going to get your heart broken."

She worried about that, too, but here she was. "I've decided to treat the whole thing like a summer fling. I know it's going to end, but I want to enjoy it while I can. I know who he is and what he's involved in. I'm not falling in love with him."

TJ's eyes rolled. "Sure. Tell yourself that. Be careful. I like Zach, but you're my sister. You'll always have me on your side."

She loved her brother so much. "Tell me what the spy kids are doing. I take it the Canadians are still napping."

TJ peeked into the room. "Yep. I don't know what Henry gave them but it's working. And that dude is way stronger than he looks. Parker's a beast, and Henry dragged his ass along. I think it's safe to say Henry's going to call Big Tag and we're all in trouble. Also, he's not your uncle. Call him Big Tag. You can be my sister, but we're not related to Uncle Ian in front of the Canadians. And…"

She knew this part. "Kala is Kara, and she's going to have to be the Kara that Kenzie plays. It's all confusing. I take it she's going to pretend to not be married to Coop. Are you and Lou together in this alternate reality we find ourselves in?"

How difficult was it to always play a role? No wonder the spy kids went hard when they were home.

How hard had it been for Zach to keep all his secrets?

"Yeah." TJ's voice went low. "A few weeks ago, Parker came to Dallas to find Kara, who you should know he calls Maggie. For Miss Magenta. He found Kala instead of Kenz, and she played nice with him to the point that she let him kiss her."

"Oh, poor Kala." Any physical intimacy would be a lot for her cousin to handle. Oh, not from her little circle, but definitely with a guy like Parker. "She did it for her sister."

TJ nodded. "She did. Kenz has it bad for this guy. Anyway, Cooper walked in and was forced to throw his fit and make some speech about how she was Parker's now, and Kala was able to switch herself out with Kenzie for a date that night. Parker knows something went down in Virginia, but he doesn't know Huisman took Kala. Only you."

She nodded. "Okay. I'll keep my mouth shut as much as possible and pretend my cousin isn't married to Coop. Now, tell me what the real plan is. Are you taking me home?"

"She was worried," TJ said. "Like sick worried about you. Zach wouldn't tell her where you were."

"He let me talk to her," Devi pointed out. "Mom is chill, and she didn't know where I was."

"Yeah, well it's been a while since Mom was in the field, and our cousin has been through a lot in the last couple of months," TJ offered. "I also think she got some feeling off her dad. Something that told her there's more going on, and she doesn't like to be left out."

"You think Un…Big Tag knew about Henry and Lucy and didn't tell anyone?"

"I think if Big Tag suspected something was up with Zach, he would play it close to the vest unless he honestly thought Zach would hurt one of us. I don't think he knew everything but he had suspicions, and he and Henry work well together. They back each other up. Henry's the only guy who knows what he's going through. So I would bet we'll have more guests soon."

And she would have to be ready for them. To play her role. Well, around the Canadians at least. She was sure her uncle would have a lot to say behind closed doors.

She was about to turn for the stairs when she decided to ask her brother the real question she wanted the answer to. "What do you think of Zach?"

TJ sighed. "I think he's in a lot of trouble. I wish he wasn't dragging my sister into it, but he's also been a good friend to this team. He lied but he never sold us out, and he had chances to. He's saved everyone at least once. Took a bullet to the chest for…"

There was only one reason her brother would hesitate. "Tasha."

The round raised scar on his chest. He hadn't mentioned he'd saved Tasha. Taken a bullet for her.

She was not going to be jealous. Nope. She was having a wild fling and so there was nothing to be jealous about.

"Yes," her brother agreed. "It was Tash, but he was the only one there and I think he would have tried to save any of us."

But Tash was special. Tash had been his dream.

And that didn't matter because she was only with him for a few weeks. A month or two. She was enjoying Zach. She wasn't in love with him.

Even if it felt like she was. "TJ, don't make it weird. I'm beyond happy Zach saved my cousin. I adore Tash, and the thought of a world without her makes me want to cry. It's a good thing."

TJ smiled like he finally understood. "Cool. I was worried because he had a thing for her, but we all get crushes. No one finds the right person the first time out."

Well, except for TJ and Lou and Coop and Kala. Oh, they'd screwed things up royally and cost themselves years, but it had always been Lou for TJ and Coop for Kala. Come to think of it, her cousin Carys had known she loved Aidan and Tristan when she was young.

Devi had some crushes but certainly no one she'd longed for years to be with. No one she would have taken a bullet for. She had never been in love with anyone the way she was…the way Zach seemed to have loved her cousin.

Nope. She wasn't going down that very awful road.

Besides, she had a mission. Or at least she was part of it until her uncle showed up and hauled her home.

"I'm not saying he's the right person. He's the right now person," she said, forcing a grin on her face. Like this was all about sex and it was good. Which it was.

"We're ready to start the debrief." Zach stood at the end of the hall, a grim expression on his face.

Because he'd heard her say it was only sex. Well, she'd told him. He hadn't walked into this afternoon with sweet promises from her.

TJ winced. "Well, let them know I'm making sure the Canadians don't lose their shit when they wake up. Which should be soon."

Zach moved in, looking into the room. "Parker's awake."

She heard a muffled curse, and she was shamelessly curious. Kara wasn't her cousin. She was TJ's sister, but Kara was just a chick on TJ's team. She could be Zach's whatever they were, but she wasn't related to any of her other relatives. There. She had this spy stuff down now.

She moved in behind Zach. There were two people laid out on Lacey's bed. Which was bigger than theirs, so she'd been holding out on them. There was plenty of room for kittens in here.

Also, Ben Parker was hot. So freaking hot.

Zach frowned her way like he could read her mind.

He was hotter. Way hotter.

Zach growled under his breath but turned toward the big Canadian. "Parker, I am not the one who drugged you, and don't blame Kara either."

Parker shoved himself to a sitting position and held his zip tied wrists up. "Of course she didn't. Who do you think I've been working with? We've been looking for you, but she has to do it undercover or the Agency will expect her to bring you in. What the fuck are you doing, man? Is that TJ's sister? I think I met her at that club last year."

The Hideout. They met briefly, though she wasn't supposed to ask a lot of questions. She gave him a wave. "It's Devi. Hi."

"She's here because Huisman wants her," Zach said gruffly. "She's in protective custody."

"Why would Huisman want her? I know why he wants Lou." Parker let Zach cut through the zip ties.

"Because her last name is Taggart," Zach replied in a no-nonsense tone.

But nonsense was fun. Also, she wasn't sure what Zach was trying to hide. There was zero way this man didn't know they were doing it. She could see Kala maybe telling him Devi Taggart was only valuable for her last name, but she'd been told Kenzie usually worked with Parker, and she would have talked. "And the whole sleeping-with-the-bombmaker's-son thing."

Zach frowned her way. "Really?"

She shrugged. "He's going to find out when we sleep together later tonight. Or did I hurt your feelings so much with the truth that you're going to withhold that glorious cock of yours?"

"I did not need to hear that," TJ said with a groan.

Parker stretched his big body and rolled his friend over. "She's right. I knew. Maggie and I have been open and honest these last few weeks, and that's why Tim and I are here and probably going to get fired for working outside of parameters. Come on, man. It wasn't that big a dose. Sorry. He's one of the best techs in the world, but he doesn't normally get hit with tranqs. Unfortunately, I do. Where is Maggie? I assume if you're here and TJ's here, she's here, too. She came."

Whoof. He said that last bit with a weird longing, and the person who was here was so not what he was longing for. She hoped. What if they had it all wrong and he was a total masochist and liked Kala instead of Kenzie? She wished Dais and Bri were here because they could discuss this whole situation over margaritas and have Nate or Zach pick them up so they didn't have to drink responsibly. But then she looked at Parker's friend. Who was super familiar. Irritatingly familiar. Well, at least she knew how they'd identified her. "That's Tim."

Zach nodded. "I think that's what he called him. Kara is downstairs, but I should warn you, they apparently needed a pilot and…"

"McKay." Ben sighed. "Then I'm going to find out if she's playing me, aren't I? I don't know if I buy his whole I can have her since she's not worth the trouble act. He was in love with her."

He was a good judge of character because Coop was desperately in love with one of the Karas. She waved it off. They could deal with that themselves. She had questions. "I mean that's Tim. The guy who saved me from the creepy dude who drugged my drink when I went to the bathroom."

"What?" Zach asked,

"What?" Her brother left his post and had that deeply worried expression he got whenever she did something super dumb. Or traveled with Daisy.

Parker sent a slightly sympathetic look Zach's way. "Sorry, man. Thought she would tell you. It happened earlier today. We were following another player in this game of ours. We found him today in a pub in town, and he was chatting up Devi."

"Eww, you make it sound like I was flirting," she argued. "Which I was not. He was my dad's age at least. Nope. I have all the troubled man romantic tropes I can handle right now. I do not need to add an age gap in there."

"Someone drugged your drink and you didn't mention it to me?" The words were carefully said. Like he had to think about them.

Oh, that was him being totally pissed at her because she hadn't given him the chance to protect her. It was a Dom thing. And she had her reasons. "It would have freaked you out. Although now I can see it also might have made you wonder about who was in town and you might have gotten us out of here before my brother found me."

"Yes, exactly. I would have found his ass on CCTV and ID'd him," Zach said, "But that is not the point. The point is someone threatened you and you didn't bother to mention it to me. Or Lacey."

Lacey was Lacey again. So many names. How did they keep them all straight? They must do some serious memory work in spy school. "I didn't think it was a big deal, and he didn't technically threaten me."

"If he drugged your drink, consider yourself threatened," her brother said with a little self-righteousness.

Like he never got accidently dosed and stuff. Rude. "Well, I didn't drink it because Tim told me not to. I bet he's not even English."

"No." Parker seemed way calmer than before. He seemed to be enjoying the show now that he knew Miss Magenta was somewhere in the house. "He's Canadian, and honestly, I'm surprised that accent worked on you. He wasn't supposed to make contact. His accent is way worse than he thinks. It's awful, but he went off script when he realized our target was trying to drug you." He gave Zach a man-to-man look. "I believe it was some kind of roofie meant to make her compliant so he could get her out of the pub. I took a look at the CCTVs around town after I alerted TJ's team that I found his sister. Somehow they narrowed it down to Wales, and they were in Cardiff waiting for word. He caught sight of her after the woman she was with left. I suspect she's some sort of operative, but I haven't identified her yet. We were doing that when the old dude showed up. What the hell? One minute he knocked on our door and was polite and seemed like a sweet older man. And then he was a fucking serial killer."

"You're not dead," Zach said with a long-suffering sigh. "I would bet trying to look into Lacey is exactly what brought Arthur to your doorstep."

"Handler, then," Parker said as though he'd suspected all along. "I could have used a heads-up, Taggart."

TJ gave him a shrug. "Dude, we had no idea. When you gave us

Devi's location we came right out, and let me tell you I wish I'd had some intel on what was happening here. I can't unhear some of that. Luckily, I didn't see anything. Well, until my sister sat down on Zach's lap and she wasn't wearing underwear. It almost set me off lunch."

She rolled her eyes. "Nothing sets you off lunch."

"Tofu does." TJ looked to Parker. "Dude, did you bring some beef? Maybe a burger or two? There is no meat here."

"We're going to talk about what happened in town today." Zach leaned over, whispering in her ear while Parker and TJ talked about the lack of animal flesh. "You're mine. My sub. You don't get to withhold that kind of information from me."

"Hypocrite," she whispered back.

"And that's ten more," he said, standing behind her. "I don't care, Dev. I don't care that you want to pretend we're not really together. That's okay. I'll take whatever you're willing to give me because I am pathetically in love with you, but you cannot keep that kind of information from me."

"How do they make like cakes and stuff? Is there no bread here?" Parker sounded a bit panicked.

Boys. She leaned back against him, not wanting to think about the fact that he said he loved her. Was in love with her. "I'm sorry, Zachary. I thought it was some random guy hitting on me, and that happens when I go into bars alone. I thought it might be different in a small town, but he was a tourist. I handled it and didn't get hurt."

"Sweetness, something's wrong because I believe that was the man the Canadians were following. Did you hear him say the target drugged your drink? If they were following him, then he has something to do with Huisman."

She hated that man. She turned and put her hands on Zach's waist. "I'm sorry. I didn't think it was serious. And Tim's accent isn't as bad as that man says it is. I found him believable."

That was the moment Tim woke, his eyes going wide, and he saw Zach and screamed.

"Hey, you're fine." Parker shook his head. "We're with friendlies. Chill, buddy. At least I think he's friendly, but he's also got an actual Red Notice out on him, not to mention all the people looking for him in North America."

Tim took a long breath and sat up. His eyes widened when he caught sight of Devi, and he went back into his perfectly serviceable British accent. "Oh, hey, mate, uhm, good to see you here."

Okay, it was pretty terrible now that she listened to him. "You can drop it Canada Tim. Also, you're a rat-fink weasel."

Tim let Parker use Zach's knife to free his hands. "Hey, I'm not a weasel. That asshole did drug your drink. I was hoping maybe you would be in a grateful mood and we could, you know, have a drink or something. I mean a drink drink, not a drugged drink. I would not do that to a lady."

Zach growled.

"Dude, he will kill you," Parker warned.

"Or I will," TJ promised. "Though I have to say I'll leave this to Zach. Cool thing is now he's the one who has to beat up the assholes who hurt you."

"Beat up?" She was surprised. Her brother was practically perfect. He never did the don't-touch-my-sister thing the way her friends' brothers sometimes did.

TJ seemed more relaxed now that he knew the Canadians weren't going to try to shoot their way out. "It wasn't many but I handled it when I had to, and now Zach can do it."

Until he wasn't around anymore. No one said it aloud, but she could feel Zach's turn.

"We should get downstairs. They want a full debrief. I think you'll find Arthur is concerned," Zach offered.

"You gonna tell me who he really is because he's not a fucking rural vet," Parker said, helping Tim up. He straightened his shirt, and she didn't miss the way he looked at himself in the mirror, trying to make sure his hair wasn't messy.

She could have told him a little mess didn't make him less hot.

But her Dom had enough stimulation for one day.

Zach held his hands up. "That's his story to tell. I thought he was exactly who he said he was until about an hour ago when my old team showed up on my doorstep. Now before we go down there, could you tell me who your target was? If he was after Devi, I have to think Huisman sent him. How the fuck does he know where I am? I've been careful. Not even her family knew where she was until today."

"Well, Bri and Daisy knew she was in Wales because she told

them," TJ helpfully pointed out.

Tim looked chipper again. "Hah, told you they didn't figure it out on their own. We got lucky. We've been following this target weirdly for other reasons. Ray White is known to work for some of the worst cartels in the world and has several warrants in Canada."

She felt Zach go still, the air around him suddenly charged with emotion, but his expression went cold. "My father."

Parker nodded. "Yes, though I didn't realize the connection until Manny separated you from your team and we all took a second look at you. The bombmaker is your mother, Shannon Reed, and Manny recently hired your father to find her. He decided that the best way to bring her in was to have you. I suspect he decided the best way to bring you in was Devi. She's on Manny's radar now. You have to be careful. He'll kill her if he can. Like he tried to get Tasha. Now he'll come after her. He didn't realize what he had all those weeks ago. He thought his plant just brought her along to control Maggie. At least that's what I got from the reports, but I suspect what I read is heavily redacted. The key is that he knows she's your weakness, and he will use it against you."

Zach's arms came up to clench her shoulders, but he didn't say a word.

Yes, her Dom had way too much stimulation, and it looked like the day wasn't over.

* * * *

Zach stood in the dining room, the small table serving as their conference room. Too small table. Everything felt too small right now. Including his skin.

I'm not saying he's the right person. He's the right now person.

It hurt. Ached. The words reminded him that none of this was going to be easy, and he had zero idea what the hell he was doing. Of course he was the right-now guy. He didn't have a fucking future.

"So you're the Lou of the team?" Devi was chatting with Parker and Tim like this was all a normal, everyday business conference and not a meeting of three different intelligence teams and the rogue agent they were all hunting or working. Like she hadn't let that rogue agent fuck her like the world was going to end.

She had poured everyone tea like this was a happy afternoon gathering and not a recitation of all of his sins. And his shitastic past. If she thought he wasn't Mr. Right before, wait until she heard about his biological dad's rap sheet.

Lou sat across from Tim, TJ at her side. "It's so good to meet other techs. We don't ever get to talk."

Tim was a puppy of a man. The kid was maybe twenty-two and looked like he smelled like maple syrup. With shaggy golden brown hair, oversized glasses, and… Was that an actual pocket protector? Anyway, he was kind of the quintessential nerd. Except he didn't mind hitting on every woman in sight.

Of course Tim probably had a squeaky-clean record and parents who didn't treat his life like a revolving door in a house of horrors.

"There's a reason." Parker was all charm now that Lou was in the room. He was polite and solicitous to both women and seemed friendly with TJ. Though naturally he looked at Zach with an air of suspicion.

Where the hell was Kala? Where was Coop? If they were off doing it somewhere before they had to pretend they weren't married, he was going to punch his brother. Not Kala. She punched back.

"We get all the techs together and you start talking about how dumbass we operatives are," Parker said with the smooth smile of a player. But Zach noticed his eyes kept looking toward the door where Miss Magenta would enter.

Instead, Arthur moved in. Henry. Whatever they were calling him.

He stood in the doorway, cold blue eyes taking in the Canadians. "Gentlemen, you can call me Mr. Bishop."

Parker sat back, and it was easy to see he was trying to figure out how to handle the older man. "Well, you're certainly not Dr. Arthur Beddoe. I can see why you picked the cover. Rural vet with a simple website. No real web presence. I suspect your target didn't pay much attention to your work and didn't go into town often, so he wouldn't run into the real Dr. Beddoe."

"And yet he seemed to deal with a bunch of health problems with the animals." Zach's head was still reeling when it came to Henry and his daughter. "I helped him vaccinate goats earlier today. Or I guess he faked that."

"The goats are perfectly safe from clostridium perfringens types

C and D, as well as tetanus," Henry announced. "And I did handle the horse's leg earlier this week. I have a vet I know who walked me through the whole procedure. I assure you no animals were harmed in the working of this op. My wife would have my head."

"Target?" Devi asked.

"He's talking about me. Mr. Bishop and his partner, Lacey Rook—almost certainly not her real name, but we won't be using many of those today—were instructed to investigate me," Zach explained. "I apparently wasn't as good at hiding my evil ways as I thought I was."

"Hey," Henry began, his gaze shifting to sympathy. "We all know you're not evil, Zachary. I know this is going to come as a surprise, but Mr. Lemon didn't ask me to investigate you because he thought you were bad. He thought you were getting in over your head and wanted someone to watch your back since you wouldn't let your team do it."

"I know his name is Ian," Parker said. "We don't have to use all the ridiculous Agency names. Let's go with first names if we're worried about being identified, though I would like to point out that Ian knows pretty much everything about me, and it doesn't feel fair."

"Then you should be better about hiding things," Henry said, taking the chair at the head of the table. "I don't like the games either, but sometimes you're compelled to play. Sometimes you don't have a choice."

Because like Big Tag's daughters, Henry's wanted to play, and he felt the need to watch over her. He wasn't so sure, though, about Big Tag's reasons for investigating him.

"So are you planning on letting the Agency know we're here?" Parker asked the question casually, but there was no mistaking the undertone.

"He's not calling anyone." Kala walked in. She stopped at the door and managed a soft smile. "Hey, Ben. Thanks for the intel. I needed to find Devi Taggart, and you came through. It means a lot to me. I'm sorry about the rude welcome. I didn't tell Mr. Bishop you were in town. I didn't want to blow your cover."

"It's fine. I would have made contact sometime tonight anyway." Parker straightened his shoulders, and his eyes seemed to eat her up. "I'm glad we're working together properly now. You look good,

Maggie."

She looked like her twin. He'd never truly considered how good an actress Kala was, but there were Kenzie Taggart vibes in the air now. She sat down beside Parker. "You do, too." She sighed. "You need to know that Cooper is on his way in. We needed a pilot. TJ can barely drive a car."

"Rude," Lou complained. Her eyes were wide behind her glasses as though she was waiting for the drama to start.

"I don't love to drive," TJ admitted.

Kala ignored him. "Also, the four of us going on vacation together won't cause any real suspicion in our handlers. They're used to it."

"So why did you need to find Devi Taggart outside of Agency overview?" Parker asked and then shook his head. "Scratch that. I get it. You don't want Zach there arrested. But I thought you didn't want the big guy to know what you were doing. I'm trying to get a lay of the land here."

Cooper chose that moment to enter, and he had forgotten to button his top button. He looked like he'd rolled around for a while with his brand-new wife. Dumb ass. Henry's eyes closed briefly as though he was holding back on the lecture.

Parker's eyes widened, taking in the state of Cooper's shirt.

"Parker," Cooper said with a frown.

"McKay," Parker returned with an equally dour expression.

Tim leaned over and whispered Devi's way. "Cooper liked Maggie and for a long time Ben thought Maggie was with Cooper, but she was all like no, eww, we pretend for ops and I like you. But Cooper got all freaked out when she almost died. Like soap opera hero freaked out."

"I did not." Cooper frowned Tim's way. "And you weren't even there."

"But the security cam footage was," Tim replied, utterly nonplussed that a six-foot, five-inch Navy pilot looked like he was going to eat him for lunch. He was too busy flirting with Devi. "It was a lot, and Ben was super sad because all he thinks about is Maggie."

"Hey," Parker began.

Devi grinned, turning that high-wattage charm on Tim. "No, tell me more, Tim. I'm new to this whole spy thing. I got involved with

Zach at a lifestyle club. I thought he was an out-of-work student my brother knew. He was trying to get a job at my uncle's restaurant. Washing dishes, but nope. He turns out to be a big old spy, and now some weird doctor person wants to murder me because my last name is Taggart. So I'm interested in how everything works. Maggie loves Ben now and not Cooper, who she just played around with."

At least she had the story down. She was having way too much fun with this. He knew she would want to call Daisy and Brianna as soon as possible.

"We don't need to get into this." Henry valiantly tried to stop the snowball that was starting to roll downhill.

"I don't think they're doing it yet," Tim whispered her way. "If they are, then Ben is awfully uptight, but now it looks like Cooper's getting some and this could become a fight."

"I am not with Cooper," Kala stated, sounding more like herself.

"We are not together," Cooper agreed. "I'm over that stupid crush."

"Yes, he is." Lucy entered with a breezy smile. She looked Cooper up and down and tsked, her British accent perfect again. "And I did not properly dress you after our reunion." She rebuttoned Cooper's shirt. "Sorry about that."

All of the American eyes went straight to Kala, who was probably about to commit murder.

"Sorry. Cooper and I worked together several times before. We haven't seen each other in ages, but let me tell you the chemistry is still there." Lucy ran an arm through Cooper's and leaned against him like he was her beloved boyfriend. "At least he won't have to sleep on the couch."

"Fuck me," Henry said under his breath.

But Parker seemed to buy it. He relaxed and leaned over, whispering something in Kala's ear that made her go pale. Still, she smiled gamely and seemed to agree.

"If you two lovebirds could sit down, I think we have a lot to talk about," Kala said in her most professional tone. "As for why I left my handler out of it, well, I've come to suspect he leaves his team out of some key decisions, so it felt like fair play. Mr. Bishop, are you or are you not working under direct orders from my handler?"

"I wouldn't call them orders," Henry replied. "I don't work for

Ian. I work with him from time to time, and I trust him. My operative, Lacey, and I were in the perfect position to work our way into Zach's world."

He could guess what that position had been. "You were already in my mother's world."

Lucy laced her fingers through Cooper's and dragged him to the table, sitting them together across from Kala, who would likely play in her entrails soon. "Mr. Bishop and I have connections in certain underground movements, including a couple Shannon Reed is involved in. My specific mission for the last couple of years has been to investigate Disrupt Europe. We've worked with MI6 trying to track down the people who attempted to assassinate several members of Europe's royal families a few years back. That was when we became aware of the bombmaker. It took us some time and another one of our associates to confirm the identity of her. At this point we believed the two missions were not connected. We knew Zach was involved in some way, but we didn't suspect Shannon Reed was his mother."

"Like Lacey explained, in the beginning we were tasked with figuring out what Zach was doing and if he was a direct threat to Ian's team," Henry continued.

"Threat?" Parker stuck on the word.

It was time for his confession. "When I was assigned as the military liaison for Ian's team, my real mission was to report back to my Army bosses and a certain contingent at the Agency who did not like the thought of Ian being in charge of a team. His team is considered experimental, and some people thought it was Ian's way of acquiring power. I was sent in to find the dirt so they could break up the team while keeping the assets they wanted. Like Kara and Lou. They would have quietly put Ian and Charlotte out to pasture."

"Is it experimental because they're married?" Parker asked. "They are married, right? I think he's referred to the redhead as his wife before."

It was as close to the truth as he wanted to get. "Yes, though there are other ways the team bucks Agency traditions. Operatives don't work with the same teams. It tends to lead to drama."

"It leads to us caring about the people around us," Lou huffed. "And not sacrificing them for an op. Which is why they think we'll fail."

Henry's brow rose. "I've heard you don't have that problem, Mr. Parker."

That caught Zach's attention. A few months back Parker had allowed Lou to be in a dangerous position in order to confirm his theory that Huisman was working with a German mercenary. Oh, he saved her after he got the bad guy to fess up, but it had been a close thing.

If Henry knew that, he was talking to Ian far more often and with more frankness than Zach had imagined. If Ian told him, then Ian trusted Henry.

Ian knew. Oh, he might not have known all of it, but he'd known. Zach hadn't fooled him, and he'd likely wrecked his whole fucking life for nothing. He could have taken it all to Ian and maybe he would have come out of it with his career and freedom intact.

Or Ian would have tossed him to the wolves, and he would already be in jail.

"I've explained how badly I feel about what happened in Dallas. I would never put Lou in danger again. I was…desperate," Parker said with a long sigh. "Believe me, Maggie and I have had this conversation, and I have apologized to Lou. That day taught me a lot about who I am and who I want to be, who I've allowed Manny to turn me into."

"From what I understand, you were childhood friends with Dr. Huisman," Henry began.

If he was this close to Ian, he would already know the story, but Zach knew a lot of operatives would rather hear the story from the person than read a report. There were so many things that couldn't be put into reports. Body language. The way a person spoke. How his eyes tightened before he started, as though he knew this would be painful.

Parker nodded. "We were good friends when we were young. Then his father was killed and he went to live in Montreal with his grandfather. When we met up again, he was different, but I didn't know how different."

"He blames Ian for his father's death," Kala explained, her eyes on where Lucy had a hand on Cooper's arm. "We believe his grandfather taught him this despite the fact that it's verifiable Ian was not working for the Agency at the time and was not in Canada. It was a rogue CIA operative who killed the elder Dr. Huisman."

"He wasn't rogue at the time," Cooper corrected. "But that's not the point. What Kara is trying to say is Huisman is a dangerous nut bag with a delusional complex when it comes to our handlers."

"He's beyond dangerous," Parker interrupted. "Don't dismiss him as crazy. He's very functional and knows how to bring people to his side. There's a reason he hasn't been arrested yet. I feel certain Ian had enough on him after what happened in Winchester."

Kala nodded. "The Agency wants to wait and see what happens."

"Huisman bad." Zach was tired of waiting. "We got it. How is he connected to my father? And how did he find me?"

"We believe he had someone follow you from the house where Miss Magenta and Miss Taggart were held," Parker explained. "We tracked you going to a small private airfield, and we also have evidence of a vehicle following you. From there he would have had a tech monitor the flights going in and out. I'm sure you tried to cover your tracks, but he has billions of dollars to play with, and he doesn't mind spending them."

Henry's expression went dark. "Then my operative's cover is blown."

Lucy cursed under her breath. "I got called into a meeting. They want me in London the day after tomorrow. I wasn't supposed to meet with my Disrupt Europe contacts for another month, but yesterday they set up a meeting saying it was urgent."

He'd fucked everything up. "Lacey, I'm so sorry."

She sighed, and at least her hand wasn't on Cooper anymore. She held them together as though she needed to make sure she didn't punch anything.

"I'm sorry as well," Parker said solicitously. The man knew how to look sympathetic. "If I realized you were Agency, I certainly would have given Maggie and her team a heads-up."

"Well, next time I'll have you take pictures of who I need you to follow. I would have recognized them," Kala replied. "And taken a step back. The truth is I have to call my handler now. I thought I could take Devi out of here, but I suspect that's going to be hard at this point."

"She needs protection." Whether she cared about him or not, he wasn't going to leave her alone. "And she needs to take that protection seriously. She had a bodyguard."

"Apparently, I had more than a bodyguard. You had someone watching me, too, didn't you, Zach?" Devi accused, but her expression was more sweetly bratty than pissed off. Something about her family showing up had put her in a good mood. Despite her telling her brother she wasn't serious about him, Zach liked how comfortable she was.

"It wasn't an intelligence person." He would tell her the whole truth whenever he could. "I hired an old Army friend of mine to keep tabs on you. That was all. I think it scared the shit out of him when he caught you shimmying out of that bathroom window and walking into a trap. He has some excellent pictures of Lena escorting you into the club. The trouble was he couldn't see the gun at your back, so he wasn't sure until they dragged you out that something had gone wrong."

Kala nodded as though he explained something important. "Ah, well, there's the secondary 911 call. He didn't stick around though, did he?"

Zach shrugged. "He called me after he called the cops, and that's when I used a friend's login to follow Miss Magenta's tracker."

"But I thought he was using something to negate our trackers," Tim pointed out. "I've been trying to find a solution because if I can't keep up with Ben in the field, I'm useless."

Lou waved her hand. "I already solved it. I'll send you some specs."

Smart Lou. Tricky Lou. "I am eternally grateful for your genius."

"And I'm happy that at least one of you listened to me," Lou admitted. "Everyone else was super freaked that Huisman would turn off Kara's tracker. I had explained it to them, but did they listen? Nope."

"I did, babe," TJ said encouragingly. "And the nanites are going to be even cooler. Lou's programmed some tiny machines to organize themselves as clothes. And if you get mustard on your shirt, they clean it up for you."

"Yes, and sometimes they decide for themselves what the operative should be wearing," Kala added with a long-suffering sigh. "I'll stick to cotton, thank you. It doesn't decide it's too hot and shift to a string bikini in the middle of a restaurant patio."

"I told you it was because of the big fountain. They thought you were going swimming," Lou argued.

"I like my clothes to not think, Lou," Kala replied.

"Oh, I'm excited to play with those." Devi practically clapped her hands together like a young girl who got to visit the castle with all the princesses.

Lou gave her a grin. "I can't wait to see some designs."

"We're getting off track." Henry seemed determined to deal with the actual problems at hand. "What do we know about Ray White?"

"I can send you the dossier I've put together on him," Tim offered. "He was a small-time drug dealer in Southern California when he met Shannon Reed."

"My mother." Zach wanted to control some of this. After all, it was his history. "She was a chemistry student at Stanford, and she decided the best way to start her career was by designing new drugs. They were more potent and cheaper, and my dad connected himself to a cartel, basically pimping out my mother's skills."

"Shannon Reed, by all accounts, was brilliant," Parker said softly, more of that sympathy easing out.

"She is brilliant," Tim corrected. "I've studied what we have on her bombs, and the construction is revolutionary."

"They kill people," Zach pointed out. "In easy to cover ways."

"But there are other uses for the things she's creating." Lou looked his way. "Almost everything humans create can be used for both good and evil. Your mother has created a structure that can be used in bombs, but also potentially in engines."

"Have we thought about the applications when it comes to potential cold fusion?" Tim asked.

Lou nodded. "I dream about it at night. I would love to get my hands on one that didn't explode. So far I've only gotten to inspect the remains. I would love schematics."

"I can help you with that. I might have some of her early designs," Zach admitted. He would feel comfortable giving them to Lou. He wasn't sure about anyone else.

"That would help enormously," Lou agreed. "But I meant what I said. All technological advances have a dark side. This one might someday give us the key to limitless clean energy."

He couldn't imagine a world where the corporations allowed that.

He worried his mother's genius would always be about crime, but this wasn't some philosophical exercise. Devi's hand came over and rubbed against his forearm, and suddenly it didn't seem so terrible to be here. "I'm glad to hear that, Lou. As for my parents, they were kind of the match made in hell. My mom did her first stint in prison after I was born. My aunt quit the military so I would have a stable place to live since my father was also in prison. She got out and everything was fine until his time was up and he came looking for her."

"And he was involved with a Mexican cartel, right?" Tim asked, looking at his notes.

"Mexican and then Honduran. My father tried to play the two off each other, and it's what led to my mom deciding the heat was too much. After her last prison stint she came home for a couple of years, but he showed up again, and that was when she hit the road." He'd been young at the time and hadn't known that his brother had been born during one of those prison sentences. Born and then adopted by Alex and Eve McKay, who had no idea how the baby they were going to raise was related to Alex's best friend Ian Taggart. Zach's aunt Joyce had worked with him in the military and thought someone in Ian's orbit would be the best guardian for the nephew she would never be able to claim. "Honestly, I know very little about what he's been doing since the last time he tried to intimidate my aunt into telling him where Mom went. I was sixteen, and he set me on my ass for trying to protect her. He should see how I plan to protect the women in my life now."

"Your father moved into arms dealing, and we think we know why," Parker explained.

He could guess. "He got my mother involved. He had no talent. Everything he had he owed to what she could do, and then he inevitably screwed things up. From what I understand my mother got involved in some underground groups, specifically ones rooted in environmental activism."

"Yes, that's where I found her," Lucy acknowledged. "Though you should know she's kept quiet. I believe she was forced to build those first bombs. Or maybe she made them for her groups. Some of the groups she's involved in blow shit up to stop deforestation. Your mom's bombs are easy to use and targeted. She could have kept any loss of life down to a minimum. Actually, now that I think about it, the way the bombs are designed would also have protected the land around the blast."

Kala had a look of grudging respect on her face. "That makes sense. So Ray gets out of prison and needs some cash and can't get it himself. He goes looking for his ex because she's always been his meal ticket. When he does find her, she's building bombs for activist groups, and he sees a new way to make her pay."

Zach groaned as the truth hit him. "My father was the one who introduced her to The Jester."

Devi gasped. "Isn't that the arms dealer person Tristan pretended to be after you murdered him and let Tris think he did it? That was sweet of you, by the way. Tris needed a major ego boost."

Not the way he would describe it. "I did it so he wouldn't know I had figured out my mom worked for The Jester. I didn't realize my dad was likely the one who introduced them. We can't know she was forced. From what my aunt says my father had power over her."

"That might have been true when she was a young woman, but I assure you she's afraid of him today," Lucy explained.

"You've talked directly to her?" Parker asked.

That would be news to Zach.

"Not yet, but I have an asset on the inside of one of her groups who has." Lucy sat back, watching the Canadians.

"And we're going to trust this asset?" Kala challenged.

"Yes, we do," Henry replied. "The asset is above reproach."

He expected Kala to argue. Instead, she took a second and then nodded. "All right, we'll work from a place of trust with Bishop's asset."

Devi slid her chair closer and leaned over, whispering in his ear. "It's Henry's wife, so you can trust what he's saying. At least that's the only person I can think of who Kala wouldn't vet herself."

It was good to have his own interpreter, but Parker was watching them, and he didn't want to give away that Devi knew more than she should. So he turned slightly and kissed her like that was what she planned on doing all along.

She stiffened slightly and then his adorable brat got into it.

"Guys, come on," TJ said.

Devi sat back with a grin. "Sorry."

"So you've made up with him for lying to you?" Parker asked.

Devi shrugged. "He's good in bed."

Well, if he wanted a deeply romantic woman, perhaps he shouldn't have fallen in love with Erin Taggart's daughter. "The question now is where do we go from here? Obviously, I've fucked up Bishop's operation."

"Yes, you have, and along with it years of undercover work," Lucy said with no small amount of bitterness. "If I'm lucky I can go home and play deputy and catch speeders."

"I could only be so lucky," Henry said under his breath.

"Well, at least we know someone is going to be happy. My mother doesn't particularly like my job." Lucy sighed as though resigned. And then perked up. "Although maybe I can work with Coop again. I've spent all my time with patchouli granolas. I miss wayward pilots who make bad decisions after too much tequila. You remember that night in Cancun? I love it when terrorists go to luxury resorts."

All eyes were on Kala again. Well, the ones who knew she was Kala.

Cooper sighed and gave Lucy a halfhearted smile and patted her hand. "Yep, fun times."

"Well, I've got more fun times ahead because Disrupt might want me dead, but I'm meeting Shannon Reed tomorrow night in Liverpool," Lucy announced. "She wants me to bring her son."

So that's what she'd been doing all day. "We're going to Liverpool then."

He hoped she had a big enough place because he was almost certain they would have more guests.

Chapter Thirteen

Devi followed Zach into the beautiful townhouse in the heart of Liverpool. It was late at night by the time they'd packed up and taken care of the animals and arranged for someone else to come to the farm. The Canadians had left earlier, wanting to split up the group so they weren't as memorable.

Parker had offered to take Kala with them.

She'd explained she couldn't leave Devi until she knew the house was safe and secure. And that she fully expected her handler to show up and soon.

It hadn't been a surprise when Henry announced her uncle and the rest of the team were waiting for them at the safe house in Liverpool.

Henry had worked overtime to keep his daughter and Kala apart. He'd managed to plan their retreat so they left as the Canadians did, and there was no time to address the fact that Lucy was pretending to be Cooper's lover. Then they broke up into groups, traveled via train, and met up here at this god-awful time of night.

She wished Zach didn't have that hollow look in his eyes.

"Tequila?" Kala asked as she set down her bag. "He doesn't even like tequila."

Lucy tossed her bag down as well and turned on Kala. "Well, I had to do something since you took him in the barn and fucked him so senseless he walked in looking like a recently used sex doll."

Kala growled. "How was I supposed to know he wouldn't check himself in a damn mirror? You are trying to get me to think you slept with my husband."

"Well, he wasn't your husband at the time," Lucy taunted.

So much drama. She moved to Zach. Despite everything she said earlier, she wanted to be close to him. She threaded her fingers through his and tilted her chin up. "Do you think there's a place for them to spar?"

He gave her a halfhearted smile. "It's a surprisingly big place for the city, but I don't think they have a room dedicated to fight club."

The Hideout did.

The train trip to Liverpool had been surprisingly short. She didn't know a lot about Welsh geography, so she hadn't known they were in the north and close to Liverpool. Lucy and Henry had taken the Jeep and managed to make it to the station just as their train pulled in.

There had been a lot of planning in that hour-long train ride. Mostly from Kala about where she was going to bury Lucy's body.

"I'm praying there's still some whiskey." Henry seemed ready to throw his hands up. "Luce, I love you. I will honor all the wishes you have for your own funeral."

"Dad, I told you why I did it," she said with a frown, obviously unused to her father being upset with her.

"You have been poking that particular bear since before she even got here," Henry shot back, walking down the long hall.

"I'm not sure they won't kill each other right here," Zach admitted.

"She's not killing anyone." Lou had her hands on a half-asleep TJ, as though she had to maneuver him to bed. "I still have the water bottle ready."

TJ yawned. "Yeah, Lucy explained why she decided to make herself Cooper's girlfriend. Now Parker definitely doesn't think you're together. What else has she done? I think it was all for the op."

"For the op? Yeah, who is the donkey named after?" Kala cracked her knuckles. "You named all of those animals after someone you knew."

"And I saved the worst for the most stubborn ass I've ever met. The Fabulous Miss K," Lucy nearly hissed.

She heard Henry say something about thanking god and someone created this mess and then she heard the dulcet tones of her uncle.

"Well, it's good to know nothing changes." Ian Taggart stood at the end of the hall, hands in fists at his hips as he looked the group over. "Cooper, you ever do Lucy?"

"I didn't even know she existed before a couple of weeks ago." Cooper looked utterly relieved to see a man who was definitely going to yell at him. "But Lucy is right. I screwed up. I was late to the debrief and didn't check myself. I wish she'd come up with something different, but at least now Parker does believe Kara and I are not together."

"Ben?" A bubblegum-colored head popped around the corner. "Ben is here? Hey, Devi. How are you after all the torture and shit?"

Ben might not be here but the gang sure was. "The evil doctor torture or what Zach did to my asshole in a barn twelve hours ago?"

Zach started coughing.

Her uncle groaned. "And if Ben was here maybe you shouldn't be bouncing in. You'll give him a heart attack."

"Yeah, well you said you would talk about letting Ben in if he proved sufficiently loyal. I would say this should prove his loyalty. He was willing to risk his job to do something crazy Kala came up with." Kenzie turned back to the room she'd walked out of. "So much gossip. Tash, Devi's doing Zach again. You were right. It didn't take long."

"Hey, I held out for weeks," Devi argued.

"Uhm, no. I held out for weeks," Zach countered.

Evil man. Couldn't he give her one thing? She moved past her uncle, who had a hand on his stomach like he might throw up. There stood her cousin. Tasha Taggart was the epitome of modern femininity. She was petite, with lush, dark hair and a figure most men would die to get their hands on. She was curvy and gorgeous, and the energy that surrounded her was calm, as though the very air understood her competence at...well, everything.

And she was loving and kind and completely unhateable because Devi remembered all the times Tasha stepped in when she needed a big sister. She went and hugged her cousin. "Hey."

Tasha's arms wound around her, pulling her in. "Are you okay? I know everyone's talked to you, and Zach has been open about taking care of you, but are you honestly okay?"

She had the sudden urge to get real. Even with her best friends she'd been putting on a front. She'd told her mom how she wasn't thinking about a future with Zach at all. Same with everyone. She wanted to tell Tasha she was lying because she couldn't think about anything but Zach's future.

But she couldn't. Not when she was the second choice to this woman. She pulled back and gave her a grin. "I'm good. It's been quiet and then Kala shows up and the world explodes. Hey, do you know why she and Lucy hate each other? I stopped going to Bliss before that happened. All I remember of Lucy and her family was playing at the park with her and her sister Poppy. I haven't seen her since we were children. Should I have recognized her?"

Tasha sighed. "Lucy is an excellent operative, and she's pretty cool when she's not in the presence of my sister. As to why they hate each other, well, she'll have to tell you. Just know that my sister can hold a ridiculous grudge, and Kenz and I are friendly with her."

Good, because she kind of liked Lucy. Weeks with the woman had proven there was a good heart under all her sarcasm and aloofness. Kind of like Kala. "Well, she's going to hate her more because she set herself up as Cooper's girlfriend so Ben Parker would buy the story that they're only friendly now. I would say she did it out of spite, but Cooper kind of walked in looking like he'd had raucous sex in a barn."

"Can we save the gossip for another time?" Her uncle stood in the middle of the living room. "I've been on the road for hours and could use some sleep, but only after we figure out what's going on."

By road he meant air. Her uncle's company owned two private jets, and she would bet one of them had been used after Henry made the call. Which brought up some questions.

"How did you get here so fast? The flight's almost ten hours," Devi pointed out.

"Well, Kala sent her mom some pictures from dinner the other night," her uncle explained. "She showed them around the office."

Kala sighed as though she knew what had happened. "Mae or Hutch?"

MaeBe Hawthorne and Greg Hutchins were the cybersecurity team at McKay-Taggart. They could hack pretty much anything, and Mae, in particular, was excellent at taking apart information on the Internet and proving whether a story was true or not.

"I asked Mae to look at it because I'm not an idiot, daughter," her uncle announced. "Honestly, I might have bought it if the pics had come from Lou or Cooper. You do not update your mom with pictures of your dinners. So Mae took them apart and proved the dinner you said you had on Wednesday was only available at the resort on their spring menu, which changed two days after you got there. You did a great job on the rest, though she suspected Lou doctored some of them."

Lou shrugged. "I told her it wouldn't work."

"Hey, I wanted to stay at the resort. They had this great buffet." TJ yawned again.

"Next time I'll disappear," Kala vowed. "I don't know why I should tell you everything when you obviously keep secrets, Big Tag."

The townhouse was big and comfortably furnished. It made Devi wonder where the family money came from. Or it could be something worse. She turned to Tasha, who seemed to always have the answers. "Is this an Agency safe house?"

If it was, they would have cameras, and Zach would be on them. If the agency was watching, they could walk in at any moment and damn it, she wasn't ready. She wasn't. She was supposed to have more time.

"My mother owns it," Lucy admitted, setting down her bag. "She doesn't typically approve of owning property, but she made an exception so we would have a European base that didn't also serve as some youth hostel. Please note she doesn't have a problem with youth hostels. I thought it could be good cover. She then cried because I think human beings could be cover and she failed as a mother. It was a whole thing."

"We are thinking about turning it into one after we're done with this phase of life." Henry settled into one of the big lounge chairs.

Her uncle frowned and sat next to him. "I don't think we get out of this phase. Even if we do, I expect my grandson to announce any day now he's joining the Agency, and wouldn't I like to come along? Come on, Grumpa. It'll be fun."

"I can't even think about it," Henry said with a long sigh. "I don't understand where they got it."

Lucy snorted.

Henry shook his head. "No. I am not taking the blame for this. I have been a mild-mannered peace-loving man since years before you were born. You never saw the John Bishop side of me. I made sure of it."

Lucy shrugged. "Tash let me read those spy high books. I liked the sound of it."

"You like copying me." Kala looked sullen as she took a seat. She crossed her arms over her chest and stared at her father. "You did not have to come after me. I am on my honeymoon. It's rude."

Her uncle's eyes rolled. "Sure, you are. I should have fucking known, but your mother convinced me it's totally normal to take your emotional support friend on your honeymoon. TJ, I expected better from you."

TJ shrugged as he dropped down to the couch with another yawn. "I don't know why. I always do what Lou tells me to, and she always helps Kala unless she decides it's too dangerous. So it feels like this is all just part of the TJ Taggart brand. Where's Aunt Charlotte?"

"Pretending everything is fine at home, including faking me going into the office," her uncle explained. "Because there's only so much Drake and Taylor can cover for us, and no matter how quiet you've been, I assure you someone will notice we're working with the Canadians. I've informed Damon we're here and asked him to cover for us. Now someone please tell me there's a plan. What were you going to do, daughter? Kidnap your cousin? Or were you going to bring Zach in?"

Devi glanced over, and Zach was standing alone in the corner of the room. He stood there as though waiting for judgment, his eyes downcast.

She should quietly go to bed. Now that everyone was here, being close to Zach would only make her look like a fool in the end.

She didn't care anymore. Something had broken this afternoon. Something cracked, and she didn't want to fix it. "She's not bringing Zach in. She was worried about me and needed to lay eyes on me. Now she's going to chill out. Well, I thought she would but she's kind of putting all her restless energy on Lucy now. We need to tap her out and send in Kenz because I think her murdering another operative would give away this game we're playing. And uncle, you're not bringing Zach in either. I want to start talking about how to get him out of hot water with the Agency."

Zach's head came up as she joined him.

This was stupid. She cared about him. Even if it didn't work out, she couldn't leave him to fate. She was smart, too. She could help. She slid her hand in his and he pulled her to him, her back to his front. She felt him breathe her in, like her scent calmed him.

"I'm not sure there is a way," he whispered. "And that's okay, sweetness. Your uncle is here, and I'm going to do whatever he wants me to do."

A little pulse of panic bubbled up inside her.

"I'm not taking him in. I've done an enormous amount of work to not be forced to take Zach in," her uncle said with a tired sigh. "I'm not the bad guy here, Devi. I was trying to let some of this play out, but your cousin has made that impossible now."

Kala's eyes narrowed on her dad. "You could have given me a heads-up that you knew exactly who Zach was and you had eyes on him."

"Yeah, I would like a timeline on who knew what and when." Cooper stood by his bride.

"I would, too." Tasha took a seat on the couch beside Lucy, and Kenz joined them.

"Make that three." Tristan Dean-Miles walked in from what Devi suspected was the kitchen. He had a tray in his hand and passed TJ a sandwich. He set the tray of snacks and drinks on the big table in the middle of the room. "You could have mentioned you knew all The Jester stuff. Would have saved me an enormous amount of trouble."

"I didn't know everything." Her uncle grabbed a coffee mug and took a long drink. "I suspected something was off with Zach early on, but it wasn't until he started taking leave and going to South America that I sicced Henry and Lucy on him."

"We were supposed to observe in the beginning, but it became clear he was looking for someone, and he was doing it in our direct orbit." Lucy took up the narrative. "Due to the nature of his ops, we couldn't exactly look into his Agency records, though we suspected he was using his position to do whatever he was trying to do. It wasn't until I made direct contact that he told me what he was doing, and even then it was months later before I got what I suspected was most of the story."

She could feel him stiffen behind her.

How hard was it for him to stand here and take all the judgment?

She leaned back against him as Lucy talked about how she slowly befriended Zach.

"None of this is going to save you, sweetness," he whispered, and his arm tightened around her waist.

A thrill went through her because she could feel the hard length of his erection against her backside. "Save me?"

"From the spanking you're going to get before we go to bed tonight," he promised.

Her ass already ached.

"I was the one who helped him find The Jester," Lucy was saying. "There are a lot of interesting people in the kind of groups I run in. Everything from genuine believers like my mom to people like Dr. Huisman, who basically want to break the world because it doesn't suit them. They often have connections. So I used some of them to find The Jester, and we put together the history between the Reeds and the reclusive arms dealer. He was the connection to Huisman. The Jester, that is."

"Did I know everything? No. Was I aware Zach had an additional agenda?" Her uncle took another long drink. "Yes. Would I have told you if I thought any one of you was in real danger? Yes, but that asshole kept nearly dying to save the team. He's a terrible bad guy. He didn't even read the handbook. He should have known getting shot for my eldest daughter would endear his ass to me."

The words hit her like a slap meant to wake her up. Oh, she was sure that wasn't how her uncle meant them, but it reminded her.

"I would have done it for any member of my team." Zach said the words so they could all hear. "I was happy to save Tash, but it could have been any of you, and we know how far I'll go for Devi."

Her uncle turned, his eyes narrowing. "It better be the distance, son. I'm not fucking kidding. If you are not serious about her, I'll kill you myself."

She was about to protest when he cuddled her close.

"I'm serious. I just shouldn't be." He kissed her hair. "I can't help myself. But we should think about getting her to a real safe house. With many guards, because she's sneaky."

That was not happening. "I'm staying. I'm literally surrounded by people who know how to protect me better than anyone at McKay-Taggart, and I don't want to put anyone else at risk."

Zach rubbed his cheek against her hair. "Well, then she stays with me, but when I go meet my mother tomorrow, I'll need someone to watch her."

"It's a public train station." She'd heard the whole plan but suspected they were about to go over it again.

Henry sat up straighter and looked to her uncle. "Nell made contact with Shannon Reed over a year ago. She's scared of her ex-husband and terrified of Huisman. We've finally convinced her to come to the UK, but she wants to meet in a neutral spot. The train station has plenty of CCTV cameras we can lock into, so coverage won't be a problem. Nell thinks once she verifies it's really her son, she'll calm down and come back here with us."

"It's the Liverpool Lime Street Station," Lucy said cheerfully. If she was tired, she didn't show it at all. "There will be tons of people. It's the central hub for the area. Mom's bringing her in from London because…" Lucy sighed. "It was less of a carbon footprint to fly to London direct than two planes from Buenos Aires to here."

"I prefer meeting her here. If we were in London, we would have to involve MI6 because Damon wouldn't be able to pretend he knows nothing." Her uncle was talking about Damon Knight, who ran the London branch of McKay-Taggart and also had a few spy kids of his own. "He'll tell us if he hears anything and try to give us cover, but we don't want to alert the Agency, and that's what bringing in MI6 would do."

"What is the point? Are we bringing her in? Protecting her? Asking her to make a couple of fun bombs for us?" Kala did look tired, but then she'd always needed her beauty sleep.

"We're making first contact and treating her like a scared deer we need to be gentle with," Henry replied.

"She's a bombmaker," Tristan pointed out. He relaxed back as he looked her uncle's way. Tris was a lovely man with dark hair and green eyes and a body he honed in the gym. "The woman has been in and out of prison most of her adult life. I don't think we should be treating her with kid gloves. She's killed people."

"She built something that killed people." Zach's tone was bland, like he didn't care. "I'm not making excuses for her, but she got caught in something bad, and you can't imagine that life. Tris, you've always had people who cared about you. Who would move mountains for you. You literally have three parents who treat you like the sun in the sky. She never had that. What she had was a genius-level IQ in a poor household where her mother didn't care about her bouts of depression, her anxiety."

"I know I have loving parents, but I assure you I do understand what it means to get caught in a life that's not good for you," Lucy said softly. "I would bet she started because she was trying to please someone, likely your father, and the truth of the matter is jail doesn't rehabilitate criminals most of the time. It merely gives them access to other criminals. They became the only people she could halfway trust. Zach, I'm with my father. I'm going to treat your mother with care. Your father is another story."

"How do you feel about that, Zach?" Uncle Ian studied Zach with sympathetic eyes.

"If you see him, don't hesitate," Zach replied in that toneless voice he used when he was far too emotional. "He already tried to take Devi. And that's my fault. The Canadians believe Huisman had someone follow me the night we broke Devi and Kala out of the house in Virginia."

"I'd like to see their data," her uncle said. "But I believe them. That was weeks ago. Why wait until now to make a move on Devi?"

"Oh, I've been sitting on that farm taking care of chickens and horses and all the kittens." She wished she could have taken one of the kittens with her. Sweet little things. "That was the first time I was allowed off the farm, and I get the feeling I'm going to pay for it. I don't know why Zach decided today he wanted to be a Dom. He literally could have picked any of the other days when I was perfectly well behaved."

She felt him place a kiss on her ear. "You're never perfectly behaved and you know it. You're a force of nature when you want to be."

Her uncle ignored them utterly. "We think Huisman has a plan he would like to execute soon. There's a meeting of the world economic council in a couple of weeks. We think he wants to disrupt it."

"But not in the traditional way," Henry continued. "He's careful when it comes to anything close to what he considers intelligence circles, but he can be a bit reckless when he's working with criminals or what we would call underground activists."

"A few months ago, we found some chatter on a couple of sites I monitor on the Dark Web," Lucy explained. "They started to talk about a group that stole a sample of weaponized anthrax."

The room seemed suddenly on edge. Oh, they knew something she didn't. "Is it Huisman's group?"

"Huisman used us for cover to steal that. My fiancé's father owned a lab that was doing some risky research." Tasha took over the narrative. "At the time we didn't realize who Huisman was. We were researching him. We certainly didn't realize he would use the raid on the business to slip in and get the formula they developed."

"Anthrax is bad?" Devi didn't keep up with medical stuff.

"Anthrax is a bacteria that occurs in nature." Naturally Lou took the scientific explanations on. "It's rare but humans who catch it usually do from contact with an infected animal. Depending on the way the spores are introduced into the body, the mortality rate is between forty and fifty percent."

That sounded bad. "So he stole some of this bacteria?"

"He stole the formula to aerosolize anthrax. What they're trying to do is take something rare with a high mortality rate and make it easy to spread and over a wide space. It could kill half a city quickly if dispersed in the right way. It would need to come from above. We think he's made his anthrax and is looking for a place to test it. What he needs is a way to deliver it."

Now she understood. "He needs something he can use as a biological bomb."

"Which is where my mother comes in," Zach explained. "She's known for targeted explosions, which sounds like it wouldn't work, but the truth is she can adapt. With the right chemistry and tech, she can ensure the spores get delivered to the city's biggest population centers."

"And if they do it in the right place, that kind of terror attack can upend the economy," Henry concluded. "If some false information gets out, a few conspiracy theories in the right ears, and suddenly the world is a powder keg waiting to go off."

It sounded diabolical. "But he can't do it without Shannon Reed."

"We believe he hasn't had a lot of luck in reverse engineering her work," her uncle continued. "I think it's frustrating him enormously, which is why he's desperate to find her now. He's on a timeline. There's intelligence pointing to him building some kind of facility in the middle of Nepal. In the side of a mountain."

"My mother is prepared to protest him. Don't discount that," Lucy offered.

"Your mother is never getting close to him. She's going back home after we talk to Shannon and hand her protection over to her son and Big Tag." Henry stood up. "Speaking of, I'm going to call her before I go to bed. I'll see you all in the morning, and I expect a full briefing on how you intend to cover the train station and the area around it. I'm looking at you, Tristan. Also, unless Kala wants to blow her cover or violate her marriage vows, Kenzie should be on the ground tomorrow when we meet the Canadians."

Kenzie clapped her hands. "Yes. I'm so excited. I haven't seen him since our dinner date. Sis, you need to tell me everything he said. Oh, have you been pretending to be me?"

Kala's brow rose.

"Are you serious?" her uncle said. "You're trying to pull this shit on me? Do I believe for one second Kala didn't tell you and you didn't cover for her?"

Kenzie's lips kicked up. "Fine. I made the deal with Ben. I couldn't figure out a way to go on the honeymoon, and she was surprisingly against me taking her place."

"Well, I didn't know," Tristan pointed out.

"No, you didn't because you are a chatty motherfucker," Kala proclaimed. "And Tash didn't know because we didn't want to put her in a bad position."

"What I'm hearing is we're the good ones, Tash," Tristan said with a smug grin.

"You're the one most likely to tell on everyone, and Tash would feel bad." Devi knew Tris well. She probably should feel weird being involved in what should be a classified debrief, but it felt more like a family reunion of sorts, and that included ribbing her obnoxious cousins.

And feeling insecure around her gorgeous cousins.

"You aren't spanking her enough, Zach." Tristan gave her Dom a frown.

"And I'm done." Her uncle stood. "There are only so many bedrooms. I'm rooming with Henry. I'm sure we can stay up most of the night drinking whiskey and talking about how our children will die."

"Fun times," Henry agreed and sighed. "I thought we would put Tasha, Kenzie, Lucy, and Devi in the bunk room."

"It's basically a tiny room with two bunk beds. Mom likes to make sure she has places for everyone to sleep," Lucy acknowledged. "I suppose that means Zach and Tristan are in the small room and the other two go to the married couples. Well, the married couple and the practically married couple."

"If you try to separate TJ and Lou, he'll wander the halls begging for hot dogs in the middle of the night," her uncle said.

She wasn't sleeping with Zach?

Guess there was more than one bed. She'd never considered how the only one bed trope would affect her life, but here she was.

Was it over? Or would they steal moments? Would he pull her into an empty bedroom tomorrow and take out all of his stress on her body?

He was going to see his mom for the first time in years. He had to be nervous about that. He had to be stressed by the events of the day. He probably needed some comfort. She had to find a way to keep them together. He would almost certainly try to please everyone by not causing a scene, but he needed her.

"No," Zach said, his tone implacable.

Her uncle turned, that one brow arching in a way that usually made her back out of the room. "No?"

"Until this is over, she's mine, and I sleep where she sleeps." He looked over at his brother.

Cooper got his arms around Kala, rubbing his cheek against her hair. "It's a family tradition. I sleep where she sleeps."

Kala's expression went tight. "What is happening to me?"

Cooper kissed her cheek. "It's called sentiment, baby. It's what you feel when you remember a sweet moment like that time when your husband wouldn't let you be alone. It's okay. You'll get used to it."

"I don't like it." But Kala leaned into his touch.

"Unless Tristan wants to watch, he can take one of the bunks," Zach announced as though that was a totally normal thing to say. Which it wasn't.

Tristan perked up. "I mean I never mind a show." He must have heard her uncle growl because his hands came up in defeat. "I will be happy in a bunk. Jeez, for lifestylers we're all a little prissy, don't you think?"

He stood and they started to break up.

Her uncle looked her way. "You know what you're doing?"

"Nope. Not in any way," she admitted.

"But you're still going to do it," her uncle said with a sigh. "He's in trouble."

"I know." She leaned back against him. "We both know we're on a timer. We're going to enjoy it while it lasts. It's not a big deal."

The sex. While it lasted. A pit opened in her gut because she was talking like he was a sex toy she had to enjoy until he was taken away from her when she knew deep down he was everything. Every fucking thing.

This wasn't some grand affair she would look back on with fondness when she found her true love.

He *was* her true love.

"Yeah, we're going to enjoy it." Zach said the words but there was a deep well in his tone. Sorrow. Regret.

Her uncle stepped back. "Fine. But I'd like a word alone with Zach first."

"You don't need to…" Devi began.

Zach released her. "Of course. Devi, I'll be there in a minute. Go and get yourself settled."

Well, that was an order. But she did understand. Zach cared about her uncle. He viewed Ian Taggart as the father figure he never had.

She really wanted to stay for that talk.

Tasha came over and took her hand. "Come on. I'll help you set up. I've been here before. It's comfy. Nell lets us use this place from time to time. It's way better than having to hide out in a hotel."

Kenzie moved in behind her. "I'll go, too."

Oh, crap. They were going to have a talk.

She looked back, but Zach wasn't saving her this time.

Chapter Fourteen

Big Tag crossed to the bar and poured out another glass. Two fingers of amber liquid that if this Henry guy bought, it was likely locally sourced and hadn't harmed the environment in any way.

Zach took it.

"Tristan, go away," Big Tag said flatly.

Tristan groaned but stood. "I don't get to watch any of the drama. TJ, hey man, tell me what happened when Kala found out Lucy was Zach's contact. Like did things explode?"

TJ followed him out. "No, but she did name this rude donkey after Kala, and that did not go well. Also, did you know geese are really mean?"

They disappeared down the hall.

Henry gestured his daughter's way. "You're not going to join in on the girl talk? I suspect they're about to corner Devi."

Lucy sighed as she stood and grabbed her bag. "I would make Kala uncomfortable, and I've pushed her enough for tonight. We need her ready for tomorrow, so I'll forgo the doomed love story portion of the evening. I don't get it. No guy is worth all of this. No offense, Zach."

Well, she was always honest with him. About things that weren't her real name or who she was actually working for. "None taken."

Henry put a hand on his daughter's shoulder. "One day you are going to meet someone who sets you on your ass, daughter, and I'm going to be here for it. Let's go call your mom. She should be in the air by now and ready to give us a heinous lecture on air travel."

Lucy groaned and walked out with her dad.

Leaving him alone with Big Tag.

"What the fuck, Zach?" Ian said with a shake of his head.

Oh, that could mean so many things. He was surprised at how heavy he felt. Earlier, he'd been light and almost happy because things felt so fucking right between him and Devi. Earlier he'd thought he still had a few weeks with her. Things were moving along with whatever Huisman's plans were, but he thought he had a little time.

He took a sip of the whiskey. He wouldn't ask for a second glass because despite Devi's insistence that they were only having sex, he wanted to remember every second he spent with her. Every touch. Every caress.

Every single thing except the fact that she didn't love him.

Her words sat on his chest so he couldn't quite breathe right. And yet he knew it was good. It was good that she didn't love him since he wasn't going to be able to stick around to protect and love her. She was being smart. She was salvaging her heart in a way he couldn't.

It hurt. It made him ache in a way he never thought he would.

But he wouldn't let it stop him. He would still go into that room with her and be her Dom for as long as he could.

"Which fuck are we talking about? The whole 'I lied to the team' fuck? The 'I got us caught by Huisman' fuck? Or the fuck where I'm the wanted outlaw sleeping with your niece?"

Big Tag snorted. "Wanted outlaw?"

"Well, there is a Red Notice out on me," Zach pointed out. "And I'm fairly certain there are BOLOs in the States."

"Why would that happen?" Ian sank down in the chair and in the low light looked every bit like a mafia boss. He would have made an excellent one if he'd chosen to go that way. "I mean I allowed the Red Notice so it looks good for Huisman, but has anyone actually tried to take you in? I know you've been careful, but I assure you there have been times you were caught on camera."

"Obviously, or the Canadians and my father wouldn't be here." His father. He was still trying to wrap his head around it. His father was close and had tried to take Devi. To drug her and do whatever to her and hold it over his head.

"Son, you look a little crazy right now. Are you thinking about murdering your father?" Ian asked as though that was a normal, everyday question to ponder at the end of a long day.

"Yes." Maybe it was normal for his life. Maybe he should embrace the fact that he was cursed and go out in a blaze of glory. Maybe that would be better than prison. Better for him. Better for Devi.

"Let Kala do it." Big Tag sat back and gestured for Zach to join him in the seat Henry had previously occupied. "She'll do it however quick or slow you like, and you don't have to get your hands dirty. I know the whole revenge thing sounds like a fun plan, but it gets murky on an emotional level. I thought about killing my father a couple of times, the first being when I was a teenager and he left us. Turned out he had a whole other family and if I killed him, I might not have met my younger brothers. Or they might have helped and it would have been bonding time. We can't look back. I'm going to give you some advice. He's an annoyance. Like a fly that won't stop buzzing around you. Let someone swat him for you and don't think twice about it. Don't make more nightmares for yourself. Let your team handle it."

The words threatened to shake his wall. The idea that someone...anyone, much less the people he admired...would put themselves on the line for him made him emotional. It wasn't happening. "I fucked my team over."

"Did you?" Big Tag seemed to think about that for a moment. "Don't get me wrong. I think you're facing some time in a ring with your brother and maybe Tris. Although Tris will probably worry about his pretty face and decide to forgo vengeance. Smart kid."

Big Tag was known for his sarcasm. Sometimes he had to ignore it and move the conversation forward. "I lied to everyone."

"Yeah, but I like to look at actions over words. I'll give you the whole Jester thing was shitty because Tristan thought he was doing something revolutionary," Big Tag said with a huff. "Like we all haven't killed international arms dealers and taken over their operations. That's Agency 101. Tristan had to turn it into some overly dramatic romantic tragedy. I blame his papa's DNA. That shit did not come from Jacob Dean. But other than that, tell me one way you've put the team at risk."

Zach had a list. He counted all his sins at night when he was trying to sleep. "I didn't tell you I knew who the bombmaker was."

"And I should spank you for it, but she's your mother." Tag shrugged him off. "It's a touchy subject. I know you won't like hearing this, but I knew you were hiding something. I could have gotten you reassigned. Do you know why I didn't?"

He had an idea. Big Tag was a strategic thinker despite all the sarcasm. "Because it's better to keep eyes on an enemy."

Big Tag frowned and shook his head like he was deeply disappointed. "You are a dramatic motherfucker, Zach. Where has this been hiding? I greatly prefer the dude who tells it like it is. Are you my enemy, Zach?"

"No."

"Then stop this morose shit and help me work this out. You don't have to be in a corner. You don't have to die or go to jail. There are far more doors open to you if you work with me and stop shutting out your team."

Emotion welled inside him. "Don't do this, Ian."

Big Tag slowed down and considered him. "What, son? Give you hope? I'm going to ask you a question. Do you care about this team?"

There was only one answer. "More than anything in the world, with one exception. I know I haven't shown it, but this team is my family. Not just Cooper. Everyone on the team."

"Have you ever turned on your team?"

"I lied."

"To protect your mother," Big Tag argued. "Also to protect yourself. I wish you had figured out who we were and come to me, but I understand that it's hard to ask for help when you've never once been able to. You were trained to be alone, to protect yourself, and yet time and time again you put your body in front of one of my kids or one of the kids I helped raise. Do you regret the bullets you took for them?"

Was this what having a dad was really like? Because his eyes were getting suspiciously watery. "Not once. I would do it again.

Every time."

"Are you with my niece because things with my daughter didn't work out? Is Devi second choice to Tasha?"

Zach snorted at the thought. "Ian, I know this is going to come as a shock to you, but they are completely different women." He shook his head and took another drink. "Tasha was a crush. She's beautiful and sweet and infinitely competent. Like a man looks at Tash and thinks there's a woman who could bring him peace. Love isn't about peace. I mean it is at some point, I hope. But I don't think I ever loved someone until I met Devi, and she is not peaceful."

"So it's all chaos?"

He shook his head and searched for the right words. "I'm not saying this properly. Probably because it's new to me. How to explain it? My feelings for Tasha were peaceful. Like admiring a painting and thinking it would be nice to live there. I didn't make a move on her. When she got together with Dare, I was genuinely happy for her."

"And if Devi found someone?"

His gut tightened at the thought of someone else's hands on her. He knew it didn't make him a very modern man, and he would control the impulse to take out anyone who would look at her, but she brought out his inner caveman. "I would take him apart with my bare hands. I would tear down everything. I would… See, not peaceful feelings. And yet, when she's close to me I'm more me than I am when she's not around. When she's with me, I feel centered and ready to deal with things."

Big Tag held up his glass. "And that is how you know it's right. I understand what you're saying. The feelings, the love… In the beginning it's all passion, but there's an undercurrent, something deep inside that tells you this one…this one could bring you something you've never known before. Isn't that worth fighting for, Zach?"

Did Big Tag think he hadn't asked himself this question a hundred times? "For me, maybe. For Devi? I'm not a good bet for her. Shouldn't I think about her first?"

"In all things, yes, but you also have to honor her and that means acknowledging that she has a say in this relationship, and the first and most important opinion she has is whether she wants to take the risk with you. You don't get to make that choice for her."

"She could get hurt." Another thought that made him sick.

"Yes, and there's no going back from that possibility," Big Tag pointed out. "Huisman knows who she is and who she's with. She's on his radar, so the only thing you do by dumping her for her own good is leave her alone."

He had to take that into consideration. His first thought was to cleave to the words like a lifeline. He didn't have to give her up. He couldn't give her up. It wasn't safe. "And if she doesn't feel the same way?"

Big Tag waved that thought off. "I know my niece. She wouldn't sleep with you if she wasn't in love with you. Oh, I'm not saying she couldn't have some casual sex. She could, but she wouldn't show you off if she wasn't serious. You went on double dates with Cooper and Kala. She would never do that with a casual fling."

They had never been casual. Not even the first night, but there was so much between them now. "That was before she knew the truth."

"And she's still standing up for you and telling me what I will and won't do when it comes to you. Stop listening to the fear in her words and watch how she acts. Watch how she defends her territory. Her territory is you. Watch how she gets jealous when she doesn't need to be. That's on you."

He'd seen it in her eyes tonight, known she got a bit tense when Tasha walked in. "Hey, I've told her I never truly loved Tasha. I told her it was a crush and I'm happy Tash is happy."

"But you held out on sleeping with her because she hurt your feelings."

He wasn't sure where Big Tag was getting his intel. "She didn't want to sleep with me."

"Liar."

Fuck. He was getting it from Henry, of course. So there was no way around this because Henry was a gossipy old dude like Tag. "Fine. I didn't want her to use me. I realized how stupid that was. I realized it didn't matter how she felt. I need this time with her. I need to have it to hold on to if the worst happens."

"Drama." Tag shook his head. "So you held out on her for weeks, and she's wondering if you really wanted her in the first place."

"I screwed up Lace…Lucy's whole op for her. When I found out Huisman had her, I lost my shit. I didn't care about anything but getting her back. I walked up to the group with the full knowledge that I might be taken in, but it was worth my freedom and whatever happened with my mom to make sure Devi was safe. How could she think I don't want her?"

"Because in her head you want her last name, not her." Big Tag held up a hand when he was going to argue. "I know that's not true. You should have figured out by now that we don't need to share blood or last names to be a family. But she heard the gossip and internalized it. Devi has a big personality in a family of them. In other families, Devi would be the leader."

He sighed. "And in this one she has Tasha and Kala."

Big Tag's lips quirked up. "I notice you didn't include Kenz."

He knew his team. "Kenz doesn't want to be the leader. She loves her people and will do anything for them, but she's more than willing to let someone she trusts take control of the situation. That's not how it is with Tash and Kala. We're lucky they don't clash more often than they do."

"Because Kala loves Tash and often just does what she wants to do quietly and behind her sister's back," Big Tag admitted. "All I'm saying is it can be hard to have these impulses and have nowhere to put them. I don't know why she's trying to get a job at some big design house when she should build her own business. It would take all those instincts of hers and give them an outlet."

"She's drawing again," he said quietly. "I think the weeks we spent on the farm helped quiet some of her doubts. Let her find her love for design again."

If that was all she got out of this, he would be content.

"I think you'll find her parents are grateful for that. They've been worried about her pinning her future on some low-level job where they won't recognize her real talents."

"She shouldn't be designing bland sportswear. There are lots of people who can pick colors for this season's polo collection." He knew what he wanted her to do, what she secretly craved. "She needs her own fet wear design business, although she's also great with wedding dresses. I wish someone with cash would maybe invest in a shop for her and a good website design."

Tag snorted. "Yeah, I'll call her uncle and see what we can do. Let me tell you, life got easier when my brother married a billionaire.

Mia is a sucker, and it doesn't hurt that they run their own club in Austin. I think if Devi would let her aunt try some samples, she might find a major investor. So what I need is someone she cares about boosting her confidence. Can you think of any way to do that, Zach?"

And they were full circle again. "Sex."

Big Tag nodded. "Take her to bed as often as possible. Play with her. Top her. Give her what she needs and those walls will come down. As for the rest of it, let me deal with it."

Hope. The man kept giving it to him. "How can you deal with it? Are you talking about the Red Notice? Or the Agency?"

"I assure you I can deal with both." Big Tag set his glass down. "You should understand that Drake and I have been presenting a somewhat made-up version of what happened. Only to our bosses. The rest of the Agency believes what we put in the official reports."

"And in the unofficial ones?"

Big Tag's lips pulled up in a slight grin. "Well, I'm known for being a ruthless bastard who takes men who are loyal to me and manipulates them into doing my bidding."

"That's bullshit." Tag always treated his team right.

"It's a reputation I haven't earned, but I find it useful from time to time. I always knew about your mother. I used the Toronto op to alienate you off from the group and split Huisman's attention. The BOLOs and Red Notices are for his benefit," Big Tag explained. "To make you look like the criminal we're pretending you are. You're undercover, Zach. If some Agency idiot brings you in, you'll sit in a cell until you're released into my custody. There will be a reckoning at the end of this if we don't stop Huisman. If we do, then no one will ask any questions."

He was damn near floored by the revelation. "But you didn't tell the team?"

"Yeah, well, I kind of wish I had now, but Drake and I decided it would look more real if we didn't bring them in. I would have to explain why I changed my MO. You see a couple of years back my brother was in trouble with a group operated by a woman who reminds me a little of Huisman. A friend of mine ended up being taken in with him. We rescued Theo and Hutch, but I asked Hutch to go back in. I knew no one would be safe while the person who took Theo was working."

He knew the story. It wasn't an Agency op, but he was sure they would know it. Big Tag had sent Hutch in to gather evidence and be his man on the inside. Hutch had been in place to save Devi's parents when it all went bad, and Big Tag had maintained the illusion with everyone, including Theo and Erin. The man knew how to use his past.

Was Big Tag's past going to save his future? "I can't ask you to do this."

There was too much at risk.

Big Tag sat back. "It's already done. I can't go back and say oops, I didn't mean that. I'm not asking your permission, son. I'm telling you what the story is. I know a couple of writers, and it's always good to edit your story. Sometimes they start over when they started in the wrong place. So you came to me when you realized your mother was involved. You had made a hash of The Jester business and wanted me to help. I asked you to valiantly go undercover, and here we are."

It sounded far too good to be true. "And all the stuff with Devi?"

"The inevitable consequences of hiring young dumbasses. They get horny and lose their minds. I'm handling it. At least that's the way Henry and I explained things to the director a couple of hours ago."

He slammed back the rest of the drink. He needed it. "Why would you do this for me? I shouldn't let you."

"That is your dumbass talking. Zachary, I'm going to tell you a secret no one likes to talk about. The most adult and masculine thing you can do is ask for help when you need it. The best thing you can possibly do for your family is let them take care of you when you're wounded, and you're wounded, Zach. I know you think it would be better for everyone if you went out in a blaze of glory, but you're fucking wrong. You ruin a lot of people if that's the path you go down. Devi never recovers. Your team will always wonder why you didn't trust them enough to let them save you."

Damn. Tears. He didn't cry. It wasn't like his aunt had beaten it out of him. She'd been lovely. His mother when she was around had loved him in her way. But the world had shown him time and time again that emotions weren't for him. But here they were.

"Ask me, Zach. You already know the answer. I know it's hard when you've always been the one who had to be strong. But this is strength. This is being strong enough to let people love you, to trust them even though there's nothing in your past that tells you this will work out. Let the people who love you make the choice to risk for you. The way you would and have for them. So ask me the question and let us be done with this part."

This part was him having control. If he did as Big Tag asked, he was trusting the man with everything. He was giving up the option of making decisions based on himself. He would have to trust that Big Tag would help him.

Like a dad would.

"Will you please help me? I'm in trouble." The hardest words to get out, and yet something freed up inside him as he said them.

"And I will make it right." Big Tag stood and held out a hand. "Take care of my niece and I'll handle this. But seriously, your team is going to give you hell forever."

The utter relief that flooded his system was a revelation. He forced himself to stand, to take the hand of the man who had been more of a father than his had ever been. This man was who he wanted to be. Stalwart. Loving. Utterly ruthless when it came to protecting the people he loved. "I'll take it. I want to come home."

Big Tag pulled him in for a hug. "Then come home, Zach. I'll make things right with the authorities. You make them right with Devi and Cooper. Everyone will fall into place. Come home."

When Zach broke, Big Tag didn't falter. He didn't retreat to sarcasm.

He was just a dad.

After a moment he felt another hand on his back.

"Come home, brother." Cooper. His brother.

"I'm sorry," Zach managed.

Cooper hugged him, enveloping him. "It's okay, but we have some things to talk about."

A long sigh was heard from his left and then Tris was joining in. "I forgive you, too."

"Tristan," Big Tag barked.

"No." Tris threw himself in. "You can keep me out of the drama but not the family love, uncle."

He heard Tag growl, but the circle got a little bigger.

He never imagined having a circle at all.

He hugged his brothers as they welcomed him home.

* * * *

Devi really wanted to know what her uncle was saying to Zach. She tried to turn around. There was a place at the end of the hall that would be perfect for eavesdropping. "You guys get settled in. I'll be there in a minute."

Kala stood in the way. "Nope. What's happening in there is not meant for feminine eyes. I'm absolutely certain my father is about to break Zach down in that way he does. I should know. He's the only person in the world besides Coop who can do it to me."

"I break down all the time," Kenzie admitted with a smile. "It feels good to let it all out. Do you want to cry? I'm worried about Ben so I'll cry with you. Normally I need a session to get going, but you have tormented love vibes right now. I think that should do it."

"You're such a menace," Tasha said and pointed to the door. "Go on, Dev. We're not listening in. Zach deserves some privacy. Believe me. I know what it feels like to have the man I love in conference with my father. Things are going to turn out okay. I'm actually happy it's my dad talking to him and not yours."

Because her uncle loved Zach and her dad didn't really know him. In her dad's mind Zach was the asshole who lied to his daughter. She would have some work to do on him.

No. She wouldn't because it was all a mess and it was ending and it was too soon and she… Devi took a long breath, trying to banish the panic. Tasha. She forced herself to look at Tasha. He loved Tasha, and she was as far from her cousin as a woman could be. She needed to remember that. Zach was in trouble and he was facing something grim, and he didn't want to go through it alone. Who would? They were friends. They liked each other. It was okay to spend this time with him.

She couldn't fucking breathe.

"I'm sure he wants to know what Zach's been doing and any intelligence he can give about his mom." Devi was happy the words came out even, and she was pretty sure she wasn't showing how close to the edge she was. She needed to survive this whole mess of a meeting and get some sleep and tomorrow they would run their op and…

"He wants to talk to Zach about you," Kala assured her.

"He shouldn't." If her uncle was going to pressure Zach to leave her alone, she was going to stop him. Anger felt way better than sorrow and fear.

She was going to lose him. He wouldn't be careful. He would fight until they killed him, and even if they didn't, he was adamant that he would turn himself in. He would be in jail for the rest of his life if he was lucky. He would probably be an asshole about it and not even marry her so they could have conjugal visits. He would tell her to forget about him. How was she supposed to forget about him? How was she supposed to go home and pretend like this time never happened? Like they never happened? Was she supposed to fly home in time for play night at The Hideout? Find a new Dom?

"She's freaking out." Kala let herself fall onto one of the two queen-sized beds in this room.

Lou plunked her bag down on the other. "She seems to be taking it well. I'm surprised."

Kenzie studied her for a moment. "Nah, Kala's right. She's freaking, and like usual she's trying very hard not to talk about it. I don't get this. It's good to talk about our feelings. I try to talk about how hard it is to love an enemy all the time."

"He's Canadian. He is not our enemy. No matter what happens, we're still family," Tasha said with a shake of her head. "Besides, I think we're now working with them, so it definitely doesn't feel like we're enemies. Didn't Dad and Mom decide you can tell Ben about the whole 'hey, I'm twins, and I'm not the mean one' thing when you're ready?"

Devi sat down, thinking seriously about letting this line of gossip begin and when her cousins were thoroughly involved in arguing, she could sneak out and go yell at her uncle for trying to take this time from her.

She could tell Zach she would run with him. She could leave it all behind and be with him. Until they ran out of luck.

"Nope, this is a discussion for another time," Kenzie announced. "We have to figure out why our cousin is so freaked out."

Uhm, because she spent several unintended weeks in a foreign country wearing underwear bought at a mini-mart in the Welsh countryside. Because she was in love with a man for the first time, and it was perfect except for all the fucking things that were wrong.

Because she'd been kidnapped twice in one year. Because she didn't have a job and she was going to have to make decisions soon. Ones she didn't want to make. Ones she didn't have the money to make. And she would make them alone because Zach would be gone. Either on the run or in a box of one kind or another. He would be gone. Gone. Fucking gone.

"I think she's going to blow." Kala sat up and sighed. "We might need a fight club."

Tash and Kenzie and Lou turned on her at the same time. "No fight club."

How long had Kala been talking about fight club? Which she was not going to do.

"I'm only saying she either needs to punch something or get laid, and I can only help with one of those things," Kala admitted and then seemed to consider. "Or…and hear me out…we trick Zach and tie his ass up and let Devi go at him."

"I'm the menace?" Kenzie pointed a thumb her sister's way. "We are not sexually assaulting Zach."

"I don't think it would actually be assault. More like a fun way to start a night," Kala argued. "Look, it worked for me and Coop, though he still complains about the flowers on his dick. Apparently dudes are real sensitive."

"Devi, are you scared?" Lou sat down next to her. "Because you've been through a lot in the last couple of weeks. Do you want to be here or do you want to go home?"

"She's not leaving Zach," Tasha said. "Oh, she can talk about how this is all sex, but she's not leaving him, and I doubt Dad is trying to convince him to leave her. He's probably talking about condoms."

Devi felt her whole body heat with embarrassment. "He doesn't need the condom talk. He uses one, but he doesn't have to. I'm on birth control."

"Oh, the condom talk can go a couple of different ways," Tasha assured her. "But it's more about talking about the heart. You see the condom is… Oww." Tasha reached over and picked up the hair tie her sister had lobbed her way. "Very mature, Kala."

"Well, you were talking about hearts and condoms, and I couldn't let you embarrass yourself," Kala replied, completely comfortable with her older sister shooting daggers her way. With her eyes, of course, although Devi had to admit if Tash had a couple of daggers, Kala would likely see it as a fun exercise. "Devi is freaking out but it's fine. We all freak out a little when we do this thing."

"This thing?" Tash asked.

Kenzie shrugged. "Yeah, that's what she calls epic love stories. She's not very romantic, and I'm with Tash. Dad's really talking about the condom we put around our hearts to protect them. Sometimes you leave that…" Kenzie ducked the flying hair tie her sister sent her way and continued as though it hadn't happened. "…off. Sometimes you have to take the leap and go with the flow."

"The flow is him being dead or in prison." Her cousins could joke all they liked, but she was still stuck. Stuck. Was that how it would always be? Would every man she met be put up against Zach and found wanting?

"Dad isn't going to let that happen." Kala seemed to get serious.

"Your dad isn't some magical god who can wave his hand and make this go away." She was on the edge. So close to it, and this wasn't where she expected to be today. She was supposed to have dinner and drink tea, and Lacey was supposed to be Lacey and they would argue about what to watch on telly and then she would go to bed with Zach and he would be all over her and she would sleep like a baby in his arms and pretend that every day would be exactly like that one.

"Don't tell him that." Kenzie sat down beside her twin. "Devi, it's going to be okay. If you want Zach, we can make it happen. I know I rejected the idea of tying Zach up, but it could work. We lock him in a room with a nice bed and then indoctrinate him with rom-coms. This is something I've been thinking about for a while. If all that's available to him is sex and rom-coms, he won't have anything better to do than fall in love. It's like brainwashing but for his dick."

Kala's eyes had gone wide, and she looked at Kenzie. "I feel bad for Parker now."

Kenzie shrugged. "I would only do it if he's being stubborn."

"I don't see how Uncle Ian is going to solve this." She stood. She wanted to be alone. She wanted to cry, and she couldn't do it here. Deep breath. Remember all the reasons why being near Zach is a bad thing. Devi plastered what she hoped was a sunny smile on her face.

"Besides, I don't think Zach is in love with me. I'm a rebound from Tash. It's been fun but it's nothing more than that."

"Rebound?" Tasha's head shook. "That's not what's happening at all."

"Marry me."

Her whole world seemed to freeze because that wasn't a question. It was a command, and it hadn't come from her cousins or Lou, who had wide eyes now, too. She was staring at the man who stood in the doorway.

"You're so fucking worried that I only love you because your last name is Taggart," Zach said grimly. "So let's change it."

Tears filled her eyes when she turned because it was clear he'd been crying. Her big, gorgeous, masculine Dom had been crying. It didn't matter that he cared about Tasha. It didn't matter that he was on the run and he lied to her. It didn't matter that they had no future. All that mattered was how her heart opened and started to beat again when he was in the room.

"See, there is no condom on his heart right now," Tasha whispered.

Tash was annoying and Devi kind of hoped Kala had endless hair ties, but she ignored all of them. All she could see was Zach.

She should run because if she moved into his arms, she would do everything he asked.

She crossed the room and went on her toes and put her mouth on his.

His hands immediately went to cup her head and hold her while he devoured her mouth. His tongue surged inside, wasting no time with niceties. He inhaled her, and she gave it all back to him.

His hands moved and he didn't bother to stop kissing her as he picked her up and began to move down the hall. He kissed her over and over. She heard the door slam as he kicked it closed and then he shoved her up against the wall and his chest was against hers, feet off the ground. He held her in place.

"Marry me."

Again, not a question, but she had one of her own. She held on with one hand and smoothed back his hair with the other, searching his eyes for the truth. "Why?"

There were so many reasons he could give, including the

conjugal visits excuse she'd come up with a few moments ago. Being his wife would make it easier for him to control her. It would ensure his place in her family. Even her father would accept him if she married him. She couldn't be forced to testify against him.

"Because I love you. Because you're in my soul and I'm not complete when you're away from me. Because if the only thing I do in this life is be good to you, I'll be satisfied."

Now she was the one crying. "Yes. I love you. I'll marry you. No matter what, Zach. If you need to run, I'll go with you. That is my only demand. I'll marry you but you can't leave me behind because you think it's too dangerous. You can't make that decision for me."

"I will never leave you of my own volition, Devi Taggart. It's you and me until the end, but your uncle seems to think that the end is going to be a long time off, so think about this, sweetness. You're going to be stuck with me," he vowed as he stared down at her. "Fuck that. You had your chance. You made your choice. I agree with your demands, so the deal is made."

Her heart was so soft when it came to this man. He was talking deals like he could trick her into staying with him. He didn't have to. She would never willingly leave him again. "I love you, Zachary Reed."

"I love you so fucking much," he growled before taking her mouth again.

Somehow the man managed to get her underwear off and free his cock and then he was inside her. And the world felt right again.

She gasped at the first long thrust of his cock, but she was already slick and wet and ready for him. She kissed him and held on to him. So tight. She could lose him tomorrow. She could lose him the next day. It didn't matter. They were together now, had made their vows, and she would let go of her fear and live with him as long as she could.

When the pleasure hit it came with a wave of emotion so strong she couldn't block it up this time, couldn't stop it. It came out as a sob, an acknowledgment of what they'd been through. The orgasm mixed with relief and anxiety and joy and fear.

She found herself on her back on the bed, Zach's arms around her as she cried.

"It's okay, sweetness," Zach whispered as he kissed her cheeks and forehead. "I'll make it right. I'll do anything to make it right. Anything but give you up. I love you."

She believed him. For the first time she believed him. He loved her and it felt like a miracle.

She clung to him while she rode out the storm and vowed to protect him, too.

Chapter Fifteen

Zach pulled the baseball cap lower on his forehead and was deeply aware of where the cameras were. The main concourse of Liverpool Lime Street Station was covered by a glass and steel dome meant to let the light in. Unfortunately, it was an overcast day and the rain pelted down, the sound a low thrum against the multitudinous voices and the clang from the trains.

"Comms working?" Cooper moved in beside him. He wore nondescript clothing. Jeans. Dark tee. Light jacket that covered the weapons he was packing.

"Testing," came the sound of Tasha's voice over the small earpieces they wore. "Zach?"

He gave his brother a thumbs-up before quietly replying. "We're a go on the west end."

Tasha and Lou were sitting at one of the small cafes, laptops open in front of them like they were a couple of travelers getting some work in while they waited on their train. Lou had already cut into the CCTV cams and was monitoring them, including several blocks around the station.

"We're a go on the east," Big Tag said. "You need to start making your way down. The train should be here in ten minutes, and it's coming in on platform six."

He'd studied the maps this morning over breakfast. With Devi in his lap, which should have been distracting, but he found she helped him focus. If she wasn't on his lap, he likely would have been watching her, trying to see if she needed anything. Or if she was plotting her revenge for the spanking she'd gotten this morning.

Liverpool Lime Street Station was technically two stations. High and Low. They were in the mainline station called Liverpool Lime Street High Station. Below was Low Station, that handled the underground and took passengers all across the city. High Station handled overland trains like the one from London his mother was currently on.

At least Henry's wife said they were on it when she texted Henry this morning.

Zach was waiting for it to all fall apart.

"Heading that way," Cooper reported back and then started to move, gesturing for Zach to join him.

Big Tag and Henry were watching from the other side of the station.

"I don't like the fact that we split up," Zach said under his breath as they walked toward the platform. "We should have left more people with Devi."

Kenzie and Tristan were meeting with the Canadians to go over what they knew about the Nepal base and Huisman's recent movements. They were meeting at a pub called The Phil. Public. Where it would be hard for someone like his father to ruin things.

Devi wanted to go with them because something about John Lennon drinking there and they had weird old loos she wanted to see, but they decided it was better for her to stay in the safe house.

He wanted to be with her, doing stupid tourist stuff and holding her hand and taking pictures so he could remember the days.

He was so tired of living in the shadows. Devi was his sunshine.

She'd waved off being stuck inside and promised to make some cookies since she was about to meet her future mother-in-law and wanted to make a good impression.

"I assure you Kala's not letting anything happen to Devi," Cooper replied. "She's been worried about her for weeks."

"The fact that she didn't even fight to go in the field tells me she's worried," Zach muttered. Kala Taggart didn't like to be benched.

Ever. He expected a big fight when her dad announced the assignments and she was left behind to guard her cousin. He expected the argument to be that Kenzie had control of where Parker and his tech were, so they shouldn't worry they'd be found out. Instead, she'd given her father a peace sign and drank her latte and promised to only maim Lucy, who was staying behind as well.

"It's not only that. She's pulling away from a lot of active field work," Cooper explained. "The last bout with Huisman nearly killed her. We're still figuring out the extent of the damage. I don't know how much longer we'll be in this line of work."

"Damage? From what Huisman did?" He'd heard about the experiments Huisman ran on Kala Taggart. First in Toronto, and then Virginia. He'd tried an experimental paralytic to keep her still while he poured yet another experimental drug into her veins. One that made her feel like she was on fire. But he hadn't heard anything about long-term injuries.

"Yeah." Cooper looked like he was checking the board for arrivals. "Her heart stopped both times. She's stable, but they're worried about what could happen in the future. I don't think she survives meeting that asshole a third time. So she's letting Kenzie take lead on the Kara construct role and she's going to transition to background."

His heart ached for her. Kala was the one who put everything into her job. Except she seemed happy. "She's okay with it?"

His brother's lips curled up. "She's started talking about the fact that she can't give her parents hellions to make their old age fun if she's dead. She's also started talking about the fact that if we take over the company, we're a McKay-Taggart who can get it on in the conference room."

It was a sweet thought and one that made his heart ache a little. "You're leaving the team?"

"Not now, but sometime in the next couple of years," he replied. "Or hell, who knows? Maybe she loves being in the background and we stay for life. I only know one thing."

"Where she goes, you go." Zach nodded as they started moving again.

"Where she goes, I go," Cooper repeated solemnly. "You okay being stuck in New York or LA watching your girl move up in some fashion design house?"

"Yes. I'm okay with whatever, but I don't think that's happening. I think she's going to be brave and follow her voice and start her own business. I think I'll be stuck in Dallas, and that sounds like heaven to me," Zach said, his heart twisting with every true word.

"Then you've never been in Dallas in August, brother." They made it to the spot.

"I'll be fine." He stood and waited with the crowd. Still a few more minutes before the train from London would be coming in. Nell told them they were in the fourth car from the front. He estimated where to stand. "The question is are you fine?"

Cooper stopped at a place fairly close to where the front of the train would end up. "Because I'm about to meet the woman who gave birth to me? I don't know. I love my mom and my mother's name is Eve McKay, but I have to admit I'm curious. Is she going to be like your aunt? Will she call me Jonathon?"

This part made his stomach twist. "I don't know. I haven't seen her in so long, I have no idea if she'll even realize who you are."

"I'll tell her. I'm not trying to hide, but I want you to know that I'm standing here with you not because I need to meet her. I'm here for you. Because you're my brother," Cooper said. "Although you should understand what that means. Hunter thinks you're super cool and if I have you as a big brother, he should get you, too. Vivi wants to meet you. I was hoping we could hang out in London when this is done so you can get to know her. Mom's worried she's into Oliver Weston, and Kala's going to threaten to take his balls if he puts one STI infected hand on her."

"Don't." Zach couldn't take much more. Not in public. The idea of being welcome, of having a family that didn't disappear for long periods of time… He just couldn't. Later when he had Devi in his arms, he would let it all out. It was safe for him, but not here when there was a job to do.

"Sorry, man." Cooper slapped him on the back. "I should remember how it feels to have one of the olds break you down. Big Tag, especially. It's like he's all sarcasm and congenial assholery and then he gives you the talk and it's like the man lays your soul bare, breaks you down, and then builds you back up again."

It was an apt description of what Big Tag had done the night before. "Well, we'll see if he can work his magic or my breakthrough is going to be spent writing letters to my wife from prison."

Cooper's brows rose in obvious surprise. "Dude?"

Zach couldn't help but smile. "I need to get her a ring, but she said yes. I'm going to trust her and hope it all works out."

Cooper smiled brightly. "It will. I promise. We're going to fix all the crap Huisman broke."

"The train is approaching." Lou's voice came over his comms unit.

He touched his ear to open the connection that would let the team hear him. "Got it. We're in position and ready. How's the underground, TJ?"

"All's quiet down here," TJ replied.

"I've got someone I'm watching," Big Tag said. "Tash and Lou, there are a group of five men walking into the front entrance. I need you to see if you can get facial ID on them. They're walking past the Boots store right now."

The train pulled in, sound humming through the space and making the floor buzz under Zach's feet.

"Where do you want to take her?" Zach asked. "We can't talk out in the open. Do you think she'll agree to come back to the house?"

Where she could meet Devi. Where he would find out how deep in she was and how hard his father would come after them all.

"She'll come back with us and we'll figure it out from there," Cooper said with a surety Zach didn't possess. "I wish we were the ones rolling in via train. I would feel better if we were meeting them at The Garden. It's got great security."

And was packed with MI6 agents who would be derelict in their duty if they didn't bring in the wanted criminals. It was precisely why Ian set it up this way.

At some point his mother would be forced to trade her expertise for safety because there was nowhere safe to keep her off the government's radar. Huisman or the Agency. They would want the same thing from her. He hoped they would have different means of achieving their goals.

"We have facial ID on one of the men," Tasha said in a completely calm tone. "He's Interpol, and we've got a couple of metro police vehicles pulling up now."

Shit. He didn't like the fact that they weren't coming in vests. They were sneaking in. Like they wanted to do this quietly. Because that was how they would bring in a rogue operative. He would bet there was someone with MI6 with them.

"It could be something else," Lou offered. "I'm not hearing radio chatter about Zach."

"Stay calm. The train is almost here," Ian said, his tone perfectly even. "Let's see where they go. It looks like a couple are heading down. TJ, blend in."

"Will do," TJ answered.

There was a little static in his ear. He started to reach for the comm.

"There are tunnels, you know." The new voice in his ear made Zach still.

A voice that haunted his fucking nightmares. He looked around as if he could see Huisman watching them. How the hell had he known?

"Is that?" Cooper began and his hand went to his jacket pocket.

"It's Dr. Huisman, Mr. McKay. How is your beautiful wife?" Huisman's voice sounded silky smooth over the comms. "Congratulations on your nuptials. I was so sorry I did not get an invitation."

His brother stepped back and had his cell out.

"Not talking to me?" Huisman chuckled over the line. He spoke English with a French accent, having spent his formative years in Quebec. "Well, that's all right. I'll see how she is myself when my men bring her to me."

Zach touched his earpiece. "Tasha? Lou?"

"Oh, I'm afraid they find themselves without connections right now. My group has some inventive men in it. Geniuses. They can ensure that certain devices in a small space cease functioning," Huisman purred over the comms. "I find it infinitely helpful. A complete communications blackout would disturb people and have them asking questions. Thank you for placing your techs where I could use the device on them but leave your comms working. This wouldn't be as much fun if I couldn't talk to you."

Don't panic. His first instinct was to pull his gun and start looking around for Huisman, but what if that was exactly what Huisman wanted? What if Huisman didn't know where he was, and a man suddenly looking around would be an X marking his spot.

"Zachary?"

He turned and his mother was there.

Older. Far more worn than the last time he could remember seeing her. Shannon Reed's dark hair had grayed, and she had it in a long braid that curled around her neck halfway down her chest. She wore dark pants and a flowy blouse, and seemed to have all her things in a worn leather backpack she slung over one slim shoulder. He registered the woman standing next to her, but she was like a blur since he could only concentrate on two things at a time—his mom and the beast that stalked them all.

"Mrs. Flanders, you need to go," Cooper said, his voice tight. "We're compromised, and he has eyes on us."

A gasp came out of his mother's mouth as she took in Cooper. "You're him. My sister told me she found you. You look like my father."

Cooper gave her a nod. "It's a pleasure to meet you, Ms. Reed. I would love to talk further, but we need to move. Quickly and quietly. Don't attract any attention."

"Where will you go?" Huisman asked. "The way I look at it, you have two choices. You can try to run, but your mother won't be able to keep up. Or you can stand there and wait for Interpol to arrest you in front of her and hope your biological brother will get her out in time. Which will you choose?"

He noticed Henry was jogging down the platform, but there was a group behind him.

Nell's face lit up at the sight of her husband, and his mother didn't seem able to see anyone but Cooper.

"Zach, we need for you to go. Now," Henry commanded. "Get down to the lower level and take the first train to pull in. Better yet, find one of the tunnels and get out that way. Cooper, you're going to need to distract them. You look enough like Zach they might think you're him if you act up a bit."

Interpol. Fuck. "I'll talk to them. I'll talk my way out of it."

"Oh, I'm afraid I won't allow that to happen, Captain Reed," Huisman said. "I'm going to have you murdered while you're in custody. One of the Interpol officers is a member of my organization. We like to recruit the authorities. Which one do you think it is? Won't this be a fun game?"

Huisman was an asshole. He touched his ear. "What do you want?"

"Well, I want the bombmaker, but it appears that CIA operative is going to take her from me," Huisman admitted. "It's all right. I have a backup plan. I hoped this would go easy." He laughed. "Who am I fooling? We both know I hoped it would all go to hell. More exciting that way. Here's how this goes. I'm going to set this place on fire and see who comes out alive. If I can't have the bombmaker, I'll take the next best thing. I think Louisa Ward already knows how to make the bombs, and if she doesn't, well I have someone new to experiment on."

Henry was hustling Nell and his mom away.

Cooper gripped his elbow, turning from the group of men obviously looking for them. "I know you're panicking. I can hear him, too, and somehow the fucker can hear us."

"Of course I can," Huisman said. "But if you get rid of the units, you won't hear what I have in store for your women. You know you would be much better at this job if you treated women as they should be treated. Disposable. Only useful for a few biological needs."

Cooper pulled his comm out and tossed it on the ground before stepping on it. "I need you to get to the next platform. There's a non-pedestrian platform between six and seven. It's used to turn trains around. It'll take you outside. From there make your way back to the safe house. I'll handle things here."

"He's going after Lou." Zach forced himself to go cold. Calm. Panic would cause more trouble than he could handle. "And if he knows we're here, than he likely knows where the safe house is. He said he would check in on Kala himself."

Cooper's jaw tightened. "Big Tag will go for Lou and Tash. Henry's getting your mom and Nell out. TJ is probably already on his way up. I need you to get the fuck out of here before they realize where you are. I know Big Tag can get you out, but it will be too late if what that fucker said is true."

"Everything I say is true," Huisman promised. "Why would I lie when the truth is so much more fun? Your safe house isn't safe, but then nowhere is safe for you, is it, Captain Reed? Mother loved her comfort more than her own son. She protected Cooper but left you as a target. Do you wonder about that?"

He started to pull the comm out of his ear.

"Tell Benjamin I appreciate the distraction." Huisman sounded positively chipper. "You know the best weapon is the one we plant ourselves. He was my best friend. That kind of loyalty never dies. Of course sending him millions of dollars helps."

Shit. Parker was part of this? Or Huisman was lying to throw him off. It didn't matter right now. What did matter was the fact that something was happening at the safe house. "He's going after Kala."

"Go," his brother commanded. "Contact me when you're safe. We'll take care of Devi." Cooper glanced down at his cell and started to dial. "Fucker couldn't jam the cell phones. Hey, babe…"

"That is cheating," Huisman said in his ear. "Well, I wanted to play hard ball anyway. Good luck, Captain Reed. I think you'll find your mother is about to be reunited with your father."

"Ray's here. He's going after Mom." Zach was about to pull his pistol and race after Henry…or race back to Devi. Fuck. He needed to get to Devi.

A dark instinct crept up Zach's spine. They had picked a public place because they didn't believe Huisman wanted to start his war yet. What if he was ready and they'd unknowingly walked onto his battlefield?

"Yeah, you need to…" Cooper began.

And the world exploded. The back car of the train on track seven blew sky high, sending shrapnel into the domed ceiling and lighting a flash fire.

There was another explosion, this one seemingly underground, and then people were everywhere. Running. Screaming. Trying to save loved ones.

"Look at them, Zachary," Huisman purred in his ear. "Rats. They're all rats, running from the flames. They aren't worthy of saving. They need a king to rule them all. You're a smart man. No one has ever helped you. Your family weighed you down. The government didn't help when you were hungry. Think about yourself this time. Bring me your mother or Louisa Ward and I'll make it so you never worry about money again. You should do it. Benjamin did."

"Tell me where you are and I'll bring her to you," Zach lied. He stood in the center of this localized apocalypse, the world falling apart around him. If he could get to Huisman…

"Oh, never mind. I don't need you now," Huisman said. "You should check on that CIA operative. He doesn't seem to have liked your father's present. Although his wife seems to be good with first aid. Tell Louisa if I don't get what I need out of your mother, I'll come back for her. And tell Benjamin I said hi. And don't worry about Devi. I'll take care of her for you."

His blood threatened to run cold.

He turned and saw his brother up ahead, kneeling on the ground with Henry's wife. Both trying to save the older man. He couldn't see what had happened.

"We need to go." Tasha jogged up to him. Her previously perfect dress was streaked with blood. "TJ has Lou. My father will stay with Henry, but we need to get out. His orders."

"We need to find my mother or he's coming for Lou." He had to shout over the noise around him as something else blew.

"They're gone, and we're not finding them in this chaos. You know what to do," Tasha ordered.

Report back to base.

What was he doing? He had to find Devi. He knew it was probably a damn distraction to get him to not follow his father.

Well, it was a distraction that worked. "We go out in the crowd and break off before they can question us. Head down. We have to get out far enough that we can call base."

Tasha nodded.

And they joined the fleeing crowd, praying everyone he loved survived.

*****

Devi glanced up at the clock and wondered if she was going to survive the experience.

"Do you have to breathe that way?" Lucy asked, staring with a frown on her face.

"Yup." Kala was laid out over the comfiest chair in the living area, scrolling on her phone. "It's how I receive oxygen. I know demons don't understand human physiology, but we require oxygen to live."

Lucy's eyes rolled. "I mean with all the sighs and obvious disdain. You know if you don't like it here, you can go join your father at the station. I assure you I can keep Devi safe. I don't understand why we can't go out into the city. It's not like Huisman is going to blow up Liverpool."

Devi sat up from her place on the couch where she sat kind of halfway watching telly and halfway waiting for the real show to begin.

Spy v Spy

Overly aggressive alpha female v overly aggressive alpha female

Kala v Lucy

Two spies enter, one survives with her hair intact.

Yeah, it was going down if the team didn't hurry up. "I can see The Phil later. I also want to go to Strawberry Fields. It looks pretty in the guide. Is there a reason the only juice we have here is beet juice?"

She'd kind of hoped for orange. Maybe some cranberry.

Both women turned her way and said in stereo, "Aliens."

No explanation. Nothing more. She searched her memory. "Is this a Bliss thing?"

"Yes," Lucy replied. "It's a Bliss thing, and Kala is a tourist."

Kala sat up, putting her phone down. "I spent almost every summer there, and a lot of Christmases and spring breaks, too. I know those mountains as well as you do. I'm sorry your sister likes me more than you. You made a mistake with Poppy. You let her meet you. If you wanted her to like you, you should have stayed away from her."

"Does anyone want to tell me why you two hate each other?" She was so curious. Zach didn't know. Cooper claimed he didn't know. Tristan had made a bunch of shit up and Tasha, Kenz, and Lou weren't talking. It was frustrating.

"I don't hate her," Lucy replied, arms crossed over her chest. "I simply don't want to hang around with a reckless asshole who will one day almost certainly get someone killed in the field."

"I do hate her," Kala countered. "She's an asshole who tried to ruin me when I was a teen."

Oh, they were getting somewhere now.

Lucy sighed. "Sure. It was all me. You did nothing."

"I responded to your taunts. I responded to your tricks." Kala looked Devi's way. "Do you know why Kenz and I went pink the first time?"

"No." Devi was so intrigued it almost made up for being left behind. "I thought you liked the color."

"I was fourteen and my mom told me I couldn't dye my hair until I was at least sixteen, and then we would talk. But then some asshole put bleach in my shampoo while my family was on vacation."

"I'm not proud of that, but I will say I was young and you told me I couldn't come with you and Poppy." Lucy's mouth tightened with the memory. "You told me Poppy needed older friends and I should find some kids my own age, but there weren't many kids my own age. I only had her. Everyone else thought I was weird. What would you have done if someone told you they were taking your sister away?"

"I didn't mean it like that, and I would punch them. I wouldn't put bleach in their shampoo. It could have gotten into my eyes," Kala replied.

"I didn't think about that at the time. I was freaking nine, and all I knew was my sister talked about how pretty your hair was, how much she liked the color. Do you think I haven't thought about what could have happened?" Lucy breathed deeply, as though she needed some strength to get through this conversation. "My mom talked about how lucky you were. And then she protested the shampoo company because you never told her you thought it was me. Why?"

"Snitches get stitches, baby." Kala sent her a peace sign that felt more like war. "I knew that even at fourteen. Besides, I didn't get it in my eyes. I only had it on part of my hair when I realized something was wrong."

Devi frowned her way. There were a few things off with this scenario. It wasn't like the shampoo would cover the scent. Not even Lucy's evil genius would have manifested so clearly at the age of nine. "Lucy might not have really known what could happen, but you did know what bleach would do. You would have smelled it. You at fourteen were practically a PI. You had already started hacking, and Kenzie was excellent at manipulating..." She pointed a finger her cousin's way because she did remember a couple of things that happened before that summer. "You said you were going to find a way to not wait two years. You complete sneaky bitch. You smelled it and put it on anyway."

Kala's lips curled up. "Kenz and I flipped for who had to do it. I lost, but Mom came through. I bravely offered to cut my hair and Kenz cried because then she would have to cut her hair, too. Mom was so upset with Kenzie's tears that we got to go pink. So…suck it."

Her cousin was so immature sometimes. Only sometimes. Or this was all part of Kala who often didn't get the nuances or know how to let go of a grudge. "So she's a kid who you left out and she's kind of mean like you and she tries to get some revenge. Again, she's nine. And her revenge leads to you getting something you've always wanted and you call her Lucifer."

"Only because her mom didn't properly name her," Kala quipped.

"I'm sorry. I was sorry when I did it," Lucy said, her tone rigid. "I felt bad and I tried to stop you, but you already figured it out. I loved my sister. I didn't want to lose her, and I never found a Lou. So there. Call me whatever you want. I'll be in the study waiting for word."

Kala turned Devi's way. "Seriously? You suck."

Devi's hands came up. "I suck? You bullied a kid."

"I didn't bully her." Kala groaned. "I didn't. Poppy wanted to hang with kids her age and not have to deal with her little sister. That doesn't mean she didn't love Lucy. It meant that during the summers she wanted some space, but she didn't know how to ask for it. So I did it for her."

"You told a kid her sister didn't want to be around her?"

"Of course I didn't. I told her to hit the road and go play with kids her own age," Kala replied. "We were teens and we wanted to hang out and not worry about baby sister getting in trouble. And now I can maybe see how she would have taken it wrong, but she was mean as shit."

"I'm trying to imagine you without your sisters," Devi pointed out because she thought Kala was being short sighted here. "You without Kenz to balance you. You have always been excellent at finding people who see you. What if Lucy didn't have that? What if Lucy's only real friend was her sister and you tried to take her away?"

"I didn't try to take her," Kala insisted. "Poppy is a person. I can't take her away."

"And how did you feel about it at nine? This is Kala after therapy. What did nine-year-old Kala do when someone threatened her family?"

Kala's head fell back and she groaned. "Do not do this to me, Dev." She brought her head back up, a stubborn look in her eyes. "We have a good thing going, Lucifer and I. We hate each other and we're good with that. The universe accepts it. Why would we change things now?"

"Because you're very, very similar but you're older and have seen more and could potentially help her. She's right. She doesn't have a Lou or a Kenz. She doesn't have a Tash or your brothers and cousins. Was she the weirdo in the weirdest town in the world?"

A long-suffering sigh came from her cousin's chest. "She was the kid who liked to play with matches and take things apart to see how they worked except sometimes she broke important things and maybe accidently blew up a shed or two. It was funny. She was always possessive. Not with things, but definitely with people and animals. She had this cat that she didn't want anyone else to pet."

"So smart, awkward socially, curious in a way most people would find annoying. Weirdly possessive." She was going to have to lead her cousin to the truth. By force. "Sound like anyone we know?"

"You think she's like Tash?" Kala asked.

Devi stared her stariest stare.

Kala growled a little. "Fine. There are some similarities, and I will admit when it comes to the job she's not entirely useless. But she's mean to me now. She named a cranky donkey after me."

"You call her Lucifer. I think The Fabulous Miss K is a way better nickname. Also, you would have liked the donkey. She would have been your spirit animal after you got over the name and you would have called her your best animal friend." She knew her cousin so well. Kala would love to hang around an animal sanctuary. It would calm and soothe her and give her purpose.

"What do you want me to do, Dev?" Kala asked. "We're never going to be besties."

"Just be nicer. Maybe don't hiss when she walks in a room," Devi suggested.

"It's a conditioned response to the addition of awfulness to my space," Kala replied.

"Maybe don't refer to her as awfulness." They had so much work to do.

"But she is," Kala insisted.

"Only when you're around," Devi shot back.

"Because I see through her..." Kala's face went a nice shade of pink. "I fucking hate therapy. It sucks and it sucks that I'm so good at it. Fine. Just fine. I'll refrain from calling out the terrible shit she does. I will try to be nice."

Devi rewarded her with a brilliant smile. "I know you can do it. And think about how proud Coop and Lou are going to be when they get back and you two are not at each other's throats. I still can't believe they left you two here together."

Devi sat back again, looking at the clock. Time was moving at a snail's pace, and she wished she could have at least sat with Lou and Tash and watched over him. But no. She had to stay put and not climb out a window.

"They don't want to further kill Lucy's cover. She can't go back to Disrupt because there's zero way Huisman doesn't know she's a plant, but she might be able to work it from another angle. I do feel bad about that," Kala admitted. "She worked her way in. She's been working at it for years."

Progress. "And Kenz wanted to be as alone with Ben as possible. Do you think she'll tell him?"

Kala's head shook. "With Tristan there? And I'm pretty sure that Tim guy was going. I doubt it. She'll wait for some weirdly dramatic time and announce her love for him and then we'll have to deal with that asshole for the rest of our lives."

Marriage had not made her cousin more romantic. "It's called happily ever after."

"I call it shit I put up with," Kala returned. "So what was all that spanking and moaning about this morning? You and Zach decide to make my dad want to die? Don't get me wrong. I approve thoroughly, but I didn't think Zach would feel the need to spank you after all the moaning from last night. Dude, you are not quiet. Kenzie cried because she said it was so beautiful, but I just wanted to sleep, man. You need to be quieter with your emotional connections."

She shrugged because she didn't care that everyone heard them. That way the group would know they were serious. "He was still upset that I didn't tell him about the whole 'a dude tried to roofie me and oops, it turned out to be his dad.' Personally, I don't think I should be held accountable for that. They don't look alike. How was I supposed to know it was his dad? No one gave me one of those file thingees, and you know they really should have."

Kala's lips turned up, an amused expression that Devi had seen on her uncle's face. "We call it a dossier."

"Well, I did not get one." And that was a real oversight on the part of the team. She might not be getting an Agency paycheck, but she was definitely Agency adjacent. Shouldn't that come with privileges?

"I think he would have been upset about anyone who tried to roofie you. He's your Dom. You didn't let him know you needed protection," Kala pointed out.

"Well, he wasn't at the time. We were kind of broken up."

"Were you?"

It had felt like a breakup. "I mean he didn't bother to tell me he was leaving. Not Dom-like behavior. But also, I didn't mind the spanking. It's kind of my thing, so I'm not going to complain, and honestly, when he goes into all the things he'll do to me if I put myself in danger again… It doesn't throw me off. He should think of worse things than taking a violet wand to my pink parts. That's sounds like a fun Saturday night to me."

Kala pointed her way. "You pull some shady shit again and it won't be your boyfriend you answer to."

The last thing she wanted was a throwdown with her cousin. Lucky for her, she knew how to distract a Taggart. "Please refer to him properly. He's my fiancé."

Kala shook her head. "You really doing this?"

"Yeah. I love him."

Kala stood and moved to hug her cousin. "I'm happy for you."

Devi reveled in the affection. Kala could be standoffish, so Devi appreciated every hug. "I'm happy for me, too. But now I have to tell my dad. My mom will be thrilled. She loves Zach. Dad, not so much."

"He'll come around when he sees how happy Zach makes you," Kala promised and moved back. "Well, if he's not in prison."

"You are horrible. Don't say that." Lucy walked in, frowning fiercely. "She does not need to hear that."

"It's the freaking truth," Kala shot back and then visibly calmed. "Sorry, Devi. I shouldn't have mentioned that Zach might go to jail."

She turned back to Lucy. "Now what put that constipated look...that worried expression on your face?"

She was trying. Not hard, but trying. "Very good, cousin."

Lucy's nose wrinkled. "What's wrong... Never mind. I know the answer. You're Kala. Anyway, I think we have a van that's circled the block four times now. I went to the safe room to chill out and watched the security cams for a couple of minutes. It could be a work van looking for an address or someone killing time."

"Or it could be trouble," Kala announced. "I'll go take a look. You make sure we're locked down."

"The security system is good. The doors are all locked, but we're not a fortress," Lucy admitted. "Well, except for the safe room. It's solid. It should survive a bomb if they dropped one on us."

"Then maybe we should get in there." Kala's head moved, gesturing for Devi to join her.

In a small room with the two of them sniping at each other? No thanks. "Come on. Can't you make sure it's a bad guy before we lock ourselves in?" She'd seen the safe room, and it locked down hard and fast and was meant for one or two people who liked each other a lot. It was kind of a panic room that locked and stayed locked for four hours after the button was pushed. Four hours of intense therapy with Kala and her Bliss twin did not seem like how she wanted to spend her day. "Please. If you lock it, we're stuck inside, and what happens if your dad wants us to move? What if Zach needs to take his mom somewhere else? He won't go without me. He'll wait and put himself in danger for what might be a dude who's lost."

Kala sighed. "Fine. Lucy, did you run the plate?"

One of Lucy's shoulders shrugged. "It's registered to a man without a record. It looks like he's a contractor of some kind, so he could be looking for a house. I don't know. I don't like it."

"All right." Kala started for the front of the townhouse. "I'll take a look. Have you informed your father?"

Lucy winced. "I don't want to worry him until I'm sure. He's got enough to deal with. He's always nervous when my mom is involved."

Kala pointed Devi's way. "You stay here."

Devi sat down and tried giving her cousin her best I-will-cause-no-trouble smile. "I'm right here."

Kala walked to the front door and stared out.

Lucy brought her laptop out. "I lost him. He turned at the end of the block, but I don't see him on the next traffic cam."

That felt like good news. "He probably found the house he's supposed to be at. So there's nothing to worry about."

Lucy didn't look sure. She was staring at her laptop. "Hey, Kala, you get that text?"

Kala walked back in, staring at her phone. "Did you run the pictures Lou sent?"

"She already has facial recognition." Lucy whistled. "I don't like that Interpol is at the train station. We should have brought her in by car, but my mother insisted on public transit."

"Hey, Shannon Reed insisted on it," Kala corrected. "Don't blame your mom. She's doing everything she can to help us. Okay. Lou and Tash are handling this. There are tunnels they can get Zach out of. Cooper will try to distract them and our dads will get Shannon out, but we have to consider the fact that Huisman is either at the station or close by monitoring. Put his picture through Tris's program."

From what she'd heard this morning, Tristan's program was some kind of upgraded facial recognition with superfast results.

"On it." Lucy's hands moved across the keys.

Kala was staring down at her phone, obviously waiting for something.

Interpol. The European police force that had a notice out on Zach was at the train station. Her gut twisted. It was too much of a coincidence. They had to be there for Zach. Who could have tipped them off? They'd been careful on the train. They were certain the cameras hadn't caught Zach, but what if they'd caught her at some point and Huisman had told the police that Zach was traveling with her? What if she was the reason Zach was about to get hauled to prison? "Where will they take him?"

"Don't worry about that now," Kala replied, her thumbs working the screen of her phone. "The team will get him out. We need to prep to move. I'm waiting for the bug-out call. Devi, go and pack what you need. We're moving out of here in ten minutes tops."

"You don't want to hole up?" Lucy asked.

"If they know we're here, all they have to do is sit outside the panic room and wait for the doors to open," Kala pointed out. "It would be one thing if the team was coming back, but we all need to move and give them a bunch of targets to try to follow. We're going to London."

"We?" Lucy asked, challenging her.

"Yes, fucking we. I'm not leaving you here. I'm the senior officer and you're going with me. I'm not going to let you fall into Huisman's hands. He would absolutely turn you and you would be a chaotic goddess who would kill us all. So get the fuck ready to move out." Kala strode away, putting the phone to her ear.

Devi stood, adrenaline starting to pour through her. Zach was out there. People were after him. "What if they try to kill him at the station?"

"They won't. They'll take him in." Lucy sounded so reasonable. "Your uncle and his team will get him out."

"But this guy, Huisman, he's known for blowing crap up, and he doesn't care who he hurts. I should know. I was in the last place he set on fire."

Lucy looked up. "First, the facial rec doesn't show him here in Liverpool or anywhere in England. Now I do have a couple of known Disrupt members entering the train station about five minutes ago, so we have two problems. I think Huisman is going to use Interpol to distract the team, and while they're worried about Zach and trying to deal with that, the mercenaries will pick off Shannon Reed or one of our people who they will offer to trade her for."

"You mean they'll try to get Lou or Tash?"

Lucy nodded. "Yes, but I assure you they're already on the move. Tash and Lou know how to handle themselves. My question is who tipped them off? Mom and Shannon are traveling on excellent faked passports. I checked as they moved through security. It should have worked. I wouldn't have allowed my mother to get on that train if I wasn't sure I had protected her. She and Shannon are wearing some tech that tricks facial recognition."

"We can't let Huisman get hold of any of us. Kala nearly died." The idea of her cousin being in that madman's hands again made her want to throw up.

"I'm surprised to hear that. All the stories around the Agency are that Miss Magenta is immortal."

"She's not. Lucy, I'm not joking. What Huisman did to her nearly killed her. It still might because we're not sure how much long-term damage he did to her heart. If he gets her again, he'll use a paralytic on her, and then he has drugs that inflict unbelievable amounts of pain on the body. I heard her cry. I heard it. If she has to go through that again, her heart won't be able to take it."

"It hurt her heart? I didn't know she had one of those," Lucy replied.

Devi needed to make something clear. "I'm not joking, Lucy. Her heart stopped both times Huisman got his hands on her. The second time she walked into it knowing what he would do because his lackey was threatening me and Cooper's mom. She knew she was going to likely die and did it anyway. I can't allow it to happen again."

"Well, then it's good she didn't go to the station." Lucy's eyes were back on the screen. "You should do what she told you and grab your bags. Pick up mine if you can. It's got everything except makeup, and I'll buy more. We need to get to London. If our fathers can't help Zach, then perhaps Damon Knight can."

Kala walked back into the room, her phone against her ear. "What are you saying, babe? You're cutting out. Damn it." She sent Devi a glare. "Hey, I was not kidding. I know you're scared but grab the bags."

She nodded and turned to the back, rushing to grab the bags. She got Kala's backpack and the canvas pack Lucy used. It was slightly open, and she could see guns and knives and some cash. She settled the cover and hefted it over her shoulder and moved to her own room. The one she'd shared with Zach.

Her heart ached. They hadn't made the bed yet. It hadn't seemed important since she'd spent as much time as she could wrapped around him. Before they'd been called to breakfast and his briefing concerning the day's mission, she'd been on her back with Zach on top of her, fucking her like a man possessed. Then he'd flipped her over, played with her ass and fucked her again. Then he'd fucked her in the shower before spending time washing every inch of her skin and shampooing her hair. She could still feel his strong fingers rubbing over her scalp. For a man who hadn't known a lot of tenderness, he reveled in it.

He couldn't go to jail.

He could die in jail. He could get hurt. Anything could happen, and she wouldn't allow it. He was hers.

She took a long breath. It was going to be okay. Her uncle had this, and Zach was a professional. He would get out and meet them in London. He would want her to follow Kala's orders now. He would not want her to rush down to the train station to try to save him. No. That would result in a not-fun spanking, and despite the fact that he'd called what happened this morning disciplinary, she suspected the next one would be a doozy.

Calm. She was a spy's fiancé, and this was the gig. Like how he would have to learn to ignore the multitudinous bolts of fabric that would sit around their apartment because she couldn't resist and someday might need that lilac-colored jersey knit she found for half off.

The floor beneath her shook, and she heard a booming sound in the distance.

What the hell? She pulled her pack over her shoulders and grabbed the other two and rushed back into the living room. Kala and Lucy were in the kitchen, and Lucy suddenly looked like she gave a damn.

"That came from the north," Lucy said.

Kala nodded. "The train station is a couple of miles north. I think we can safely say Huisman is no longer playing. That's a declaration of war. We have to move. I'll run a magnet over the computer in the office and send out a text to let Tris and Kenz know to run. Shit."

It took a moment for Devi's eyes to register the small hole in Kala's torso. It was on her left side, right above her hip, and blood bloomed.

She hadn't even heard the window above shattering. When she'd first walked in, Lucy had explained the lower windows were all bullet resistant, but the picture windows that let light in were normal in case they needed a way out. Someone found a sniper position and took advantage.

Lucy cursed as Kala stumbled and fell, her head striking the island. She slumped to the floor, still bleeding.

"Damn it. Throw me my bag," Lucy shouted. "Do not walk across the floor. He's got a shot at anyone in the living room. Stay where you are."

Devi nodded and tossed the bag across the room. It landed near her cousin's body. "Is she okay?"

"I don't know." Lucy grabbed her bag. "I need to get you out of here."

She felt another shaking and one more boom from several blocks north. It could be something else.

But deep down she knew they were caught and someone was about to come through that door. "Can you stabilize her?"

"She's unconscious because she hit her head. The bullet is pretty much in the best possible place. Lower left quad is where you want to get shot if you have to. Yes, I could stabilize her, but I have to get you out."

She heard a pinging sound and realized it was coming from the door. "They're here."

They stood on opposite sides. The living room with its comfy chairs and sofas and coffee table was a chasm between Devi and Lucy and her cousin.

"They're coming through the door, and they will take me." Devi had heard this scenario a million times. "They will want to use me to bring in Zach." Another ping and then someone was banging on the door. Kicking it, probably. "They'll bring Kala in and she will die. They will kill you. Please. You can get to the safe room."

She couldn't because it would mean running across the space, and she could see more than one red dot prowling around, looking for a target. How many guns did they have on three women?

Lucy glanced at the door and frowned at whatever she saw there. "You honestly believe she'll die?"

Devi nodded. "She will die. Please save her, Lucy. They won't kill me, and Zach will find me. Take her to the safe room and lock it down. Stabilize her. Cooper will come for her. Let me give you the distraction. If they have me, they don't need her."

"She's going to kill me." But Lucy wrapped her hands around Kala's wrists and started pulling her toward the safe room. "Try to get out if you can. The windows above the beds can be broken. They're safety glass, meant for quick escapes. Be careful and call someone. Kenzie, if you can. Tell her where we are. This should be you doing this. You should be in that fucking safe room with her."

The door finally gave way, and she heard the sound of men

rushing in as Lucy disappeared with Kala.

She recognized that man. Zach's father stood in the living room. His mask was off, his predator unleashed. Two men showed up behind him, both with guns in hand.

Devi stood there, trying to give her cousin a chance. "I already called the police."

Ray White's lips curled up in a smirk. "They have better things to do. Trust me. When my boss decides to distract, he does it well. They're all down at the train station trying to find the terrorists. And he made sure there's an Interpol team there so everyone is trying to save their fucking brothers. Gotta love cops," he said with a chuckle. He glanced around, his eyes stopping on Kala's backpack near Devi's feet. "So where is Kala Taggart?"

Devi shrugged. "She went out for breakfast."

"She got shot. Tell me they didn't kill her." Ray walked in, acting like this was a normal visit between friends. "They were specifically told to not kill Miss Magenta. The boss likes her. I think he's got a little crush." He nodded to the others, and one of them took off the way Lucy had gone.

Please let her be in the safe room. Please. Please let her sacrifice mean something. "What do you want with me?"

He looked her up and down, the way a man does before he makes his move. It was gross. "Well, honey, I think I want to find out why my son is willing to risk the world for you. Right before the bombs started exploding, my boss might have implied to Zach that I was at the station and after his mom. So that probably threw him off and he won't see the real men ready to take her into custody. She's got a soft spot when it comes to Zach."

"He's her son." Her heart was pounding in her chest. Panic threatened, but she remembered all the training her mom had given her. Her parents hadn't let her go off into the world without learning some self-defense. The biggest part was to not panic.

"Yeah, that's been helpful over the years. I shoulda knocked her up more," Ray said. "I think when she knows how our son feels about you, she'll do what we need. Of course if we catch Zach, then it'll just be fun to watch him squirm. Thinks he's better than his father. I'll show him."

The sound of gunfire blasted through the townhouse, and Devi took the chance. Lucy was fighting and she was smart. If she only had to deal with one…

Devi took off for the back rooms. The doors were heavy and they locked. She slammed the bedroom door closed and locked it, reaching for the only chair in the room and propping it against the door. Immediately it started shaking.

Devi ignored it and grabbed a towel, wrapping it around her hand and climbing on the bed. Thank the universe she had some of her father's height. She pulled the thin lamp, turning it over and using the heavy base to break the window.

She was halfway out when she felt hands around her ankles, pulling her back.

She hit the bed as her hands were gripped behind her.

"Don't you dare kill her," Ray was saying. "She's all we got since that bitch killed Greg and locked herself in. We have to go. Now. Knock her out, but don't you fucking kill her."

Devi kicked and fought, but when the man brought the hilt of his gun down on her head, she slid into darkness.

Chapter Sixteen

She was gone.

They were both gone, but Devi...his Devi was in the hands of a fucking madman, and he hadn't been here to protect her.

Zach stood in the living room surrounded by his team, but he had never felt more alone.

Because this was his fault. He had brought her with him for selfish reasons.

"I have a private aircraft leaving twenty minutes after the attack." Lou was on her laptop. "I believe they're going to Nepal, which vibes with the intel the Canadians gave us. Are you sure we shouldn't be at the hospital?"

The question was directed at Kala. Who probably should be at the hospital.

When they'd returned to base, they'd found it eerily quiet. The door had been kicked in, and for a moment he thought Devi had made it to the safe room. Big Tag knew the room was in use, and they all believed their people were in there.

"I'm fine. Lucifer's pretty good at stitching people up," Kala replied, her eyes on her own laptop.

Then the door had opened and only Kala and Lucy had emerged.

"It wasn't as bad as I thought at first." Lucy stood beside Tristan, who was also working the web to find information. "There was so much blood I thought the bullet was lodged in her, but it was more like a heavy grazing of her left side. I think they had orders to not kill her. I know the dude I shot was pissed he couldn't get his hands on her."

"Which is precisely why you should have left me and taken Devi into the safe room," Kala said through gritted teeth.

Lucy's eyes narrowed. "We had a sniper situation. I couldn't get her across the living room without exposing her to gunfire, and she basically begged me to save your lousy ass. Which I am regretting right now."

Cooper sat beside his wife. "I am eternally grateful, Lucy."

Kala frowned his way.

Cooper shook his head. "Devi knew you wouldn't last another round with Huisman. Those drugs of his are primed to kill you this time."

"Well, now he'll use them on Devi," Kala announced.

"We don't know that." Big Tag paced, waiting for word that the plane was ready. "He was torturing you for very specific reasons, the chief one being you're my daughter."

"I think it was more than that." Zach found the will to speak. He'd done nothing these last few weeks but sit around and think about Emmanuel Huisman. "Huisman is a red pill misogynist of the highest order. He genuinely believes women are good for breeding and serving men and nothing more. Kala challenges his world view. He treated Carys differently, from what I've been told."

"Well, he was about to cut her fingers off with a straight cutter," Tristan said, every word tight. "But I do get what you're saying. He's fascinated by Kala. He wants to break her."

"I'll break his dick the next time I see him and then we'll see how toxic his masculinity really is," Kala vowed.

"Eve agrees." Big Tag continued to move like he couldn't stand to be still. "I talked to her a few minutes ago. She's built a profile on him. I think she would say Zach is right on the money. His only real interest in Devi is going to be in controlling Shannon."

"I should have let them take me." It was killing him. Those moments in the train station could cost him everything and all because he followed his instincts and fought when he should have conceded.

"And then they would have still tried to take Kala and they would have simply shot Devi." Big Tag moved in front of him, putting his hands on Zach's shoulders. "I know where you are, son. I've been there far too often, and I can tell you that trying to run different scenarios that might have changed things will do nothing to help her. Throw your guilt out. I need you to be the soldier you are. The operative I trained you to be."

"See, I was thinking he's taking this pretty well," Tris pointed out.

TJ finally looked up from his phone. Zach was almost certain he was texting back and forth with his parents. "He looks calm, but underneath he's losing his shit. Like I am."

At least one person got him. It was good that it was Devi's brother, though TJ had to blame him, too.

"Ben thinks he's ready to move." Kenzie had asked to bring the Canadians in, but Big Tag wanted time to assess the situation. She was staring down at her phone. "Ben and Tim are on their way to Nepal. Maybe I should go with them."

Big Tag sent his daughter a stare that could have peeled paint.

"Fine," she said and sat back down. "But it wasn't about Ben. I think we need to get there as soon as possible and figure out how to save my cousin."

"We're lucky we're not in custody," Big Tag announced. "Drake is losing his shit because we're not supposed to be here, and now we're in the middle of the biggest terrorist attack in Europe in this century."

Twelve dead. Countless injured. Billions in property destruction, and Huisman was just getting started. There was something more. Something he hadn't told them yet. The team knew Huisman had been in his and Cooper's ears, but they hadn't told them everything.

"Huisman claims Ben is a double." Zach forced himself to say the words. "When he was talking to me before he blew the station all to hell, he pointed out that none of this was possible without Ben's help. He claims they're still friends, and Ben has been with him all along."

Kenzie waved him off. "Huisman lies. Ben has done nothing to hurt us. He's risking his job to work with us right now."

"He's being a reckless asshole because he knows damn well he's going to need a key card and code to even approach the facility," her father said. He looked Zach's way and gave him a slight shake of his head, which Zach took to mean they weren't talking about this now. Not while Kenz was here. Tag directed his attention to Lou. "Lou, you have the schematics, right?"

Lou nodded. "I thought I would do a presentation on the plane where I have you all as a captive audience. But yes, this facility Ben claims is actually a front for Huisman is Disrupt Asia's climate base. It's supposed to house a bunch of scientists and climate professionals who are studying the Himalayas for signs of climate change. It's built into the side of a mountain, and from what I can tell it used to be a Chinese secret base. Disrupt bought it years ago, so who knows what changes Huisman's made. The security system runs on key cards and codes. I'm surprised he's not using biometrics."

"Tech can be difficult in an environment like that. Also, he would have to bring people in to set it all up, and not dayworkers. He would need specialists," Tristan explained. "From what I can tell they only recently started to use this place. At least Huisman's visits began roughly a year ago."

Henry walked in the room, sliding his phone into his pocket. He walked slowly, having taken a knife to his side. Luckily he'd deflected it, and Big Tag had stitched him up. "I've talked to the director. What happened at the station today has sent shockwaves through the Agency."

"I'll bet it did. Well, at least they can't deny who Huisman is anymore." Big Tag finally stopped moving, leaning against the bar. He ran a hand over his head. "I bet your talk went as well as mine."

"He's pissed that Lucy's cover is blown, and I don't think he's buying what Drake's selling," Henry admitted. "But the good news is now this team is considered the subject-matter experts, and you're kind of unassailable since no one else has clocked as much time on Huisman as you. You've got the go to get to Kathmandu. They have an agent on the ground who's going to run logistics for you."

Tag nodded. "We need to find a way to access the inner base and get the intel to Parker. At least those were my orders."

Could they trust Parker? "How much does Parker know about what went down today?"

"Parker is being told an American team will meet him there, but he knows nothing else," Henry replied. "But you should understand we're working with the Canadians on this. We've agreed to provide backup and share intel. The important stuff."

"He doesn't know they have Devi and my mom?" Zach asked. The world felt like it was running in slow motion.

"No, and it's going to stay that way because no matter what my daughter says, we have to look into the allegations," Big Tag announced. "The Canadians' mission concerns Huisman and ensuring he can't do whatever it is he plans on doing. Our mission is to support theirs. On the surface."

"Our real mission is getting our people back," Kala surmised.

"Then why are we working with him at all?" Kenzie's lips flattened into a stubborn line.

"Because we keep our friends close," her father said, "and our enemies closer. Kenz, you're going to be in charge of working with the operative on the ground. We'll fly into Kathmandu, get what we need, and hopefully meet the Canadians in a day or two. I'm going to hope bombmaking takes some time."

Time was the one thing they didn't have. He didn't like Big Tag's timeline. Not one bit.

"All I care about is getting Devi and my mom out of there." Zach wanted to be on a plane now. He glanced over at Lucy, who was excellent at putting together logistics at a moment's notice. It wouldn't be the first time she'd helped him out.

Cooper stood and pointed a finger his way. "You are not ditching us and making a run for the facility. Lucy, if you help him, I'll find a way to make your life hell."

Lucy's head shook. "Well, you already did by bringing your psycho wife here and ruining years of undercover work. No. I will be going home with my parents and licking my wounds. I can't help anymore. I have to figure out what I can do and hope I don't get fired."

"She's been ordered back to Langley, and so have I." Henry's expression was grim. "We're taking a flight back tonight. My wife... Well, she's pretty emotional right now since she's worried she somehow screwed up."

"I'll talk to her, Dad." Lucy crossed her arms over her chest, a defensive position. "None of this is her fault."

"No. It's not." Henry held a hand out to Tag. "I'm sorry it's gone this way. If you need me, I'll tell Langley to go to hell."

Tag's head shook. "We need to go in fast and tight. Kenzie will handle the Canadians. Lou will work tech. Tash, you need to find us a base of operations close to that mountain. Zach and Cooper's only job is to get our people out. Tris and I will find the anthrax and ensure Huisman can't use it against anyone. Henry, we'll talk when we get back. I'll handle things through Drake for now."

Kala held up a hand. "Uhm, hello. Still here."

"Still shot," Tag countered. "I should send you back with Henry."

"Please don't," Henry said.

"I'm not going anywhere but to Nepal." Kala stood, and if her side was bothering her she didn't show it. "I'll stay in the background, but I'm not going home. My cousin is out there, and my team needs me."

They started arguing, but Zach couldn't take it anymore. He stood and walked back toward the bedroom where it was apparent Devi had tried to get away. There were tiny pieces of safety glass all over the bed they'd shared. Proof of how low he'd brought her. She should be home and safe. She should be applying for the internships she wanted or working on her business. She should not be trying to survive being kidnapped by a fucking terrorist.

"Whatever you're thinking, stop."

Zach turned and Cooper stood there, his mouth a flat line. "I'm thinking I got my fiancée killed."

"She's alive. I know she's alive, and we're going to save her." Cooper walked in, avoiding the glass by the bed. "From what I can piece together, she saved Kala and likely Lucy, too."

"Devi shouldn't have to save anyone. I should have been here. I shouldn't have left her." The guilt was starting to eat him alive. He felt so fucking numb, and he knew it was a way to delay the pain, but it was coming for him.

"Devi would always save whoever she could. Don't make her less than she is. And if I'm reading Huisman right, Devi was likely taken to force Shannon to do Huisman's bidding. I think he was trying to take either you or me. I had to fight off a guy."

"You mean you killed him."

Cooper shrugged. "It was him or me. He had a syringe. Lou will run it through one of her many instruments and come up with what was in there, but I think we all know it was a sedative. It's how Huisman works. He didn't get either of us, so Devi will have to do. I suspect he always meant to try to get Kala back, and Devi was an insurance plan. We can't blow the place up if Devi and your mom are there."

That was an excellent point. He needed Devi alive.

"He'll hurt her." Every possible scenario was going through his brain at this point.

"Not if Shannon complies. Do you think she will?"

He hoped she would, to a point. "I think this is my mother's worst nightmare. I don't know. I don't know if she'll shut down. She's capable of anything. The truth of the matter is I don't know her. I know the facts about her life, but she's been in and out of mine for so long that I don't know if she'll build a bomb to save the woman I love. I only know I put her in this position."

"You didn't," Cooper insisted. "Look, man, I know how you feel. I know what it means to do something and have the consequences be so over the fucking top you can't imagine it. I didn't mean for anything to happen and yet it did, and I was a fifteen-year-old kid."

He knew something of what his brother was talking about. He and Kala had a fight when they were teens and it ended with her being kidnapped so her cousin would have to walk into a trap. They'd been estranged for a long time after.

Was Devi out there wishing she'd never met him? Wishing he hadn't walked into her life and wrecked it?

What was she going through? What was his father putting her through on that plane? Would he dump her body at the end of this like she didn't matter? Like she wasn't the whole world?

"Zach, you have to calm down. You need to be clearheaded throughout this." Cooper studied him for a moment. "Maybe we should rethink our plans. I know it's hard for me to think straight when Kala's in danger."

"You are not leaving me behind."

"Technically, you're not part of the team right now. You're AWOL. Have you thought about that?" Cooper asked. "You could be arrested at the end of this. I don't think Big Tag has worked his magic yet."

"He doesn't give a fuck." TJ stood in the doorway, his face pale as he looked at the window. "Zach doesn't care about anything but getting Devi back."

TJ should be pissed at him, too. "Man, I'm so sorry."

TJ shook his head as though he was shaking off some thought. He walked into the room and gave Zach a big bear hug. "I know. I am, too. One of us should have stayed, but this is the job, man. She should have been safe with Kala and Lucy. Huisman threw us a curve ball, and now we have to do everything we can to deal with the problem. So you're going to take a deep breath and we're going to do the job. There is no failure here. There is only one purpose, and we will achieve it. No matter who we have to get through."

"I know the Agency is probably going to make a big deal out of ensuring this op is as quiet as possible, and that means keeping the body count down, but everyone in that facility knows what's happening," Cooper said. "From what I can tell they fired the real scientists a year ago. This place isn't about climate change. It's a bioweapons factory."

"So we take them all out and then it'll be real fucking quiet," TJ vowed.

Funny, goofy TJ could turn on his soldier self when he wanted to.

"But Zach, you have to consider the fact that they'll want you to come in," Cooper pointed out. "If you go in…"

He might never come out, but he was having some faith. "If I go in and I don't come back out, you have to promise me you'll take care of Devi. I have to do this because I need to clear my name if we're going to have any chance at the life she deserves. But if it goes wrong…"

"Then we'll have a job to do," TJ said, putting a fist out.

"And we'll get it done, brother." Cooper's fist joined TJ's.

His brothers. Somehow he'd found this amazing family. He pressed his hand to theirs.

He wouldn't let them down.

* * * *

As kidnappings went this one wasn't terrible. At least the accommodations were pretty good.

Devi looked around the sleek private jet. There were three men with lots of guns and a pilot with guns, and then there was Zach's dad who had...yep, more guns.

It was gun party central.

"So you're my son's girlfriend." Ray White sat in the chair opposite her.

She had to figure out how to play this. What she wanted to do was throw bile and vitriol this guy's way. Her head hurt. She was being kidnapped...again. She was on her way to who knew where, and her future mother-in-law was drugged and buckled into a seat toward the front of the plane. They wouldn't let her sit close to Shannon. She wanted to fight. But she'd seen how Huisman handled Kala. He'd loved her bile. It made him want to hurt her more.

She knew nothing about this man.

She knew nothing at all. Everyone kept looking to the back of the plane like they were all waiting to see a predator emerge.

She had the feeling Huisman was here, and that motherfucker was waiting to make an entrance.

"I don't think he calls you dad." She glanced over at Shannon Reed. She'd tried to make her more comfortable.

"Only because she kept him from me. She kept the other one from me, too. I didn't know about my other boy until Dr. Huisman told me. That bitch ruined us."

"I thought she hid your other son because you were in trouble with a cartel and she was trying to protect him." Logic might not work, but she was going to give it a go.

"I would have protected them. I would have protected them all." He stared at Shannon like she was a work of art. Or a deeply held regret that threatened to drown him.

"You were in prison," Devi pointed out.

"I had plenty of connections."

She wasn't sure what his prison connections would have done to a cartel that wanted to hurt his family, but she wasn't going to argue. "Well, you certainly do now. You have Huisman. How did you meet him?"

Calm. She sounded calm. That was how she was going to play this whole thing.

She hoped Zach was calm. She needed him on his game because

she knew without a doubt that he was coming for her. It would be up to her uncle to keep her brother and fiancé from running in without a plan. They would rush in and try to kill everyone when they needed to be surgical.

All she had to do was survive.

"He came looking for me." Ray's voice brought her back to the moment. "He knew I could bring Shannon in. I've been following that woman for most of my life. I can find her anywhere."

She'd been in hiding for years, but again, she wasn't about to argue with the criminal. Also, he hadn't brought her in. Nell Flanders had.

She hoped her cousin was alive. She remembered something about Lucy taking out the other guy and locking them in, so she knew they'd made it at least that far.

Devi looked out the window. It was dark, and she had no idea where they were going.

Where was Zach? Was he okay?

"You found her today," Devi agreed, leaning over to see if she could tell if Shannon was starting to wake.

"She'll be out for hours. Unlike you. You're being an awfully good girl."

Oh, she didn't like that, but she gave him a wide-eyed stare. "I don't want to die. I'll do what you ask me to, though I don't know why I'm here."

"You're here because these men could not bring in the person I wanted," a deep voice said.

Sure enough, every eye was now on a place behind her. Damn. She was about to meet the man, the myth, the terrorist dickhead.

Emmanuel Huisman stepped into her line of vision, putting a hand to the back of Ray's chair. He was an attractive man in his early thirties with intelligent eyes that held a hint of his cruelty.

"I suspect the person you wanted was my cousin," she replied quietly.

Huisman's lips curled up as though he was remembering something infinitely lovely. "Well, that was for personal reasons. It had nothing to really do with the mission, though Ray here was smart enough to at least bring me someone. Yes, I did want to get my hands on the stronger half of Ms. Magenta. I will never understand why my dear friend Benjamin is fascinated with the other one."

That was news to her. "I don't think he knows."

Now his smile was vibrant and bright. "Of course he does. I told him, but that's a matter for another day. I simply don't understand why my dear friend would want the bland and boring when he could have the extraordinary."

Her gut tightened at the thought of Ben Parker working for this man. "He's helped us."

Huisman sank onto the seat beside Ray and wagged his finger her way. "You are not a part of *us*. You are not on that team. You are Ian Taggart's much-indulged niece. Benjamin has not helped *you*. Now the question becomes has he helped the team? Or did he maneuver them into the position I want them in? Time and time again. I'm actually disappointed Taggart fell for it. I suppose I made him up to be far more than he truly is. Rather like that woman at the front of the plane. She doesn't look like the person who can change the world."

"I suspect that's because you don't believe women can."

Huisman's head shook. "Oh, not at all. I know women can change everything. For the worse. Women manipulate men. Like our friend here. Shannon kept his children from him. A child needs his father. I had mine taken from me. My father, that is. By your uncle. Look how I turned out."

She was not about to go there. "Zach did fine without him."

"Ah, Captain Reed." Huisman's voice turned silky smooth. "I tried to reason with him. When I captured him in Toronto, I meant to spend some time with him, get to know each other. I thought he, of all the people on that team, might see reason."

She was pretty sure they had different definitions of reason. "Then maybe you shouldn't have tortured the people he cared about and put him in handcuffs."

"Well, he managed to kill all of my men while he was handcuffed, so I suppose I'm lucky he ran." Huisman gave a negligent shrug like he wasn't talking about life and death and trauma. He sobered. "Still, I would have preferred to bring him in. Or his brother. That was the original plan. I think Shannon Reed will do anything for her sons, but I can pivot. I can still make this happen." He turned to Ray. "Does it bother you that neither of your sons has your name? Names are so important. It's a man's right to name his sons."

It was clear to see Ray was uncomfortable. "I named him Zach. I didn't get a chance with the other."

Huisman tsked. "I'm talking about the family name. It means something. Women are vessels to be used and discarded. They are pawns for their fathers to move around and strengthen his family line. Your sons do not have your name. One has the name of his vessel and the other carries a stronger man's name."

Ray's eyes narrowed. "He ain't stronger than me."

A low chuckle came from Huisman. "I assure you Alexander McKay has better control over his family than you do, my friend, though he was only able to produce one weak girl child. His sons all came from other men."

"Who hurt you?" Devi knew this was a mistake, but the words were out of her mouth before she could stop them. "I mean as a child, because it's clear you have problems. Was your mother a terrible person?"

Huisman went still. Preternaturally still, and Devi braced for an attack.

And then he took a long breath and sat back. "My mother was a whore. After my father was murdered, I was sent to live with her for a brief time before my grandfather took control. She was far more interested in finding a man than in being a mother. In the short time I was with her, she brought in three different men."

Ah, that's who physically hurt him. It was apparent there was all kinds of psychological harm, too. "I'm sorry you went through that. There's nothing worse than a chaotic childhood."

One side of his mouth turned up. "Is that how you're playing me, Devon?"

Now she was going to be honest with him. "I'm not playing at all. I'm simply trying to understand the man who will likely kill me."

"Well, at least you're realistic. And my childhood prepared me for the real world. While my mother was absent, at best, those men she clung to taught me a lot about how the world works. Only the strong survive, and the ideas placed in the heads of humans about building communities and families are constructed by those who wish to pretend the world is something it is not. For far too long smart men have allowed the weak to rule, have allowed the idea that independence makes us equal. I'm going to show the world that this is not true. It was better when we had a king to rule us."

She knew where he wanted to put the crown. "I suppose you're the king."

"Of course. I mean I can't rule the entire world by myself. I've picked my dukes and vassals from my brethren. When this is done, we'll carve up the world and it will be a calmer place. Imagine an end to wars and famine. Well, unless a famine is required to remind the slaves of their place."

She was sitting with a madman. "Since I'm probably not going to be around to see this new world order, tell me, how are you going to accomplish it?"

He seemed to think about it for a moment and then leaned toward her, an unholy light in his eyes. "I'm going to start a war in Asia and watch the world burn. Once I get the right bombs, I'm going to deploy them over select Asian cities to deliver a deadly form of anthrax. I believe with the proper use of Ms. Reed's bombs, we can take out fifty percent of the population of Bangkok in moments. The same with Taipei and Kathmandu."

Ray clapped his hands together like he was going to enjoy the carnage. "I can't wait to see that."

Devi was confused. "But won't that make everyone mad at you?"

Huisman waved the thought off. "Oh, they won't think it's me. I've already started several rumors in intelligence circles that the Chinese are planning something big. The Chinese government was more than happy to work with the Huisman Foundation and later with Disrupt Asia. It gave us access to certain systems that got us into other systems. They use artificial intelligence a lot in China. Sometimes it's about taking over control. When the attacks occur, a broadcast will go out. The president of the People's Republic of China will take credit for the attacks. The deep fake is chef's kiss. Truly remarkable. Along with all the data and files I've planted deep in their systems, the world will have no choice but to attack China."

And the world would explode. "When are you going to use the nukes? I suspect you have control of those, too."

"I have a few of my own," he admitted. "Those systems are harder, but I assure you I can make it look like it came from China. You know I don't actually have to send a nuclear warhead to say, Washington, DC. I only have to make it look like it's coming."

"Because the US would respond if they thought it was coming," she surmised. "You don't think they would wait to verify it was real?"

He laughed at the thought. "You honestly believe your government will wait when they believe they are about to die? I mean perhaps if they did it would prove me wrong. I don't know. We will see if I'm right. Now let's talk about how you're going to bring Zachary Reed to me. I think he might need a little help."

"Why wouldn't you have Ben Parker bring him in? Zach would believe it." She didn't. He was lying for some reason. She'd seen her cousin and Parker. He might be a spectacular actor, but why wouldn't he have made a move by now?

The crack across her face shook her to her core. She could handle pain, but that man had damn near broken her jaw.

She cradled her cheek, tears filling her eyes.

"Perhaps I will send him your body parts." Huisman stood, sneering down at her. His hand clenched in a fist, and Devi prepared for the pain. "When he gets your hands, he'll do whatever I want."

"Stop or I won't help you at all." Shannon Reed stood on shaky legs. "You don't lay another hand on her."

Huisman turned, his eyes widening. "You are supposed to be asleep."

Her gaze went a bit unfocused, but she stood her ground. "You think you're the first person to try to drug me? I assure you I can handle more, and I know you'll probably give it to me, but understand if that young woman is hurt at any point, I will let you kill me before I'll build a single bomb for you. I didn't write down my process for this particular bomb and it is different from the others. I stopped documenting my work after some early schematics got out. It's all in my brain now, and I'll find a way to blow my brains out before I give you anything if you hurt her."

Huisman's face went a flaming red, and Devi could see he was considering whether he was going to use those fists on Zach's mom.

Devi moved and quickly. She put herself between the two. She wasn't going to let Zach lose his mom. Her hands came up as though she could placate the beast she found herself with.

There were suddenly a whole lot of guns pointed their way.

"There's no need for violence," Devi said quietly, the words tremulous. She forced herself to breathe. "I'll be good, and Ms. Reed is going to do what we need to do. I think you'll find if you send Zach a body part, he won't be able to be reasonable. Send him proof of life and let him know I'm good, that I'm being taken care of. That's how you deal with Zach and my family. You're right. I'm not a part of that team. I'm a fashion designer. I'm not going to give you any trouble."

She felt Shannon's hand on her shoulder. She wasn't sure if she was trying to give her support or needed the support herself, but she appreciated the fact that she wasn't alone.

Huisman backed down. "We'll record proof of life when we get to the base. If you step out of line in any way, I will make you wish you were dead. I will allow all of these men to have a go at you."

Shannon tried to move to her side. "And I will make sure my bomb explodes in your face. You won't see it coming. I'll be clever. I will not let you harm my boy this way. He loves her. Nell told me all about her."

She hadn't even thought about Lacey...Lucy's mom. She'd met her a long time ago and she was the sweetest woman. Was she okay? Had Henry gotten her out?

Devi pushed the questions aside because she couldn't know and wouldn't trust anything these men told her. She needed to bring the heat level down. "I'm not going to cause any trouble. I'll help Ms. Reed. I'm good with my hands, so you shouldn't cut those off."

Huisman snarled and turned and walked toward the back of the plane. She heard a door slam shut.

A sigh of relief went through her. Somehow all those men with guns didn't scare her nearly as much as the one who didn't carry at all.

Shannon stumbled and Devi caught her, helping her back down to a chair.

"Hello, baby." Ray hadn't moved at all, and his focus was entirely on the woman he'd put through hell.

Shannon brought her hand up, giving her husband the finger before she slumped back.

Ray chuckled like she amused him. "It's so fucking good to see you, too, babe. We're going to work a few things out."

Devi sat down and found herself holding Shannon's hand even as she slipped back into sleep.

She vowed she would do whatever it took to protect Zach's mom.

Chapter Seventeen

"I don't like this plan." Big Tag paced the floor of the house they were renting on the outskirts of Kathmandu. "Or rather I don't like this timeline."

From the small windows Zach could see the mountains in the distance, including the one where Devi was being held. Where she'd been held for the last three days. Seventy-two hours where she might be tortured. He had no idea what she'd been forced to endure while they'd been moving things into place and waiting for Ben Parker to let them know he was going in.

Zach was done waiting. "I'm turning myself in, and I'll do it whether the Canadians are ready or not. We honestly still have to think about what Huisman said. I find it interesting that they were so gung ho days ago they couldn't wait for us, and now we're twiddling our thumbs waiting for them."

"Kenzie only got the key card a few hours ago," Big Tag pointed out. "And Huisman set a time limit. You still have twenty-four hours before you turn yourself in."

"Parker is being cautious." Kala sat at the small dining room table, watching them with hooded eyes. "I know. I don't like this feeling. I'm giving him the benefit of the doubt. I should be all

Parker's a traitor, but it doesn't add up. I've worked with the man. He's had several good shots at taking us out or handing us over, and he hasn't. This is Huisman bullshit meant to divide us."

"I tend to agree," Big Tag said.

He didn't know Parker the way Kala and Kenzie did. He wasn't the operative in the field. He was the guy who moved in when it all went to hell and they needed someone to start blowing shit up.

Sitting on his hands was killing him.

"She looked good in the last video." TJ stood in the doorway that led back to the bedrooms. Lou and Tristan and Tasha were set up in what they called command central. Tris had already gotten into part of Huisman's security camera system.

They could see the workspaces but not his private residence, which was deep inside the mountain. They couldn't see what was most likely his torture chambers.

Last night he sat up watching the monitors, waiting for any sign of her. He'd watched as she carried something from the loading docks back to the halls where there were no cameras to be hacked.

She'd been steady and calm, and beyond looking tired, there were no outward signs that she was being harmed.

But some scars were hidden.

"She's acting," Zach replied. "She's staying calm so we don't get freaked out. We won't know what's happened until we get her back."

"Coop's on it. He has to find a helo that will work at that elevation. He's meeting a guy today who thinks he can get us one without Huisman finding out. The man has eyes everywhere," Kala said with a sigh. Her twin was currently sleeping, having had a long night of flirting with Huisman's guards so she could get a working key card to his inner office. "We checked and we're all up to date on the anthrax vax."

The military had taken care of the men. He, TJ, Cooper, and Tris had it as part of their military medical protocols.

"Yeah. I make sure all my puppies get their shots. And we're all covered with Lou's new trackers," Big Tag announced.

"I put it in Tris's ass myself," Kala agreed. "Whiny man baby. Like it hurt. But we all have to understand that we don't know what he's managed to do to the anthrax. We know Dare's dad's company made it more easily inhalable and concentrated, but the bacteria itself was basically the same and should be covered by our current vaccines."

"However, Huisman works in medical tech. We know he's got some doctors in Disrupt who specialize in bacterial infections," Big Tag continued with the bad news. "Who knows what they've managed to do."

"We will once we get in there and Lou downloads everything she can get her hands on." TJ moved to the table. "I'm going to shadow Lou. Cooper's going in behind Zach. He'll stay back until the team goes in, but he'll have eyes on you."

Zach was surprised. He'd expected TJ to fight to be there with him. "I thought you would do that."

"Don't need to. You love my sister. Cooper's not going to let his brother die. So I can protect my girl. You need to understand there is no one else on earth I would leave this to, and that includes my parents. I love them, but it's been a long time since they were in the field. And my uncle is old."

All eyes moved to Big Tag, who simply shrugged. "I would argue but even I can hear my knees creak. And I'm pretty sure I know what sciatica is now. However, we need Coop to stay close to the helo. He's the only one who can fly it. I'll go in with Zach and try not to hold him back too much. TJ, you should understand I will absolutely tell your mother you think she's too old."

TJ went a little pale. "I didn't say that. I said she was out of practice."

"Not what I heard." Kala's lips tugged up.

"Yeah, I definitely heard him say his mom was super old," Tris concurred as he walked into the room.

TJ was going to be his brother-in-law. "I'll let your mom know everyone is being mean to you. And TJ, I will get her out of there."

"I know you will. And Devi knows where the cameras are." TJ sat down and pulled one of the energy drinks laid out on the table toward him. "I looked through the footage you flagged last night. Did you see when she stopped and reached down and tied her shoe? Her shoe wasn't untied. She pretended for her guard. She stopped right where the camera would pick her up and while she was down there, she flashed a peace sign."

"Whoa, didn't she and Bri and Devi used to send each other

coded messages?" Kala seemed to think. "When they started dating they would try to be in the same places for the first couple of dates."

TJ nodded. "A clenched fist meant save me. A peace sign let them know she was okay and they could relax. She's okay, Zach. She's strong, and I think maybe your mom is helping her. I saw them going into the dining room together. She was holding your mom's hand."

Tears pierced his eyes. Was his mother working hard to ensure his girl was okay?

"The question becomes why risk bringing Zach in at all?" Big Tag put his fear into words and then winced. "Damn it. He's got something up his sleeve. Something that will make Zach or this whole team look bad."

"We can't worry about that right now," Zach replied. "All that matters is stopping him and getting Devi back."

"I think he's more likely setting up Ben." TJ sighed and took a long sip of the energy drink. "He's not my favorite guy or anything, but I know he's not working for that fucker. Otherwise, why would he have put us all in harm's way to make us believe Huisman's the bad guy?"

"I don't think we're the real targets. He's playing with us, and I don't like it." Big Tag looked Zach's way. "I think you have the potential to get close to him. We all know the minute he realizes we're raiding the place he'll leave, but you might get into the same space. Langley wants us to bring him in."

"I'm going to kill him," Zach vowed. He didn't care what Langley wanted.

Big Tag nodded. "Do it. Any of you. If you get the chance, take the shot. We're not playing games anymore. Take him out and we'll let Henry's team deal with the fallout at Disrupt. I think MI6 is planning to send an agent in to take Lucy's place. Once Huisman is done, we're out of this mess."

The door came open and everyone in the room went tense until they realized it was Cooper. He walked in and shrugged out of the jacket he was wearing. "I've got us a helo, but we're kind of stealing it. I'm afraid this is going to have to go down today."

Big Tag sighed. "I'll go inform Drake. Someone wake Kenzie up. I'll let Drake be the one to tell the Canadians it's go time whether they're ready or not."

Cooper put a hand on Zach's shoulder. "You ready, brother?"

Zach nodded. He was ready to get his girl. No matter what he would make sure Devi was safe.

* * * *

"It's done?" Huisman stood in the lab, arms crossed over his chest and eyes on his prize.

Three small bombs he meant to explode midair over three heavily populated cities here in Asia.

Shannon turned from her place at the high table where she'd been working diligently. Or rather seemed to be working diligently. Devi happened to know Zach's mother could have finished this project two days before but she kept putting it off, forcing Huisman to collect more "parts."

She'd done a good job of buying them a little time. Time for Zach and the team to move into place and make plans.

Devi had to hope they were out there and they'd worked their magic. Last night when she'd been allowed to go to the loading docks to pick up a package for Shannon, she'd taken a chance. She'd stopped in front of one of the CCTV cams to tie her shoe and flashed a peace sign, hoping her brother would remember the signals she and Bri and Daisy used when they were younger. She hoped it told TJ that she was safe and they could take their time. Rushing in might get someone killed. It was all she thought about when she lay awake at night. She thought about her cousins dying. Her brother dying.

Zach's big body cold and still.

"I need to..." Shannon began.

Huisman held up a hand. "I need you to think about what you're going to say next. If it's anything beyond *yes, sir, it's ready* we might have a problem. My patience only lasts so long. Your son is coming soon. My men are picking him up in the village below us. They can treat him with care or they can be careless with him. It's up to you. I need him alive, but I don't need him unharmed."

Devi's stomach threatened to turn. She'd spent her days mostly locked in this lab with her future mother-in-law. She'd only been allowed out to gather things Shannon needed or when they ate in the small dining hall. Then they were shadowed by guards. For the most part, they'd been left alone to work. There was a guard on the door, and they had to deal with Huisman's creepy check-ins.

They'd been offered separate rooms to sleep in, but Shannon insisted on keeping them together. She didn't even like sending Devi off to grab the parts she needed. Zach's mom was watching over her like she was something precious.

Of course Devi had to protect her, too. Zach's father was almost always around. Always watching Shannon with greedy eyes.

And now Zach was coming.

She knew deep down he wouldn't be coming alone. Things were about to get complex.

"They're ready. All you have to do is slide the canisters in. They're wired to respond to the detonation and will release in an umbrella pattern that will give you maximum coverage." Shannon's arms crossed over her chest. "Why do you need my son? I told you I would do what you wanted."

"Ah, but you didn't do what I wanted," Huisman said, facing off with her. "I wanted you to teach me how to make the bombs. I wanted you to document your process."

"I couldn't do that and get them done in time. You gave me a few days to basically invent a new system. The bomb itself wasn't made to disperse biological weapons." Shannon seemed fragile at first, but now Devi understood how strong the woman was. "I assume you'll want more at some point."

Huisman stared at her like he was trying to decide how the rest of this conversation was going to go. If Devi had learned one thing about this man, it was that he was mercurial. Cautious one moment. Utterly reckless the next. "You assume correctly, and that is the only reason I don't kill you now. Well, that and I'm going to need leverage to get the captain to do my bidding."

The reality hit Devi. This had been his plan all along. "You're going to make him do it, aren't you? You're going to make him drop the bombs."

"Well, I'm certainly not going to do it myself. I'm going to tie Captain Reed to the Chinese and implicate his boss, Ian Taggart, as well. It shouldn't be too hard. His wife has Russian syndicate ties," Huisman explained with a smirk. "Most of the materials you used in those bombs were brought to me by that same syndicate. You'll find that mobsters don't take the time to vet who's paying them. They don't care, but I do. There's a clear trail. Tying him to the Chinese and making your uncle look like a double agent will be far trickier, but I think there are some people at the Agency who will believe anything to get Ian Taggart behind bars and out of their lives."

She was horrified because she knew he was right. There were people in the Agency who would love to see her uncle fall. "Zach won't do it."

One shoulder shrugged. "Then he will watch you die in a horrible way."

"If he has to choose between me and a million people, I assure you he's going to choose the people," Devi said and realized her mistake the moment she made it. She'd been so good at keeping her damn mouth shut, but she was starting to fray. Something would happen and it would happen soon.

Huisman turned on her like a predator scenting prey. "Then he will not be useful to me either, and I will still find a way to pin it on his dead body. Do I make myself clear? Miss Taggart, this is not a negotiation. If Captain Reed complies, you will be allowed to leave. He will be allowed to leave. I would honestly rather have him alive and on the run, but I can manage it. So if you care about him at all, you will cry prettily and convince him."

She wouldn't. She would try to save them both, but she wasn't about to allow Zach to kill millions of people to save her own skin.

"He'll do it." Shannon moved between them. She did it a lot. She placed herself between Devi and whoever was coming at them. "I assure you my son will do anything to save his fiancée. He'll get it done for you."

Huisman stared at her for a moment, the air ripe with potential violence. "He better, and Ms. Reed, if those bombs do not work, I will let your ex have you. I've kept him on a leash. For an old man he still has quite the sexual drive."

"They will work," Shannon replied, the tremor in her voice the only sign she was affected by his words.

"You should hope so. I will inform you when your son is here. Perhaps seeing you will make it easier for him to make the correct choice." Huisman turned and walked out.

Devi got a glimpse of the guard outside the door and then it clicked closed again.

"We can't let Zach use those bombs."

Shannon reached out and took her hand. Her voice went low. "You are going to let Zach do what he needs to do to get you out of here. If I could have found a way to fake the bombs, I would have, but he's monitored us far too closely, and despite what I said he could probably reverse engineer it at this point. He's had a camera watching us for days. The last few adjustments I obscured with my body, but it won't take much for him to figure out what I did."

"Shannon, he's talking about killing millions and starting a war that would kill millions more." Devi couldn't get a grip on the enormity of what that man was planning to do. He was going to burn the planet and for nothing more than revenge on his perceived enemies. He was going to take down her family.

"Sweetheart, if there is one thing I have learned in this life, it is that we can only do so much and the rest is fate. Maybe if it was only me, I would leave this life. I've hidden and wasted years because I was too afraid. I thought Zach would be better without me. I know Cooper was better without me. If you weren't here, I would set that bomb off. I would kill us all and make the world a better place."

It sent a chill down her spine, but she had to consider it. She had to consider that her life wasn't worth the lives of everyone who would die next. "Could you do it?"

It would save her family since they were absolutely on the ground somewhere. Likely in Kathmandu. They would be there when the bombs went off. They would breathe in the air and they would die. She could make sure that didn't happen.

Shannon's chin came up. "I could but I won't. Those bombs are connected remotely to a computer that will control its detonation. Any computer is hackable. But I'm putting this in the hands of fate and my son, who is the absolute best thing I ever did. Sometimes I'm sure he's the only good thing I ever did. I will not let the woman he loves sacrifice herself. Besides, it's not like he's given me access to the actual canisters. The ones he had me design around are empty. They don't contain the anthrax."

"But these do," a masculine voice said.

Shannon tensed, and Devi knew who was standing in the doorway before she even turned around.

Ray. He was the shadow always haunting them.

She worried he was hunting them.

Now it was her turn to stand in front of Shannon. He'd obviously come to take the bombs now that they were done.

This was happening. Anxiety pressed against her, but she forced herself to stay calm. "You should take them and go. I think Huisman is getting impatient."

"Huisman is fucking insane," Ray said with a chuckle. He nodded to the two men who stood behind him, and they moved in quickly, taking the bombs. Ray held back. He had a thin metal canister in his hand, one that would fit neatly into the space Shannon had built at the base of the small bombs.

So small to be so deadly. Shouldn't something that could kill millions have more weight? Be harder to carry?

One of the men took the canister from Ray, promising to deliver it to Huisman.

Shannon waited until the other men stepped out before looking to her ex. "Ray, you have to stop this. I know you don't care about many people, but you have to know this will affect you in the end, too. If he does this, the world ends."

Ray's gray head shook. "The world changes. It doesn't end."

"The one we know will end," Devi said. "We won't ever go back."

"Little girl, I've spent the majority of my life working my way up. I've found the best way to make myself rich and powerful is to take from other people. When Huisman gets what he wants, I'm going to be a king, and I don't care that my kingdom will be on fire. It will be mine and I will finally have what I deserve." He stared at Shannon for a moment. "And you will be there at my side. I will make sure of it. You should know I won't care that you don't want to be there. In so many ways that makes it sweeter. So this better work or he'll take it out on all of us, and anything that he does to me I'll take out on everyone you care about."

Tears filled Shannon's eyes. "They're your sons, too."

"Nah. They ain't nothing to me but a way to control you," Ray admitted. "And the second one, I don't even know him. Zach was a disappointment. I'm sure the other one is, too."

"You're a fucking monster," Devi spat.

"Watch your mouth," Ray shot back, his eyes narrowing.

"Watch your back." There was a time to lay low and a time to fight like hell. It was looking like the latter.

Shannon quickly got between them. "Don't lay a hand on her. Huisman needs Zach to do this job, and he'll be pissed if Zach hesitates because his fiancée is hurt."

A feral smile crossed his face. "Well then I'll have to wait until the job is done. Then maybe we'll see what my son finds so intriguing. I have to admit I wouldn't have thought he would go for the athletic type. I like my women more womanly, but it might be fun to make him watch."

"Don't you dare," Shannon said.

"I dare and so much more," he snarled her way.

There was a pinging sound that always preceded an announcement. "All security report to the loading dock."

"Well, that will be our boy. I think it's time to get this party started." He turned and started for the door.

It was time. No matter what Shannon said, she had to try. Even if it killed her.

If she was dead, Zach wouldn't be forced into an unthinkable position.

She might not be a spy, but she'd been raised by two soldiers.

When Shannon turned away, she reached for the hammer Shannon had used earlier in the day and moved into position, following Ray. She was sure Huisman would have loved to ensure they had access to nothing, but tools were required to make bombs, and no one had come to pick them up the way they usually did at the end of the day.

He was sloppy because he had too many balls in the air, and she'd made him think she was harmless.

So it was time to do some harm.

She heard Shannon gasp but it was too late. She kicked out, catching Ray firmly in the back and sending him straight to the ground. Before he could get up, she brought that hammer down on his head. Hard. Twice. Blood spewed and Devi took a step back as Ray twitched and then went still.

"What did you…" Shannon stared at the man on the floor.

Devi had to stay focused. They needed to get out of here. She just murdered someone. Murdered.

She had killed Zach's dad.

No. She fought for her life. She was fighting for her family. Deep breath. She needed the key card, and she hoped the fucker had a gun.

Shannon was shaking but seemed resolute. "He wears his gun in the small of his back. Always has. We need the key card, too, and we have to move because even though they're preoccupied with Zach, they're going to see the tape. You run. I'm going to destroy those bombs."

"I'm going with you," Devi said, reaching in and pulling out the gun. It was a semiautomatic, like the one her mom had trained her on. She checked it and flicked off the safety before grabbing the key card. "We need to stick together because we only have one key card and one gun."

Shannon nodded slowly. "Okay, but sweet girl, if anything happens, you have to let me go. If I'm not alive at the end of this, I can't make more bombs for him. I wish I could promise you I won't, but we both know I'll do it if it means saving my boys."

Devi nodded and grabbed the key card.

Shannon stepped over her ex's body like he was a bit of trash.

Devi followed and prayed she wouldn't have to make that choice.

They opened the door and she heard a blast from somewhere in the complex. The floor beneath her shook, and she knew Zach was here.

Chapter Eighteen

Zach wished like hell they'd zip tied his hands in front rather than the back. It made it hard to punch a dude.

Huisman stood in the big loading bay looking every bit like a fucking Bond villain. All the asshole needed was a white cat and maybe an eyepatch and he would be set.

Devi was somewhere inside. Not somewhere. From the intel Kenzie had dug up, she was likely being held in one of the labs close to the center of the compound.

"Hello, Captain Reed. It's good of you to join us." Huisman's lips curled up in a satisfied smirk. "Welcome to Disrupt Earth. It's what I like to call this place."

This place was stark and streamlined for work and not comfort. Huisman was surrounded by several men cosplaying soldiers. At least that was Zach's take. He could buy that a few of them had real military training, but most of these men looked sloppy. A few even seemed uncomfortable with their weapons.

The intel was correct. Huisman's army was a ragtag group of mercenaries, and not top paid ones. These were men he culled from the bottom or hired from local towns. Likely he'd wanted to make sure no one in his employ had ties to intelligence agencies. He thought he could tie up their loyalty with money and the prestige of working in a place like this.

The dude highly underestimated Kenzie Taggart's ability to flirt and roll a guy.

"I want to see Devi Taggart and my mother." Time. He needed to buy the team a little time to get everyone in place.

They'd picked him up on the outskirts of Kathmandu, and he was surprised they hadn't roughed him up more than they had. He'd had his hands zip tied and a coarse fabric bag tossed over his head. That was the moment he knew Huisman was going to play this to the hilt.

Because if Ben Parker was working for him, wouldn't he know they had the location of his base here?

They were risking a lot for Kenzie's crush. If Huisman was telling the truth, this was one big-ass trap, and they were falling into it.

If he was lying, what Ben Parker did next would prove if he was an ally or the enemy.

Parker, who had told them he was ready to infiltrate Huisman's pain palace. He was supposed to meet the American operative deep inside the base. He would be coming in via air ducts.

Kenzie would be entering with a little more shock and awe.

"I think we can arrange that," Huisman said. "After we discuss your part in this."

It was hard not to look around and get more of a lay of the land, but he forced his attention on Huisman. "I thought my part in this was to show up and probably get murdered by you. Or stuck in a cage and used to make my mother work for you."

"Your mother is a stubborn woman," Huisman said with a tsking sound. "She claims my timeline was far too short to build a how-to manual. And she seemed to notice the cameras and where they were placed. There were a few things she did that I couldn't see. Naturally it was all to the delivery system. A delicate operation, that if done improperly could explode in my face. Smart woman. I can't toss her body off the side of the mountain. So yes, I do need you to ensure her cooperation with the next round of my plan. You see, she was right about the time crunch."

"The World Economic Forum is slated to meet next week. You want it in chaos." He knew that much.

"I want it burning, but I'll settle for chaos. That's where the next bomb goes off," he admitted. "I told your mother I needed three, but I think I'll keep one. The whole world will be talking about the double agent who set this all in motion for Beijing. When the WEF is hit with the same thing a week later, the West will go to war with the East."

The man liked to talk. It would be his downfall one day. "Parker is taking the blame for you?"

Huisman chuckled. "Ah, I should have said rogue *American* agent. I think you'll find you now have five million dollars in a bank account in the Caymans. I have a friend in the States who is planting all the evidence even as we speak."

Well, that shouldn't be a surprise. Huisman knew how to use his assets, and he would see Zach's separation from his team and his real life a definite asset. After all, hadn't that been his plan all along? "What am I supposed to do? Strap a bomb to my chest and blow up the city?"

"Heavens, don't be so dramatic. You're going to take one of my helicopters and deploy the bomb from the air. I'll provide the pilot, of course. And a few guards to ensure you do your job. You see, this is how I know it will work. Your mother understands it's you who will be setting it off, and she didn't even scream and cry and try to fix it. So I'm sure she hasn't sabotaged the bombs." Huisman neatly summed up the impossible position Zach's mother had been put in. "Once it's revealed you are working for the Chinese, I won't even need you to be the one to plant the WEF bomb. Everyone in the world will be hunting you down, and they won't look to me at all."

"Somehow I think my boss will disagree." A mistake. He needed to play into Huisman's dreams. "He might hate me right now, but he'll back me up for his niece's sake alone."

A low chuckle came from Huisman. "Well, he can disagree all he likes, but I happened to buy all of the parts for these bombs from a very specific Russian syndicate."

Fuck. Now that was something they hadn't counted on. "Denisovitch. Ian doesn't have anything to do with Dusan Denisovitch's criminal activities."

Huisman shrugged. "Good luck proving that. I think you'll find the world will be happy to have someone to pin this on. They will do anything to keep their peace, even ignore the truth. They will certainly ignore the train that's barreling toward them."

Two men entered the space. Zach recognized the bombs they held. His mother's.

Shit. This was happening, and he prayed Parker was already in the building. Prayed Parker was exactly who he said he was because if he wasn't, they were all dead.

Or his team would be dead and he would be forced to do everything Huisman commanded him to do because he couldn't let him hurt Devi. Zach wished he was a better man but he wasn't. He realized he would let the world burn if it meant sparing her a second's worth of pain. He knew his baby was somewhere in this complex begging him to not do this. She would tell him her life wasn't worth the thousands that bomb would take.

He wouldn't listen.

His mind was racing with the possibilities. "I want Devi with me. What guarantees do I have that I won't come right back here to her dead body?"

"What guarantees do I have that you won't simply dump the bomb in the mountains and take your girl with you?"

"Well, I can't fly a chopper for one, so I assume your pilot and your guards will take care of that. It's not like I can get rid of the pilot. I admit I've gotten good with light aircraft, but you know damn well it takes an experienced pilot at these heights and wind conditions. I'm surprised you can fly this high up." His brother had assured him it wouldn't be a problem. After all, they were "borrowing" a helo built for these conditions.

"I assure you we can do everything I say we can. Now do you want to see her before you leave?" Huisman seemed ready to get down to business. "Your mother can give you all the instructions on how to deploy this. You will be assigned a pilot and a guard. If my explosion doesn't happen within forty-five minutes after takeoff, I will have Devon Taggart killed and I will give your mother to your father. He's eager. I've kept him off her until now. Personally, I don't see the appeal since she's old and fairly useless except for her bombmaking skills. She's certainly not sexually attractive. Now the young Miss Taggart..."

Zach didn't care about his hands. He could use his whole body to kill the fucker.

Strong arms gripped him, holding him back.

Huisman's head shook, and he looked at Zach like he was nothing more than an animal. "This is why you fail, Captain Reed. Tell me something. Did you follow my instructions, or did you tell Mr. Taggart where I am?"

Zach could breathe again.

Parker wasn't lying.

If Huisman didn't know the Taggarts were here in Nepal, then Parker was on the right team.

Or he was screwing with the boss.

No. He was going to trust his team's instincts. He was going to trust Kenzie. Well, Kala didn't think Parker was lying. He could trust that.

"I only told my brother. He helped me get away." Not a lie. When they realized Huisman would likely have someone watching him, he made his way from Liverpool to Kathmandu on his own with some forged passports and trying to duck Interpol as well. If Huisman looked, he would have seen someone matching his build and rough features checked into a rathole in a bad part of the city. "Big Tag isn't exactly happy with me right now. I think you'll find he's back in England trying to figure out where his niece is."

"So he will be hunting you, too." Huisman clapped his hands together and pulled his radio. "Make a general announcement. I need the rest of security down here at the landing bays. We're going to be launching in less than an hour."

An hour. Cooper was waiting until the right time. The wind patterns changed, but there was some research done on the best time to fly. Cooper would make the call. From there he had to hope the Canadians were in place. They came up without a helo. They'd been camping down the mountain for days, waiting for the right moment, studying the security protocols. They were coming in through a cave system, and then would get into the air ducts that would absolutely seem way too small. Tim would do fine, but Parker was a big bastard.

The announcement came over the loudspeakers that seemed to be everywhere. In seconds there were at least twenty men dressed in fatigues spreading out across the space.

Huisman gestured around. "My army. We're small right now. Most of the men I employ are based around the world. I didn't want attention, and we don't need more. That's the key. Don't overestimate. That's how you trip up. I've found small teams are better." He looked back. *"Louis, où est Ray White?"*

A young man stepped up, a tablet in his hand. His fingers moved over the face of it. *"Il est toujours dans le laboratoire. Ou du moins sa radio."*

His father was still in the labs. At least his radio was. That was what the younger man said in French.

Devi was in the labs. His mom was in the labs. "Is he alone in there with them?"

Huisman ignored him. *"Va le chercher et amène-le ici avec la fille."*

Bring them. The man nodded to one of his fellow minions and they started walking toward the double doors. They swiped a key card and the doors opened.

He would need to get one of those. Of course it would be helpful to have hands.

Huisman stepped onto a raised dais and looked around at his assembled army and began to speak. "Today we take the first step in creating our new world. A world where you are no longer ground under the feet of people who don't deserve to lead you, who ignore your needs and raise up people who should lick your boots."

Women. He was pretty sure Huisman was talking about women. When Eve McKay had done a profile on him in the early days, she talked about how his whole life seemed to be defined by the trauma of watching his father be killed, but Zach wanted to take a long look at that man's relationship with his mother. Huisman hated Big Tag, but he hated women more.

Which was why he had to find a way to save Devi. His father hated women, too. He wouldn't put it past the asshole to hurt her in every way just so he could tell Zach he'd done it.

What had she already been through? Would he find her huddled in a corner trying to survive?

Then he heard the gunfire and realized she wasn't in a corner at all.

Huisman was interrupted in the middle of his evil villain monologue. He frowned toward the double doors. Another volley of gunfire and then one of the men who'd left to bring Devi back staggered in, holding his chest and reaching for help before falling to the ground.

That was when he heard the thud of the chopper rapidly approaching.

There was genuine shock on Huisman's face. *"Occupe-toi de ça. Tuez-les tous."*

Take care of that. Kill them all.

Zach started to move because the hands had come off him, the soldiers doing their king's will. From the open bays, Zach could see the help approaching. TJ, Lou, and Kenzie would have been dropped at the site where Tim was set up. Tasha was back at base since there were only so many seats on the helo, and they were bringing two more back if they got the job done.

He could see Kala Taggart standing on the landing skid, an AR-15 in her hands. She began to give her husband cover by peppering the bay with bullets.

Huisman grabbed Zach's arm. "If you think this will save you, you're wrong. I have plans in place for such a scenario. I will blow this whole base sky high and send those spores into the upper atmosphere and see what happens."

Chaos erupted around them. "Guess Parker isn't on your side after all."

Huisman's eyes narrowed as they moved to the double doors. "Not all is as it seems, Captain. As everyone here will learn."

Huisman stopped, his shoulder jerking. Hit. He'd been hit. He dropped Zach's hand and pulled out a small device. "If I'm going down, so is everyone. You might be protected with your Army vaccines, but I don't think your girl has had one. And perhaps I've managed to change it enough that it will still kill you."

He pressed the button.

Kala was on the ground, having jumped down as Cooper began to land. Big Tag came out behind her, and father and daughter started spraying the place with bullets.

Fuck. He had to get to the bombs.

"Huisman," Kala shouted. "Let's see who wins this time, asshole."

Huisman actually scrambled back. He looked over to the table he'd set the bombs on. "This is far from over."

Huisman raced through the doors.

Zach tried to get to him, to pull him back. The doors locked and then a signal began, a clanging sound that told anyone listening to it that the world was going to explode.

He turned and got his hands on the handle, but it was locked.

"Damn it." Kala rushed up. "Did that fucker get away? You were supposed to stop him."

"With what hands?" It looked like she and Big Tag had taken out a good deal of Huisman's security team. "Where did the rest of them go? He had at least twenty guys."

"They ran." Big Tag was in all white, the arctic version of fatigues. The combat uniform looked good on him. Kala's vibrant hair contrasted with the white of her uniform. She'd pulled off her balaclava when she moved through the bay. Likely because she wanted Huisman to know she was there. "It's what happens when you hire mercenaries. Come here, Zach."

Big Tag pulled a knife and quickly sawed through the zip ties.

"We have to get through that door. Devi's back there, and I think she might have a gun." He moved to the nearest downed soldier and pulled the key card off him. "Shit. Huisman started a timer for the bomb. It's going to explode and kill everyone in here who isn't protected."

"We don't know we're protected." Cooper ran up, holding an extra semi and offering it to his brother. "The intel Parker gave us said there were significant changes to the anthrax they took from Dare's father's lab. Huisman has been experimenting. I know we don't care about the soldiers, but there are workers from town in here. Cleaners and cooks. They don't know what goes on here."

Tristan stood at the table with the bomb. He had his greatest weapon with him. While Tris was deadly with a gun, he was a hacking god. He pulled his laptop from the pack on his back. "I can already tell you it's on a timer. It's set for forty-five minutes, which I suppose is what Huisman thought it would take to get out of here and find the right spot over Kathmandu. This is complex. I might need Lou."

Big Tag touched his ear. "TJ, are you in position?"

Zach wasn't waiting. They could handle the bomb. He needed to get to Devi. His girl was out there, and she was fighting. He had to give her the best chance for survival, and that meant having every security asshole in the place chasing him instead of her.

He slapped the key card to the door and started to push through.

Tried to push through.

"Damn it. He's shut the key cards down," Zach shouted back. "I can't get out of here, and Devi can't get in. She's got to know we would have to enter the facility from the landing bays. She'll be making her way here."

Unless all that chaos wasn't about Devi and his mom escaping. Unless all that gunfire had already taken her out.

He couldn't think like that. He threw his shoulder against the doors, trying to force them open.

"Hey." Cooper was suddenly beside him. "You can't let the panic take over. She needs you calm. She needs the soldier right now."

"Comms are down." Big Tag's face was set in harsh lines.

"I can get the doors open. Everything but the inner rooms Huisman uses are on the same system. It's not complex," Tris explained. He moved to the doors and had the key card reader open in seconds. He plugged his laptop in.

"I think you should be working on the bomb," Big Tag said. "Even a simple system will take time."

Tristan hissed. "Damn it. I have to unlock them one by one. And I'm getting some kind of code. Huisman enacted a protocol. I think he might have a fail-safe in place."

"I assure you Lou is working on it. I don't have to talk to them to know that Lou won't let us down," Big Tag reassured them. "Tris, get this one open and then you're on the bomb. I'm going in with Zach. Cooper…"

Cooper nodded. "I'm going to fly it out and have Tristan disarm it in the air. We can't let it detonate here. It's almost certain to get down to the village below. I'll find a spot to minimize the chance of avalanche."

His brother was going to fly the bomb out? They were at the upmost range of the helo. "You can't risk it. You just got married. I know I'm not the pilot you are…"

"Eww. Don't do that." Kala frowned his way. "No gross self-sacrificing stuff. And he did get married, which is why I'm going with him. So is Tris. He's good under pressure."

The doors clicked, proving her point.

Tristan unplugged his laptop. "You're on your own. Hopefully Lou's figured it out. It's simple but death by a thousand cuts since I'm pretty sure she'll have to open the doors one by one. They'll be worried about getting Kenzie to Parker first. Be careful. If we don't die, we'll come back and pick you up."

Big Tag looked his daughter's way. "Take care of them, baby girl."

"Always," she promised. "Also, you should know Kenz is planning on telling Ben everything, so we'll probably be happy if we blow up. We won't have to do the family bonding crap with him. I bet he's a chatty motherfucker." She looked at her husband. "Let's do this. Where you die, I die and all that, babe."

"I'm not going to let us die." Cooper held a hand up. "Go get your girl. I'll be back when Tristan shuts this bomb down, but I'm not risking doing it here. We don't know if Huisman can't override."

Another volley of gunfire forced his attention back to the job at hand. "Coop..."

"Save it, brother." Cooper didn't seem to want an overly emotional good-bye. "Go."

Big Tag pushed the door open and stepped out into the hall. "We're going to work our way to the lab. That's their last known position. Do you remember the schematics?"

He'd studied them, but he also knew they were the basic building plans and could have changed. Still, they'd ID'd the labs. From watching the CCTV cams, he knew basically where he wanted to go. He moved left. Somewhere in the distance, he heard shouting and then it went quiet.

"We make a left at the intersection," Zach said softly. "It'll take us back to the labs. Shouldn't there be more security?"

Big Tag moved to the wall, sliding along so his back was protected and he had the best angle. "Good. Let's do it. And I'll be shocked if most of his security doesn't take off. He's hiring mercenaries. They require two things—pay and the knowledge that their jobs aren't going to go bad. That's the difference between a mission and a paycheck. And that's why my fucking team works. Not a one of you would ever run. Well, except you, and even then you stopped and took care of Lou and Aidan in Toronto. That was impressive, by the way. You took out five guards, and most of them with your hands in cuffs."

"They weren't well trained." Talking was calming him down. "And you're right. The minute they figured out it was going bad, they tried to run. I couldn't let them."

He couldn't let them now either because he wasn't sure where Devi was and if they would encounter her. A security guard turned the corner and his gun came up.

Zach shot him without hesitation and picked up his key card because they might work on different doors.

He took out two more in the hallways as he and Big Tag made their way deeper into the complex. Big Tag took down his own. Every now and then they would meet someone who had to be on the cleaning staff. Big Tag would tell them to take cover. Or try to since there was a language barrier.

It was tense, and they had to find a way through two doors on their own before the third took one of the keycards.

Lou. Thank the universe for Lou.

A door opened to his right and Zach turned, but Ian put a hand out, stopping Zach from firing.

Kenzie stood there wearing Lou's latest contraption. She was in all white, but that could change since her clothes were made of nanites. It wasn't what she'd been wearing when they'd dropped her off. She smiled that smile she used when she knew she was caught and was going to brazen through it. "Hey, Dad."

Big Tag's eyes narrowed. "I issued you a perfectly acceptable combat uniform. What happens if that fucker sets off an electromagnetic pulse and all those nanites are suddenly on the floor?"

She gave him an even brighter smile. "I'll distract everyone." Her father growled but she shrugged. "Well, it worked for Daisy. Oh, and Lou got the comms back on, but she didn't want to interrupt you when you're like murdering people. I know it's fun for you."

Tag sighed. "Yeah, not so much anymore, kiddo. You see your cousin?"

"Lou's looking for her," Kenzie replied. "She's got the CCTV cams back up and made sure they're recording. She and Tim are now working with Tris. I've got to get this to Ben, though he doesn't know it's me coming."

"You're working." Big Tag could really put the judgment in there.

"I know, but you should be aware…"

"You're going to tell him. I agree. It's time." A wolfish grin lit the big guy's face. "And then all our cards are on the table, and he and I can have a real talk."

Kenzie went a little pale. "I'll have to deal with that later." She touched her earpiece and winced. "And they're down again. Lou told me Huisman has weird programs running. She's worried about some signal that's coming from his inner base. I have to go. The last time we saw Devi she was moving toward the cafeteria. She's got Shannon with her, and Aunt Erin is going to be proud of her. I don't think that blood is hers."

Zach felt his stomach bottom out. "Blood?"

Big Tag's head shook. "Go. Meet back at the helo. If there's a helo. The Canadians better have their own ride."

"I'll let him know." And she was gone, disappearing down the hall.

He had no idea how Big Tag stayed so fucking calm. He was never allowing his kids to… He was going to have kids with Devi. He was going to have a family with her. Marry her. Be a husband. Live a life. "Sir, I need you to know I'll do whatever you say if you'll help me come home."

Big Tag nodded. "I know you will, but we have to get her first. You remember the plan?"

Oh, he did. He took a long breath because one of the things Big Tag had come up with was a plan to deal with his mother's situation. It was brutal and would be hard to get through. Especially since he couldn't prepare her for it. "I'm ready."

Big Tag's hand went to his ear. "Lou? TJ? You there? You're breaking up…what? Yes. We'll go. Tell me…" He cursed under his breath. "And they're out again. Huisman's got something up his sleeve. I don't like this. I don't like it at all. Everything's too fucking quiet. We need to get to the cafeteria. Lou says they're holed up there but someone's sneaking up on them. We have to move and fast."

Zach took off, praying he made it in time.

* * * *

The quiet was eerie.

Devi walked into the cafeteria warily, eyes first on the other side and then roaming the room, trying to see where her potential attackers might hide.

They'd almost been caught once already, and she'd had to fire at the man. She thought she might have hit him. Her nerves were frayed, and she wanted nothing more than to get through all of this and see Zach again.

"We have to go through the cafeteria to get to the loading docks." Shannon was right behind her. "You're sure they're here? It sounded like the doctor wasn't bringing Zach in until later, and I know he wouldn't allow him to bring his team."

No one was in the dining area. Not a surprising thing since it wasn't exactly dinner time, but usually there was someone getting coffee or a soda. Nothing. The lights were only half on, and one of them flickered.

If the power went out, they were in a mountain. The darkness would be endless.

"I assure you they wouldn't be shooting only at Zach." She had the insanest urge to run for it, but she took a deep breath and checked the instinct. She moved around the perimeter where she could at least be sure no one was behind her. Shannon followed.

Up ahead she could see the hallway they were trying to get to. The double doors were closed, but there were two windows. The hall was still well lit, but the one behind her had gone dead.

She walked slowly, watching for any movement.

"I think Huisman has been trying to drive a wedge between Zach and the team," she explained quietly. "He's told Zach a bunch of lies. Huisman's an arrogant prick who thinks everyone will believe him. He thinks a lot of his own intellect, and it worked for a long time because my uncle is a patient man who doesn't move until he's sure. Now the evil doc is going to get a full dose of my family, and he better be ready for it."

"I'm afraid Huisman is ready for anything," Shannon said as she moved behind Devi. "I don't like a couple of things I've noticed about this place. There are wires that don't go where they should, and I'm fairly certain he's rigged this whole place to blow if he wants it to."

Devi forced herself not to curse a blue streak. That asshole.

"Well, that would be typical Huisman. I was recently a guest at a house he owned, and he torched it the minute he realized things were going bad. I think we're playing into his hands and that's the real problem. I know we're taking him blowing up his own house as some kind of win, but what if it's a game for him and we keep playing? What if he's rigged our lives so he wins either way? He blows up the world and gets to be the dung heap king he seems to want to be, or he keeps his enemies in a continual state of chaos so none of us can enjoy the lives we lead."

"My darling girl, you've described every narcissist I've ever met." Shannon sighed. "And there were so many of them."

She stopped when she heard a volley of gunfire. She saw someone run by the window, but the person wore all white and had the hood up, covering her face. Her. She knew that had been a woman.

Huisman didn't have a bunch of women running around. He had some women from the village below who did cleaning work, but they didn't wear arctic white parkas that had a vaguely military look.

"My cousins are here." Hope surged hard through Devi. "I don't know which one, but she ran by. Likely looking for my uncle. I know they won't all come in together. They'll have at least two different entry points."

And if her cousins were there, then Lou would be, too. The first thing Lou would do would be to cut into the security cams.

She looked around. She'd gotten to know where the cams were. It was a risk but one she was willing to take. She moved away from the wall and faced the camera in the corner, waving her arms. She held up the gun so Lou would know she was armed.

"I don't think it's on, honey." Shannon stayed by the wall, a grim expression on her face.

Devi stopped bouncing like she was on a deserted island trying to flag down a plane. "Why do you say that?"

"That one moves, and it's not moving. It was working when we first walked in, but it's dead now." Shannon seemed to think, and whatever was going through her head did not lift her mood. "Something's happening, Devi."

"I'm sure it's my uncle. He likes to shut down systems. Or all the gunfire hit something important."

Shannon's head shook. "No. I've studied a lot of military philosophy and how battle plans are mapped out. Your uncle would have a plan, and it wouldn't consist of taking the power out. Doing that would lock us in when he needs to move quickly. Remember when Huisman brought us into his residence?"

It had been their first full day here, and Huisman had them brought to his sleek and technologically advanced apartment. He'd had one of his staff bring them tea, which she did not drink, and had told them the rules. "I remember."

"I studied the place. I'm absolutely certain his bedroom is wired to act as a safe room like the one you told me Nell's daughter had in Liverpool. The door had a specific panel that goes beyond a simple keycard or even biometrics. I'm worried Huisman is going to lock himself in his safe room and blow up one of the bombs. Even with a vaccine, I think it will kill everyone who comes into contact with it."

"There's a vaccine? Did I get it as a kid?" If there was a damn vaccine, what was everyone worried about? She still didn't get the whole bioweapons thing, but she was going with it.

"It's not the kind of vaccine they give to kids," Shannon said as they moved around the back wall, avoiding the area that led to the kitchen where they had no line of sight. "Mostly military or medical professionals and first responders who might come into contact with it. You and I will die quickly, but with the way the winds blow, everyone in the village below will likely die as well."

"You think he would destroy this whole place?" Were they on borrowed time or had Zach already taken him out?

"Sweetie, you said it yourself. I believe if that man thinks he's going down, he'll take everyone with him."

They needed to find Zach and get out of here. She was sure they had brought a helo and hadn't climbed the mountain. Cooper could pilot anything that flew. He would have brought them up.

She was not panicking. She was calm and cool and steady. She was Erin and Theo Taggart's daughter. She was Captain Zach Reed's fiancée.

No. She stood there for a second, and something deep settled in her.

She was Devi Taggart, the sum of all those parts, but her own person. She was made from everything that happened to her and how she handled it. She was made from love, but she was her own person.

If she survived, she wasn't going to sit and wait for some design house to notice her.

She would build her own. She would build a house for her creativity, a home for her soul, and she would let her family help her. A home for her husband and children built on her strength and her dreams.

But she had to survive first. It had only taken three damn kidnappings, but she was ready to move on with faith in herself and her family.

"Then we have to figure out how to stop him. If he blows the place up, we won't exactly have time to get out. The team will have to split up," Devi said. "So how do we stop it? If we pull the wires, would that help?"

"We need to find his system." Shannon's voice was quiet but certain. "I'm sure he has one system that controls the entire base of operations."

Devi had paid close attention when she was allowed out of the lab. "I think the control room is one floor down."

Shannon's head shook. "He wouldn't keep this in the control room. It's in one of the four rooms that make up his residence. One floor up. That's where we need to go. That's where he'll have it."

"Do you think it's possible we can shut it down remotely?" Devi asked.

"I find it hard to believe he doesn't have a wireless connection. He's obsessed with technology. Being able to remotely detonate is one of the things he wants from me. I told him I couldn't do it in the time he needed, but I could," Shannon admitted. "He wants to be able to stand anywhere in the world and have power over some place far away. He's a megalomaniac. I know he's smart, but his downfall will be his arrogance. He views everything as a game, and he doesn't imagine he can lose."

"Then we need to find where he would keep the controls and let you try to shut it down," Devi said.

Shannon's head shook. "Honey, I'm excellent at a lot of things, but not computers. I use them but I don't hack. We need a hacker."

They were almost to the door, and Devi had the keycard out. "Luckily, I'm pretty sure we have at least one working right now."

She pressed the key card to the reader but got nothing. "Damn it."

She was about to turn and tell Shannon they needed a new plan when a face appeared in the window in one of the doors.

Huisman. She gasped and stepped back because... Well, first because it was shocking that anyone was there, and also he was covered in blood, a hole in his forehead.

He grinned, a ghoulish expression, and then slowly peeled off the hole on his forehead and wiggled it in front of her. *"Ces imbeciles."* He winked, and she worried he had a way in. "Tell your uncle I hope everyone enjoys my countdown. Tick tock. I wish I could have changed the timer, but I still think this will work. You have less than an hour to find your way out of here, little mouse, or the whole place falls down. Enjoy the maze."

She tried the keycard again. Locked. She saw Huisman's shadow disappear as he made his way to whatever insane exit plan he'd put into place.

"He's already set it in motion," Shannon said, her voice hollowing out. "Zach needs to get out of here if he can."

"He won't. He won't leave me." She knew it deep in her bones. If she died here, he would go down trying to save her.

So she had to survive.

"How do we get these doors open?" Devi asked.

"I don't think we do." Shannon studied the keycard reader. "I think we need to worry more about the power going out completely and us being truly locked in. Once he gets out, I suspect that's what will happen. He might have the bomb on a timer, but he'll also have some remote way to control the rest of the building."

"Devi!"

She turned and her body seemed to lift. Zach was there. His face was in the window, their bodies separated by these fucking doors, and there might not be anything they could do about it. She pocketed the key card and put a hand to the window, wanting so badly to be able to touch him. "You have to get out of here."

She could see her uncle trying to use the key card from the other side.

"I'm not leaving you." Zach's beautiful face was stark in the sputtering lights.

"Huisman ran that way. He has some kind of plan, and he's going to blow the whole mountain. You have to get the team out of here." She would beg and plead. Anything to save his life. Their lives. She would give hers up so her family could live. "Tell my parents and my brother I love them."

"I'm not leaving you," Zach reiterated.

Her uncle stepped away, his fingers at the comm in his ear.

"I love you, Zach."

"Move back." His jaw went tight.

Her uncle stopped him. "Lou is working on the system, but she's got another problem."

Devi nodded. "He's got a way to blow the whole compound, and that will send the anthrax out into the world. But he told us it's on a timer."

"Lou, is there a timer?" her uncle asked, touching his ear again. Then he cursed. "The comms go in and out, and I'm pretty sure Huisman had protocols to fuck with the key cards. Sometimes they work. Sometimes they don't."

"Chaos," Shannon said. "It's what he bases his world view on. I suspect he's the only person in the facility with a master card that works all the time. He's likely set up a rotating system that shuts down security levels. Sometimes they work. Sometimes they don't."

"So we try again in a few minutes?" Devi asked.

"No. I get this fucking door down." Zach's eyes suddenly went wide. "Devi, behind you."

She turned and gasped because Ray White was walking through the doors they'd opened. He was covered in blood and looked like a damn zombie.

Unfortunately, he didn't move like one, and he'd found more than a working keycard. He seemed to have found another gun along the way.

"Bitch," he cursed and raised the gun.

Devi leapt, throwing her body to the right and behind the first of the long tables that dotted the cafeteria. It wasn't a large room. Just enough for roughly forty people to take a break if they needed one. She would have to move and fast.

"Ray," she heard Shannon say. "Don't hurt Zach this way. Don't hurt our boy."

She couldn't see Ray. She gripped the gun, thankful she managed to not drop it. Devi crawled along the side of the table to the end. Tilting her head down, she could see Ray's boots and Shannon's sensible shoes. They were too close. Why wasn't Shannon hiding?

She heard something heavy hit the doors. Zach. He would try to get in.

"Our boy? The one you took from me?" Ray asked, his voice low and gravelly.

"He's still your son." Shannon's voice was soft but steady.

How many times had she been put in a position where she had to placate this man so no one got hurt? Zach's mom was a study in tragedy. She'd made the mistake of falling in love with the wrong man, and there had been no going back.

Another bang and pop and she realized Zach and her uncle were shooting at the door, trying to get it to give.

It wouldn't. It was too well built.

"I think him watching me kill his bitch will be a fitting punishment for betraying his father," Ray said, but she watched his leg twitch.

He wasn't all there. What she'd done earlier with the hammer to his head was probably still going to kill him, but it would be too late.

"Of course, maybe it's time I took care of you, too," he said in a growl. "Look at you, Shannon. A gun to your head and you stand there. Ain't no fight in you at all."

But this was how Shannon fought. She'd gone on the run to protect her family, given up the life she could have spent with them so this man didn't infect them all. Sometimes bravery was simply standing tall and not giving in.

And sometimes it was standing up and taking the fucking shot no matter what.

Devi got to her feet. The man was clearly not thinking straight because he didn't even turn and look for her. His eyes were on the woman whose life he'd ruined.

"I always was your god," he said, blood caking his face. "You always thought you were so smart, but I was your god and I'll be the one who kills you."

"Not if I kill you first, fucker." She needed him to look her way.

He turned slightly and Devi fired. Once. Twice. She saw Shannon move away, stumbling back. Ray shot, too, but it went wide and at least one of Devi's hit. His chest. Though he wore a dark shirt, she could see the blood, see the way his hand went there, and he dropped the gun as his body started to fall.

Shannon picked it up and scrambled to her feet. She stood over him and put a bullet in his brain. The room went quiet, the only sound Zach still trying to get in. Shannon looked her way. "We should have done that last time. You okay?"

"Devi!" Zach was screaming her name.

He couldn't see her. He didn't realize she was unhurt. She nodded Shannon's way and rushed to the doors. "I'm fine, babe. He didn't hit me."

Zach put a hand on his chest like he needed to restart his heart.

Her uncle gave her a thumbs-up. "Good shot. Your parents are going to be proud."

She sniffled, tears beginning because they were still in an impossible situation. "You have to run. Zach, we have no idea how we're going to get out. We'll try."

But they would have to navigate a maze with a hundred doors that might or might not work. They wouldn't know they were stuck until they hit the end and were trapped. Zach could go back the way he came. He could get to the landing bays.

Zach's head shook. "I stay with you."

He put his hand to the window.

She put hers there too, against his, save for the cold of the slightly now cracked glass. Huisman had thought of everything. Bulletproof glass. Doors that could withstand anything. A chaotic system they would never be able to navigate.

A buzzing sound hit her ears and the light on the pad next to the door went green.

Devi's eyes widened and her hand shot to the door, opening it in an instant.

And then she was in his arms.

"Yeah, it's open, Lou. We've got them," her uncle was saying. He held the door open for Shannon. "You got a handle now?" He nodded. "No. We can't risk a helo battle at this height, and we need to get our people safe." He frowned. "What? Are you fucking kidding me? Yeah, we're coming in."

Zach hugged her so hard she could barely breathe.

Huisman had planned for everything.

Everything except Louisa Ward.

Devi was still shaking as she held on to the man she loved.

"All right, people. Let's head to the landing bays. Lou's set up there now since she's managed to take over the entire system, with one exception." Big Tag's head shook. "The kids are going to kill me."

Zach's head came down and he kissed her softly before dropping his forehead to hers. "Never again, Dev. I can't handle it. You are out of the kidnapping business."

She was. Although he could kidnap her whenever he liked.

Ten minutes later she stared at the screen Lou had managed to pull up.

The whole group was around it. Cooper had landed the helo moments after they made it to the bays. Kala had walked up like holding a bioweapon in her lap until her teammate could defuse it all while flying at a high altitude in an experimental stolen chopper was an everyday occurrence.

"Tris nearly had a heart attack," Kala said, joining them. "What the hell is that? Seriously? What is my sister doing? Ewww. Lou. Make the nanites put her clothes back on."

Zach snorted and then averted his eyes because Kenzie really was all naked.

"Wow. That's cool." Tim from Canada was with them. He looked to Lou. "You programmed those?"

"Hey, there's a gorgeous, naked woman on screen and you're looking at my girl like you could eat her up?" TJ complained.

"Tell me when it's over." Her uncle stood way out of the line of sight of those monitors.

"Shouldn't we be running?" Devi asked.

Lou waved the thought off. "I've rewritten everything. I've got the CCTV's up and running, and I've locked all the doors. I made two keycards that will work on everything except that door. Yeah. I'm talking about the one Kenzie and Ben are in. It's like the Liverpool safe room. It's on a timer. Now from what I can tell they actually could open it from the inside if they looked around enough, but they're preoccupied."

"What's that thing on the side?" Cooper asked.

Tim looked up, perfectly chipper. "Oh, that's the bomb that was supposed to blow up the whole place. So here's what happened. Ben made his way to Huisman's rooms, but when he got there, Huisman was dead on the floor."

"We just got the cams up in there, so we thought he'd pulled a Hitler in his bunker move," Lou admitted. "But then after Ben and Kenz hit the safe room button and got locked in, that asshole got up and ran. In their defense it looked really good on camera."

"He should have put an extra bullet in him." Zach had an arm around her and his mother's hand in his. "Like you did, Mom. Thank you."

Shannon leaned against her son, and Devi felt her reach around him so she touched her as well. "Your girl did so good."

"Yes, she did." Zach kissed her hair.

"I'm surprised he didn't." Big Tag paced, his eyes moving, checking all the entrances. "Lou, can't you tell my daughter she's making a sex tape? Did she even try to defuse the bomb?"

Lou nodded. "Oh, yeah. She did, and so did Ben, but then they figured out they couldn't fix it and now they're having end-of-the-world sex. Wow, he is very flexible."

"Lou," her boyfriend barked.

Lou shrugged. "You know she'll want me to tape this and keep it for her." She turned to Ian. "They think they're about to die. I can't get comms in there. Believe me we've tried. I thought they could use some music. I know she's always thought they would do it the first time while listening to her girl power ballad playlist."

"So what is the timer at now?" Kala asked with a resolute sigh.

"Oh, they're down to like five minutes." Lou held out the key card like she knew what Kala would ask for next. "You should head that way if you're bringing her back here. I think they're almost... Yep, they're done. When the light goes green you can use the key card to get in. Oh, and I stopped the bomb, but the timer itself was surprisingly intricate. I decided to let it go since getting the doors open through the complex was more important."

Kala frowned at her bestie. "Also, it adds a mega shit ton of drama to their first time. Awesome. And they say Brianna is the writer. Tim, come on. This is where you leave us."

Tim stood but looked around like maybe he would get a reprieve, and then he got a good look at Kala. His whole attention had been on the screen and then Lou. He stared for a moment. "Uhm…" He looked back at the screen. "I have questions."

Kala put a hand on his slender shoulder. "Twins, Tim. We're twins, and I'm the evil one. So we're going to go get your boy and you two can freak out together and he can tell you all about his afternoon love countdown."

Tim started walking with her. "I mean, I could do that in the helo. I was hoping to catch a ride. Mountain climbing kind of sucks."

Cooper snorted and followed them. "We'll be back."

The door had closed behind them when she heard the sound of a chopper in the distance.

Devi tensed.

"It's okay," Zach assured her. He leaned over and whispered in her ear. "They're going to take my mom, but it's okay."

Her uncle put a hand on Shannon's shoulder. "Ms. Reed, you're about to meet Drake and Taylor Radcliffe and a couple of soldiers who are going to escort you to a site where they think you'll be safe. They'll explain everything in the helo."

Shannon shook her head, fear on her face. "Please, Mr. Taggart. I would rather die than have to work for anyone. I won't make another one. Not even for the Agency."

The chopper landed in the bay, and Devi started to move.

Zach stopped her. He pulled her close and whispered in her ear. "It's all for show. They're going to take her to a black ops site and then when the coast is clear, they're going to move her to Bliss. She's going to stay there from now on, and we'll put the word out that she's working for us. We're doing it here because Huisman will see it. He's still watching us. So cry a little for me."

She was the one who was going to sell it. The rest would be in on it. She pulled back and shook her head. "You can't."

She played the scene out, putting all her adrenaline and fear into it. By the time they took Shannon away, she was weeping in Zach's arms.

He carried her to their helo. He sat down, cradling her on his lap. "You were perfect."

She sniffled.

"You were excellent, niece." Her uncle took the copilot seat. "There's a place for you if you decide to give up the whole clothes thing."

"Abso-fucking-lutely not." Zach's arms wound around her.

"Oh, hey, maybe not on the missions' part, but I definitely need her on the design front." Lou looked cheerful now that they were out of range of the security cams. "I think the field test went well."

"I think Kenzie might have thought about her mission more if she'd been wearing a chastity belt," her uncle complained.

The pilot door opened, and Coop hopped in. "Is Shannon off okay?"

"She's good. Drake's explaining it to her before they go to the first site," Zach explained. "And he's smoothed things over with the base we stole this sucker from."

"Excellent. Jail was not how I wanted to end the day." He started his precheck.

Kala stepped into the back, followed by a glowing Kenzie.

Kala looked at Devi and made a gagging sound before taking her seat.

Kenzie sat down beside her.

A laugh went through Devi because she felt safe and warm. "Just tell us."

"She doesn't have to. We saw it," TJ complained.

Kenzie ignored them and told her tale.

Devi sat back, utterly happy with where she was.

Zach still had things he would need to do. Huisman was still out there. Her cousins were in danger.

But as long as they were together, they would win.

Epilogue

Dallas, TX
Many years later

There were days when Theo Taggart wondered what his life would have been like had he not had his past ripped from his brain. Days when the memories that were still gone would surface and whisper along his mind like a ghost trying to take him to the past.

He'd learned long ago how to deal with them.

Despite the crowd milling around Top's private banquet hall, he let the world shrink down, followed the training that had become so engrained in him by the deeply caring professionals who had created whole protocols to help him deal with his trauma.

In that moment he thanked them. Kai and Eve. He said a quiet prayer of gratitude and began the process.

He took a long breath and let the memory flow over him. A vision of the most beautiful woman in the world punching him in the gut assailed him. He could practically feel the air whooshing from his lungs.

Damn, that woman took his breath away. He didn't fight to stay in the memory, simply let it be.

"You okay, Dad?"

He opened his eyes and his baby girl stood there looking up at him. She was her mother's mini me at one point, though there was zero doubt that kid had a lot of his soul. "I'm good."

"What was it?" Devi Taggart-Reed might be a mother of two and wife with many years of happy marriage under her belt, but she remembered her childhood.

They talked about what happened to him. Even when she and TJ were kids. He'd never hidden the fact that it was hard for him to remember most of his life before Hope McDonald had experimented on his brain. He'd gotten back a lot, but it was by using methods like this one. Not chasing the memory. Simply letting it come, feeling the emotions connected to it, and then talking.

Sometimes he wasn't completely sure if the memories he had from those methods were true or some variation his brain created to fill the void.

He no longer cared. All that mattered were the feelings. The love. The passion. The deep sense that this was right and he was home.

"I got a little flash of how your mom and I met the first time."

Devi grinned. "You mean the first time she kicked your ass."

He couldn't help but laugh. "Yes, that is absolutely what I mean. That woman took my breath away within seconds of meeting her."

He looked across the elegantly decorated room and found her. His whole fucking beautiful life stood there in a black sheath dress that clung to her curves and made his mouth water. Her glorious red hair had only a hint of steel in it after all these years. But then he was pretty sure the woman was made of it. He'd never met a woman stronger than Erin Argent, and the joy of his life—the salvation of his life—was that he'd made her love him so much she dragged him back from hell.

His brothers often teased him about being the girl in their relationship. They could be toxic assholes sometimes, but he loved them. It never bothered him because he quite liked being Erin's prize. It was a good thing to be.

"She likes to tell everyone how she did it. I believe it was an elbow to your solar plexus," Devi said, sounding infinitely amused. "I know this is well-worn territory, but I still wonder how you thought it was a good idea to raid your brother's company in the middle of a workday."

"I wonder about it, too." Because he really couldn't remember. It was odd what came back and what didn't. What surfaced at the strangest times, but lucky for him his baby would tell him stories. "I believe your mother would say I was an arrogant shit who stormed her castle and thought I would get away with it."

It wasn't true. He had been on a CIA team and following orders, though there had been something deep inside that told him when Ten Smith had ordered them to storm the building because he mistakenly thought his sister was in danger, he'd been excited. Not because of Erin. He hadn't met her at that point. But at that point they'd met Ian Taggart and knew about Sean Taggart, and he thought he would have wanted to get to know his other brothers. He liked to think he'd been a young dumbass and the world had seemed like an adventure.

How odd to have gone through all of that and be right back here. Where his knees creaked and he had to worry about cholesterol and the world still seemed like a big, gorgeous adventure.

Devi threaded her arm through his and leaned her head against him. "Well, I personally think having parents who had an epic love story led your kids to find their own. At least with me and Zach. All Lou had to do was lay out a trail of sandwiches to get TJ to fall into her web."

He snorted because that was so not true. "I think Lou would say there was a lot more to it."

Devi and Zach had been much simpler. Zach had seen her, fallen in love, fucked it all up, and then wooed her back by kidnapping her and keeping her with a bunch of rescue animals. It had taken TJ and Lou years.

Louisa. His sweet daughter-in-law. He'd always worried about her working with the Agency, but she'd survived something horrific in those last few months when the team had fought Emmanuel Huisman and she still thrived. It had taken a while. It had taken love and therapy and a family surrounding her, but Lou had beaten all those beasts back and she was a wife and mom, and more importantly to the world, she was Lou again.

Devi stood up straight and her hand came out, catching the five-year-old trying to race by at breakneck speed. "Mitchell, what did I tell you? You cannot run around Top like it's a park."

"But Uncle Lucas lets us." His grandson had the Taggart looks. Blond. Blue eyes. A smile that belied what would absolutely someday be a sarcastic wit. "He says the olds need a jolt of... It was something that starts with an A. I don't know but Thea does."

Thea Calliope Taggart. His first grandbaby. She had TJ's smile and eyes, and thank the universe her momma's intellect. Thea ran the little cousins' group with smarts and kindness and joy. She was eight and would one day rule the world.

"And what did Thea tell you?" Devi asked.

Mitchell shrugged. "That I shouldn't listen to Uncle Lucas because he's going to get us in trouble with the grumps."

"Do not let your grandmother hear you," Devi said, glancing around.

"Eh, I'm okay with it." The light of his life was suddenly beside him. Erin looked down at their grandbaby and winked. "If Big Tag can be Grumpa, I probably deserve Grumpma."

She made him smile. He leaned over and kissed her. "You do not, sunshine."

"Only for you, babe." Erin knelt down with a grace that always took his breath away. She put her hands on Mitchell's shoulders. "Sweetie, you should totally call your Uncle Ian an old. You should go do it now."

Mitchell's eyes had gone wide, and he shook his head. "Thea told me I should never say that word around any of the grands. I'm supposed to call them grands if I want to survive."

Damn, that kid was cute. How did he have grandkids? How was his heart so damn full? Every time he was certain his soul was as full as it could get, someone put another baby in his arms and his soul grew.

"Thea is very smart." Erin winked and stood. "Come on, buddy. I think your Uncle Lucas put out the kid's buffet, and he promised to make plain hot dogs this time."

Because Lucas Taggart believed in elevating every food. He loved his nephew, but he was a food snob. Sometimes a bag of chips was just a bag of chips.

"Seriously?" TJ walked up with a tiny toddler asleep on his shoulder. Ella Taggart was three and the youngest of TJ and Lou's brood. Their middle kid, Jonah, was likely running around with

Cooper and Kala's small army. He still wasn't sure how those kids would go. They would either protect the world or become amazing supervillains. Theo was deeply interested in either outcome. "He always tries to mess with the perfection that is a hot dog. Like it doesn't need to be elevated. I swear he's gotten to be even more of a food snob, and given who he married I thought he would soften up."

The fact that Lucas had gotten married at all was a miracle, but then it all seemed like a miracle to him.

"Come on. Let's go and get my boys their dinner." Erin winked back at Theo, taking Mitchell's hand.

Devi's head shook. "You are choosing the kid's buffet over your father's birthday dinner? You know it's Wagyu ribeyes with potato puree and grilled asparagus, right?"

Her brother was already walking away, his hand on his daughter's back. "I was going to eat both, sis. Happy birthday, Dad, and you, Uncle Case."

"Thanks, kiddo. Erin, you are looking gorgeous." Case Taggart was his twin, though they were fraternal. They looked a lot alike, but they had never been able to fool anyone like their nieces had.

Erin gave him a wave. "You and Mia better be at my house for dinner on Sunday."

"Will do," his brother promised.

"We're having dinner on Sunday?" Zach walked up, his big chest covered with a baby carrier and Theo's latest grandbaby, who watched everything with wide eyes. Erika Reed was almost one and seemed to think the world was one big ball of fun.

"We are." Erin stopped and kissed the top of Erika's head. "Theo's going to make a brisket."

News to him, but he was happy to do so. "It'll be a big one."

His kids could eat. He watched as his wife walked away. Damn, that woman was gorgeous. The years rolled by but his wife simply got more beautiful.

"Awesome. It's been a week. Devi's got a massive order and we've been living on takeout," Zach explained.

Devi's company, Tag, was considered one of the world's premiere luxury lingerie and fet wear lines. Zach Reed had learned how to run the business end so Devi could spend her days designing. It turned out to be an excellent partnership. All of his fears dissolved when he'd realized how much Zach loved his daughter.

"Well, there's only good stuff tonight," Devi promised with a grin. She slid her hand against her husband's, tangling their fingers together. "Let's find a place close to your mom. I can't believe she got on a plane."

"Well, Big Tag sent a private jet for her and managed to get Henry and Nell on it, too. Let me tell you the carbon offset he had to buy to make that happen was a lot of fun to get by the new CEO," Zach said with a chuckle. "Your cousin says you owe her some serious fet wear."

It was great to see the kids were keeping up all the family traditions, including ribbing each other at all times.

"Watching Kala and Coop take over McKay-Taggart gives me hope that one day my brother-in-law will be able to retire," Case said as they watched Zach and Devi walk away to find his mom.

Shannon Reed. He'd spent a lot of time with the brilliant, troubled woman. They had a lot in common, though it might not look like it on the surface. Trauma had molded so much of their lives, but he'd had the right partner and that had made all the difference. He was so glad she'd been able to spend these later years in the peace of Bliss, living in a cabin with her sister and enjoying the love of her new family. She taught science at the school and had found a real home.

Like he had.

Home, Theo Taggart had found, wasn't really a place. It was people. It was family, no matter how that family formed.

"Drew is never going to retire. He's going to drive the younger generation crazy." Case's in-laws ran a huge tech company that now employed one Louisa Ward-Taggart. He would forever be in Drew Lawless's debt for building an office in Dallas for his research and development branch. At first the job had been a cover for Lou's Agency work, and then it was a refuge and blessing for her whole family.

"I don't know." Case smiled and put a hand on his brother's shoulder. "He gets jealous of Big Tag and Charlotte's adventures. I think big brother has the right idea. Let the kids take over and we'll spend the rest of our lives traipsing around the world with our wives and friends."

It sounded perfect, and what his wife didn't know was that it might be his birthday, but she was getting the present. "Does Mia know?"

"Does my wife know that we're spending the next month on a yacht in the Mediterranean?" Case grinned. "No. It's going to be a surprise. She finished her latest book last week, and she could use a break. She asked if we could spend some time here in Dallas so she could hang out with Erin."

They would spend plenty of time together. Just in a different place. "And Ian promises he'll fly Sean out when we're anchored in Greece. He and Charlotte are touring the islands for the next couple of weeks. I see a fishing trip in our future."

Case looked over the restaurant and let out a deep breath that let his twin know he was getting a little emotional. "How the hell did we get here, brother? We grew up in a trailer park."

Theo shrugged. "Dude, you're asking the guy who got his memory wiped."

Case laughed, the sound booming through the room and bringing their older brothers to join them.

"Hey, are we making fun of Theo?" Ian asked.

"We should be making fun of Luke for those hot dogs," Sean said with a shake of his head. "They're Wagyu. I cannot convince that kid that a hot dog can just be a hot dog. Also, one of the kids got into the mustard. Luke made it himself and put it in a bowl. So now the buffet is an art project."

Ian put a hand to his still taut belly. Big brother still had a hell of a metabolism. "Wagyu hot dogs sound kind of good."

Case nodded. "They do. What do you say we join the kids?"

"I'm pretty sure yesterday I was a kid," Sean complained.

Theo followed his brothers.

The world was a beautiful place when surrounded by friends and family.

* * * *

Kenzie, Ben, and all the New Recruits will return in *Love and Let Spy* coming March 24th, 2026. Click here to purchase.

Author's Note

I'm often asked by generous readers how they can help get the word out about a book they enjoyed. There are so many ways to help an author you like. Leave a review. If your e-reader allows you to lend a book to a friend, please share it. Go to Goodreads and connect with others. Recommend the books you love because stories are meant to be shared. Thank you so much for reading this book and for supporting all the authors you love!

Love and Let Spy
Masters and Mercenaries: New Recruits, Book 6
By Lexi Blake
Coming March 24, 2026

Canadian operative Ben Parker met the woman of his dreams while working undercover in Australia. That operation, to take down Emmanuel Huisman, was the singular focus of his life until he met Maggie. Now the hunt for his former childhood friend turned international terrorist often feels like what he does in between chasing the magenta-haired American spy he can't stop thinking about. She's the woman of his dreams, when she isn't being the stuff of his nightmares. Sometimes she is sweet and deliciously responsive to him, and other times she pushes him out of a plane without a parachute.

Kenzie Taggart knew Ben Parker was the one for her the minute she saw him. Unfortunately, he didn't meet her first. He met her twin sister, Kala, and they had to keep the secret. No one outside of their team knows they're twins. Everyone believes the operative known as Miss Magenta is one person. Kenzie can't tell the man she's falling in love with who she really is, but she also can't afford to lose him.

When faced with certain death on a joint operation in Nepal, Kenzie reveals the truth about "Maggie" and they spend their last minutes alive in each other's arms. It was perfect, and then a miraculous rescue leaves them in a difficult situation. Kenzie couldn't be happier that Ben knows the truth, but so does Huisman. He's determined to burn down the world, but not before he ruins his old friend and his newfound beloved. As Ben and Kenzie cross the globe in their quest to stop the madman, they might have to choose between saving the world and saving each other.

About Lexi Blake

New York Times bestselling author Lexi Blake lives in North Texas with her husband and three kids. Since starting her publishing journey in 2010, she's sold over three million copies of her books. She began writing at a young age, concentrating on plays and journalism. It wasn't until she started writing romance that she found success. She likes to find humor in the strangest places and believes in happy endings.

Connect with Lexi online:

Facebook: Lexi Blake
Twitter: authorlexiblake
Website: www.LexiBlake.net
Instagram: www.instagram.com